THE VILLAGE OF C

Adam Millard

Published by Crystal Lake Publishing
Tales from The Darkest Depths

Website: www.crystallakepub.com

WELCOME
TO ANOTHER

CRYSTAL LAKE PUBLISHING
CREATION

Join today at www.crystallakepub.com & www.patreon.com/CLP

"The more things change, the more they stay the same." - Jean-Baptiste Alphonse Karr

ONE

Neverville, 1974

It never rains but it pours. At least, that's what old Freddie Carson's mother used to say when something went wrong. And old Freddie Carson's mother, God rest her soul, was wont to use such prosaic aphorisms whenever she could. No matter the situation, Alice Carson had had a proverb for it. Whenever an eight-year-old Freddie complained about turning in for the night, it was, "Early to bed, early to rise, makes a man healthy, wealthy, and wise." If he made a mistake, "You've made your bed, now lie in it," made an appearance. "Know which side your bread is buttered on," was usually reserved for those rare occasions Freddie mustered up the courage to complain about something, which wasn't very often as his mother's temper was short and would often result in a paddling from one of her slippers.

And now, standing in that barn with Walter Creswell, Joan Lockwood, and Eric Majors, and the bodies of those two poor girls—blood, so much bloodstained hay strewn across the ground, viscera spread across the wooden plank walls—"It never rains but it pours," had never seemed more apt.

"Such a shame," Joan said, finally breaking the silence. Her liver-spotted hand was pressed against her flat chest, occasionally clutching at her thick knit cardigan, though her eyes never left the bodies of the mutilated girls, and there was something there that suggested much of her grief was simply an act, perhaps a means of justifying to herself that yes, she was truly remorseful, and not the person who had just almost decapitated one of the girls with a shovel while Walter and Eric had gone to work on the other with pitchforks.

Eric placed one hand on Joan's shoulder and sighed heavily. "You know we had no choice," he said. "Those girls shouldn't have been here. They should never have come to Neverville." He wiped blood from his forehead and turned to Freddie. "And you should have taken care of this," he said, reproachfully. "If we hadn't caught up to them tonight, it wouldn't have been these girls we'd have to bury. It would have been two of our own."

"Give him a break," Walter said, finally dropping his pitchfork. The sound of it hitting concrete rang around the barn. "We got them in time, didn't we? No harm done."

No harm done. That was another of Alice Carson's favourites, Freddie remembered. Though it was usually accompanied by the removal of the slipper anyway, because, "A lesson lived is a lesson learned."

"I lost track of them," Freddie said, for he had somewhere between John Guest's greengrocer's and the barn in which they now stood. "When I caught up to them, they were standing at the side of the old dirt track with their thumbs out. Lord knows what they were doing. Figured they were trying to get help, but you know no one comes that way. When they saw me, they got all kinds of excited. It was as if they'd never seen a horse and cart before. Managed to get them on board, but when they realised I wasn't going to let them leave Neverville, when they saw the knife, they just fucking jumped off of the cart like a couple of goddamn maniacs. Chased them down to here, and that's when you all showed up."

"It's a good job we got here when we did," Joan said, bitterness in her voice. "You quite clearly couldn't organise a piss-up in a brewery."

Freddie had never liked Joan. Her jowly face, her unkempt hair scraped back in a tight, silver bun, the way she always seemed to have white froth at the corner of her lips. If Joan had dropped down dead as a result of tonight's misadventure, instead of one of those girls, he wouldn't have batted an eyelid. The other ninety-nine villagers might have shed a tear, but not Freddie. Yet it wasn't just her looks which fueled Freddie's hatred for Joan Lockwood. There was one other thing, one major thing which he could never forgive her for.

"What's done is done," Walter said. It was almost as if he was trying to compete with Alice Carson's endless repertoire of idioms. "The girls are dead. We're all safe—"

"For now!" Eric snapped. "What if more of them come? What if they come looking for these two? For all we know they left a trail as clear as horse shit. The last thing we need is more outsiders, because you know what that means? More holes to dig, and I don't know about you, but I've pretty much had it up to here with digging holes." Up to here was, as his raised hand suggested, above his own head.

Freddie knew that Eric hadn't picked a shovel up since the sixties, but decided against fuelling the fire. "No one will come looking," he said. "They're just a couple of stupid girls who unfortunately wandered off the beaten track."

"You'd better hope so," Eric said, poking the air in front of Freddie's face with a tobacco-stained finger. Freddie could see that the man was on the verge of a coronary, had been for many years due to his borderline obesity and fifty-a-day habit. Even now he was sweating beads. After a few more seconds of grimacing, Eric lowered his hand. Calmly, he said, "There are a hundred people in this godforsaken village. One hundred souls, and it's our job to preserve them."

"And there are *still* that many," Walter said, motioning to the battered and bloodied bodies of the two girls. "We got them in time, and that's all that matters right now."

"Well, next time we might not be so damn lucky," Eric said, turning to leave. Halfway to the barn doors he added, "If we hadn't got to them, we could have been burying your wife, Walter. Or Joan. Or you." He stopped for a moment, as if anticipating a response.

Nobody said a word.

"Get them gone," Eric said. "And I don't want another fuck-up like this. We were lucky tonight, but Neverville might not be so forgiving of us next time." And with that he was gone. A few seconds later there came the sound of a horse whinnying and then hooves on the trail as Eric left the farm.

Freddie didn't know what to say. Maybe it *was* his fault. Perhaps he should have taken care of the girls earlier, when he'd spotted them leaving The Wheatsheaf.

Fuck that, he thought. There were ninety-nine other people in the village, each one at risk of losing their own life as a result of an outsider. Why didn't Albie Moss, the landlord of the inn, blow them away with his musket the moment they walked through the door? Why didn't any of his regulars—and it had been around 9.00 P.M., so there would have been at least ten of the piss-heads frequenting the place—drag the girls into the cellar and put an end to them right there and then? Why was it up to just him, Eric, Joan, Walter, and a couple of the other old boys to slaughter the trespassers?

"Because the rest of them don't have the fucking stomach for it," Freddie muttered.

"Huh?" Joan was crouched and stripping the girls of their jewellery, because even the dead couldn't rest in Neverville.

"Nothing," Freddie said. "Let's get this over with. There's a patch in the field I was gonna use for potatoes. Guess all I'm growing there now is more misery."

"Always so dramatic," Walter said. To Joan he added, "And will you stop robbing them? Goddamn, what's the matter with you?"

Joan sniffed and pocketed two rings and a necklace. "Trinkets are no good to them anymore." She straightened, her bones cracking audibly as she moved. "And besides. It's Eve's birthday coming up." Eve was Joan's daughter, and cut from an entirely different cloth. Freddie didn't hate Eve one bit; she was just another victim of circumstance, a girl who wouldn't hurt a fly if you held a musket to her head and gave her an ultimatum. "Wouldn't want to disappoint my precious little girl."

And there it was. The thing for which Freddie could never forgive Joan Lockwood.

Eve.

Innocent, precious Eve Lockwood.

TWO

"Hold her legs, for Christ's sake!" Doc Renfield yelled as he dabbed at his forehead with a dirty rag. "I can't do this alone!"

There were four others in the room besides the doc: Francis 'Frannie' Mills, Joan Lockwood, Freddie Carson, and Jack Lockwood—the man responsible for all this chaos all because he couldn't keep his dick in his pants long enough for him to realise what a mistake he was making and consider the moral predicament he was forcing upon the whole village.

The woman whose legs needed to be held, for Christ's sake, was Joan Lockwood's, who was screaming like a banshee and bucking like a prize bronco. It wasn't, Freddie thought, just her legs which needed holding. He doubted four lengths of rope and a quart of barbiturates would stop her from writhing so violently.

Freddie took hold of her left leg anyway as Jack Lockwood grabbed the right. With her bottom half now pinned to the bed, Joan grabbed the pillow and pulled it tightly to her face, stifling her screams somewhat.

"Why would you do this?" Freddie shouted, either at Jack or Joan or both, for they were both responsible. "After all these fucking years, after everything we've—"

"It just happened!" Jack screamed, the cords on his neck tautening. "We didn't plan for this to happen. Don't you realise we've been in agony these past few months? We didn't know what to do!"

"But you knew what to do nine fucking months ago." Freddie was not in the mood for self-pitying bullshit. This was selfishness, pure and simple. Something Jack Lockwood was an expert in, the sonofabitch. "You knew what was going to happen when you filled your wife up with...fuck!"

"Stop!" Joan screeched from somewhere beneath the pillow, her muffled plea making it through six inches of goose down feathers and emerging as *ftop!* It would have been funny under other circumstances, but not now. Nothing would have been funny now.

"She's right," Frannie said from beside Doc Renfield. She had assigned herself as an assistant, but so far had only proven herself worthy of such a role by handing the doc the filthy rag he was using to mop away his sweat. "None of this is going to help. We just need to get that baby out of her and take care of it as quickly as possible."

Joan's ass came up off the bed and she snatched the pillow away from her face. Freddie thought she looked evil in that moment, almost demonic, as if possessed by something centuries old. "My baby!" she hissed. "Don't kill my baby!"

"She's delusional," Jack said, mainly to the doc. "She doesn't know what she's talking about."

Freddie pressed Joan's body down onto the bed, which took every ounce of effort he could muster, and said, "Joan, you know it has to be done. Your mistake must be erased and as soon as possible."

"It's the only way," Frannie added, taking one of Joan's sweaty hands and kissing it softly. "You are a smart woman, Joan, and I consider you a dear, dear friend. I will be with you through all of this. You will not be alone. I will take care of disposal myself, and it will be treated with the utmost care and respect."

It was then that Joan began to wail uncontrollably. Tears spilt from her in an endless torrent and her mouth was forced wide open, revealing two rows of decaying and yellowed teeth, though no noise came out. Her tongue, Freddie saw, was bleeding from where she had been chewing at it from the pain. Then she screamed again, before saying, "Just get it out of me! Just get it out of me, if that's what you're going to do!"

If that's what you're going to do? Freddie knew there was no other option, no alternative to what they were suggesting. At least none that any of them were willing to consider. One hundred people, not one more. That was the ancient curse of Neverville, so unless one of the villagers had died in the past ten minutes and it was yet to be reported, this really was a one-option decision.

"Now hold still, Joan," Doc Renfield said. "We're almost there. It's crowning."

"Almost done, dear," Frannie said, gripping that sweat-drenched hand tighter. "Just a few good pushes and it'll all be over."

Freddie, who was trying desperately not to get kneed in the chin by Joan's physical protestations, felt a sudden pang of guilt, for it was he who would be digging the hole for this...this thing about to be born into a world it would never know. He had lost count of the number of bodies he had buried on his land, but pretty soon he was sure he would be digging a new grave and come across an old one, the remains of someone wrapped in filthy sheets, now no more than skeletal remnants, long forgotten by the world beyond Neverville's borders.

At least I'll only need to dig a small hole for this one, he reminded himself, as if that would somehow provide him with comfort. Of course, it didn't. This was a baby, the most innocent of all beings. There was a way of dealing with outsiders which helped the villagers justify their actions, and that was to remember that they had sinned. At some point in their lives, these people had done something inherently bad. They were philanderers, adulterers, child abusers, blasphemers, rapists, arsonists, drug addicts, prostitutes, and money launderers. They were the lowest of the low, the scum of the earth, worse than any man or woman in Neverville could ever be, and therefore worthy of their punishment.

Deep down, though, they all knew this was not true. Amongst the slaughtered there were hundreds of innocents, people who had gotten to where they were in life without so much as a parking ticket, but if you thought about that, if you considered it for one second, you were not only risking your own life but that of the entire community. And that simply could not happen.

Joan screeched and pushed and the baby's head emerged slowly from her like pus from a squeezed cyst. It was the first time any of them had witnessed childbirth, and Freddie had to fight to keep his breakfast down. There was something so alien about the whole process. A body materialising from another body, a soul from a soul. For almost nine months this creature had been growing, developing, feeding from the inside, perhaps even dreaming, if that were possible. And now here was its head and its little slits for eyes, and it had no idea what an unceremoniously short existence it would have. And that thought was the thing which tipped him over the edge.

He rushed to the corner of the room, where Joan Lockwood often sat and knitted, judging by the needles and balled wool on the dresser next to the armchair, and upchucked.

"For fuck's sake, Freddie!" John cried as he tried to hold down both of Joan's legs now that the left one had been suddenly abandoned. "You're cleaning that up before you leave, you bastard."

Wiping drool and remnants of breakfast from his chin, Freddie took deep, measured breaths. "I'm cleaning up enough of your mess today," he said. Perhaps a little unfair given the delicate nature of the situation, but true, nonetheless.

"One more good push," the doc said, for there was nothing apparently slowing down this birth, not even the stench of Freddie Carson's breakfast making its second appearance of the day. "You're almost there, Joan."

Freddie returned to assist, and no sooner had he wrapped his big, work-worn hand around Joan's ankle there came a bang from downstairs. For a moment everything stopped. Joan even ceased screaming momentarily. Only the sound of heavy breathing filled the room.

"Expecting someone else?" Freddie asked.

Jack shook his head. "No one else knows about this, and we were hoping to keep it that way. Why do you think we've kept Joan hidden these past few months? The last thing we wanted was to piss people off."

But there was somebody else now in the house, and they were making their way up the creaky stairs. It was faint, as if the approaching person was of slight build, but footsteps nonetheless.

"We can't stop now," the doc said. "Just hold her still, and Joan, give me that one last push, yeah?"

"Frannie, go see who's coming," Jack whispered. "If you can, get them out of here. The fewer people that know about this, the better."

"Okay." Frannie, seemingly reluctant, let go of Joan's hand and left the room. Joan once again pressed the pillow to her face to stifle her moans of agony.

The baby, who would never be named and would be buried on Freddie's farm by lunchtime, slipped somewhat effortlessly the rest of the way from its host, and Doc Renfield did something to separate the two, but Freddie was no longer paying attention, as muffled voices came from the hallway. One of them was Frannie's, of course, but it was the second female voice with which he was most familiar.

And true enough, a second later the two women entered the bedroom. Frannie had a bemused countenance, as if to say, *What was I supposed to do? Hit her over the head with a skillet?* Alice Carson, on the other hand, looked serene, beatific, as if she hadn't a care in the world. Either that or she had lost her marbles completely.

"Mother, what are you doing here?" Freddie said, finally allowing Joan's sweat-drenched ankle to slip to the mattress beneath. "You shouldn't be here."

Alice smiled, ignoring her son completely as if he hadn't spoken at all. Her eyes were fixated upon one thing, and that was the new life now bursting into raucous tears between Joan Lockwood's still-spread legs. Alice's smile broadened, almost into a rictus grin, and Freddie would have been lying if he'd said there was something deeply unsettling about it. It was a face he would never forget.

"Isn't it beautiful," Alice said. To the doctor, she added, "Healthy?"

"For now," said Jack. "Mrs. Carson, you know what has to happen to this child?"

Alice smiled serenely once more and shook her head. "I don't think so. It won't be that way."

By the time Freddie had moved halfway across the room to where his mother stood, it was too late. She had produced the knife from her apron and ran the full length of the blade across her throat.

Freddie wasn't aware of screaming, but would later learn that he had shaken loose dust from the rafters with his roar of anguish.

Blood was now geysering from his mother's neck, raining down on the wooden floorboards with a sickening pitter-patter. Alice dropped to her knees and then toppled backwards, gargling, choking on her own blood. As Freddie reached her, he too went to his knees and immediately pressed his hand to the wound.

The baby continued to scream between Joan Lockwood's legs.

A second later, Doc Renfield was there, pushing Freddie aside so he could help, easing Alice down to the floorboards, but there was too much blood and the filthy rag he had been using to mop his brow was sodden with crimson a second after applying it to the deep cut. "She's gone through the carotid!" he said. "I can't stop the flow!"

"Do something!" Freddie cried. "Help her!"

Alice's bulging eyes looked at nothing in particular, and everything at the same time. Her wet gargles became fewer and farther between, and then she stopped making sounds altogether. But her eyes remained wide until Renfield closed them with two fingers. Blood no longer pumped from Alice's open neck; merely seeped, like the last dregs of oil from an oiler.

"I'm sorry," the doc whispered, but the baby was shrieking so loudly that Freddie didn't hear it.

"We all are," Frannie concurred.

For the longest time Freddie was unable to speak. His mouth opened and shut, but nothing came out. Before he could finally ask the obvious—"Why would she do this to herself? What just happened? Why?"—Joan Lockwood spoke from her prone position on the bed.

"She did it for us," she said. "For our baby."

Little Eve Lockwood.

"My precious little Eve," Joan said.

One hundred souls, and not one more. Order was restored, but Freddie was motherless, and it was all the Lockwoods' doing.

This was exactly one year before Jack Lockwood lost his marbles and precious little Eve would only ever know her father as The Burden in the Bedroom.

12

THREE

Yorkshire, 1974

Mike Denver was half asleep when the telephone rang. He glanced at the clock on the bedside table, at the neon green numbers: 12:23 A.M.

Any phone call received at an hour with A.M. in it was never a good one. Other than the glowing green light from the clock, the room was cloaked in darkness, and before Mike made it to the hallway and the phone hanging on the wall there, he had stubbed his toe on every piece of furniture and almost tripped up over the ottoman at the foot of his bed.

"Hello?" he groggily said, anticipating the worst but half-expecting it to be some dipshit unable to dial the right fucking number in the dark.

"Michael?"

There was only one person who still called him Michael.

"Mom?" Mike was confused even more now; he hadn't spoken to his mother in almost a month, not since he moved to Yorkshire to become, "The Number One Car Salesman of the North." And now here she was, calling at a godawful time of night (morning), and was that a quiver in his mother's voice?

Something was wrong.

"Michael, I'm sorry to ring you so late, but I didn't know who else to call."

"That's okay, Mom," he assured her, stifling a yawn. "Is everything okay? You sound—"

"It's Kelly," his mother said, and now Mike could hear that everything was not okay, not by a long shot.

"Kelly? Is she okay? What's going on?"

"She's been missing for three days, Michael," she said, her words broken with grief.

Mike momentarily considered the fact that this was all just a nightmare, that he was safe and sound in bed and would wake up at any moment never having spoken to his mom at all. "What do you mean missing?"

"She went for a sleepover at that Rebecca Jones's house, you know Rebecca? The one with the strange mouth?"

"It's a cleft lip, Mom," Jack said, his heart now racing with concern.

"Well, that was three days ago and your sister never came home. Neither did Rebecca. Her father said they were going to some other girl's house, but Michael...neither of them came home, and I've been frantic—"

"What about the police?" Mike asked, realising how stupid that was. Of course she had called the police. Probably two days ago. Probably had Interpol on standby, too, knowing his mother.

"A missing person's report has been filed and they're looking into it, but this isn't like your sister. She wouldn't do this. It's been three days, Michael, and with Jennifer missing, too... I'm worried sick something's happened to her."

Something has happened to her, Mike thought. *She's gone missing.* And when a seventeen-year-old girl and her best friend go missing at the exact same time, the results are seldom positive.

"What about Jennifer's family? Do they have any idea where they went, the name of this other girl they were heading for?"

"That's the thing," said his mother. "They didn't give a name. Sam Jones doesn't even believe there *is* another girl. He's a wreck. We *all* are."

"Okay, Mom," Mike said. "I'm coming home. I'll be there in a couple of hours."

"Really?" She seemed relieved, but what did she expect of him? That he would just offer some friendly advice, maybe an, "I'm sure she'll turn up eventually," and hang up the phone? What kind of a brother did she think he was?

"I'll be there by four, Mom," he said. He wiped sweat from his brow. When he'd started to sweat, he wasn't sure. This was all a bit much to take in at 12:25 in the morning. "I love you. Everything's going to be all right."

But when his mother answered with, "You know, I'm not sure it is," Mike didn't know what to say, because he agreed. He simply hung up the phone and rushed back to the bedroom to dress.

Something terrible had happened to Kelly. Jennifer, too. And if the police were struggling to come up with anything concrete, what chance did he have?

He had to try, though. He knew that much.

This *was* a nightmare after all.

FOUR

Neverville, 1974

There it came. The familiar thump from upstairs. He was hungry again. He was *always* hungry these days, and yet when she tried to feed him, most of it ended up down his chin or in his lap. Jack Lockwood was 'The Burden in the Bedroom,' and Eve hated him. She hated the sight of him, the terrible smell that surrounded him, the way he grunted and groaned as she read to him at night, something her mom told her was, "beneficial for his recovery."

Jack Lockwood was never going to recover, and both Eve and her mother knew it. He was one step shy of being a complete lock-in, his brain turned to mush twenty-odd years prior. He was a stranger to her; she had been a baby when he'd done the most stupid thing imaginable.

Eve had taken to sleeping in the downstairs living room, for she hated to be near to him for any longer than was necessary. But Mother insisted that she take care of this man, to feed him and bathe him, to clean the insides of his ears and nostrils daily, to empty his commode—how she hated that terrible ancient contraption, almost as much as its contents, which filled up far too quickly for a man who drooled most of his food down his body—because Joan was frail and too tired to do it herself.

There was nothing frail about her. Her mother had simply tired of caring for him: The Burden in the Bedroom. So now it was Eve's job, and she resented them both for ever bringing her into this world, to endure a life as the youngest person in a cursed village.

Thump, thump, thump.

"Coming," she said. "You old, evil bastard." The last part was under her breath. His brain might be mush, but he was semi-aware of what was going on around him. Just. She was certain of it.

Into the kitchen she went to boil and mash some potatoes. Her mother was spending the night at Frannie Mills' place, playing bridge and drinking moonshine with Mae

Creswell. They did that once a week without fail, leaving her alone in the house with the man who would have been her father.

She poured a glass of milk for herself and carried the potatoes upstairs, almost on tiptoes. He heard her coming, though; his hellish groans enough to give her gooseflesh.

"It's potatoes again," she told him as she entered the last room at the end of the hallway. It was always potatoes for Jack. Occasionally she'd make a soup from whatever she could find in the larder. Anything thicker than potatoes and he was liable to choke to death.

And good riddance, Eve thought, unceremoniously. Her life, and the lives of the other villagers, would be much easier if a piece of improperly chewed meat got wedged in his windpipe. And it would be an accident, too. At least that's what she'd tell her mother. *It was only potatoes, Mother. I swear, just potatoes.*

She knelt beside him, and instantly knew that he had filled his commode once more. The stench was overwhelming, and it was all she could do not to throw up all over his legs. "We'll get that changed after you've eaten," she told him, spooning a small mouthful of spuds from the bowl and hovering it just in front of his face before forcing it into his mouth. He groaned with pleasure before the potato trickled from the corners of his disgusting mouth.

"More potatoes tomorrow," she told him. "I'm afraid the larder's looking a bit barren. But you don't really care, do you, as long as it's food. Probably can't even taste it, can you? There's no salt in it. No salt in the house today, I checked all the cupboards. Can you believe that? No salt at all?"

She didn't know why she talked to him during his feeds. Perhaps it was to mute the slurping sounds he made as he sucked the food down, a horrible noise that often made her gag. One thing she couldn't do was look him in his dead eyes, which were always bloodshot for some reason.

"Mother's out for the night, and I'm really tired, so you must sleep after you've eaten." She knew he wouldn't. There would be more thumps from upstairs as he mustered up the ability to lift one foot and drop it down again.

I could put a pillow over his face, she thought. So easy to suffocate him, go downstairs to sleep, and when Mother returns in the morning and finds him, I can feign surprise and explain that he fell asleep after his potatoes and I retired for the night. He must have gone peacefully in the night. Her mother would be distraught for a while, but she'd get over it soon enough. Eve would of course get over it immediately.

Another spoon of potatoes, another half-spoon in his lap. She wasn't going to bathe him tonight. He could sit in his congealed mess until tomorrow. Eve was far too exhausted to carry buckets of water up the stairs.

And then, after emptying his commode, she said the same thing she always said to him before leaving him alone for the night.

"Goodnight. You did this to yourself, you old fool."

Because Jack Lockwood had done this to himself, and locked in as he sat on that commode day after day while his daughter spoon-fed him mashed potatoes, he relived his mistake over and over, like a short but terrifying horror film.

Neverville, 1953

It was a bitter winter, one of the coldest on record, and almost the entire village was crammed into The Wheatsheaf for warmth. Joan Lockwood was not; she had a one-year-old baby to take care of, and the breastfeeding was beginning to take its toll on her. Jack, on the other hand, had spent much of the past year avoiding the child. The constant crying, the shitting and pissing, it was all too much for Jack, and so he had created a new life for himself, right there at the inn.

"Colder than a witch's tit out there," Eric Majors said as he sidled up to the bar. He ordered his moonshine and tried to engage Jack in conversation, but Jack was not in the mood for inane repartee. He wasn't in the mood for much of anything these days, thanks to that goddamn baby. If only Alice Carson hadn't slashed her own throat at the birth, he'd be dancing around the inn singing fun little ditties and enjoying the festivities, but that wasn't the case. He was a shell of his former self, and the constant arguments with Joan weren't helping matters.

That morning, she had chastised him for staying out all night and then returning home in the early hours only to pass out on the front doorstep. So, what was he going to do tonight? The same? It didn't matter anymore. She'd chew a hole in his trousers just for farting in the wrong direction. Only yesterday she had reminded him that they hadn't made love since Eve was born, and he'd reminded her of what had happened the last time. That screaming little fucking thing. She hadn't taken too kindly to that, which was why he'd spent the best part of the day and night discussing the ins and outs of weather systems with Albie Moss, who was in his usual grumpy mood. They had made a fine pair, at the bar bitching and moaning about frost and gale force winds, stopping only to occasionally sip at their warm drinks.

Jack liked Albie, though. You could talk to him without any reprisals or expectations. You knew what you were getting with him, which made him the best landlord in the village. The fact that it was the only inn in the village had nothing to do with it.

"Did you hear what I said?" It was Eric again, who hadn't stopped jaw flapping since he'd got through the door.

"I was miles away." Jack wished Eric was miles away, preferably in a different country. He considered Eric his closest friend, perhaps only friend, but Jack was not in the mood tonight.

"Reckon this shit's going to go on until February. I bloody hope not; I've only got enough firewood to last until December." He sighed and shook his head. "How's that kid of yours? Little Eve?"

"Little Evil, you mean," Jack replied, perhaps a little too tersely, almost as if he had been saving up for the right moment to call her that. "How do you think she is, Eric? She's pissing all over the house. She's hanging off Joan's tit morning, noon, and night, and she's giving me the worst headaches I've suffered in all my years. I'm telling you, she's the worst thing to happen to this village, and as much as I take responsibility for putting my dick where I shouldn't have, that old bat Alice Carson is as much to blame as we were."

Eric was no longer listening, though. In fact, he was shaking his head and his eyes were wide. *Don't go any further.* And the reason for that was, Freddie Carson, whose mother had perished so that Eve could live, was standing not three feet away and had seemingly heard the entire tirade. And he did not look happy about it.

Freddie was and had always been a big guy; years of toiling on the farm, day in, day out, made him that way. Jack Lockwood was not a big guy. Years of doing nothing much had made *him* that way. And now Freddie had turned to face him, and Jack's heart was in his throat, for it wasn't going to be much of a fist fight, and it wasn't.

Freddie swung once, connected perfectly with Jack's chin, and he went down like a sack of potatoes. He hit the floor so hard that something broke, and he wasn't sure if it was part of him or the floorboards.

For a moment he blacked out, such was the viciousness of the right hook, but he heard a scuffle and the sound of glass smashing as fellow punters rushed in to prevent Freddie from delivering more damage, and they must have succeeded as none was forthcoming.

Vision came swimming back and, when it did, he saw the faces of all those men and women staring down at where he lay. Some of them were shaking their heads with disapproval, others were smiling, as if they had been waiting for this moment for years, and today was the day. Albie Moss had come round to their side of the bar, still nonchalantly polishing a glass with a dirty cloth.

"Help him up," Albie said, hoping that someone would volunteer. Fortunately, two men did, and Jack was presently back in an upright position; whether he would stay that way was another matter completely, for he was so unsteady on his jelly legs that it took the two men all of their strength to hold him up.

"Why don't you piss off home, Jack," Albie said. "And when you can keep your trap shut, I'll think about unbarring you."

Jack wiped blood from his lip, or was it his nose? Both? "Wait, you're barring me?" he slurred, a result of both drink and concussion.

Albie sighed. "It's been a long time coming, Jack. You come in here every day, every night, mouthing off and pissing off the other punters. You're a drunk, Jack, and with Joan and the babbie at home, too. You should be ashamed of yourself. You should be ashamed that you don't appreciate that babbie. She shouldn't even be here, and wouldn't be if it weren't for Freddie's poor mam."

That was when Eric chimed in with his two shillings' worth. "Do you have any idea how many of us would give our right hand to have a baby? How lucky you are? And she's beautiful, Jack. How can you hate her so much? How can you hate her at all?"

Then it was Walter Creswell's turn to speak, apparently. Jack was too busy still trying to steady himself to care by now. "That kid of yours is the first to be born in the village in decades, and you spend your days here, fucking up your life with cheap booze."

And now Freddie. "You should be ashamed of yourself, Jack Lockwood. My mother sacrificed herself for little Eve. Now get out of here, before I do something I might regret. And by that, I mean definitely won't regret."

Jack was, for want of a better word, flabbergasted. He was clearly being ganged up on by these ignoramuses. And how dare they! And heading the gang was Albie Moss, with whom he'd been "mouthing off" for hours yesterday, and who he had liked up until now. Well, he wasn't standing for it, and he wasn't going home to his so-called wife and that little creature that everyone else seemed to adore so much. To hell with everyone.

"I don't need any of you," he said, then spat a globule of blood onto the floor and wiped his swollen lip once more. "You have no idea. None of you. What it's like. Fuck all of you. And Freddie..." He was being brave or stupid by now, but it didn't matter. Nothing mattered in that moment, not anymore. "I meant what I said. Your mother ended more than one life that day."

Freddie lunged for him. Fortunately, there were plenty of men around him to hold him back, and perhaps that's why Jack had had the balls to say it.

"Just get out of here," Albie said. "And you know what? You're never welcome back. Ever."

The severity of the situation was yet to dawn on Jack, for he relied on the drink to get him through the day. Without Albie's moonshine, he was fucked. There was no way he could operate sober, not here, not with that screaming monster at home. He never wanted to be sober again.

Without uttering another word, he staggered out of The Wheatsheaf. When he got outside, the raucous revelries began anew within, celebrations that he would never be a part of again.

Whether it was the concussion, the tremendous amount of alcohol he had consumed throughout the day, or a moment of utter madness, Jack Lockwood would never know, because in that moment he didn't return home to his wife and daughter. He went, at pace, in the opposite direction. Before he knew it, he was running, somewhat haphazardly, through the village. Past the grocery store, past the church, past Freddie Carson's farm, on and on he went. He wasn't fit in the slightest, and so he occasionally slowed to a fast walk, before taking off again. A man on a mission.

At the edge of the village was the forest, and he scaled the wooden fence there and ran through the trees. Off in the distance he could still hear the faint sound of singing and merriment from the venue he had, up until fifteen minutes ago, frequented daily. Those bastards! Those utter bastards!

Through the trees he ran, sweating and panting, cursing every single villager, as if they weren't already cursed enough. He tripped over fallen trees, lost a shoe in a mud patch, almost lost an eye to a protruding branch, but never stopped running. It would all be over soon. *I'll show them,* he thought. *I'll show them all!*

And now he did slow. Almost to a halt, but not quite. The trees gave way and the moon and stars were once again visible in the purple-black sky above.

He smiled as the rocks came into view, boulders systematically placed centuries ago by the villagers' ancestors.

The Neverville border. These boulders surrounded the entire village to prevent vehicles from getting in, to dissuade outsiders from entering the village, and they worked for the most part. You had to be a decent climber to get in, or find a sweet spot where the boulders were smaller, and this was the first time Jack had seen them; he never came this close to the border, but tonight was different. Tonight, he wasn't thinking straight, and tonight he was going to do something no one else had ever tried.

He began to climb.

It wasn't easy. Finding footholds was problematic, especially with just one shoe and his level of intoxication, and he fell the first three attempts. Undeterred, he tried again, and on the fourth try he managed to pull himself up and onto a jagged outcrop. With renewed vigour, he clambered to his feet and was now standing, right there on the border of the village.

"Fuck you all!" he cried, probably not loud enough for anyone he'd left behind to hear, but it felt good. He spent the next thirty seconds staring at the sky; the stars, the moon, the wispy indigo clouds passing overhead.

And then he jumped outward, out of Neverville and into the night beyond.

At least, that was the plan. Instead he bounced off an invisible force, something that could not be seen, but he felt it. He felt it as he hit it, and he felt the ground as it came up to meet him. Still in Neverville.

And then came the darkness.

It would be almost a week before he was found, lying there at the border, insensible, drooling. There had been no search party, no active quest to find him; it was by chance two villagers had decided to head into the forest and beyond to mutually masturbate one another, away from prying eyes and loose lips.

So, Jack Lockwood *had* done this to himself.

And spent the next twenty-one years reliving this nightmare in full, over and over, an unrelenting vision that began where it ended and showed no signs of ever reaching a denouement, while his daughter pushed unsalted potatoes into his lopsided mouth.

FIVE

Montgomery, 1974

Mike pulled up to his mother's house a little over three hours after their telephone call. It was still dark, and would be for a few hours longer, and Mike was just glad to have arrived in one piece, for the combination of darkness and weariness had almost put him to sleep on the motorway. Cold air from the Marina's air-con was probably the only thing that had kept him alive.

It was a warm night for mid-September, and certainly much warmer down here than it was back in Yorkshire. These Southerners didn't know how good they had it.

His mother answered within five seconds of his knocking, as if she had been waiting for him in the hallway, and she probably had been because she frantically hugged him no sooner than opening the door. It was unfamiliar; he hadn't been embraced by his mother since he was a child, and even then it had been infrequent, perhaps if he'd fallen from his bike and grazed a kneecap, or if he'd done particularly well on a school test.

"Oh, Michael!" she cried into his ear, sobs wracking her entire body. Tears dampened Mike's cheek. His sideburn was almost drenched by the time she released him.

They went inside, and the first thing Mike noticed was how little anything had changed. The furniture was all the same; the same chair he'd bounced on when he was a child, the same walnut bureau his mother always kept her letters in, the same breakfront filled with the same plates and the same bone china cups they had never eaten off or drunk tea from. It was like walking into the past, a museum of his former life.

With a tray of tea and biscuits sitting on the beaten-up coffee table in front of them, it was time to talk, but where to start? "Tell me about the last time you saw her," Mike said, which seemed as good a place as any.

His mother sighed. She looked as if she might cry again. Mike hoped not; it wasn't getting them anywhere, and they needed to get somewhere fast, if there was any hope of finding Kelly and Rebecca alive.

"She seemed happy," his mother said. "Glad to be seeing Rebecca. Happy that I was trusting her to stay over for the night..." She trailed off there and shook her head. "I shouldn't have. It's all my fault."

"Mom, none of this is your fault, but we have to try to figure it out." He drank half of his lukewarm tea down in one gulp, placed the cup back in its saucer, and continued. "What was she wearing? I need you to be specific. What did she have on when she left for Rebecca's?"

For a moment his mother just stared at the wall, and Mike lost all hope of getting to the bottom of this easily. Then she blurted it out. "It was a pair of cream bellbottoms!" she said. "And a white tee shirt."

"Was there anything written on the shirt?"

"One of those bands she likes!" his mother said. "One of those noisy ones I can't stand."

That didn't narrow it down much. Hard rock was all the rage, and fortunately Mike liked to listen to it, too. "Led Zeppelin?" he ventured.

She shook her head. "No, I'd have remembered that."

"AC/DC?"

"Uh-uh. It was...it was Bad something-or-other."

"Bad Company?"

"Yes! That's it! Bad Company. But the tee shirt just said Bad Co in black writing."

Mike was relieved; they could have spent all morning going back and forth with hard rock bands, and he really was tired, having not slept since 6 A.M. the previous morning. "Okay, and what about shoes?" he said, knowing he was setting himself up for failure, and he was.

"I don't know," his mother said, her face morphing into sadness, as if it was something she should have paid particular attention to.

"Were they black, white, red?"

"Black, I think," she said. "But I'm not a hundred per cent sure."

The clock on the wall chimed once as it reached four, startling Mike. It was the same old clock they had always had, but its chime was as loud as ever.

"Okay," Mike said. "What time did she leave?"

"It was getting dark, but I knew she'd make it to Rebecca's before it was pitch, so I guess it must have been before seven."

Mike knew the Jones house was just a few streets away, only because it was the house where the girl with the cleft lip lived, and girls with cleft lips weren't ubiquitous in Montgomery when he was growing up and he and his friends were partial to a soupçon of bullying to make themselves feel better for their own misgivings. So, Kelly would have made it to the Jones residence sometime between seven and quarter past. Another mental note made, another piece to the five-thousand-piece puzzle he was trying to put together.

Blindfolded.

With his hands tied behind his back.

"And she didn't call you when she got there safe?"

"You know what our Kelly is like," she said. "I didn't want to seem overbearing. Like I said, she's not a child anymore. Seventeen is a bit old for check-ins."

Our Kelly? Mike liked that. He also liked that his mother was still talking about her in present tense; she still had hope, which was a good thing. Once hope was lost, they really had nothing else to hold onto.

"I'm going to go over to the Jones house later on, talk to Sam about Rebecca, maybe find out if there was anything strange." His mother had said during their telephone call that Sam Jones doubted there was a third girl at all, and if that was the case, and he suspected something was amiss, why didn't he press them further? Why did he let them leave when it was getting dark if he had an inkling they were lying to him?

"I spoke to Sam yesterday," his mother said. "He sounded drunk. I think it's hitting him really hard."

"Well, drinking's not going to help," Mike said. "And when was the last time you spoke to the police?"

"They came to me first, yesterday, then went over to Sam's. The questions they asked me! It made me feel sick! Like they thought I wasn't telling them everything I knew."

Mike knew that wasn't the case; their intrusive questioning was a good thing. "Did you tell them what she was wearing?"

"I couldn't!" his mother almost screeched. "I was under too much pressure. I thought they were going to arrest me. I told you because you're my son, and it just came to me. I'll telephone them and tell them what I've just remembered. Do you think they'll be open now?"

"It's a police station, Mom," Mike said. "It's not a supermarket. They're open, but I want you to leave it until later, in case you recall anything else. Okay?"

She nodded. "Do you...do you think..."

Mike knew where she was going with this. She was going to ask whether he believed Kelly was dead, that the police were going to find her next year floating down a stream somewhere, or dig her up on the moors. It was a question that Mike didn't want to be asked, and certainly didn't want to answer, because his answer would upset his mother. He didn't believe his sister was still alive, no. Or Rebecca Jones. This was most likely a salvage mission, and there was no way he could tell his mother that. It would break her already fractured heart.

"Do you have any recent pictures of her, Mom?" Mike said, deflecting from her unfinished question. "Anything from the last few months?"

Jude stood, went across to the bureau, and opened it. Its hinges squeaked. It was the same noise it had always made; all these years and she had never gotten around to oiling the damn thing. She came back to Mike with a handful of photographs and began sifting through them. Mike could see it was hard for her, seeing her missing daughter's face in every snap. Eventually she arrived at one which she had decided was the most recent. "I think this one," she said, handing it over. "Will that do? Is it clear enough?"

Mike examined the picture. It was a little out of focus, but not that the features were too distorted. His mother had always been a terrible photographer. Their childhoods, if the pictures were to be believed, were a mishmash of blurry backgrounds, blurry foregrounds, light spills, and ghostly orbs, the kinds of photographs you found in serial killer scrapbooks.

Mike shuddered. It was not the right time to be thinking about serial killers.

"We'll talk more in the morning before I go to the Jones house," Mike said. "Try to get some sleep, if you can. I'll do the same." Though he knew that damn clock would wake him up on the hour, every hour, until he finally gave up on sleep altogether.

"You're a good boy, Michael," his mother said with the tiniest of smiles. "I love you."

"I love you, too, Mom," he said as she pushed herself up from her armchair. She was only fifty, but looked and moved more like a woman about to enter her twilight years. She had, it seemed, aged twenty years in just three days.

Mike slept a little, and the clock didn't wake him with its clamorous chime the way he predicted it would. His mother was still sleeping in her room when he left for the Jones house at eight, and she looked, for the moment at least, peaceful.

He really didn't know what would happen to her if his worst fears about Kelly and Rebecca were true.

Sam Jones was drunk when he answered the door, blurry-eyed and dressed in a filthy white vest and his underpants. He was still clutching the whisky bottle in his hand; its contents were severely depleted. When he saw Mike, it clearly took a moment for him to recognise the boy who had become a man, the little shit who used to hurl insults at his daughter with his friends.

"Michael?" he said. "Michael Denver?" He seemed suddenly ashamed of the bottle in his hand and tried to conceal it behind the door, which had only been half opened.

"I need to talk to you," Mike said, although seeing the current state of Sam Jones, he didn't imagine their conversation would result in anything productive. When his mother had told him about Sam's drinking last night, he had no idea how bad it was. Eight in the morning? Jesus Christ.

"Is it about Rebecca?" he said, panic suddenly filling his face. He looked like he needed a wash, a good shave, and a few days of uninterrupted sleep. Mike was annoyed, simply that Sam only mentioned his daughter, as if Kelly was of no importance.

"It's about both of them," Mike said. "And I don't care if I'm interrupting your mid-morning *soirée*. We need to go over a few things." Mike was surprised at his assertiveness. Since when did he talk like that? He was a car salesman, not CID. He hadn't had a fight since high school, and he'd come out worse than the other boy. If Sam Jones was sober, he'd probably be able to demolish Mike in a few seconds, but in his current state, Mike felt he had the man beat.

After a few seconds of contemplation, Sam opened the door fully and stepped aside. He no longer seemed concerned about hiding the whisky bottle; he looked more concerned about the angry young man knocking on his door at eight in the morning, though Mike doubted Sam knew what time of day it currently was. Or what year.

The house stank of booze and stale cigarette smoke. It was sickening, the smell of some seedy pub an hour before closing time. On the armchair in the living room, an ashtray overspilled with smoked butts. The chair was surrounded by empty bottles, most of which were top shelf, though there were a few beer cans. A solitary fly buzzed around an open container of untouched takeaway food; Mike guessed Sam had hoped to be able to eat something, had taken one look at the food and had changed his mind. No, he'd opted for a liquid diet instead. The cornerstone of any healthy regime, especially in the middle of a crisis.

Sam cleared the sofa of newspapers and clothes—although Mike wished he would put some of them on, or at least a pair of jeans—and urged Mike to sit. "I'd offer you a drink," he said, "but I guess it's too early in the morning for you." He gestured with the whisky bottle.

"You'd guess right," Mike said. *A little early for most humans*, he thought

Sam sat in the armchair opposite; Mike was relieved when the man placed the bottle down at the side of the chair; he couldn't face a serious conversation with a man still seeking to get soused.

Sitting in front of him was not the formidable man Mike remembered growing up. Sam Jones had always been fearsome, the kind of guy to tell you to get off his lawn if you so much as accidentally kicked a ball there and had to retrieve it. He was, if Mike remembered correctly, some sort of factory worker, manual construction, perhaps a welder, and was often seen dressed in dark blue overalls and covered in grease and grime. Mike and his friends had been stupid to even think about taunting 'cleft lip' Rebecca, but when you're a kid, you know an adult can't beat the living shit out of you, no matter what you do. The law forbade it, and therefore they were far braver than they had any right to be.

Mike recalled, on one occasion, that he and Gavin Williamson were out on their skateboards. It had been a great day; sunny, warm, the kind of day that ice cream vans compete for custom, their chimes a constant chorus around the neighbourhood. They must have been about twelve, although Gavin was a few months older and therefore their fearless leader, and it had been Gavin's idea to skate around to Earl Street to see if 'cleft lip' Rebecca was out. Mike hadn't really wanted to, but he knew that Gavin would mock him if he didn't, so he went along with it.

As they approached the Jones house on their boards, Gavin at the front, of course, Mike saw her. She was only seven years old back then, for Christ's sake, but that didn't make a difference. They had locked on to their target and were moving in for the kill.

Mike wanted to stop, play no part in what was about to happen, but he knew it was too late to back out. They were almost upon her; all that was missing was the two-note theme tune from Jaws.

She looked so innocent, sitting on the grass in front of her house, a doll in either hand. The wheels of their skateboards thundered along the concrete, so Mike couldn't make out what she was making the dolls say, but Rebecca's cleft lip was moving so they were definitely saying something, conversing with one another.

Mike had no idea what Gavin had in mind, that was until his friend, without slowing on his board, crouched down and scooped something up from the ground.

This was going to be serious, something that could get them both into a lot of trouble. Mike knew that, but boys will be boys.

They were level with the Jones house when Rebecca looked up and saw them, and Gavin's arm came back, and with all the force he could muster, he launched something toward the unsuspecting girl. Fortunately, the pebble fell short of its intended target, but it bounced up and caught Rebecca somewhere in the face.

Her head rocked back ever so slightly, and for a moment Mike thought they were going to get away with it; it couldn't have hurt that much. Yes, it was just a nick. The pebble must have been no bigger than a penny. Thank God for that.

And then the screaming started, by which point Gavin was already kicking his way out of there as fast as his board could carry him. Mike was still metres behind, though, so when Sam Jones came running out of the house, still in his dark blue overalls and with his face blackened from a hard day's graft at the factory, it was Mike that he saw, skating away from his squealing, injured daughter.

"I know where you live, you little shit!" the enraged man had bellowed, and Mike thought, *I know you do! My sister plays with your daughter!* Mike was terrified that the man would run him down, drag him from his board, and stamp on him until his brain popped out of his ears. He was relieved to find that when he looked back, Sam Jones was too busy consoling his wailing daughter to pursue the assailants.

That had been ten years ago, but it felt like only yesterday, and now 'cleft lip' Rebecca was probably dead, and so was his sister, and the man sitting in front of him, lighting a cigarette and regarding Mike with solemn eyes, was half the man he used to be.

"I guess we're in the same boat," Sam finally said through a haze of blue-grey smoke. It was a strange way to begin the conversation, but it was true, nonetheless. They were both missing a loved one, both clueless as to their whereabouts, both unsure what to do next. Same boat, indeed. The only difference was Sam was in no fit state to take the helm. Mike didn't even think the man was capable of holding an oar.

"Mom called me last night," Mike said. "I drove down this morning."

"That your Marina out front?" He slurred slightly, but not enough to concern Mike. Perhaps the man had only just begun his day of drinking, and was yet to reach peak toxicity.

"Yeah," Mike said. "One of the perks of working at a car dealership. Comes with the job."

"Nice car," said Sam. "Bit of an upgrade from that skateboard you used to piss around on."

Shit, he remembers, Mike thought. *After all these years he remembers that one day in the summer of '64.* And then Mike wondered how many times, over the years, Sam Jones had thought about that one moment, that solitary misdeed that had probably not even left a mark on his daughter's face. Or had he only recently recalled the event, cast up from the recesses of his mind because it was a memory of his absent daughter?

"Yeah," Mike said, solemnly, unable to look Sam in the eye. It was time to change the subject, get back to the matter in hand. "Mom said you talked to the police. What did you tell them?"

Sam took a long pull on his cigarette and sighed. "What do you think I told them, kid?" he said. Mike didn't like being called kid, but he let it slide on account of the situation and the palpable tension in the room. "I told them everything. I told them what time they left. What Rebecca was wearing. I couldn't remember what Kelly was wearing, because I wasn't paying that much attention, but Rebecca had on her favourite stuff. Blue jeans, black tee, black leather jacket. Not real leather; I'm not made of money, but good enough to pass as genuine. I told them that they had arranged to go to some girl's house for a sleepover. I didn't get the girl's name, but I didn't think much of it at the time."

"Were you drunk at the time?" Mike asked. It wasn't meant to be reproachful, but it sure came out like it. And when Sam didn't respond right away, Mike knew the answer.

"Things haven't been good for me these past few months," Sam said, nonchalantly waiting for the ash to fall from his cigarette and into the already overflowing ashtray. "They laid a load of us off at the factory. Agency staff are cheaper, apparently. Can you believe that? Twenty years of service and nothing but a fuck you later."

"So, you started drinking?" Mike said. "Why not go out and get another job?"

"Welding's all robots these days," Sam said. "I don't even know how to operate a damn microwave." The ash finally fell from the tip of his cigarette and he took another long pull. "I had to sell my own car to keep up the payments on this place. And you know what? I never once told Rebecca about any of it. I pretended I was still going to work because I didn't want to worry her. I had a fund, you know, to fix her mouth, and fuck if I didn't almost have enough to get it done, and then I lost my job and had to use it all up to keep the electricity on. And now she's fucking gone, kid, and I lied to her. About everything. I lied."

Then Mike saw something he never thought he would. Sam Jones, the formidable sonofabitch he'd once skated away from as fast as he could to avoid a certain mauling, broke down in the most uncontrollable fit of tears he'd ever witnessed. The man was broken, doubled over in his armchair. He looked like he was going to upchuck, but no. He Just kept sobbing, his shoulders and back bouncing up and down. Yet Mike didn't feel awkward; he felt ashamed. Embarrassed he wasn't doing the same.

We're in the same boat.

After almost a minute of this, Mike decided to say something, and it wasn't perhaps what he intended, but it did the trick. "I guess it's not too early for that drink."

Sam straightened up, looking confused at first as he wiped the tears from his eyes and face. Then he smiled just a little. "Sounds like a plan," he said.

So they shared a drink and talked about Kelly and Rebecca and where they might be. When Mike broached the subject of the mystery third girl, Sam repeated what he'd told Mike's mother. "I don't even think there was a third girl."

"So they lied about where they were going," Mike said. "Which means it was somewhere they knew they shouldn't have been going."

"Yeah," Sam said, that one word lasting almost a full three seconds. Mike knew why; Something important had just occurred to Sam, something which might lead somewhere, a new piece to the puzzle, or perhaps Mike was just being optimistic.

"Wait here a second," Sam said, stubbing his cigarette out and setting his glass down on the floor. He left the room and, judging by the heavy footfall, headed upstairs. When he returned a minute later, he was holding something. Envelopes, around a dozen of them. Opened letters. "She found them," he said, and Mike could see that Sam was genuinely perturbed. "She must have found them and read them and..." He trailed off there and shook his head.

"What?" Mike said as he stood. This was something after all. "What is it?"

Sam held the letters out to Mike. He was visibly shaking. "When she left me, Barbara promised she'd never get in touch again. Never try to contact Rebecca. Said she'd give me the divorce as long as I kept the freak kid. Can you believe she called Rebecca that? Her own daughter a freak kid."

Mike took the letters from Sam and read the address of the one on top. Thumbing through them, he saw that they were all addressed to Rebecca Jones. "She sent these?" Mike said, though it wasn't quite a question. "Your ex-wife, Rebecca's mom?"

Sam nodded. "They stopped coming about a year ago," he said. "I thought she'd finally given up. My heart raced every single time the mail came, just in case Rebecca got to it before me, but she never did. I managed to hide them from her. I kept them in a shoebox in my wardrobe but she must have found them. Why would she be going through my shoeboxes?"

"More importantly," Mike said, "why didn't you just throw them away?"

"I wanted to," Sam said. "But she deserved to know who her mother was. Eventually. I was going to give them to her on her eighteenth birthday and let her make her own mind up about the woman who abandoned her. I was hoping she'd make the right decision without my interference. Seemed only fair."

Mike admired Sam for that. Giving a second chance to the woman who called her own daughter 'freak kid' seemed a little *more* than fair to Mike. He doubted he would do the same.

"So, you think she found them?"

"She *must* have," Sam said. "I only ever opened the first one to see who it was from. Overprotective father, and all that. After that I stopped. I knew they were from Barbara. These have all been opened now. She's read them all."

"Okay," Mike said. "Then I guess we need to read them."

So they did. And the first thirteen were just updates. What Barbara was up to, where she had been, how sorry she was for leaving all those years ago, how she wished things had been different, how Sam was a good father and that she hoped he was doing well, blah-de-blah.

It was the final letter, postmarked eleven months ago, which contained the break-through they were looking for.

"I'll be damned," Sam said. He was still shaking; hadn't stopped since he came downstairs.

"Me, too," Mike concurred, for there right at the end of the letter (which had been yet another one filled with updates and apologies) was an address. No phone number, just a physical address.

If ever you want to get in touch, I've got a nice house now. I'd love for you to come visit some time. I completely understand if not, but I know I'd love to meet up in person, so if you're ever in the area, my door is always open.

"Sonofabitch!" Sam said, reading the letter over and over in disbelief. "She's gone to meet her mother."

"And took my sister along for moral support?"

"Sure looks like it," Sam said.

Mike read the address one more time. "Staylittle," he said. "Not sure where that is, but I've got an A to Z in the car. How sober are you feeling, Sam?"

"Pretty damn sober right about now," he said. "I've always wanted to ride in a Marina."

SIX

Neverville, 1974

Eve sat on the rocking chair in front of the house. She didn't want to go back inside; The Burden in the Bedroom was having one of his needy days. God, how she hated when he was in one of his demanding moods. She'd already fed him, changed, him, washed him, read to him; the only thing she hadn't done was what she wanted to do, and that was put him out of his misery. Put them all out of his misery.

So, she'd poured the last of their milk into a large tumbler—making a mental note to head over to Freddie Carson's farm that afternoon to see if his cows had been productive enough that morning for a pint or two of the white stuff—and had taken to the porch, where she felt more relaxed and unburdened and satisfied. *Let the old bastard stamp on the floor all he likes. I can't hear him out here.*

A few passersby had wished her a good morning; more than a few had ignored her entirely, and she knew exactly why. She was an outcast. She was the only villager under sixty. Her mother was the next youngest in Neverville, and she'd only been sixty for a few months.

It wasn't that the other villagers hated her. She believed it was more that they envied her, that they were all perhaps approaching the latter years of their lives, and she was just starting hers. What they didn't realise was that Eve Lockwood was terrified, for she would, unless some fatal accident befell her or one of the other villagers lived well into their hundreds, be left all alone in the village. At some point she would be the last, for however many years that may be, and something like that plays on your mind.

On the other hand, having the run of the village seemed somewhat appealing. She could grow her own food, live wherever she wanted to, walk around the village without people whispering curiously behind her back. Neverville would be hers. Hell, even the village contained her name: nEVErville. She could even change it to Everville. She could do whatever she wanted and without a care in the world. And the best part is, there would be no The Burden in the Bedroom. He'd be long gone, his awful commode burned as firewood. She would delete all memory of him; it would be as if he had never existed, and that suited her just fine.

"Eve?"

Snapping out of her reverie, Eve saw her mother staggering toward the house. She looked a little worse for wear, barely making it along the path without kicking up the flowerbeds. It must have been a good night with Frannie and Mae, while Eve was wiping The Burden in the Bedroom's ass and filling his face with bland spuds.

"I called you three times," Joan said. "I thought you were ignoring me on purpose."

"I wasn't," she said. "Why would I?" *Apart from the fact that you left me at home with that thing upstairs yet again, while you were out drinking and playing cards with the ladies.*

"How was your father last night?"

"Don't call him that," Eve said, setting her empty glass down on the porch.

"Oh, come now, daughter of mine!" Joan said, quite jovially. Eve put that down to the previous night's moonshine. "He is your father. He has always been your father, and will always be your father."

"Mother, that thing is not my father. He is a donor. That is all. And now he is the bane of my entire life." And that, she thought, was an understatement. That her mother was even minimising the effect The Burden in the Bedroom had had on her life, her upbringing, her growth into the young woman she was today—nothing like the woman she would have become had he not been there—was insulting.

"Your father was a good man," Joan said, serious now. "He deserves compassion, care, love—"

"Then why don't *you* give it to him?" Eve said. She was sick of being treated like a chambermaid, a factotum to her so-called father. "The best thing that could have happened to him and this family is that the curse had released him fully. Instead, look at what we are left with. This is no kind of life for anyone."

Joan didn't reply straight away, instead gave her forthcoming words careful consideration. Eve didn't know what was worse; upstairs with The Burden in the Bedroom or out here with She Who Cannot Be Reasoned With.

"It won't be like this forever," Joan finally said, morosely. "Your father...he will not live a full life, not the way you and I will. Which is why we need to make the most of it while he is still with us." She paused for a beat. "And yes," she went on, "I have left a lot of the work for you. I forget myself, sometimes, and it's unfair, unreasonable to expect so much of someone so young."

Patronising, Eve thought, but the sentiment was there.

"I will try to do more, to ease the burden on you." She meant it, too. Eve knew when her mother was paying her lip service. It was all in the eyes. The pupils. The way she glanced away to the right after speaking.

"We're out of milk," Eve said, no longer wishing to continue the conversation. Their little *tête-à-tête* had come to an end.

Joan smiled. "Freddie's cows are doing well this season," she said. "I'm sure we have nothing to worry about. Why don't you head on over there and see? I'll check on your father."

Eve sighed, for that had been on her agenda anyway, though not so soon. Though, if it meant her mother tended to The Burden for a while and allowed her a little respite, she wasn't going to turn it down.

She stood, but before she could say goodbye and set off for the Carson farm, her mother grabbed her by the arm, stopping her in her tracks. "Before you go, and I know you don't like to celebrate, not in the proper way, anyway, I trust you have not forgotten your birthday is approaching."

Eve hadn't forgotten, no matter how hard she had tried. There just didn't seem any point to it. She was going to be a year older. Another year had passed since that poor woman had sacrificed herself for Eve. Whoopee-fucking-doo!

"I hadn't forgotten," Eve said.

"Good." And with that, Joan reached into the breast pocket of her blouse and retrieved something. "Now, I was going to wait for the day to give you this, but now seems as good a time as any. Plus, it might cheer you up a little." She held the thing—Eve couldn't see, for it was clenched in her mother's tight fist, what she held out to her. Eve placed an open palm beneath her mother's fist and watched as the shiny thing fell into it.

"It's a ring!" Eve said, inspecting the object. "I've never had a ring before! Never thought I would *ever* have one!" She immediately searched for a finger it would fit snugly on, which happened to be the middle finger of her right hand. Once on, she examined it more closely.

The design was an octagon, with lines moving outward from the centre stone, a clear ball of glass. "What is this?"

Joan smiled. *I know something you don't know.* "That is a diamond," she said. "And it is almost as precious as you. Almost, but not quite."

"A dy-mand," Eve said, holding her arm out fully and taking in the magic. "It's beautiful. It's...it's...where did you get it from?"

Joan chuckled. "Never you mind," she said. "Let's just say it didn't come cheap. Had to really work for that, I did."

Eve shrugged. "I love it," she said. "It's my new favourite thing." And she really did love it. And in that moment, she was reminded that she loved her mother, too, though her mother was now her second favourite thing. "Thank you."

"You're very welcome," Joan said. "Now run along to Freddie's for that milk. It's still early, and you know how quickly it goes."

Eve hugged her mother and almost skipped off along the track. It was moments like these that she forgot about how bad everything was, how much she dreamed of change, in whatever form it came, and about her future, which would unquestionably be spent wandering the village alone searching for things to do to keep her lonely little self occupied.

The events that would transpire later that day, however, would soon remind her of why hope does not exist in Neverville.

SEVEN

En-route to Staylittle, 1974

Mike had made a call to his mother to tell her what they had found at the Jones house, and she had answered promptly; she must have got out of bed shortly after he left. She seemed elated by the news, but Mike had reined her in a little, told her not to get her hopes up. They didn't know for sure that they weren't embarking upon a wild goose chase. It seemed a little too good to be true, but it was all they had to go on.

His mother had insisted on telling the police this new information when she called them, "As soon as I get off the phone with you." Mike convinced her not to. This was a slim possibility. It was something and nothing, and to have the police tear over to Sam's ex-wife's new house so early in the morning would be presumptuous and reckless. Which was why *they* were going. If it turned out to be nothing, then no police time would be wasted. After careful consideration, his mother had conceded.

"Besides," Mike had told her, "it's not far at all to Staylittle." Forty-five minutes with moderate traffic. He would update her as soon as he knew more, and goodbye.

As it turned out, there was almost zero traffic, and they arrive in the quaint little village of Staylittle. In fact, as they drove through the endless fields peppered here and there with trees and sheep, Mike felt like he had entered an episode of *The Twilight Zone*. When it's a relief just to see a Post Office or a Baptist church, you know you're on very desolate ground.

"We're never going to find the place," Sam said, anxiously from the passenger seat. "This place has less life than the local cemetery."

"We'll find it," Mike assured him. Twenty minutes later, and with no soul in sight, they decided to turn around and head back to the Post Office, where they encountered an ancient man wearing a flat cap and tweed suit. The room smelled of boiled sweets and newspaper print, but once again they were the only people there. It was as if this entire village had been left in the dark ages while the rest of the world moved on without it.

"How may I be of assistance?" the man asked from the other side of the counter; he was seemingly grateful of the company, for his grin was so broad it almost touched at the back of his head. His teeth, the ones that remained, were discoloured, and Mike could smell aniseed on his breath as he spoke.

"Yes, um," Mike said, motioning to the letters in Sam's hand.

Sam stepped forward and took over. "Hey, old feller," he said. "We're looking for a house here in the village—"

"Ah, we have houses here in the village, yes," said the man. "Is there a specific one you are looking for?"

Mike could see Sam wanted to swat the man from the way his grip tightened on the letters. "Yes," Sam said. "We have an address right here. We were hoping you could point us in the right direction."

"Well of *course* I can, young man," the postmaster said, accepting one of the letters from Sam. "What kind of a Post Office would we be if we didn't know precisely which houses to deliver mail to?"

If Sam doesn't hit him, Mike thought, *there's a damn good chance I will.*

"Now, let me see," said the postmaster, taking up a pair of spectacles and setting them on the bridge of his bulbous nose. Then he held the letter as far away from his face as possible, leading Mike to believe the spectacles were as usual as a chocolate teapot. After a few moments, in which Mike and Sam exchanged a mutual glance of exasperation, the man said, "Ah, yes, I know where you need to be." He handed the letter back to Sam, but said no more.

"Well?" Any moment now, Sam was going to deck the old man and then rob the place for good measure.

"Ah. Yes, which way are you facing in your vehicle?"

"That way," Mike said, pointing east.

"No, no, no, no, you need to be facing that way," the postmaster said with something akin to a Mephistophelian smirk. "You'll never get to where you need to be if you're facing that way."

"Okay," Mike said. "We'll turn around."

"Yes," said the man. "That would work in your favour. And then when you have done that, you need to drive for about half a mile and take your first left. You will see, on your right, a row of caravans. Ignore those. Carry on for two hundred or so yards, and you will see the house. Big white thing. The woman who lives there hasn't been there for long, but she is such a lovely lady."

"Try living with her," Sam muttered under his breath.

"Huh?"

"Nothing," Sam said. "Thanks for your help. You've been...an experience." And with that he turned and walked at pace for the door.

Back in the car, Mike and Sam made fun of the man and his ways. Not because they were mean; it was to ease the palpable tension. They were minutes away from finding out whether to call off the police search, or if they had made the journey to the ends of the earth, or whatever this place was, for nothing.

Mike took the first left onto a nameless track—back in the real world they would have called this 'someone's driveway'—and as the man said, there on the right were four caravans, each at various stages of disrepair. It seemed in Staylittle, even the structures committed suicide.

"I can't believe she moved...*here*," Sam said, glancing out through his open window at the passing field.

Mike couldn't understand how anyone could live so rurally. This wasn't just cut off from the world; it had been excommunicated. The sheep outnumbered humans a thousand to one, perhaps more, and they hadn't even had so much as a sniff of a pub, let alone driven past one.

After a few hundred feet, the house came into view, and when they saw it, standing there alone, set back from the trail, Mike realised why people moved to places such as Staylittle.

Seclusion. Peace and quiet. Not to mention the fact you could buy what amounted to a mansion for the same price as a one-bedroom flat in Yorkshire.

The house was immense. Contemporary and country all at the same time, Mike was surprised the place didn't have its own chapel. "Now we know why she moved here," he said. "Jesus, Sam, how much did she get in the divorce."

Sam shook his head, but was unable to take his eyes off the approaching house. "She got nothing because I *had* nothing," he said. "We just went our separate ways, as in I kept Rebecca and she got to go off and live a new life." The bitterness in his voice cut through the car like a steak knife through butter. Whatever happened in the next half hour, Mike realised it was not going to be a pleasant experience. There was certainly no love lost between Sam and Barbara, at least on Sam's part.

Mike parked in front of the house and Sam flicked his cigarette butt unceremoniously out of the open window before winding it up. They exited the vehicle at the same time and made their way toward the door. Even that was huge.

Posthaste, Sam rang the bell, and the melodious yet annoying notes of Greensleeves came from within. They both sighed and waited nervously for a response. Mike prayed that it would be Kelly who answered the door, that this nightmare would all be over and they could all pile into the Marina and head back to the disparate normality of Montgomery. He knew that Sam would be praying for the same, substituting Kelly with Rebecca. Either would do, so long as they were here. Together.

Safe.

A moment later, the door swung open and Mike's heart fell into the pit of his stomach. Disappointment stood there in her oversized kimono and with her hair in rollers. She went to tell them that she wasn't interested in whatever they were selling, until her eyes fell upon Sam, and she fell silent.

"Is she here?" Sam said. He was breathing heavily again, shaking, and on the verge, Mike thought, of a full-blown embolism.

"Sam," Barbara said. "What are you doing here? I almost didn't recognise you."

"Cut the bullshit, Barb," Sam said, retrieving the letters from his inside jacket pocket. He held them toward her, not offering, but accusing. She had started something with these letters, and it had culminated in this. The disappearance of two young girls and a county-wide search that seemed to be going nowhere fast. "Is Rebecca here?"

Barbara looked confused, pulled her kimono tightly around her, as if fearful that something might fall out, although it was nothing at least fifty per cent of the men standing in her doorway hadn't seen before. "Why would...why would Rebecca be here?"

"She *read* these!" Sam said, his voice growing louder. "She found them, and she read them, and now she's missing, Barb!"

Barbara's eyes widened with surprise. "She's missing?"

"Yes!" Sam said. "And this young man's sister, Rebecca's best friend, is missing, too, so if she's here—"

"She's not here, Sam," Barbara said. "And I haven't sent a letter for...what do you mean she found them?" It seemingly dawned on Barbara then what was going on, and Mike's suspicions were true. This was not going to be a peaceful reunion. "She never got the letters because you kept them from her." It wasn't a question.

"Of *course* I kept them from her," Sam said. "For now, at least. I didn't want her to get hurt all over again, or get her hopes up of one day meeting you only to find out what a vindictive little witch you actually are."

Barbara's mouth fell open into a wide O. Under other circumstances, Mike would have found it comical, but he was grieving internally in that moment.

Kelly wasn't here.

Rebecca wasn't here.

Hope wasn't here.

"This is no coincidence, Barb," Sam continued. "Those letters were sealed in my wardrobe until last week. At some point between then and now, she opened them, read them, found your address, and has since gone missing, and my Rebecca would not just up and disappear unless she had good reason to."

"Neither would Kelly," Mike said. "But I know for a fact how close those two were …are…and that if Rebecca asked Kelly to, say, go somewhere with her, it was a matter of emotional support, she would do it." Now it was him accusing Barbara of lying. Not in so many words, but he might as well just have come out and said it. *You're fucking lying, you kimono-wearing sadist! Where's my damn sister?*

"I swear to God, they're not here. I wish they were! When I put my address in that letter, I never for one moment thought she would come all the way out here to see me or…reconcile. It was a gesture. An empty one, at that. Just to let her know that when she was ready, and if she ever felt the urge, she would know where I was."

Sam stuttered for a moment as his brain worked overtime. Unlike Mike, Sam seemed to have placed all his eggs in one basket. He had pinned his hopes upon finding Rebecca and Kelly with Barbara. It seemed the only reasonable explanation. Mom leaves girl. Girl forgets Mom. Mom sends letters. Dad hides letters. Girl finds letters. Girl finds Mom. Dad finds Girl. The end.

"She's really not here?" Sam said. His voice had risen an octave. Here was that broken man again, the one sitting in his armchair, doubled over, smoke trailing upward from the lit cigarette in his hand as his back and shoulders bounced and bounced and bounced.

"She's not here," Barbara said, solemnly. "I'm so sorry, Sam," she said. "I wish I could tell you something, anything, but I really don't know. I haven't heard from her. Never thought I would, and I feel terrible." She paused for a moment, then said, "Look, come inside. Whatever's happened between us is done. That girl is still my daughter. Come on. Inside. We can try to figure it out. I've just made a fresh pot of coffee, and Lord knows you two look like you could use some."

Sam didn't speak; he was visibly still in a terrible state of shock, so Mike accepted on their behalf and followed her into the house. A moment later, Sam staggered, broken and dejected, through the door, closing it slowly and quietly behind him as he did so.

If the exterior of the house was something to behold, the interior was as close to perfection as you could probably get outside of a manor house. In the hallway, a pair of large wall mirrors hung on either side, their shape evoking that of the doorway arch. A two-seater bench sat against one wall. Various paintings lined the walls, but Mike knew nothing about art unless Banksy had had something to do with it.

In the living room, which was where Barbara had led them, mahogany bookcases sat against one wall, while various floral couches, each one replete with wooden legs, created a square at the centre of the room, in which sat a large, varnished coffee table. There was more artwork, too, and several pieces of porcelain sitting upon the huge fireplace on the west wall. The ceiling was higher than most churches, and Mike found himself wondering just what Barbara had done to be able to afford such a beautiful place.

"Back in just a moment," Barbara said, and then left the room, leaving Mike and Sam to survey their surroundings in awe, though Sam looked pallid and not at all interested in the décor. He slumped onto one of the sofas and stared off into nothingness.

Mike thought about reassuring Sam, but he himself was dejected. The only difference was that he had not made the mistake of getting his hopes up. The one thing you quickly learn as a car salesman is that, no matter how interested a potential buyer is in a new ride, no matter whether they've got cash on the hip and are already perusing the contract, there's a good chance they will not follow through with the purchase. It happens more often than you'd think. Even after a test drive, with the client as excited and making plans for a trip to the coast, there is always the possibility some small part of him, a niggling at the back of their mind, will tell him that he doesn't need it. He is simply having a mid-life crisis. What would the wife think if I pulled up in this tonight? So, Mike had conditioned himself not to assume anything, regardless of the positive signs.

And that was why he was not pale and on the verge of tears. Dejected, sure, but the eggs in only one of his baskets had been broken.

After sitting in silence for longer than Mike was comfortable with, Barbara returned with the much-needed coffee. She set it down on an ornamental fabric doily at the centre of the coffee table and urged them to help themselves and that there was more milk in the fridge if they required it.

It was Sam who spoke first. Low and emotionless, a hint of scorn in his voice. "Nice place you've got here, Barb," he said. "Marry a rich man, did you?"

She scoffed. "No, no, I never remarried," she said, taking a seat. When you each have a sofa to call your own, you know you've done well in life. "You remember you used to do the football pools every week, without fail?"

Sam nodded. "You used to tell me I might as well just chuck my money straight in the bin."

She smiled slightly. "Well, after we...after I left, I started doing it. I don't know why; it was just that I had spent all those years watching you, the hope you had every Saturday, I decided why not."

"And you won," Sam said.

She nodded. "Took a few years, but I finally got all the results," she said. "What's worse is that you knew exactly what you were doing. Which teams were likely to win, draw, or lose. I was just guessing. I don't even know who Hartlepool are, or whether they're any good. I was just doing it to... I don't know. Keep the good memories of us alive."

Mike expected a curt remark from Sam, or at least a grimace of discontent, so when Sam's expression softened slightly, and the corners of his lips turned ever-so-slightly upward, it came as something of a surprise. "Lucky bitch," he said. It was affectionate.

"Unlucky prick," she replied.

Mike didn't know whether to leave the room or not in that moment; it wasn't a romantic rekindling he was witnessing, merely a snapshot of what life would have been like for them back then, a memory played out in real-time for Mike to experience first-hand.

Their marriage must have been a tumultuous one for Barbara to just up and leave, and not all of that could be attributed to the fact her daughter had a cleft lip. Was Sam drinking heavily then, too? Did that play a part in their demise? According to Sam, Rebecca had been no more than a baby when her mother had departed for pastures greener. What drives a woman to desert their offspring so casually? If Sam had been a little fist-happy, it would be one thing to leave, but why leave your disfigured daughter anywhere near a man capable of such brutality? And Sam didn't strike Mike as being a wife-beater. A man-beater, certainly, if required. A boy-on-a-skateboard-beater, yup. If he'd been quick enough. But a wife-beater? Not Sam.

"Okay, well, let's talk about Rebecca," Barbara said, sipping elegantly from her coffee mug. She really had gone from rags to riches. People from Montgomery don't sip, they slurp, and they don't drink expensive percolator coffee, they have it from a jar like normal people. Show them a doily and they'll try to wear it. "How was she? You know, before..." She trailed off.

"Beautiful," Sam said. "The most beautiful girl I could ever have wished for in every sense of the word."

"I told her you were a good father," Barbara said.

"I read the letters." Sam slurped from his coffee before continuing. "But she already knew that. One of the reasons we were so close was because I treated her as an equal.

I encouraged her to follow her dreams so that she wouldn't end up like me, a jobless middle-aged nothing with a drink problem.

"She liked to cook. *Loved* to cook. Some of it was edible, too. I'm pretty sure she'd just started seeing some lad from college. Dave something-or-other, but whenever I mentioned him, she quickly changed the subject. That's how I knew she liked him. She was into rock music, just like Mike's sister. The number of times I had to tell her to turn it down, she'd burst her bloody eardrums, I lost count. If I'm being honest with you, I didn't mind the stuff she listened to. Better than all those crooners you used to subject me to.

He shook his head. "I never heard her say a bad word about anybody," he said. "Not even you. Whenever she asked about you, I always told her the truth. That you and I had grown apart and that when you left, we agreed that I would take care of her. It was for the best. And she was always okay with that, when she should have been screaming at me, pleading with me to tell her why you felt like you had to abandon her. But she never did. She simply accepted it because she knew that as long as she had me, everything would be okay.

"And now it's not okay. I couldn't keep her safe, Barb. I tried; I really did—"

"It isn't your fault, Sam," Barbara said. "You did everything you could for her and more."

"Okay," Mike said, for he had heard enough, and neither Sam nor Barbara had realised it, but they had spent the last five minutes talking in the past tense. Every time Mike heard a 'was' or 'did', Mike almost chewed his tongue off. "Say they intended to come here. Say, for one second, they came on foot, hitchhiked some of the way, maybe jumped on a bus, whatever. How would they get here?"

Barbara considered this for a moment before speaking. "The nearest bus route to Staylittle runs through Pennant, about four miles up the road. If they'd got to Pennant, it's possible they could walk it from there, but I don't think there's a road some of the way. They'd have to have cut through fields, woods, muddy trails. Does that sound like something Rebecca might have done? Your sister, Mike?"

"Yeah," Sam said, and Mike concurred. "Providing they knew where they were headed, and if it was the quickest way to get there."

"Kelly's really good with maps," Mike said. "She did an orienteering thing a few years ago. There's no way they would have made it all the way out here without forward planning. And Kelly would have made sure no stone was left unturned. Bus routes, A-roads, B-roads. She knows her east from her west just by looking at the direction the clouds are blowing in." He knew that wasn't possible, but he was trying to let them know just how good his sister was at getting to places.

"They would have had access to the library at college," Sam said. "Sure, there's a huge archive of stuff there. They could have found everything they needed. And bus routes and timetables are not a problem. Couple of smart girls could have figured out which buses to get, where to get off, which direction to walk, how long it would take, what time they would get here if they walked at a certain speed."

"Yeah," Mike said. "That sounds just like Kelly."

"So, you still think they were trying to come to me?" Barbara asked. Perhaps she now felt responsible for all this, somehow. If they had been trying to reach Staylittle, and something had happened to them en route, then was it her fault for including her address in that final letter?

"I think so," Sam said. "Like I said, Rebecca and I were close. We told each other everything. The only thing, the one thing she would keep from me, is this, because she knew it was the only thing, the one thing, that would hurt me."

Barbara nodded, as if she understood. "So, what next?" she asked. "What happens now?"

"Can I use your telephone?" Mike asked, remembering that he'd promised his mother he would call her as soon as he knew more. It wasn't good news, but it wasn't necessarily bad news, either.

"My line's been down for almost a week," she said. "Staylittle doesn't really have the most reliable of services. The only other telephone I know of is at the Post Office. I'm sure Mr. Crenshaw will let you use it, if you ask nicely."

"Fuck that," Sam said. To Mike he said, "Let's just go to Pennant, park up, and walk back this way with a fine-tooth comb. You think like your sister and I'll think like Rebecca. What would they do? Would they go around something? Would they stop for a rest?"

"Stop for something to eat?" Mike said, nodding. "That's not a bad idea. Mom gave me a recent picture of Kelly. Might jog someone's memory if they passed through."

"Okay," Sam said. He was, Mike noticed, completely sober now, and he preferred him that way. They were two men, now, not one and a half. "Then let's get moving." He stood, and Mike followed suit. "Barb, I'd love to say it's been nice to see you again, but, well, you know."

"Please find her," Barbara said. She looked genuinely concerned. "And let me know."

"We'll come back here if we find or hear anything," Mike said. She was Rebecca's mother, after. Not much of one, but blood is thicker than water, or something along those lines. He wasn't sure whether that applied here.

Barbara showed them out and waved them off sadly from the front of the house.

"Do you think we'll find anything?" Sam asked, lighting up the cigarette he must have been itching for inside Casa Barbara. He rolled the window down and exhaled smoke into the countryside.

"If there is anything to find," Mike said, "then I have no doubt we'll find it."

He pointed the Marina toward Pennant and pushed the needle as far as it would go.

EIGHT

Neverville, 1974

"Goddammit!"

That was the third body Freddie had accidentally dug up in a month. Up until twenty years ago, he hadn't thought about marking them out. He had been a little too optimistic. There was no way his land would ever be overflowing with the dead. These outsiders would stop coming through here eventually. Maybe the world beyond the stones would figure it out and stop cutting through the cursed place. But they never did.

Almost a quarter of the field to the left of the barn was lined with small rocks, and he knew not to dig or plant there. Nothing wholesome grows from the dead, at least nothing he'd be comfortable eating. He thought this patch, two hundred feet in front of the barn, was clear, but they had been doing this for so long that it was impossible to keep track. Sure enough, this was an old one. Nothing more than disarticulated yellow bones. For the life of him, Freddie couldn't remember burying this poor fucker. And why would he? He'd already forgotten what was written on that poor girl's bloodied tee shirt, and she was a newbie.

"Fuck!" Freddie was not happy. This was where he was going to plant his germinated pepper seeds. Three rows of them. Lord knows how long the village had been living off the same peppers. Decades. And now he couldn't even consciously put them in the ground where he'd planned to, thanks to whoever the hell this was, or had once been. If this carried on, the whole village would starve to death. Without anywhere to plant, there is no food. Without food, there are no villagers. He would have to raise it at the next village meeting, because land was growing sparse, and Freddie knew for a fact that there was a suitable stretch at the rear of Frannie's place. The soil was tougher there, but that wasn't his concern. It was about time the rest of the fuckers contributed.

"Hey, Mr. Carson!"

Freddie turned to find young Eve striding toward him at pace. She looked strangely happy. It suited her, and he would tell her so in a moment, but for now he kicked dirt over the uncovered remains; she was far too innocent to see something so grim at such an ungodly hour.

"Eve!" he said. "A little early for you, isn't it? Everything okay?"

When she reached him, her smile grew even broader. "You could say that," she said.

For a moment, Freddie got his hopes up. That Eve's sudden jubilation had been brought on by Jack Lockwood's demise. He knew how much she loathed the man, had even told him so on more than one occasion. How much she had wished the border had taken him, the way it had taken curious people a hundred years before, and not left him a vegetable. What was it she called him? The Beast from Upstairs? Something along those lines.

"Well, go on, girl. Spill the beans. Can't stand around here all day looking pretty. And of course, by that, I mean me." They both laughed at that; it was a nice shared moment.

Eve held her hand out, and when Freddie saw the ring on her finger, he almost cursed out loud. "Oh," he said. "Wow. That's, um, that's a nice ring." She clearly had no idea of its origin, that Freddie had only recently buried its rightful owner. Joan, the thieving little minx, had taken it from that poor girl and gifted it to Eve.

But look at the joy it's brought her, Freddie thought. The girl was positively beaming. He didn't think he'd ever seen her smile so much. What did she have to smile about, though, really?

Just this ring, it seemed.

"Well, I think it's almost as radiant as its wearer," Freddie said, which hurt a little but he wasn't about to put a dampener on Eve's morning. "And happy birthday for next week, though I'm sure I'll see you before then."

"I'm sure you will," Eve said, still admiring her new jewellery. "If The Burden in the Bedroom allows it."

That's it! The Burden in the Bedroom. And that, Freddie thought, was the most apt name for Jack Lockwood. Still, he wouldn't wish what had happened to that sonofabitch on his worst enemy. Imagine, every day in that room, slowly dying, simply waiting for the darkness. The most one could hope for is that one doesn't know anything about it. Just utter oblivion.

Until the end.

"What can I do for you this fine morning?" Freddie already knew her reason for being at the farm; she needed either milk or eggs. Milk he could do, eggs were a little thin on the ground. For some reason his bantams were giving him the runaround. The foxes were out in force this season, and they'd been scratching and clawing at the coops in the dead of night, when the chickens were resting. He'd put it down to fear. Pure and simple fear. The foxes were frightening the eggs back into the chickens.

"I finished the milk this morning," Eve said. "I was wondering if you had any to spare."

Freddie smiled. "I'll have to look in the book," he said, taking a small, black pad from his shirt pocket. He flicked through the pages, though it was all for show. He had no intention of actually checking under the Lockwood name. Eve was far too nice. Too nice for her own good, and far too nice to be a damn Lockwood. He knew the Lockwoods had gone over on milk, potatoes, onions, eggs, and pretty much everything else they obtained from Freddie, and if it wasn't for Eve, they would have been going hungry and thirsty right about now, and he wouldn't have given a rat's ass about it. "Ah!" he said, settling on a random page. "It says here that you've reached your quota for milk and aren't due another pint until…" He paused for effect. "Some point next spring." He closed the book and pocketed it.

"Oh," Eve said, clearly disappointed. "Um, well, I'm sure—"

"I'm messing with you!" Freddie said. "Come on, we'll sort you out with a pint."

On the way back to the house, Eve asked him what his plans were for the patch he had been digging. Was it tomatoes? Strawberries? Beans, those really long ones she loves so much? When he told her there was a good chance he wouldn't be able to plant anything there, that the soil was tainted, too sandy (was as good a lie as any), she seemed really interested.

"Thinking of taking over the farm once I'm gone?" he joked.

"Maybe," she said. "But I don't like to think about it being anything other than Freddie's farm, so let's not talk about it."

That, he thought, was very sweet of her. He knew that one day it would be Eve's farm. The whole village would belong to Eve Lockwood, unless someone else came along and she decided to allow them to stay. Maybe a nice young man. She could start a family of her own. A community of her own. The next generation of Neverville, in which Eve Lockwood was an elder. A leader.

Never more than a hundred.

She knew that.

"Can I stick around for a while?" Eve asked as Freddie handed her the milk jar. "It's early, and I've finished all my chores for the morning."

"You sure your mother won't mind?" Freddie asked. He would be happy of the company, that he knew, and there was no better company than Eve Lockwood, as far as Freddie was concerned

Precious little Eve.

"She's just got back from a bridge night," Eve said. "Pretty certain she's going to be passed out solid for the next couple of hours." And she performed a cute little dance, pleaded with Freddie to allow her to assist him with his morning's work.

"Okay, okay," he relented, although there was never any doubt she would get her own way. "But you're not gonna like what I've got in store for you. Those pigs aren't going to muck themselves out."

"Trust me," Eve said. "I've been mucking one pig out for the past ten years. Pretty sure I've got the hang of it."

Freddie laughed. "I guess you have, Eve Lockwood," he said. "I guess you have."

Jack Lockwood ran and ran and ran. With every step farther away from The Wheatsheaf he got, his hatred of the villagers doubled, the resentment toward his wife and that screaming little creature intensified.

He knew what he had to do. Knew that he would go over the boulders, and either escape to the world beyond or kill himself trying. He didn't care which. Anything was better than Neverville. Anything was better than returning home to that witch and her spawn. Their spawn.

Through the trees he ran. Moon. Stars. Nothing. Moon. Stars. Nothing. Clouds. Stars. Clouds. Moon.

His face was sore from where Freddie Carson, that piece of shit, had connected with it; his ego was sore from where that sonofabitch Albie Moss had dented it. But the pain was going to end soon. All he had to do was keep running. Keep on heading through the woods to the boulders.

Run.

Run, Jack.

He tripped, snagged his leg on some vines, and sat for a moment breathlessly untangling himself. Somewhere and owl hooted, and Jack hooted back before erupting in a fit of laughter. Once free of the vines, he ran again. Sweat stung his eyes, impaired his vision, but time waits for no man, and that border beckoned him. Sang to him like a siren.

He reached a clearing, gasped and slowed to a stop as the woman sitting there in her armchair snored and snored and twitched as she slept. He didn't recognise her at first, for she had aged quite badly since the last time he had seen her, but then he realised who it was. There was no doubting it; the features had simply gone south a little.

It was Joan. The woman he was trying to escape. Older, perhaps twenty years older, give or take a few. Her hair was now almost entirely white, and she was all jowly, like some expensive breed of dog. She looked like what his wife would look like if you left her in front of the fire for too long.

She murmured something incomprehensible and shuffled in the chair, but her eyes remained shut. Jack slowly made his way toward her, being careful not to wake her with the crunching of dead leaves underfoot. Joan had always been a light sleeper, unless she'd had alcohol, in which case you could lead a marching band through the house and she wouldn't bat an eyelid.

A twig snapped, and Jack thought she would surely awaken, but she didn't. Just licked her puckered lips with a semi-black tongue and continued to sleep the good sleep.

Standing right in front of her now, he wondered what she was doing here in the middle of the night and why she had aged so drastically. And what of Eve? Where was their daughter, the thing that screamed incessantly and shit and pissed when she wasn't doing that? Surely she hadn't left Eve at home to come out here and sit in her armchair in the middle of the woods?

Of course not.

This was all an illusion brought on by his haunted surroundings and the alcohol he had consumed. Perhaps Freddie had hit him hard enough to knock something loose, after all, and this was the result.

I tripped! I tripped and got caught in the vines! And that, he thought, made perfect sense. He must have hit his head on something after falling, and everything that followed was not real because somewhere back there he was still lying, all wrapped up in undergrowth and weeds, having this bizarre dream about his impossibly aged wife snoozing in an armchair in the clearing. In a moment he would wake up, free himself, and continue on to the border where he would meet his fate, one way or the other, but for now he was going to enjoy the moment. He was going to do to Joan what he had always wanted to, and it would make no difference because this was just a dream, after all, and you can't hurt people in dreams, no matter how hard you might try.

He reached down, slowly, slowly, brought his hands in toward her throat. Smiling, even though it hurt to smile so broadly, he felt the warmth of her neck as his fingers brushed against it, and then his palms, and when her eyes shot open he knew he had to be quick, because Joan was quick and would ruin the whole thing for him if she co uld.

He squeezed, so hard that he thought her eyes might pop out completely. Her tongue did, which made him laugh out loud. Oh, Joan! If you could see your face right now! You would be laughing, too.

But she wasn't laughing. She was bucking in the chair, kicking out at him with everything she could muster, and making a godawful noise that reminded Jack of Alice Carson, lying on the bedroom floor as the blood seeped out of her like so much tar.

"It'll all be over in a second," Jack said, no more than a whisper. "It's just a dream, Joan. It's my dream, and you're trying to ruin my dream, just like you and that little brat ruined my life."

He squeezed even tighter as Joan clawed at the backs of his hands in an effort to break free. The scratches hurt. Stung like a sonofabitch, but there was no way he was letting go. Not until she fell silent and still. Not until he had murdered his dream wife where she sat.

Joan managed to wriggle free of his grasp, just long enough to suck in a lungful of air and hiss, "Wake uuuuup!" but then he had her again, and this time he gripped so hard that she threw herself back. She was almost horizontal on the chair now, her legs wrapped around him the way they had been on the night of Eve's conception, but this was not consensual. Joan didn't want to die, and she continued to fight, even though it was fruitless.

"Just fucking die already!" he screamed into her terrified face. Off in the distance the owl hooted again, a single note, but what Jack heard was, Go on, Jack. Kill her! Kill her! Kill her !

"I will!" he replied, a string of drool now stretching from his lips down to Joan's terror-stricken face. And he was about to apply the coup-de-grâce *when all of a sudden his head snapped sideways. Pain shot through his entire body and then everything went dark for the second time that night.*

The last words he heard before unconsciously enveloped him fully was, "Are you okay? Mother, are you okay?"

Eve stood over The Burden in the Bedroom, the candelabra still in her tremulous hand. Her mother slowly pushed herself up in the armchair, rubbing at her neck and throat. She looked to be in shock, which was a perfectly natural state, given that the man who had they had been tending to for more than two decades, nothing more than a fleshy mannequin capable of the occasional grunt or stamp on the floorboards, had been up. Had walked across the bedroom and had tried to throttle her as she slept.

"Are you okay? Mother, are you okay?" She lowered the candelabra and reached down to assist her mother into a sitting position, but when her mother brushed her off, she decided it best to leave her to it.

Jack mumbled something from the floor, and Eve raised the candelabra again, ready to strike. And she would, if it came to it. Would even enjoy it, after all the years of misery she had had to endure on account of his stupidity. But there was no second utterance; her father fell silent once again, but she could see he was not dead. His shallow breaths could be heard in the now otherwise silent room.

"What...how?"

Returning home from Freddie's farm following a morning of semi-hard drudgery (Freddie had gone easy on her, she knew that, but she had enjoyed it all the same), Eve had taken the milk to the kitchen. That was when she had heard a commotion upstairs and had raced up, two steps at a time, to see what was going on. Upon entering the room, she had found The Burden standing over her mother, hands wrapped around her throat. He had been squeezing the life out of her. Eve had reached for the closest thing she could find, which happened to be the candelabra, and had raced the length of the room and swung for the back of his head.

"I don't know," said her mother. "I was sleeping. The next thing I know he's up, and he's trying to kill me."

This was all too much for Eve to take in. Twenty years in a vegetative state and then capable of not only standing, walking, but able to almost kill her mother. Her brain just couldn't fathom how such a thing was possible.

"Is he dead?" her mother asked, her face returning to its normal colour.

Eve shook her head. She wished he was; walking, cognizant, talking, it really didn't matter. She still wished he were dead, and cursed herself for not doing it when he had been nothing more than a meat person sitting on a full commode. "He's not dead," she said. "Mother, he's more alive than he's been in decades."

"That wasn't your father," her mother said. "He would never hurt me like that. I don't think he knew what he was doing."

"Seemed to know exactly what he was trying to do," Eve said, setting the candelabra down on the floor. "It was a good job I came back when I did, otherwise..."

"I'm okay, Eve. I would have been able to get him off."

She was defending him. He had tried to kill her and here she was making excuses for it, because at some point The Burden would wake up, and they would have a go at playing happy families, and harbouring a grudge, and rightfully so, was not conducive to that.

"Mother," Eve said, for she was about to draw a line under this right now, before it went any further. "I do not want to be in the same room as that man. I do not want to be left alone with him, and I will not do another thing for him as long as I should live."

Her mother looked hurt. Abandoned. Conflicted. "Eve, we don't even know what state he is going to be in when he comes around. This could have been...there might be a perfectly reasonable explanation for this."

But Eve didn't care. She didn't care if The Burden had, by some method only science could explain, found his feet again and, without ever regaining consciousness, unwillingly attacked her mother. She didn't care if it was just a freak occurrence. She didn't care if he had been carried across the room by fairies and forced to commit such an atrocious act by the Devil's own hand. The Burden had made her feel unsafe before he started moving around again. If he was able to walk, to wander freely, and his mind was filled with violence and murder, then of course she wanted nothing to do with him. Her mother was blinded by love for the man. She was not, for she had seen the hatred in his eyes as he stared off into nothingness and mashed potatoes dribbled down his chin. She had listened to his incoherent grunts as she'd read from The Bible and The Epic of Gilgamesh and The Iliad. He had been angry asleep, and now that he had awoken, he was positively enraged.

"I suggest we lock him in," Eve said as she made for the door. "As you said, we don't know what state he will be in when he comes around." She had an idea. He had just been thwacked about the back of the head by something hard and heavy; he was not exactly going to offer warm embraces.

Her mother silently considered this for a moment, and then nodded. "Just for now," she said. "Just until we know what's going on."

That was good enough for Eve. For now.

And so, armed with nails and a hammer, they set about securing the bedroom door from the outside. The Burden would, Eve assured herself, be weak. Years sitting still in that chair would surely have affected his bones, his muscles, the flow of blood around his body.

But he had seemed so strong standing over her mother, as if the twenty-year rest had done him the world of good and now, he was burning off the excess.

Once finished with the bedroom door, they went downstairs and drank tea. "I'm going to see Doc Renfield," her mother finally said as she washed the crockery. "He might be able to shed some light on the situation."

"But, mother—"

"Until I speak to him," her mother interjected, "I don't want this to go any further. There are a lot of people in this village who do not think your father is a good man—"

"He just tried to kill—"

"And I will not have his name bandied around as if he is some sort of...*lunatic*. Do you understand me, Eve?" She slammed a clean teacup down on the counter so hard that it shattered, sending shards of china in all directions. She had cut her hand, but didn't seem to notice.

"I understand," Eve said, even though she didn't. And he *was* a lunatic. Not just for what he had just tried to do, but for leaping at the border. Those are not the actions of a sane man.

"And there is one man that this will hurt more than any other," said her mother. "And I know how fond you are of him, so it's in everyone's best interests that this goes no further, at least until Renfield's taken a look at your father."

Freddie Carson was the man to which she alluded. And no, Eve did not want to do anything to upset Freddie. He had always been overly nice to her, when the rest of the village had kept her at arm's length. And out of everyone, Freddie had the most valid reason for treating her differently. It was his mother who had committed the most selfless sacrifice Neverville had ever seen, taken her own life so that Eve might live. And yet Freddie had never so much as given her a sideways glance or, as far as she was aware, said a bad word about her to another soul. So no, she would not hurt the man, and if that meant keeping The Burden's sudden awakening a secret for the time being, then so be it.

"Okay," she said. "But mother, I hope you know what you are doing."

Her mother's silence and inability to maintain eye contact suggested that she had no idea what was going to happen now.

The nightmare, it seemed, had just come back to life.

NINE

Pennant, 1974

Finding a parking spot for the Marina had been the easy part. There was a boarded-up pub whose car park was empty, save for a rusty white transit that looked as if it hadn't been moved in years. Someone had graffitied WASH ME on its side and red paint; its tyres were flat on all sides, and the passenger window was cracked so that a spiderweb stretched out from the centre. Seagulls hovered overhead, screeching and calling to one another. Somewhere nearby, a scrap collector drove through the streets, calling out to anyone who might have "old iron" to dispose of.

"You happy leaving the car here?" Sam didn't look convinced; in fact, he looked mortified at the very thought of it.

"It'll be fine," Mike said. And if it wasn't, well, it was a company car, on company insurance. The dealership wouldn't be happy about it, but making those fat cats happy was not high on Mike's list of priorities right now. And besides, there was a new Escort out next month, and he was thinking of trading the Marina in any way. The graffiti bandit, if he were to return, would be doing him a favour.

With the car suitably parked in what amounted to a war zone, Mike and Sam began to walk back toward Staylittle. Four miles was not far if you were just walking, but they were not. They were searching. For anything. For something one of the girls might have dropped. For clues. For signs that they had been here at all.

After about a mile they came across a coin-operated launderette, the kind that stays open all day and night to accommodate everyone's washing regime, but that was back in Yorkshire. Down here in the middle of nowhere, there probably wasn't much call for a launderette to stay open twenty-four hours. Or even six.

"Is it worth it?" Sam asked as Mike headed for the run-down washateria. "Doubtful they decided to get their shit dry-cleaned on the way to Barbara's."

"We said we were going to try everything," Mike reminded him, and although it was highly unlikely the proprietor had seen his sister or Rebecca, or would remember them even if they had, they had to try. This was the one occasion that Mike was glad of Rebecca's facial disfigurement; it made her more memorable, more significant. People would have seen her coming and perhaps commented once she had passed them by. As Mike knew all too well, children could be particularly cruel, perhaps remarking a little too loudly before being hushed by an embarrassed parent. These things all worked in their favour, and they had to capitalise on them, no matter how small the odds of anything actually coming of something.

The launderette was warm. Machines whirred and spun and the distinct smell of detergent hung in the air. An old lady came out to greet them, but when she saw they weren't carrying anything, no bags or basket, she looked confused, and somewhat disappointed.

"May I help you?"

"Um, maybe," Mike said, producing the photograph of Kelly from his pocket. "We're looking for two young girls. We believe they might have passed through here a couple of days ago." He showed the old lady the picture, but if she recognised Kelly she showed no sign of it.

"Don't get many young ones in Pennant," she said. "I would have remembered someone so pretty."

"My daughter was with her," Sam said. "You might remember her. She has a cleft lip."

"A what?"

"It's a facial disfigurement between her top lip and her nose," Sam said.

The woman frowned. "That doesn't sound good," she said, gritting her teeth and hissing slightly.

"Oh, it's great!" Sam said. "She *loves* it."

"Sam," Mike said, before things got out of hand. To the lady he said, "So you have no recollection of two girls passing through here a few days ago?"

"No, young man," the lady said.

Mike thanked the lady and they left the launderette and its pervasive atmosphere of steam and lavender soap. It was a relief to get back outside to the gentle morning breeze, even though they had only been in the launderette for a minute or two.

"Well, that was useful," Sam said.

"We should have brought a picture of Rebecca," Mike said as they began to walk.

"Because they'd remember such a weird face?" Sam said, though there was nothing malicious in it.

"Just that it'd be easier to show them than it will be to explain every time," Mike said.

Sam lit a cigarette and took a long drag. "Yeah, well, to be honest I thought they'd definitely be with Barbara."

"I know," Mike said.

All your eggs in one basket.

A little farther down the road was where they found their first clue, or at least what Sam was certain proved that the girls had come this way. To Mike it was just another hair bobble, but to Sam it needed to be bagged, tagged, and placed in evidence.

"That could be anyone's," Mike said, staring down at the luminous green loop in Sam's palm. It was dirty from where it had been lying on the pavement.

"I swear," Sam said. "She bought a whole pack of these just last week. All bright colours. Orange, yellow, green. Look, it even has some hair trapped in it. Light brown, just like Rebecca's." He pulled two strands of hair free from the bobble and examined it more closely. Mike was still not convinced, although he wanted to be.

"If it was hers," he said. "Why would she have taken it out? Why would she have put her hair down?"

"*I* don't know," Sam said, irately. "Maybe she wanted to show her mother how long her hair had got. I'm not a fucking detective, Mike, but this is hers. I know it is. Does this look like the kind of place people walk around with neon fucking hair ties?"

Mike had to admit that it didn't. Pennant looked like the type of place where the men had little to no hair and the women held their silver buns up with bobby pins. Maybe that was being a little unfair on Pennant, since they'd only been there for fifteen minutes or so, but Mike was usually a good judge of character, and Pennant was severely lacking in that department. It made Staylittle look like Dubai.

"Let's keep going," Mike said. "Put that in your pocket for now, and if you say it looks familiar, then I believe you, but let's not get our hopes up, yeah?"

Eggs.

Basket.

"Okay," Sam said, pocketing the bobble.

They had been walking for a further minute or so when a dog began to bark somewhere nearby. Sure enough, a man emerged from what appeared to be an alleyway. He wore a flat cap and a wax jacket, as if he knew something about the forthcoming weather that they didn't. A grey beard covered the lower portion of his face; the moustache was yellowing, as if he had smoked for the past fifty years. At the end of the lead in his hand was some sort of large, black terrier, but Mike had never been very good with dogs. He could tell you the horsepower of a 1973 Ford Cortina 2000 GXL, but to him this was just a black doggy. A big black doggy.

When the man saw them, he did what all polite members of society do at this hour of the morning when they encounter other human beings: he gave them a polite good morning and a nod of the head.

"Morning," Mike said.

Sam didn't speak. His hand remained in his pocket, and Mike knew that he hadn't let go of that bright green bobble since he'd picked it up from the pavement a short while ago.

"Are you from around here?" Mike asked.

"Born and bred," the man said. He came to a stop in front of them; the terrier (big black doggy) sniffed at them and tried to tug the man away as if it had somewhere better to be.

"We're looking for someone," Mike said.

"Two girls," Sam added. "They might have come this way a few evenings ago. Around eight? Maybe a little later?"

The man yanked at the lead and the dog shot back toward him with a yelp. Not the greatest method to obedience train a dog, but it had the desired effect. The terrier fell in alongside the man and sat patiently.

"I saw a couple the other night," he said, removing the flat cap and scratching thoughtfully at his head. "I was out walking Banjo over by the boulders. Must have been going on nine by then, though. I thought it was strange, seeing two young lasses out by themselves at that time of night."

Sam perked up then. "Did you recognise them?" he said, frantically. "Are they from around here?"

The man shrugged. "I don't know who's living around here anymore," he said. "All of my friends are dead. There could be all sorts in these houses." He then went on to use every racial slur Mike had ever heard, and at least a dozen he hadn't.

"Was this one of them?" Mike asked when the man was finished being an intolerable xenophobe. He showed the man the picture of Kelly.

"I think so," he said. "Yeah, mind you, I could be wrong. They all look the same to me."

Had this man been this way, or had it been instilled in him from an early age by bigoted parents? Either way, Mike severely disliked him. And if Mike disliked him, Sam was ten seconds away from clocking the old timer on the chin. They had about thirty seconds left to get as much information as possible before things escalated. It would be difficult extracting information from an unconscious racist.

"The other one," Sam said. "She had a facial disfigurement. Can you remember?"

The man nodded. "Oh, that's what that was," he said. "I thought she was pulling faces at me. Yeah, that sounds like them. I was picking up Banjo's shit and they were laughing about something. Giggling like little girls, they were. I thought they were laughing at me, and was about to give them a piece of my mind, but when I stood up, they were gone."

"Gone? What do you mean they were gone?" Sam's uncontrollable shakes had returned. They were onto something. Not only that but it seemed they had a positive identity on both Kelly and Rebecca.

"Well, I had my back to them. I always walk along the boulders for Banjo's last walk of the day. Like I said, I was bagging up one of Banjo's blooters and they were giggling by the boulders. When I turned around, they were gone. They must have gone over."

"Gone over?" Mike said. "Gone over the boulders?"

"I'd say so," said the man. "Ain't anywhere else they could have gone. But it's a bit of a climb. Must be really good at it, those girls. I don't even know what's over there. Never interested me to find out, either."

"You couldn't do us a favour and point us in the direction you last saw them?" Hope had surged up inside Mike once again. It had to be them. The man said one of them looked like they were making faces at him, and he didn't recognise them from Pennant. He wasn't stacking all his eggs in one basket just yet, but there were only a few in reserve just in case it turned out to be another nothing.

"Well, it's not far," the man said. "I'd say about half a mile, but you have to take a few turns to get there. If you have a pen I could—"

"We're really good with directions," Sam said, eager to get moving.

The man looked dubious, as if he was about to tell them the way to El Dorado, so when he said it was a right, a left, and a right, then straight on until you see a line of boulders and a row of treetops beyond, Mike was almost disappointed.

"But you boys shouldn't go trying to climb over those rocks," the man said as he fished a treat from his jacket and fed it to his dog. "Ambulances struggle to find this place. They'd have to get a helicopter out to you, and that's just a waste of taxpayer money, especially since you've been warned."

"We'll be careful," Mike said. "Thanks for your help."

"No worries. I hope you find what you came looking for." Banjo, sensing the conversation was over, stood and tugged at the leash and the man staggered forward a few steps before regaining control of the beast. They watched him go before either of them spoke.

"Sounds like them, Mike," Sam said. "*Has* to be them."

"Maybe," Mike said. Sam hadn't considered the consequences. If it was them, what had prevented them from reaching Barbara's? Something between here and there had gotten in the way, and he doubted it was some sort of annual three-day outdoor festival. If it had been Kelly and Rebecca, and they had gone over those boulders as the man said, then something had happened to them.

In the summer of '60—there had been talk of some massive new band about to come out of Liverpool and Elvis was number one again with *It's Now or Never*—and Mike's birthday party was in full-swing. All the family were there, and lots of people that Mom and Dad made him call Aunty or Uncle, even though he knew they were just their friends, people his father went to the pub with, people who his mother had around for tea and scones every now and then. Mike was eight then, and so had got to pick twelve children from school, but only twelve, his mother told him. They weren't made of money. He had gone along with it, if only because he knew that in order to attend the party, each child would have to furnish a gift. It was the done thing. You didn't arrive at someone else's party empty-handed. You would be gossiped about by the other parents, ridiculed by the other children. So, Mike knew that by inviting twelve classmates, he was guaranteed more gifts. There was a method to his madness, even at such an early age.

So, Mike had obviously picked Kevin first. They had been best friends since nursery school, and would be best friends for the rest of their lives, unless (and they always joked about it) one of them died a horrible death. And then he had picked the other eleven at random from his class, none of whom he would call real friends. They were just the kids he spent the most time with in an average day, which automatically gave them a free pass to the party, in descending alphabetical order; there was nobody after Lucy Taylor. He had run out of free passes at T.

That was the summer Kelly had gone missing. Only for fifteen minutes, but long enough to drive everyone at the party into a frenzy. One minute she had been next to the buffet, trying to reach up for a cupcake, and the next she was just...nowhere. They looked everywhere for her, and eventually found her in the dog's kennel, with a plate of cherry Bakewells. She didn't even like them, that was the thing, but she had piled a paper plate up and had hidden herself away so that she could work through them. She was the dragon protecting her gold in that kennel, while at least two dozen adults and thirteen children hunted her down. Mike had hated Kelly for pulling such a stunt on his special day. In his mind, it was all for attention. She was making his birthday party all about her. He hadn't seen the funny side when everyone else did. He wasn't relieved when they had found her with icing all across her lips and an empty foil tray in her hand.

But what. Mike thought as they walked in the direction the man had told them to. *I would give to find her right now, hiding away somewhere, full of mischief and with icing across her lips. What I would give to tell her he was sorry, for reacting the way I did at that birthday party all those years ago. What I would give to make today all about her.*

The wind picked up and the sun disappeared behind grey clouds.

It looked like rain.

TEN

Robert Renfield had awakened early that morning for church. He wasn't religious, or at least hadn't been until recently, but for some reason the first thing that crossed his mind when he got out of bed was God. To be more exact, the existence of God. If witches were real, and he knew that to be true, then was it possible that a higher being was responsible for all this? For everything?

Renfield had the most extensive library in the village, comprising mainly medical books and journals and tomes on philosophy and psychology. They had been passed down to him by his father, who had received them from his father many years before Renfield was born. The villagers had full access to his library, on the proviso they returned the books in precisely the same condition they had been in when they had taken them out. There weren't a great number of adequate readers in the village, perhaps a dozen who could string a sentence together competently, and so it was easy to keep track of which books were where without making too much of a fuss. It was nice to be needed, not just as the village's medicine man, but also for educational purposes. Renfield liked nothing more than perusing the titles with a fellow villager, suggesting which book would meet their requirements most aptly. It gave him an incredible sense of wellbeing.

But what none of the villagers would find amongst his shelves and shelves of books and journals was a *Bible*. Nothing alluding to spirituality or religion. He had always, and would always be, a man of science. A man of reason and methods and conclusions. The planets were up there amongst the stars; man had seen them; therefore, they were real. There was life deep within the oceans, impossible creatures of varying beauty; man had seen them; therefore, they were real. God was a supposition, relying solely on man's faith to will Him into existence; man had never seen Him; therefore he was a *possibility*, but no more real than visitors from space or time travel. Renfield would be first in line to apologise should the rapture occur and prove him wrong, but until that day, he would continue to remain skeptical, believe in what he knew to be true, what had been proven by science and medicine without discord.

And yet he had gone to church that morning, and it wasn't even Sunday, because something had drawn him there. Perhaps it was simply a change of scenery he needed. The same four walls were driving him to distraction, and there were only so many times one could wander alone in the woods, contemplating life and the mortality of man, before it became more of a chore than a pleasure.

The church seemed welcoming to him, which he guessed was the impression they were going for. Only a dozen villagers could read out loud from a book without sounding like three-year-olds, but at least half of the hundred attended church regularly. Especially on a Sunday, when Father Calhoun gave his longest sermons and the service was concluded with homemade baked goods and a good old catch-up. Were those who attended all devoutly religious? No. Did they enjoy a soft scone with butter and jam? Most decidedly. Frannie Mills made the best raspberry jam, though Mae Creswell's marmalade came a close second—and jaw flapping with their neighbours about the weather or so and so and what they had been up to? The church wasn't merely about God and the belief thereof; it was about community, the coming together of people so that they didn't go wholly mad.

Father Calhoun was in rather jovial spirits that morning, ushering Renfield into the church with all the warmth and passion he could muster. He seemed surprised to see the good doctor there, especially since it wasn't even Sunday, and Renfield thought, *I'm just as surprised as you are, Father.*

Victor Calhoun was one of the oldest in the village at seventy-nine, but he had the mannerisms and exuberance of someone half his age. His body might have been frail—he was shaped like a question mark now, and walked slowly but deliberately wherever he went with the aid of an exquisitely carved cane—but his mind was just as sharp as ever. He had presided over every marriage, every death, every christening and blessing that had ever occurred in Neverville. In his entire career as a man of the cloth, Calhoun had never been absent for Sunday service. Come rain or shine, he had been at the pulpit reciting passages from the *Bible* and bringing a little light to the villagers' lives and never once asking for anything in return.

It was only once Father Calhoun had welcomed him into the church that Renfield suddenly realised why he was there. It was not the church he was being drawn to at all, but the confessional. And it was not God to whom he wanted to confess, but the old man leading him between the pews toward the altar. There was something he needed to get off his chest; Eve's approaching birthday had reminded him that he had never, in the twenty-two years that had passed, told anyone his true feelings. Being one of the village elders, Father Calhoun was the most appropriate man to unburden on, despite his insistence on believing in things and devoting his whole life and purpose to unproven doctrine.

"I have a confession to make," he told Calhoun as the old man set about lighting candles and scraping wax from pew upholstery. "Well, not a confession, as such. I simply need to speak. Out loud and have someone listen in return."

"I can do that, Robert," Father Calhoun said with an amiable smile. "My ears are the Lord's ears."

It's not the Lord's ears I want, Renfield thought.

Once settled in the confessional, Renfield felt a sudden tenseness. An amalgam of emotions overwhelmed him, and for an instant he considered apologising to the good father for wasting his time and making his exit. But then Father Calhoun spoke, and some of those anxieties lifted; there was a lilt to the man's voice, a calming element which put one at ease the moment he opened his mouth. Renfield decided to stick it out, to do what he had come here to do and feel better about himself for the rest of the day.

"Father, I have done terrible things..." It was a little early to be trailing off, but he realised he was simply allowing Father Calhoun the opportunity to respond. The old man did not disappoint.

"Robert, I am afraid we all have," he said. Renfield could just about discern the shape of Calhoun through the latticed partition, and saw that the man lowered his head as he spoke. "When given no choice, we sometimes must decide between what is good, and what is right. I believe we have done what is right."

Renfield sighed. "Not always right," he said. "I, for one, believe that we could have done things differently. This place will forever be cursed, and what if it is? Will it always be this way? So much death and misery. We haven't even begun to lose our own yet, but it will happen. Sooner rather than later."

There was a pause, and Renfield realised what he had said. He'd meant nothing by it, but he had reminded Father Calhoun that his days were numbered. It was only a matter of time before he, before all of them, met their maker, if there was one. The difference between the two men in the confessional was that only one of them had the right to absolution.

"This place is forever," Father Calhoun said. Renfield thought he might have used that one in a sermon once or twice before. "When we are gone, we are gone. Ashes in the wind. The good Lord takes us into his embrace and holds us there for all eternity. Is that not a comforting thought, Robert? Is that not what this life is for? So that we may become what we were always destined to become?"

No, that was not comforting at all. Renfield liked the ashes in the wind part, it was the rest of it, the uncertainty of it all, that terrified him.

But he had not come here to wax lyrical about the ins and outs of Christianity. He had come here to unload about a specific thing, something which had been irking him for many years.

"It is Eve Lockwood's birthday soon," he said. "I've been thinking about her a lot recently. She borrows a lot of books from my library. That girl is interested in everything. It's marvellous!"

Eve was a regular visitor to his shelves. Completely self-taught, she devoured everything he had to offer, from Plato's *The Symposium* to Hutton's *Theory of the Earth*, from Shakespeare to Babbage. He wasn't certain she understood some of it, but he had to hand it to the girl; she was trying a lot harder than anyone else in the village.

"She is a remarkable young lady," said Father Calhoun. "We are extremely proud of her." If the collective 'we' meant the entirety of the village, then the good father had been blinded by his love for everyone. Eve was not revered by all; she was often maligned. Even despised by a few, and Renfield could not help but feel more than a little responsible for the things she had to endure daily.

"You are feeling guilt," Father Calhoun said, breaking an otherwise unbearable silence. "For helping to bring her into this world."

"I think about it every day," Renfield said. "The night in that bedroom, what Alice did, and then what Eve's father did when she was just a babe in arms. It was all a result of my silence."

"It was fate," Father Calhoun said. "Alice Carson, the Lord bless her and may she forever be at peace, had lived her life to its fullest. She had sacrificed herself so that another might experience the joys and wonders she had."

She had slit her own throat and bled to death on the Lockwood's bedroom floor, Renfield thought. *Doesn't sound very joyous or wondrous.*

"And there is a difference between silence and patience, Robert," Father Calhoun added. "Have you ever considered that you were waiting for a reason? Waited for the child to be born so that something, perhaps a miracle, might happen?"

Renfield had thought about this at length. There had been ample opportunity to terminate. He had known about the life growing inside Joan Lockwood for months, and yet he had waited. Had he been anticipating a death in the village? Was there some ulterior motive to his diligence? And while contemplating this made him feel a little less uneasy about the situation, he always arrived back at the same conclusion.

He had been negligent.

"There was no miracle that night," he said, solemnly. "Only more misery, and that poor girl has lived a life of misery because of it."

"You know that isn't true, Robert," Father Calhoun said. "Alice Carson was the miracle. Eve Lockwood was the miracle. Your bringing her into this world with ten fingers and ten toes intact was the miracle. Why minimise it? Everything that happened on that night was exactly as it should have been. Alice would not want you to feel like this about it, would she? Did she not give her own life of her own accord?"

"I thought the church was against suicide?" Renfield said. "No place in heaven for anyone who commits such an act?"

Father Calhoun cleared his throat. "I believe the Lord made an exception for Alice Carson and the selfless act she committed that night," he said. "Self-sacrifice is one of the greatest acts of love mankind can ever show. 'For whoever wishes to save his life will lose it, but whoever loses his life for My sake, he is the one who will save it'."

Renfield didn't do *Bible* talk, but he got the gist of it. "So you think Alice did the right thing?"

"Well," said Father Calhoun. "Only she knew whether she felt it was the right thing to do, but I like to think that she did. Eve Lockwood has to live with that knowledge hanging over her every day, knowing that someone gave up their own life so that she could exist here, and never once have I had to offer her counsel. Never once has she come to me and asked for forgiveness. And I never want her to. She has made her peace with existence; isn't it time you made yours?"

All at once Renfield felt claustrophobic, trapped inside that wooden confessional as if held against his will. Sweat beaded on his forehead, and he wanted nothing more than to escape. He had gone from four walls to a different four walls; there would never be freedom. Not from this wooden box, not from his library's four walls, and not from Neverville. All that remained was the ultimate containment, a wooden box of different sorts.

It will happen, sooner rather than later...

"Is there anything else you would like to discuss?" Father Calhoun sounded tired all of a sudden; the jovial mood he'd been in when Renfield arrived all but gone.

"I don't think so," Renfield said.

They exited the confessional—Renfield couldn't believe how good it felt to get out of that confined space—and discussed the particulars regarding that Sunday's service. Holy

Communion, morning prayer, sung Eucharist, sermon, *Gloria*, et al. Renfield found himself wondering who would be responsible for the flapjacks.

"And Son," Father Calhoun said as they slowly made their way toward the doors, "you know where I am, where the Lord is, should you require further assistance."

Renfield thanked him and headed out into the morning.

He arrived home just as it started to rain, and had just removed his coat and shoes when there came a knock at the door. He wasn't expecting anyone, but the urgency with which they knocked suggested it was not someone returning a book.

Over the years there had been many urgent knocks on his door. When Mae Creswell took a nasty fall last year and almost broke her hip, Walter had come hammering and banging as if he wouldn't be happy until the foundations lifted out of the ground. When the landlord Albie Moss dropped a moonshine barrel on his foot, he'd limped all the way across the village from the inn. He needn't have bothered; his blackened toenail had already fallen off by the time he arrived. There were ninety-nine villagers, excluding himself, and he had treated each and every one of them at some point over the course of the preceding decade. All except for Eve Lockwood. He hadn't had to tend to her since her birth.

Renfield answered the door, and was quite taken aback to find Joan Lockwood standing there. Should he tell her that he was just thinking about Eve and, lo and behold, here was her mother? He didn't think it was necessary, and so plumbed for the more widely acceptable, "Can I help?"

Joan tilted her head slightly to one side. "Is it possible to speak inside?" she said. "Only what I have to say may come as a bit of a shock."

"Sure," Renfield said, leading her into his home. Once inside she wasted no time in flooding him with information. She was frothing at the lips as she spoke, as was her wont.

She told him about how she had returned home from a night of drunken bridge and had fallen asleep in the armchair in Jack's room. And how she had been rudely awakened by attempted asphyxiation at the hands of her formerly braindead husband. How Eve had handled him with some aplomb. How they had barricaded Jack Lockwood in the room, where he was sure to come to and not be very happy about any of the above. Renfield listened intently, but he struggled to arrive at a suitable conclusion as to why and how Jack could suddenly emerge from a twenty-year stupor, and why, upon doing so, the first thing he would decide to do was strangle his wife as she slept.

"Where is Eve now?" Renfield asked. "Please tell me you did not leave her alone in the house."

"She's safe," Joan assured him. "We must have put fifty nails in that door and door-frame. I don't care if he's possessed by the ghost of Zeus, there's no way he's getting out of that room unless we let him."

"Windows?"

"Ah." She waved a hand dismissively toward him. "Those windows have been rotted shut ever since we moved in. Never been able to get the blasted things open. That's why it's always hotter than an Arab's flip-flop in there. That and two decades of accumulated breath."

"Who else knows about this?" Renfield was suddenly overwrought. If news of Jack Lockwood's sudden and miraculous rebirth got back to Freddie Carson, it was impossible to know how bad things could get.

"I came straight to you," Joan said. "It was only an hour ago he had his hands all over me. There's no need to be telling anyone else about this, not yet. It might not be anything."

It sounded like something to Renfield. Jack had risen from the almost-dead after two decades. Not only that but he'd had the strength and, for some reason, the motive to try to murder the woman who had helped take care of him all these years. If it hadn't been for Eve's quick thinking, it was likely that this conversation wouldn't have been happening right now. Joan would have been sitting in her chair, eyes wide open and lifeless, and who knows what Jack Lockwood was capable of if that was his first port of call. Killing the only person in the village who loved him.

"Would you come over to the house and take a look at him?"

To Renfield, that sounded like an absolute nightmare. The man had just emerged from a twenty-year trance. The last thing he would want is someone poking and prodding at him with medical instruments. And Joan had already been on the receiving end of Jack's fury. *Imagine what he might try to do to me.*

"I can try to talk to him first," Renfield relented. It seemed like a fair compromise, and one which would keep his kneecaps intact. "Through the door, of course. Try to assess what frame of mind he is in, how he feels, his mental cognizance, that sort of thing." It was the best he had to offer, and she could take it or leave it. He hoped she would leave it.

"Sounds like a good place to start," she said. "Doc, I really think he'll be okay. It must be terrible for him. All those years unable to do anything, unable to move, and then..."

"I'm not suggesting for a moment that your husband will be permanently damaged by what he has been through," Renfield said, "but the mind is a fragile thing. If he has been aware of everything that has been going on around him all this time, but couldn't do anything to show you, then there is a chance that your husband will have been affected in a negative way that might be beyond our control."

"What are you saying, Doc?"

"I'm simply suggesting that we might not be able to get him back," Renfield said. "Not to the way he was before. Not to anything resembling normal."

He was speaking the truth, and from Joan's expression he gathered that she wasn't ready to hear it. "We have to try," she said. "There has to be something we can do to help him."

Renfield, in that moment, was reminded of his own father. The man had been all there, inasmuch as he knew where everything was, had no trouble remembering faces and names, and could speak perfect Latin. He was one of the most intelligent men in the village, and a young Robert Renfield had worshipped the man who had taught him everything he knew about medicine and science and life and philosophy.

Then one day, his father began to act strangely. He started to refer to Robert Renfield as Junior, even though his father's name was Bruce. He started to become increasingly irate whenever Robert's mother was near him, often flying off the handle at the most innocuous comments. Eventually, he lost it completely and attempted to drown Robert in the tub, an ancient cast-iron thing that took up an entire room in the house. If not for his mother, Renfield would have perished that evening. She had rushed in and struck his father with the flat iron she had been pressing clothes with in the next room.

After that, his father hadn't been much of a man at all, and for a spell the village was without a doctor. It was chaos. People did not know who to turn to if they became sick or if they injured themselves. They had no one to advise them on the best medicines to take or the best exercises to recover accordingly. His father was just not capable of making scientific decisions. He stopped speaking Latin, when once every other sentence had been peppered with it. He began to disremember people's names, became confused at the simplest of things, and his frustration exhibited in the only way it could.

With more violence.

When his father died, Robert Renfield took up the mantle. He had learned enough to be able to treat the villagers' minor infirmities, all the while learning more and more and pushing himself. There had been no way back for his father, not once the disease in his mind had taken hold. Sure, he showed signs of recovery. Occasionally he would slip in a Latinism, or call Robert by his real name, but these instances were few and far between and it never lasted. The madness was always there, lying dormant, waiting, giving them all a false sense of hope before cruelly snatching it away again.

And that, Renfield thought, could be precisely the problem with Jack Lockwood.

"I'll be over in a little while," he told Joan. "Go, take care of Eve. She must be just as confused as you are right now."

"Beyond confused," Joan said. "I'm concerned about both of them, Doc. Just when I think things can't get any stranger around here, something like this happens to prove me wrong."

Ain't that the sorry truth, Renfield thought. Neverville never ceased to surprise him, and for the most part that was not a good thing.

Once Joan was gone, Renfield searched his books for answers. At first, he discovered nothing of note, but after almost half an hour of looking, he came across an article on the subject of GPi, or General Paralysis of the Insane. Apparently, it was all too common in asylums across Britain in the 19th century. Renfield read the article in full and, by the time he had finished, was still none the wiser as to whether it was relevant to Jack Lockwood and his mysterious rebirth.

He closed the book, placed it back on the shelf, and put his shoes and coat on. If he had been drawn inexorably toward the church that morning, it was the complete opposite here. He wanted to distance himself from the Lockwoods, hide in the woods and hope they didn't come looking for him. He could feel it in the atmosphere; something terrible was about to happen, and not just to him or Joan or Eve, but to the rest of the village.

By the time he left for the Lockwood house, he had worked himself up into such a state that he wasn't sure if he would be any more useful than the ninety-nine other villagers. With the weight of the world on his shoulders, he staggered through the rain, all memories of his father's awful demise dissipating like the raindrops soaking into the material of his coat.

ELEVEN

The boulders, 1974

Sheep bleated as Mike and Sam walked through the mud, rain coming down on them in sheets now. The wind howled and the rain attacked them from all directions. Mike thought they wouldn't have been any wetter if they'd thrown themselves in a lake. His jeans clung to his skin, rubbed at his crotch, and his coat was heavy and slowed him down. Sam was struggling, too. Mike had never heard such expletives from a man's lips like those that came from Sam whenever he almost slipped in the mud. It was hard going for them both, but at least Mike hadn't reverted to swearing at the sheep just yet. Sam, on the other hand, had decided they were his enemies, laughing at him, and so whenever one came close or so much as looked at him, he told it to, "Fuck the fuck off!" or asked, "What the fuck you looking at, you woolly bastard?" It would have been funny under other circumstances, but with the rain and the mud and the wind and the sheep and the nature of the mission they had embarked upon, there was nothing remotely funny to be found anywhere.

"We're lost," Sam said, his voice barely discernible over the howling wind. "Fucking racist old bastard got us lost."

Mike knew they weren't lost. It was impossible to be lost if you knew the direction you had come from. At worst, they would have to return to the road and start again. It was inconvenient, for sure, but there wasn't much they could do about it.

To occupy his mind as they walked, Mike wondered whether the Marina would still be in one piece, or if it was already up on bricks, stripped of its wheels and with a catchy slogan spray-painted along its side. Something like POSH TWAT or DAZ WOZ EAR. Pennant didn't look the sort of place to harbour vandals, and yet someone had abandoned that transit a while back and someone, with all the artistic flair of a geriatric monkey, had graffitied on it, and while he didn't want the same fate to befall his beloved Marina, it wouldn't be the worst thing to come out of the day

"There!" Sam had stopped a few metres ahead, and was pointing toward an endless wall of high boulders. There seemed to be no end to them, and from the bank Mike and Sam were currently ascending, and the distance between them and the boulders, they appeared to be somewhere between eight and twelve feet high. In some places they were sharp, jutting up toward the grey sky like stone blades. In others they were rounded, weathered, like a bottom row of rock teeth. A bank of fog drifted across the boulders, and they disappeared momentarily before coming back into view.

"Looks like boulders to me," Mike said, breathlessly. He knew he was out of shape, but climbing that hill had convinced him that when this was all over, renewing his gym membership would not be a bad thing.

Sam picked up the pace. He was surprisingly fit and healthy for a man of his age. All those years of manual work had paid off. The man had spent the last few days drinking and rotting in his house, and now here he was, looking ready and able to conquer K2 while Mike lagged behind, gasping for breath and blinking raindrops from his eyes like a madman.

When they reached the boulders, Mike turned and leaned against one. He needed a moment to compose himself; Sam was already trying to find a way over, searching the boulders for anything to grip onto, looking for crevices they could use to push themselves up. Mike was glad of the temporary respite.

"I don't think they came over here," Sam said, hands on hips and examining the boulders. "Rebecca's a good climber, but I doubt whether even she'd get over this."

Mike had to agree. Kelly was pretty athletic, but there was no way she'd have made it over these boulders. "Let's keep moving," he said. "Maybe they get lower further down."

Sam concurred. They decided to head west, sticking to the wall of rocks which seemed to go on forever. It was only when Mike looked back that he saw they had already lost sight of their starting point. The boulders weren't one long row, after all. They were circumnavigating the exterior of a massive circular wall.

"What the hell is this?" Sam said, almost slipping on a sheep shit.

Mike didn't know. Whatever it was it hadn't been on the map, at least not that he'd noticed. The old racist had professed to not knowing what was beyond the boulders, and he lived within its vicinity. "All I know," Mike said, "is that I'm wet, I'm hungry, I'm thirsty, my legs are hurting, and I need a piss so bad I might pass out."

"Just go," Sam said, stopping so that Mike could relieve himself, which he did posthaste. "Do you ever feel like the whole world is against you? Like there's someone out there just laughing at everything you do?"

Mike tucked himself away and zipped up his jeans. "Can't say that I do," he said. "I'm more of a glass half full type of guy." Which was the truth. He had never been one to wallow in self-pity. What was the point in that? What will be, will be, and that's all there is to it.

"It's just all of this," Sam said. Mike thought he was stalling to catch his breath. Understandable, he thought, given the distance they had walked and the pace with which they had walked it. "I feel like I'm being taught a lesson."

By who? Mike thought. Things like this happened every day, to thousands of people. He didn't believe for one second that it was personal. It was just their turn. "Mate, I don't know you that well, but you seem like a stand-up guy. Worked hard all your life, raised Rebecca on your own and did a damn good job of it. You have no reason to be hard on yourself. What's happened these past few days has happened. That's all there is to it. What happens next is down to us." He was starting to sound like a therapist, or what he imagined a therapist might sound like should he ever require the services of one. After this, anything was possible.

Sam sighed heavily. "You're right," he said. "I just want to find Rebecca and go home."

Best case scenario, Mike thought, and that was all they could hope for.

"Let's keep going," Mike said. The rain had abated a little, or the boulders to their right were preventing it from spraying in at them. Either way it no longer felt as if they were being hosed down by riot police.

They continued, neither of them talking. It was all Mike could do to remain on his feet; the quagmire underfoot sucked at his trainers, pulled him down and refused to let him go, and when it wasn't doing that it threatened to send him skidding down the embankment. He had to keep his wits about him to determine what the earth was going to try next.

In front, Sam bent down to pick something up from where it was resting against the boulders. It was a small black plastic bag, and there was something inside it. Mike knew exactly what it was.

"Looks like the old racist doesn't mind picking up after Banjo," he said. "But then just leaves it behind." Surely that was doing more harm than good? At least a shit would have eventually decomposed. A plastic bag out here in the middle of nowhere would take years to rot, if it ever would. He wondered how many of these bags the bigot had left behind; the man was a walking, talking carbon footprint, with seemingly about as much love for the environment as he had for those of a different ethnic persuasion. In other words, the man was a total prick and Mike hoped that when he died, Banjo ate him.

"Looks fresh," Sam said, before tossing the bag against the boulders. It hit with a wet *thwuck*! before dropping and nestling in a puddle. "Reckon the girls went over somewhere here?" He began to look for footholds and grips, and didn't have to look for long.

The boulders were slightly lower here—still almost seven feet high, but more manageable than some of the rocks they had passed—and unlike the many perfectly round stones used to create this barrier, these were jagged, as if they had been carved out in places. They were certainly scalable, with a little effort and care. If the girls had gone over the boulders, as the man said they almost certainly had, then this was the place they had done it.

"Okay." Mike ran his hands along the wet rocks as Sam took a step back to survey the wall at a distance. He lit a cigarette. "It'd be much easier if it wasn't pissing it down. This whole thing is slippery, and I'm hardly wearing the right shoes for it."

"I'll get you up first," Sam said. "You can help me up once you're on top."

It sounded like a plan, but Mike wasn't sure he could pull Sam's weight up. He was a big guy, perhaps three stone heavier than Mike. "Maybe you should go up first," he suggested. "You can pull me up." Now *that* sounded like an executable plan.

"All right," Sam said, flicking his half-smoked cigarette away. Orange embers were carried away on the wind, fading to nothing before they touched the ground. "Let's do it."

Sam had never climbed in his life. That became apparent almost immediately. He found a crevice, slipped out of it. He reached up and took hold of a jagged protrusion, yet couldn't grip on once his full weight was off the ground. Each time he failed he came up with a new combination of profanities. It was not going well at all, and Mike was about to suggest an alternative plan when Sam managed to wedge his foot into a tight aperture and push himself halfway up the rock.

"Got it!" he grunted, frantically searching for the best place to go next. Mike moved behind him, pushed his shoulder into Sam's ass, and held him in place. The last thing either of them wanted now was to fail.

"To your left," Mike said, noticing the outcrop that Sam should have been aiming for next. He had been right; Sam was a lot heavier than he looked. Mike's feet slipped in the mud, but he held firm and managed to dig his heels in to prevent them both from sliding down the hill and back to square one.

Sam must have seen the rocky offshoot, because a second later the weight eased on Mike's shoulder and Sam inched farther up the wall. He had to hand it to his sister and Rebecca; they had been determined to get over this wall. Whereas most people, most *normal* people, would have searched for a way around, they had opted to move linearly, the most direct way to Barbara's house, and this was apparently it.

"Push!" Sam said. "Push me up!"

Mike grabbed Sam by the soles of his muddy shoes and, with every ounce of strength that remained, forced Sam upwards. Sam was muttering something, perhaps words of encouragement, to himself, but Mike couldn't hear him over the howling wind and the racing *hush-thump* of blood in his ears. And then the soles of Sam's shoes were no longer pressing down into his palms, and Sam's legs were scrabbling in thin air, steadily upwards, as he managed to grab a hold of something at the top of the boulder and drag himself up.

Mike breathed a sigh of relief; that was a lot more difficult than it had looked, but at least one of them had made it.

"Jesus fuck!" Sam said from the top of the boulder he now rested on. "I really ought to quit smoking."

Mike didn't think that was the whole problem. Smoking, drinking, eating, ruminating, wallowing. It was a plethora of unhealthy choices. "Reckon you can help me up?"

"Been humping steel most my life," Sam said. "Think I can manage a scrawny little waif like you."

Mike sniggered. "I don't know," he said. "Think this coat weighs three times as much as it did earlier."

"Give me your hand." Sam reached down for him. "Put one foot in that hole there and reach up for me. I'll do most of the work, but you need to push up."

Mike did as he was instructed, and was surprised by how strong Sam actually was. He had to do very little work to get up. Sam almost pulled his arm out of its socket. Within moments they were both sitting atop the wall of boulders, staring into the trees on the other side.

"Some kind of abandoned forest?" Mike said. "But why would they build a wall around it?"

"We don't know that the wall goes all the way," Sam said. From their vantage point it was still impossible to tell, but to Mike it seemed to stretch on into the ether. Even through the fog he saw that it appeared endless on either side. There certainly wasn't an easier way in than the one they had just found.

Then why wasn't it on the map? Why hadn't it been marked clearly when such trivial things as minor trails and farmers' fields had? This looked like an entire forest, a place of natural beauty, and here it was, cordoned off with no easy access and no markings to suggest it was even there.

Solemnly, Sam said, "How were the girls not terrified coming this way?" It was a very good question, for it would have been dark by the time they got to this point. Yet they had persisted, climbed over the rocks and headed into a forest that led to somewhere or nowhere. And if the boulders did go all the way around, what was to say they would find a way over on the other side? What was to say they would find their way back to this place? They could still be trapped in there, Mike thought.

He had a nightmarish vision of them then, slumped against a tree, shivering and soaked to the bone. Kelly was skilled when it came to orienteering, but she was no survivalist. Three days without food and water would have rendered them both weak, resigned to the fact that they were lost and trapped, relying on someone to come to their rescue. Not only was it possible but it made perfect sense.

He thought about her hiding in that kennel with crumbs around her lips and her nose tipped white with icing. He thought about how she might look now, all covered in mud with her knees pulled into her chest, trying to beckon a passing squirrel with a stick so that they might live to fight another day.

"Are you ready?" Mike said, but he was already lowering himself down the other side. Without answering, Sam followed suit.

A strange sensation suddenly washed over Mike as his feet made contact with the ground on the other side and he stepped away from the boulders. Loneliness. Helplessness. It was a feeling that he had never experienced before, and he didn't like it at all. His body seemed to vibrate; every bone, tendon, muscle, organ trembled, his own personal earthquake, and the farther he moved away from the boulders the worse it got.

"I don't feel good," he said, and he didn't. He felt queasy. His mouth filled with saliva, the way it often does in those brief but terrible seconds before vomiting. He took deep and measured breaths and closed his eyes, willing the nausea away. The cold rain spraying his face helped to regulate his temperature, otherwise he would surely have succumbed to the sickness.

When he opened his eyes, he saw that Sam had dropped to his knees and was up-chucking violently yet somehow not making a sound. Years of practice as an alcoholic, Mike guessed, and wondered how many times Sam had been doubled over the toilet bowl, silently vomiting whisky and beer so as not to alert Rebecca to the problem.

"You okay?" Mike asked once Sam was finished.

"I think so," he said, wiping a string of drool from his bottom lip. "Man, that was pretty fucked up. I was okay, but then—"

"You touched the ground."

Sam nodded. "I don't like this place," he said. "There's something not right about any of this, or those boulders."

He was right. Mike could feel it. The air was much thicker here, heavier. Why would they both feel it, the palpable strangeness of this place, if it weren't true? And it all started with the boulders. Had the girls felt it, too? Had a sudden and inexplicable nausea washed over them as they touched down on the other side of the boulders?

Mike didn't know, but he knew one thing was for certain. This place, whatever and wherever it was, had been cordoned off for a reason. "You good to start walking?"

Sam nodded, but he still looked pale and, more concerning to Mike, more than a little afraid. "Yeah," he said. "Let's go."

They headed into the trees, unsure of their bearings but doing everything in their power to walk in a straight line. Mike was the first to call out the girls' names. After that they took it in turns, but there came no reply from anyone.

They're not here, Mike thought. *They were, but they're not anymore.*

He called out louder, hoping to hear her his sister's voice in return, wishing for a miracle that he somehow knew would not happen, and trying desperately not to lose hope for all their sakes.

TWELVE

Neverville, 1974

Freddie and Albie were standing at the bar supping moonshine when Dennis Wainwright limped into the inn. Freddie had enjoyed his morning with Eve and had decided to top it off with a couple of pints before returning to the farm to slaughter one of his lambs. It was the one part of the job he hated but it was necessary in order for them to eat. Man could not survive on vegetables alone, or as his mother used to say in her infinite wisdom, "A louse in the cabbage is better than no meat at all." It was one of those Alice-isms that didn't need much explanation. Sure, a cabbage is fine, but it lacks purpose without meat, no matter what form it comes in.

"How's the leg?" Albie asked Dennis as he poured a pint for the newcomer.

"Giving me a bit of gyp this morning," Dennis said. "I swear it's this rain. I think I need oiling. Or putting down."

Freddie and Dennis had grown up together, had played together in the woods when they were knee-high to a grasshopper, had been educated together, and fished together regularly down at the pond on the days Freddie wasn't tending to his animals or planting and Dennis wasn't overseeing the smooth operation of the watermill on the east side of the village. Dennis was a couple of years younger than Freddie, but the years hadn't been kind to him. Riddled with arthritis and gout, Dennis Wainwright kept Doc Renfield busier than any of the other villagers. His fingers no longer functioned as a unit, jutting off at impossible angles, and his legs were so swollen that he had taken to cutting slits into the calves of his trousers just so he could leave the house with a modicum of dignity. It pained Freddie to see him like this, but what could he do? They were all growing old together; it was inevitable.

It had always been inevitable.

"Get that down your neck," Albie said, setting the glass down in front of Dennis. "Put hairs on your chest, that will."

Dennis snorted. "Got plenty of those," he said. "My problem is that they keep falling out every time I sneeze."

The Wheatsheaf was surprisingly quiet for a lunchtime. The menu board behind Albie announced a Tasty Meat Soup as the lunchtime special, and perhaps that was the problem. The locals would eat almost anything, but it wouldn't have hurt for Albie to let them know exactly what cut of meat had been used in the soup. Or at least what animal.

Apart from Freddie and Dennis, there were two other patrons—Edith Frewer and Liz Slocombe—who were drinking gin at a nearby table and discussing knitting patterns. So, the inn was quiet, so quiet that Freddie considered asking Albie for his rendition of Amazing Grace.

Dennis had turned up in the nick of time, for Freddie was already thinking of heading back to the farm to take care of business. Now he had someone to talk to for a while, and although his stomach was growling at him, there was no way he was staying for the mystery soup.

"Fishing tomorrow?" Freddie was planning on spending the day at the pond if the weather picked up. There was absolutely nothing fun about sitting in the rain for hours, hoping for a bite. You got wet, and you got cold, and therefore you got miserable.

Dennis shrugged. "Might as well while I can still hold the rod." He held up his hands and Freddie tried not to recoil in horror, or show any sign that the gnarled mess of fingers and knuckles affected him either way. "One thing's for sure," he said. "My piano playing days are over."

Freddie laughed slightly. Dennis Wainwright had never played the piano, or any musical instrument. "I guess so," he said. "On the bright side, at least you don't need your hands to boss those lackeys around at the mill."

"There's always that," Dennis said. "Trouble is, they're all getting too old to put in a hard day's shift. I'm lucky if half of them turn up for work, and the ones that do are either coughing their lungs up or moving about the place like half-crippled crabs. It's a wonder this place has any power at all."

Albie sat on his stool behind the bar and joined the conversation. "It's only a matter of time before it doesn't," he said. "Unless you get young Eve up there and show her the ropes."

"The mill's no place for a lady," Dennis said, visibly shuddering at the thought. He was old-fashioned, still believed that a woman's place was in the home, which was probably the reason he had never been married or, to Freddie's knowledge—and he had known him all his life—felt the sweet, loving embrace of a woman. If Dennis had seen the way Eve Lockwood had thrown herself into the work at the farm that morning, he might have changed his tune. She was ten times more able than any of them, and a hundred times sharper of mind. There was nothing that girl couldn't do, which was perhaps the reason why people like Dennis strived to keep her down.

"She'd have that place ship-shape in no time," Albie said, taking the words out of Freddie's mouth. "Let's face it, Dennis. If you can do it, anyone can."

"It's a skilled job," Dennis said, sipping at his moonshine. "Takes years of experience. I still haven't learned everything yet."

"Well, you'd better hurry up," Freddie said. "Hate to say it, but you're running out of time."

"Very funny. At least you'll both have the pleasure of being at my funeral."

Freddie patted his friend affectionately on the back. "We'll have to get a coffin specially made," he said, "the way your legs are going."

"Ah, don't be bothering with no coffin," Dennis said. "Just stick me up in that field of yours. Besides, I can't afford anything special. Reckon not many of us can, these days. No, you can tie a rock around my ankle and drop me to the bottom of the pond." He smiled at that, as if the thought was crossing his mind for the first time and he quite liked it.

Freddie, on the other hand, was thinking about the fish. It wouldn't be good for them, swimming around a corpse, feeding from what remained of Dennis until there was nothing left. And people had to eat those fish once he caught them, which couldn't be healthy. By proxy, they would each be eating Dennis, at least at the beginning. Albie's mystery soup was only marginally less terrifying than the thought of eating the decaying body of Dennis Wainwright.

"Can we change the subject?" Albie said as he ran a dirty rag across the bar, though he remained seated as he did it. It was too early for physical exertion, and the inn was too quiet to pretend to be doing anything in order to appear busy. Albie had always been a procrastinator; don't do today what you can put off until tomorrow, that was his motto, and oftentimes the state of the inn reflected this. If you weren't sticking to the floor as you walked across the room, or your elbows weren't fusing with the counter as you ordered more drinks, that was good enough for Albie.

"Oh! Yeah, I had the worst nightmare ever last night!" Dennis lit a cigarette made from tobacco from butts he had probably smoked a dozen times already. It barely lit; he was practically just burning the paper. "Well, it wasn't really a nightmare. She was in my room, standing at the foot of my bed, just watching me, and I couldn't move. I was whimpering, I knew I was whimpering, but it was as if I was stuck to the bedclothes."

"Dennis," Freddie said. "You know we don't talk about Her. It was just a dream." Who was he trying to convince? Had he not had the same dream once or twice? Unable to move as She watched him from the shadows at the corner of the room? "And I thought we were going to talk about something nice."

"I know," Dennis said. "It just gave me the scares, that's all. It was so real. I even saw Her face, all nasty and filled with hate."

"Dennis," Albie said. He had heard enough, and Freddie was glad the landlord was intervening before it went any further. "What with your gout, your arthritis, your funeral, and now Her, I'm starting to think you're trying to piss me off."

Dennis laughed a little, but it was nervous, false. "Fair enough," he said. He raised his glass and held it in the air. "Here's to us."

"To us," Freddie said, clinking his friend's glass with his own. Albie, *sans* drink, simply tapped the bar with his hand. "Another one please, Albie."

After that, the conversation became lighter, less intense, and Freddie all at once felt at ease in the company of his friend. They discussed horses—Dennis tried to convince Freddie to give him one of his at a discount, but Freddie was having none of it, and besides, what was Dennis going to do with a horse?—and conversed at length about building a small cabin down by the pond to save them carting their tackle and gear down there every time they wanted to fish. It would, they decided, be more than just a storage unit. They would be able to sleep there, should the urge strike them to partake in a little night fishing, taking it in turns in a bunk while the other continued to fish late into the night. It would have a canopy, so that they could shelter if the rain became a nuisance, and in the summer it would shade them from the sun and keep them cool. Freddie built a picture of it in his mind as they planned it out, and it sounded like a dream. But he knew that, like most of their dreams now, it would never come to fruition. They had left it a little late in the day to start laying out plans to build things. It was just talk. Something to fill the silence. Like the ladies sitting a few tables away discussing stain removal and the best pattern for a winter cardigan. None of it mattered. Stains would eventually fade, and if it got too cold in the winter, you just put another layer on. Their dream cabin down by the pond would forever be a nice idea, but nothing more.

Dennis had just started to prattle on about his gout again when the door flew open and in came little Wanda Hill. Wanda was not a dwarf, at least that's what Doc Renfield had told her, but she was the smallest person in the village by a good two feet. And she swayed as she walked, side to side like a stick insect, as if her thighs were too big for the rest of her legs. Whether it had something to do with her size, Freddie didn't know, but Wanda's voice was high, too, and wholly unnatural. There was definitely something wrong with her, despite Doc Renfield's official diagnosis, but no one ever mentioned it. The whole village knew she was different; they had gotten used to it, and so what if she had some underlying factor that made her that way? She was one of them.

She said her hellos to everyone in the room in that strange, high-pitched voice of hers, removed her sodden coat and ran her fingers through her drenched hair, then hopped up onto the empty stool at the end of the bar and drummed her stubby little fingers until Albie placed a drink in front of her.

"Everything okay, Wanda?" Freddie said. He could see that something irked her, and if it meant he wouldn't have to listen to another gout diatribe from Dennis, Freddie was more than willing to find out what it was.

"I don't know," Wanda said. "Well, I mean, maybe."

Freddie was intrigued. "Stop dangling carrots," he said. "What's the matter?"

Wanda turned the glass around in her hands and scratched at her chin, where a small silver beard had begun to form. "Well," she said. "I was getting my washing in earlier, you know, because of this rain. I was too late. My smalls were already soaked."

It took every ounce of Freddie's resolve not to make a joke about Wanda Hill's smalls, since that was everything she wore. But she seemed perturbed by whatever had happened, and now was not the time for smart remarks.

"I was getting the stuff off the line when I heard something."

"You *heard* something?" Dennis had given up on his useless cigarette and crushed what remained of it between his crooked fingers.

"What was it?" Freddie sipped at his fresh moonshine, enjoyed the warmth as it slipped down his throat.

"Voices," Wanda said. "Coming from over the back."

Wanda lived at the edge of the forest. For some reason she liked it there, away from the hustle and bustle of the rest of the village. Perhaps she knew she was different and had made herself something of an outsider because of it. The house she lived in had always been there, and she had merely adopted it as her own, its distance from the village proper just enough for her. Freddie thought she had made a good choice, for it must be nice living out there. Peaceful. With the trees to her rear and very few passersby.

"That's the forest," Albie said.

Nothing unusual about that, Freddie thought. People often walked through the woods. It was one of the best things about the village. He would go up there himself sometimes, purposely to get lost amongst the trees. "Hardly news, Wanda," he said. "You must hear a lot of voices from back there."

She nodded. "Yeah, but I didn't recognise these voices. And they were shouting. They were calling out, as if someone was lost in there."

That was strange; anyone who went up there regularly would know those trees like the backs of their hands. Even if you somehow got turned around and ass backward, it was easy to find your way down to the trail again. All you had to do was listen for the machinery from the mill and start walking toward it. And if the machinery wasn't operating, what the hell were you doing in the forest at that time of night to begin with?

"Maybe it was the wind," Albie said. "Voices can carry on the wind like that. I've heard things before, too. Like when one of those white things flies over. Sounds like thunder, sometimes." They had all seen the white things in the sky, the trails they left behind. Some of the more religious villagers believed them to be a sign from God, but not Freddie. He didn't know what they were. Some sort of air vehicle from the outside world was his guess, a reminder that although time stood still in Neverville, beyond the boulders the world continued to progress. He didn't like to think about it too much.

"It was coming from the forest," Wanda said. "I might be small, but my ears are normal size."

"You say they were calling out," Freddie said. "What did you hear? How many voices did you hear? Who were they calling out to?"

"It sounded like they were calling out girls' names," Wanda said. "Two voices, but there might have been more. They were calling out Kelly, I think, and something else. I didn't get the other one. But I know what I heard, and that was it. Two men's voices."

Freddie's heart began to race. There was no one in the village called Kelly; everyone knew everyone. It was easy when there were only ninety-nine other people to remember by name or face, and it was even easier when you had had seventy-something years to memorise them.

"That's not what she heard," Dennis said. "And even if she did, maybe someone renamed one of the dogs and it got away from them. There's a perfectly reasonable explanation for it."

"Maybe," Wanda said, as if the dog theory made more sense than the alternative.

Freddie and Albie exchanged a look that said neither of them was convinced. To ignore this would be irresponsible. Maybe someone's dog had slipped its leash. Maybe it had become lost up there, and its careless owner was trying to call it back. Maybe, and this was a big one, the voices had travelled on the wind from beyond the boulders. Freddie had never heard anything other than bleating sheep on his many sojourns through the trees, but it was possible and couldn't be immediately ruled out. But the way Albie Moss looked at him now told him exactly what the man was thinking, what he wanted Freddie to do.

"Where's that musket of yours?" he asked Albie.

"Got her right here," Albie said. He reached down beneath the counter and retrieved the matchlock musket, something that had been handed down through the Mosses for generations. It was a relic from some long-ago war or other, but Freddie knew how to use it, had hunted outsiders with it on more than one occasion. "And a whole box of iron balls." He set the box down on the counter next to the musket and flipped the lid open.

"*We* made those," Dennis said, seemingly pleased with the craftmanship of his men.

Freddie downed the rest of his moonshine and stood. If there was somebody up in the forest, more than one person if Wanda was to be believed, then he felt compelled to do something about it. The mishap with those two girls the other night necessitated some sort of atonement, if not to appease Eric Majors, who had been visibly and verbally annoyed with him, then to prove he wasn't going soft in his old age.

"Do you want me to gather a posse?" Albie said, handing the musket across the counter to Freddie. "You know how much they love a good hunt."

Freddie shook his head. "I don't think that's necessary," he said, pocketing the box of iron balls. "It might be nothing." He *hoped* it was nothing; it was too early in the day to be gunning down outsiders. And it wasn't the weather for digging holes, though at least the soil would be soft. *Every cloud has a silver lining*, his mother's voice said to him. "I'll just go take a little look-see."

Dennis stood then, wincing and making a godawful hissing sound, as if he had trodden on a bed of nails. "I'll come with you," he said.

Freddie placed a hand on his friend's shoulder. "You stay here," he said. Dennis, with his numerous physical ailments, would only slow him down, and he was slow enough already. And besides, only one of them had a musket, and Dennis struggled to hold onto his pint. Giving the man a blade and expecting him to be able to grip it was ludicrous.

"Yeah, finish your pint," Albie said. "Freddie can take care of this."

If there's anything to take care of, Freddie thought. He continued to hope that Wanda was mistaken, that the voices had come from beyond the boulders or that someone was calling out to a recalcitrant animal.

To Wanda, Freddie said, "Two of them, you say?"

"That's what I heard." She held up two stubby fingers, as if he didn't know what that looked like. In all honesty, Freddie was surprised she could count that high. "And they didn't sound old, like us."

"Wanda, how can a voice sound old?" Dennis had returned to his stool, resigned to the fact he was superfluous to this particular crusade.

Wanda shrugged. "Ain't none of us that can shout that loud without coughing up a lung," she said.

Freddie had heard enough. The only way to draw a line under this was to go up there and find out for himself. He had the musket, he had the iron balls, and he had a reason for doing it alone: to shut Eric Majors up once and for all.

He said his goodbyes and received his good lucks, and left the inn with the musket slung across his shoulder and the iron balls rattling around in the box in his pocket.

The rain drenched him almost immediately, but it no longer bothered him in the slightest. He pointed himself in the direction of the forest and began to walk.

THIRTEEN

Neverville, 1974

As Freddie and Albie and Dennis sat in the Wheatsheaf, before Wanda had made her entrance and thrown the entire day into darkness, Doc Renfield arrived at the Lockwood residence, still cursing ever getting out of bed that morning. It wouldn't have changed the course of events, of course. He would have still been inexorably drawn to the church, where Father Calhoun would have proceeded to kiss his self-pitying wounds and urged him to think about things a little differently. He would have still been soaked to the bone. Jack Lockwood would still have awoken and tried to kill his wife. Nothing would have changed. It was, for want of a better word, fate, and although Renfield didn't believe in religion or a magic mystery man in the sky, there was no denying the existence of destiny, that predetermined events beyond a person's control were a thing, and that he was a victim of circumstance just as much as the next man.

To deny fate would be arrogant; to believe that one had control over everything that happened around them, that was simply absurd.

When Joan came to the door, she looked visibly shaken. Eve stood behind her looking more like a little girl than Renfield had ever seen her before. Even as a child she had appeared fierce, capable of taking on the world, but now she looked lost, her eyes imploring him for answers, her downturned mouth a precursor of tears.

"He's been awake for a while," Joan said, ushering Renfield into the house. "Thought he was going to break the door down. And he's been screaming the most hideous things."

Eve offered to make a pot of tea, but Renfield politely declined. He had to get to work as quickly as possible. "I can't hear him now," he said, for he couldn't. There was no sound from upstairs, no screams or bangs. It was eerily silent, which made Renfield even more uncomfortable.

"He's been doing this," Eve said. "It's like he's exhausting himself. His outbursts are violent, and I'm not sure he can keep them up for long."

"He called me a wicked cunt!" Joan said. "He knows how much I abhor that word, but he kept saying it over and over again, that he would finish the job and plant me up at the farm with the others."

Renfield recoiled a little at Joan's use of the C-word. Only an hour or so ago he had been at the church in the presence of a self-professed Man of God. Now he was here with a foul-mouthed mother and wife. The disparity was remarkable.

"I don't think he knows what's going on," Eve said. "It's as if he's possessed."

Renfield didn't believe in possession, either. Jack Lockwood's body and mind had not been taken over by anything but his own madness, which science and psychology could explain. There was no reason to give in to supernatural fantasies when there was a perfectly reasonable explanation right in front of them. Eve was frightened, he could see that, and Joan was equally so, but was seemingly more concerned about the names she had been called than the man behind them. Eve, Renfield concluded, since she was a smart girl, hadn't meant that her father was possessed by an otherworldly being. She had merely meant he was not in control. There was a body in the cart but the horses were the ones doing the steering.

"I think we need to restrain him before anything else," Renfield said. "I would like to perhaps get another man present. That's not to say I don't think we are capable, between the three of us, of overpowering him. Just that I am not a very physical man, and your love for him might compromise our attempts."

"I don't want anyone else involved," Joan said, staidly. "You understand why."

Renfield sighed. He knew that Jack Lockwood was not the most popular villager in Neverville. He had, at one time or other, pissed on the shoes of just about every one of them. Even Doc Renfield.

Twenty-five years ago, before Eve was even conceived and Jack had made a vegetable of himself, Renfield had treated Joan for a case of influenza. He had been summoned to the house by Jack Lockwood himself, and over the duration of three weeks, had utilised everything he had to keep her from succumbing to it. He also succeeded in keeping Joan and Jack away from the other villagers to prevent the disease's spread, and was greatly relieved, and more than a little vainglorious, when no one else in the village contracted it. He had prevailed where, according to his books, entire countries and continents had failed before him. It was a remarkable feat, and when Joan recovered fully, she could not have been more grateful.

She deified Doc Renfield as some kind of demigod, her worship of him manifesting in all manner of over-the-top gestures and statements. She would bake for him and arrive at his house with baskets filled with loaves and cakes and sweet things. When she deemed that as an improper display of recognition, she tended to his garden when he was not there, fetched him milk from Freddie's farm and left it on his stoop, often accompanied by a little note explaining that she was forever in his debt and would do anything and everything she could to show her thanks.

Eventually, it all got a little much for Jack, who had always been a jealous man and apparently saw his wife's sudden infatuation with the doctor as more than meets the eye. The problem was, to Renfield it was nothing more than it was; Joan was grateful to still be alive, thankful that the doctor had looked after her so well, had not left her bedside for the better part of a month, putting himself at risk of contracting the disease in the process. But to Jack, it was much more. It showed all the signs of infidelity. Baked goods today would lead to sexual offerings tomorrow. It was, in Jack's mind, the natural order of things, and he wasn't about to allow Renfield to come in and defile his wife, nosiree.

It started out as nothing more than an evil eye here, a muted utterance there, but Renfield had seen it coming. He knew exactly what was going on, and wanted to say something to Jack before it went any further. He had no interest in Joan, or any woman in the village, for that matter. He had his library and his mind, and to him that was far more important. So, he had, during a village party at which most of the villagers were in attendance, taken Jack to one side and tried to get through to him.

Jack's response?

Well, it had gone about as well as Renfield had expected. The man was enraged, and had set about Renfield with all the fury of a box of lit dynamite. There had been punches and kicks and elbows and knees, and Renfield had made himself into a ball to protect himself until the villagers came to his rescue. Jack was still shouting about how Renfield was ruining his marriage and that the other married men in the village needed to lock up their wives, for this man was not to be trusted. Fortunately for Renfield, the villagers knew he was not capable of such malpractice, and Jack was temporarily ostracised. This only drew further resentment from Jack, who spent the next two years ignoring Renfield completely, even though he had done nothing wrong. This new arrangement suited the doctor, who found it almost impossible to forgive the man who had inflicted such a savage and unwarranted beating upon him in front of the entire village. Not only had it been demoralising, it had hurt like a sonofabitch.

Jack Lockwood was not a good man, despite what his wife thought of him. The other villagers knew it, and the other villagers would be quite happy at the news of his death. To hear that he was back, that he had returned from his purgatory and was now a bubbling ball of rage and pure hatred, would cause unnecessary tumult the length and breadth of the village.

It was no wonder Joan wanted to keep it a secret.

"Okay," Renfield ceded. "But if it's true what you've said, then the man in that room is no longer your husband." To Eve he said, "No longer your father. And you have to set aside all love you hold for him so that we can get this under control."

"That'll be easy enough," Eve said.

"Eve!" her mother cried. "Show a little compassion. For me."

But Eve, Renfield noticed, was not ready to be as forgiving as her mother, and she had only known him as the mostly harmless incapacitated man in the chair; she had only heard of her father's wicked ways through hearsay and gossip, and had forged her own informed opinion of him accordingly. Eve had decided, from a very early age, that any man crazy enough to try to go over the boulders was not a man with all his sandwiches in the picnic basket.

"He's dangerous," Eve reminded her mother. "Don't forget that, Mother."

Joan huffed. If that was the best excuse she had for him, Renfield didn't rate their chances of overpowering the man very highly.

"Come on," Renfield said, realising that they were getting nowhere fast. "Do you have anything we can tie him up with? A length of rope, perhaps?"

"There should be some in the outhouse," Joan said. "I'll go and fetch it."

When she returned with six feet or so of rope coiled around her arm and shoulder, Renfield inspected it. There was no room for error here, and any negligence could result in any one of them getting hurt or killed. "Looks strong enough," he said. "Let's do it."

Outside the bedroom door they stopped. Renfield looked at the boards that had been hurriedly hammered into the door and frames. There was no way Jack would have gotten through it, but there was also no way they would be able to get into him without alerting him to their presence. This was going to be even more difficult because of the ladies' impeccable handiwork.

"I want you to talk to him," Renfield said.

"What?" Joan said.

"Convince him that we're here to help."

"We've tried that already," Eve said. "It just makes him angrier. I don't think he cares too much about being helped right now."

"Then try to make him realise that we're not going to hurt him, at least."

"But we are," Joan said, no more than a whisper. "That's what we're going to do. That's what the rope is for."

"I just need him to get away from the door so we can rush him as soon as we get through. If he thinks we're going to hurt him, he's going to come at us before we even get a chance to restrain him." Renfield didn't like the fear that had crept into his voice. He recalled the pain he had felt after that beating at the party, remembered Jack's balled fists coming in at him from the right and left and underneath. It all came flooding back, and he couldn't deny the fact he didn't want to be on the receiving end of a second mauling by Jack's hands.

"Okay," Joan said. "If you think it will help."

Renfield didn't know whether it would help, but he knew that they had to try *something*.

Joan stepped up to the door, listened for a moment for any hint of a sound from within, and when none came, she proceeded to speak. "Jack? Jack, can you hear me? Jack, we're not going to hurt you. We're here to help take care of you. Jack? Jack, can you hear me?"

Silence.

Renfield motioned to Eve, as if the sound of his daughter's voice would have a different effect. Eve looked unconvinced and wholly terrified at the thought. "It's okay," Renfield assured her. "I won't let anything bad happen to you. To either of you." Although he realised he was reassuring himself as much he was them.

Reluctantly, Eve stepped up to the door and sighed. Joan took a few steps back as Renfield set about removing the first few planks from the doorframe.

"Father, can you hear me?" If Eve had looked like a little girl when Renfield saw her downstairs, she sounded like one now. Innocent, sad, confused, she might as well have been telling her mother that she had accidentally broken a china teapot or, in a bout of overzealousness, fallen from a wall and soiled her best dress. She paused for a response, and when there came only silence repeated the phrase two more times.

He's being clever, Renfield thought. In not answering, he was making them question their approach, slowing them down so that he could formulate a plan of his own. Jack didn't know that Renfield was present; the doctor had been very careful not to speak too loudly. It gave them the element of surprise when they came through the door. If he was simply expecting it to be his wife and daughter, he was about to be sorely mistaken, and that, Renfield thought, might just be enough to throw him off for that split-second, that brief moment they would have between success or failure.

Renfield set another board down. He would need an iron crow to pry the main boards off, and whispered to Eve to go and fetch one, or something similar. As she descended the stairs, Joan continued to call out through the door, growing increasingly frustrated when there was no response. Renfield had to remind her to remain calm, that the mere raising of her voice was likely to exacerbate matters.

"He's in there!" Joan cried.

Renfield nodded, confirmation that he knew that.

"Why's he not answering? I'm his wife, for Christ's sake!"

Renfield nodded silently once more. *You're also the person he tried to kill earlier,* Renfield wanted to remind her. *You're lucky to just be getting the silent treatment right now.* He urged her to continue trying, as fruitless as that might be, and she did her best but her frustration was palpable.

Eve returned with an iron crowbar and handed it to Renfield. It was heavy, and would make for a useful weapon if it came to it. But they only wanted to subdue Jack, not knock the brains out of his ears. Renfield would strike him in the kneecaps with the bar; it would be enough to take the savage man down without causing permanent damage.

The first board squeaked as the nails pulled out of the doorframe. Jack, on the other side of the door, would have heard it, would know that they were removing the barricade. Time was of the essence; there was no point in pussyfooting around now.

"Jack, we are trying to help you." Joan continued to tell him what they thought he wanted to hear, and she was, Renfield thought, doing a convincing job of it. But then she would become discouraged once again by his silence, and bitterness would take over as she reminded him, "Just who the hell do you think you are? Ignoring me like this."

Renfield removed all but one of the wooden planks from the door. One good kick and the door would fly open; that final plank was their last line of defence.

He urged the women to take a step back. Joan had picked up the rope and now held it like a cowboy about to lasso his horse. Eve nervously twiddled something around and around on her finger, but the shadows in the hallway made it dark and Renfield couldn't see what it was. "On three," he whispered, heart racing in his chest. The bannister behind made it impossible to get a good run-up to the door, but he had room to bring his leg back, and that was enough. It had to be.

Joan and Eve nodded in unison. It was now or never, and while Renfield much preferred the latter option, he knew that the safety of the village hinged upon them getting this right.

"One..."

Still silent beyond the door, but he was in there. Joan said there was no way out other than the shuttered door.

"Two..."

Eve whimpered a little, terrified, uncertain, perhaps hoping this was all just a terrible nightmare from which she would awaken as soon as the doctor's foot made contact with the door.

"Three!"

Renfield gave it everything he had, bringing his knee up into his body and throwing his leg out as hard as he could possibly muster. The door flew open, the splintered plank shooting off and almost hitting Joan Lockwood squarely in the face. All three of them barrelled into the bedroom, ready for war. Renfield shouted for Jack to get on the floor, but Jack couldn't get on the floor, because Jack was not in the room.

What followed was a few seconds of panicked confusion as they surveyed the room, anywhere that Jack might have been hiding, but he was not there. He had seemingly vanished into thin air. A miracle that science could not explain, much to Renfield's chagrin.

Then Joan brought everything back to reality, and all was well with the world again. Renfield's world of science and perfectly reasonable explanations, anyway. "The window!" she gasped.

Rushing across the room, still gripping the iron crowbar ready to strike if Jack should suddenly appear from some shadowy corner, Renfield saw that the window-pane was almost entirely gone, smashed through. Shards remained, jutting upward from the sill. There was fresh blood on the glass, a sign that Jack had cut himself as he made his escape.

Renfield looked out through the window, at the ground in front of the house and then along the trail and into the distance, but there was no sign of the escapee.

"Do you see him?" Joan cried. "Oh, God! Is he there?"

"He's long gone," Renfield said, and the coward in him was glad of that, for it meant no violent confrontation right now. He turned to Joan; Eve was still standing in the bedroom doorway, had come no further into the room. "You must have heard the window go through," he said.

Joan looked shocked. Her eyes were fixated upon the smashed window, and Renfield saw that she was trembling. "He was banging," she said. "Smashing the room up. I didn't think he'd break the window."

Of course, he'd break the window, Renfield thought. When an animal is in a cage against its will, it will look for any weaknesses in the structure. Joan said the windows had been stuck shut, but Jack hadn't let that prevent him from getting out.

Renfield heaved a sigh of...relief? Disappointment? Both? "He's out there," he said. "And who knows what he's capable of."

"We have to find him," Joan said, rubbing her arms as if a chill had suddenly come over her. "If anyone sees him—"

"We'll find him, Mother," Eve said.

"This whole village is in danger," Renfield said. He wanted to scream it from the rooftops that there was a lunatic on the loose, that they all knew him well, for he had wronged them all, and now he was free, not just of the mental prison that had kept him confined to his bedroom for the past twenty-something years, but his physical prison, too.

Jack Lockwood was a free man, and he was capable of just about anything.

"Damn!" Renfield said.

There was a flash of lightning and then, a second later, thunder shook the foundations of the house. Doc Renfield was starting to wish he believed in God; in that moment, they needed as much help as they could get.

Those bastards! Who did they think they were, blocking him in that room like that? They thought they could keep him there, the way they had kept him there all these years. How many years? How many years had he been sitting in that chair? They must have fed him, kept him alive. There was congealed potato down his shirt, and his trousers were full of shit. Cold shit that now slipped down his trouser legs as he ran through the rain.

He had to get off the trail. Had to find somewhere to hole up for a while, figure out his next move. Out here he was a sitting duck. If he was seen, it would all be over. The villagers would come after him, and that couldn't happen. There was only one thing on his mind, and that was putting an end to that witch and that witch's daughter. They were not his family. They were the enemy, and when he was done with them—and he would make it slow, so that they too could experience the pain and helplessness he had felt since he had leapt from the boulders—he would take care of that sonofabitch Freddie Carson.

And Albie Moss, for if Albie hadn't interfered that night and banished him from the inn, none of this would have happened.

Don't forget that stealer of wives, Doc Renfield. Yes, it would be a pleasure to end that man.

Jack would kill them all for what they had put him through, make them suffer as much as he had and then some. It would be strategic; he was a general now, the leader of his own confederation, but first he had to get off the trail, out of this godforsaken weather, and he knew exactly where he should be, where he could lay low for a while and formulate his revenge without intrusion.

The church doors were shut when he arrived, but one good push and he spilled into the building and almost went over as his feet slipped on the floor. The sound of pipe organ music came from somewhere. Father Calhoun, Jack thought, was practicing for Sunday's service, and that was a good thing, for it had covered the sound of his arrival.

At least, he thought it had, but when the pipe organ suddenly stopped playing, Jack knew that he had not gotten away with it. Footsteps echoed around the church, accompanied by the heavy *click-clack* of a cane as it met with the floor, signalling the vicar's approach.

Jack thought about hiding, ducking down beneath the pews and remaining out of sight until Father Calhoun returned to his organ, but then a voice in his head said, *Why should I? Fuck that!* which somehow made perfect sense to him. He could handle Calhoun.

Instead of hiding, Jack began to walk along the aisle, humming to himself as he went. When he saw the confessional at the edge of the room, he laughed, for he had much to confess and very little inclination to do so. Where would he even begin? Was attempted murder a forgivable sin? Of course it was. You could kill a thousand people, sit in that box for one minute, and still go to heaven. At least that's what they had all been led to believe. What kind of stupid fuckery was that?

Father Calhoun appeared in front of the altar, and when he saw Jack Lockwood walking toward him, he stopped dead in his tracks, gasping audibly with shock. "Um, Jack?" he said. "Jack Lockwood?"

"Don't you recognise me?" Jack said, grinning. "Yes, Father. It's me. Back from the dead. And it's not even Easter! Turns out this resurrection malarkey is an all-year-round thing."

Calhoun recoiled a little, gripped his cane as if it were a crucifix and Jack was a creature of the night. "This is remarkable!" he said, forcing a smile. "It's so good...so good to have you back."

"It's good to *be* back, Father," Jack said, and it was. "I guess you could say my little absence from reality has done me the world of good. Apart from all the years of nightmares, reliving the hell over and over while the village went on without me, I'd say it was the best thing to ever happen to me." He paused for a moment to consider something. Perhaps the good father could shed some light upon his little departure from existence. "Say, how long has it been, Father? I mean, when was I last in here? This place?" He motioned ambiguously at the church around him.

"Um, Jack, you don't know how long it's been?" Calhoun was clearly uncomfortable with the distance between them closing, and took a few steps back toward the altar.

Jack laughed. "What's it been?" he asked. "Five years? Ten?" For all he knew it could have been ten years. A whole decade of semi-unconsciousness while, in his mind, he must have run through those woods fifty-thousand times, been punched upside the head by Freddie Carson that same amount.

"It's been twenty-one years, Jack," Father Calhoun said. "Since you last graced these walls with your presence."

Something caught in Jack's throat, and for a moment he feared he would choke upon it. Father Calhoun must have noticed his discomfiture, for his face dropped a couple of inches with concern.

"Well," Jack said, trying not to let this terrible new knowledge affect his newfound sense of purpose. "That would make me sixty-five. I guess I should have known it was longer than five years. You look like a sack of worms compared to the last time I saw you. And how long have you had the cane, Father? Not very Christian of your God, is it, punishing one of his own like that? And don't give me that, 'The Lord works in mysterious ways' bullshit. He's crippled you good and proper, and kept me in purgatory for longer than I care to think about. Does that sound like the work of a loving being?"

Father Calhoun was speechless, his mouth opening and shutting but nothing coming out. It was, Jack thought, hilarious. All those years of chattering and desperately trying to convince the villagers that they needed God in their life, that Jesus would always be there for them regardless, and that Neverville wasn't, in fact, cursed, but blessed, blessed to be set apart from the rest of the world, and now he was speechless. Jack felt a sense of pride at being able to shut the fucker up.

He moved closer still, enjoying the moment. "This village is sick," he said. "And you people are the disease bringing it to its knees." Jack knew that he was detested by everyone that knew him, but that was because he spoke the truth, saw past all the bullshit that blindfolded the rest of the village, and they didn't like it. "We are an abomination, deserving of this curse, and you, Father, are giving these people false hope with your promise of eternal paradise."

"I forgive you!" Calhoun cried, staggering back, away from the altar, his cane the only thing keeping him from going all the way over. "What happened to you was not your fault, Jack! I forgive you!"

Jack snickered. "I don't ever recall asking for your forgiveness," he said. He was almost upon the vicar, could reach out and take him by the throat, if he wanted to. But not just yet. It would be too easy.

A rumble of thunder shook the church. Several of the candles at the altar suddenly went out.

"Did you pray for me, Father?"

"Uh—"

"Did you ever, while I was *non compos mentis*, pray that I would be okay?"

Father Calhoun gasped for air. He had shrunk a couple of inches over the years, and Jack now towered over him. "I pray for everyone," he finally managed.

"Specifically," Jack said. "Has my name been uttered out loud in one of your sermons? Have you ever asked Him to save me?"

A flash of lightning and then more thunder.

"I prayed for your wife," Calhoun said. "For Eve. That they may find peace."

And that was just the problem. Jack was so loathed that even a man of God had forsaken him. Again, not very Christian, but it was what Jack had come to expect.

He reached down and snatched the cane from under Calhoun, and the old man toppled to the ground, moaning helplessly as his frail body connected with the tiled floor with a heavy thump.

The cane was much heavier than it looked, its ornate carvings suggesting a lot of work had gone into its manufacture. As Jack examined it, it was all he could do not to erupt in a fit of laughter; various religious sigils ran the length of the cane. Alpha and Omega, cross and crucifix, Ichthys, Chi Ro, The Good Shephard, each more intricate than the next. Did Calhoun think this gave him power, this stick whose sole purpose was to keep the man upright? Did he believe that it would protect him from the village's many evils, those things which they refused to acknowledge and were regarded by many as taboo? The curse? The witches? The boulders? The centum?

"One hundred, and not one more," Jack said.

He raised the cane, revelled for a moment in the fear this elicited from Calhoun, and then brought it down hard on top of the vicar's head. There was a meaty thud as it connected, and Calhoun made a sound that delighted Jack before his elbows gave way beneath him and he landed on his back.

Jack beat him again and again with the cane, until eventually Calhoun stopped moving and convulsing. When he was satisfied the vicar was finished, Jack went to the church doors and made sure they were locked good and tight. No one in their right mind would be out in this inclement weather, so it was probably unnecessary, but he wanted complete peace and time to think, and this was the perfect place in which to do it.

All alone in the church, Jack waited. The time would come to even the score against the villagers.

"Twenty fucking years," Jack sighed as the thunder rolled around and over the village. He extinguished all the candles and took a pew near the front, sitting in the darkness and loving every senseless minute of it.

FOURTEEN

Neverville, 1974

Mike didn't know how long they had been sheltering under that same tree, but it was keeping the rain off of them, and that's all that mattered. They were both drenched through, and Sam didn't look well. They had decided to find somewhere that provided cover, at least until the rain eased up, but it didn't look as if it would abate any time soon. So, they had sat at the base of a tree on protruding roots that were neither dry nor comfortable.

"Fuck, I wish we'd brought food," Mike said. His stomach had been aching for a while, and all he could think about was fish and chips and mushy peas. He was thirsty, too, and annoyed that they hadn't picked something up back at that Post Office in Staylittle. "You hungry?"

Sam grunted. "Of course I'm hungry. I'm hungry and pissed off, Mike."

A drop of rain managed to find its way onto Mike's neck and crawled down between his shoulder blades like an icy finger. He thought about how different things were just this time yesterday, and now look at him. Hiding from the rain beneath a tree in some walled-off graveyard in the middle of nowhere. And while things had been very different for him this time yesterday, Kelly had already been missing for several days. Rebecca, too. Not knowing about something did not alter the fact that it had happened; it just meant that you were oblivious to it. If his mother hadn't called him in the middle of the night, his life would have continued as normal. He would have gone to work, would have tried to convince people that they needed this particular car, that it would bring them joy and adventure, that they could afford it because, "We offer a finance package to cater for everyone!" He and Sam would not have reconciled after all these years; those memories of Kevin whipping the pebble at an innocent Rebecca Jones as she made her dolls talk to one another on the lawn in front of her house would have remained buried deep in his mind.

"I could use a drink," Sam said. Mike knew that he wasn't talking about water. He had noticed Sam's shakes worsening as the inevitable withdrawals set in.

"You're doing great," Mike said, but he couldn't imagine what Sam was going through right now. Addiction, for Mike, had never been an issue, unless you could be addicted to success. The euphoria that came with watching a contract being signed, he supposed, was similar to how Sam felt when he opened a fresh bottle and poured it out into a glass tumbler. He didn't know if that was a fair comparison, so kept it to himself.

"Yeah, great," Sam said, sardonically. "She's out there somewhere, and all I can think about is drinking. That's not normal, Mike. I'm so fucked up."

"You're not fucked up, mate," Mike said. Bringing up Rebecca alone, divorcing Barbara, losing his job, it had all contributed to Sam's drinking, and while it was no excuse, it certainly hadn't helped. "Have you ever thought about AA? There's got to be a Montgomery chapter?"

"Fuck all that," Sam said. "Talking about feelings and spiritual awakenings. I'd rather eat my own shit."

Mike laughed. "Jesus, Sam!" he said, wiping raindrops from his forehead.

"It's true! I'm not partnering up with some twitchy, seven-stone sad-case who thinks that three litres of cheap gut rot a day makes him a bad person, just because his mom told him it wasn't right. Those people collect those little pebbles, 'Oh, look at me! Ten years sober and all I've got to show for it is this lousy bit of rock!', and think they're better than everyone else because they've managed to turn their lives around." He gnawed nervously at his fingernails for a second, biting something off and spitting it out before continuing. "I'm fully aware that my drinking is a problem. It's been that way for a while, and I want to do something about it, but not right now. I can't do it right now, Mike, because my body feels like it could shut down at any minute. Even now I can feel it. Maybe that's why I was sick back there."

That's not the reason why, Mike thought. That was something else entirely.

"I know what Rebecca was looking for when she found those letters from Barbara," Sam said. "Empty bottles. I've been hiding them for years, and she'd always find them, because she's not stupid. But even when she found them, she wouldn't say anything, because she would know that I would know that she had found them, and that would be enough. Like she would move them slightly, or take the cap off, and we'd both know."

Mike understood how this little arrangement worked. Neither of them wanted the confrontation, the argument that would come from verbally broaching the subject. What Rebecca was doing was far cleverer, perhaps hoping that her silent efforts would have some sort of knock-on effect and change the man she loved so dearly without ever having to mention it aloud.

Sam laughed a little. "This one time, I thought I was being so smart. I had three empty bottles I knew I couldn't get rid of. The bins were already full of rubbish, and they weren't due to be collected for a few days. I knew the plank underneath the kitchen sink cabinet was loose. All it took was a little pull and I had the perfect place to keep them, at least until the bins were empty. So I did. I stuffed them in that little secret compartment and put the wood back. No way she'd find them there, right?"

"But she did."

Sam nodded. "Filled them up with water and put them back," he said. "I didn't know until I came to get them a few days later. When she got back from school that day, everything was normal. We both acted like it was, anyway, but she knew that I knew that she knew, and it was this whole thing we had going on. Almost like a game. And that's why she'd been going through my wardrobe. That's why she'd found those letters from Barbara, and that's why I feel like a fuck-up, Mike."

He blamed himself for this. For all of it. If he wasn't hiding bottles around the house—some twisted game of cat and mouse that neither of them spoke of, yet both knew was taking place—then she wouldn't have been looking in his wardrobe, and she wouldn't now be missing.

"You can't blame yourself for any of this," Mike said. "But you need to stay focussed, okay? You're feeling like shit right now because your brain is telling you that you haven't had a drink in a while."

"Look!" Sam held up his shaking hand for Mike to see, as if he hadn't already noticed it. "One glass of whisky makes that go away. Three glasses and I'm fucking normal again."

"Ten glasses and you're about as useful to me as this fucking weather," Mike said. He knew he sounded scathing, but he had to get through to Sam somehow, and if tough love was what it took, then so be it. "Mate, it's not my place, but I will help you. Once all this is over, I'll fucking help get you clean, if you want to, that is, but right now we're going to have to get through it." He held up his own hand, which was shaking, too, though not as violently as Sam's. "That's adrenaline," he said. "And fear. And cold. And uncertainty, and I'm going to use that to find my sister."

They both lowered their hands at the same time, and Mike thought he saw something in Sam's expression that suggested he understood.

"You're a good kid, Mike," Sam said. "I wouldn't have hit you, you know."

"What?"

"If I'd caught you that day, when you were on your skateboard. I wouldn't have hit you. I'd have made you apologise to her, probably would have made you sit there and play with her dolls, but I wouldn't have hit you."

Mike smiled. Being forced to sit and play with Rebecca and her Barbies would have been far more humiliating than a beating, and it would have been no less than he deserved. "Just so you know, it wasn't me that threw the stone."

Sam nodded. "Just so you know, and you'll know this when you've got a kid of your own, it doesn't matter who threw the stone."

And that was that. Neatly underlined and nothing further to say about the matter.

"Looks like the rain's easing up a little," Mike said, looking up through the trees at the dark clouds above. They were moving peculiarly, unnaturally quick, or was it the earth's rotation that had quickened? Of course that wasn't the case, but here in this strange forest, Mike's imagination was working overtime.

"Let's get out of this fucking forest," Sam said, pushing himself up from the ground. "Can't be much farther, not if we keep going that way." He motioned in the direction they had been walking, but there just seemed to be more trees, their branches dripping with rain, their trunks glistening.

The thunder was moving away, and for that Mike was grateful.

Freddie walked slowly through the forest, the musket slung across his back offering no peace of mind whatsoever. He was careful not to tread on anything that might alert anyone to his presence; twigs and dead leaves were given a wide berth entirely, although it was impossible to remain completely silent. The rain helped, and the occasional rumble of thunder allowed him to press on without having to worry too much about the odd crunch or rustle.

Since entering the forest, he hadn't heard anything. No shouting, no voices—male or otherwise—and he began to once again hope that Wanda was mistaken or that what she had heard had come from a lot farther away than the woods.

As he meandered between the trees, thoughts of more innocent times danced through his mind. As a child he had played here. His mother and father had forbidden him from going too close to the boulders, and had laid pieces of rope across the ground, the line which he should never cross. That damn rope had stretched almost all the way across the forest. There must have been almost a mile of it, and Freddie had always wondered where they got it from. It wasn't only his parents that used the rope as a safety net. Everyone's parents told their children not to cross it, that it was there for a reason. Some of them made up stories about all sorts of nasties and evils that lived on the other side of the rope, putting the fear into their children, as if they weren't all terrified enough by the village and its curse and the boulders and what happened if you got too close to them.

One day, in a fit of excitement and lunacy, Freddie and Dennis had crossed the rope. They had been provoking each other for weeks, calling each other names—Scaredy-cat! Chicken! Poltroon! Sissy!—until finally, Freddie had had enough. He went over that rope without a second though, never once believing that the stories of the Boogeyman that lived on the other side were real. And even if he was, Freddie was a brave boy, brave enough to step over the rope, much braver than Dennis Wainwright, who had stood there on the right side of the rope looking at him as if he had lost his marbles.

After much taunting, Dennis had joined Freddie on the other side, and they soon realised there was nothing there to fear. It was just the other side of the rope. The terrifying tales of shadowmen and trees with limbs that would reach down and pluck you from the ground were nothing more than the senseless falsehoods of deceitful parents.

Over the coming weeks, Freddie and Dennis had constructed a den of their own on the wrong side of the rope, far enough away from the myriad other structures in the woods that had been hastily thrown together by the likes of Walter Creswell and Frannie Mills. Those were, Freddie had told Dennis one summer, absolute shit. No, they would build something extraordinary, a den like no other. And when they had crossed that rope and entered uncharted territory—where the Boogeyman most certainly didn't live, and neither did the forest goblins or the ghoulish tree-dwellers—they had found the perfect spot for it where none of the other children dared to tread. It was theirs; there would never be any fear of coming back to it only to find that someone had set it afire, or had smashed it to pieces in a fit of either jealousy or out of pure selfishness.

That den—The Lair Beyond, they had called it—was their sanctuary, and remained upright and habitable for almost a year, until their parents got wind of it and all hell broke loose. Had they not been warned? There were bad things beyond the rope, things that would eat them and pull them apart before they even got close to the boulders. Alice Carson had beaten Freddie to within an inch of his life, and Dennis's father, who was not known for his compassion either, had inflicted such a severe pummeling upon Dennis that the poor boy couldn't walk right for months after.

The Lair Beyond was deconstructed and used for firewood, and Freddie, Dennis, and the other children of Neverville never set foot across that rope again, not because of the myriad evils that lurked beyond, but because they feared a much more palpable threat: the wrath of their parents.

That den had stood somewhere right around where Freddie now walked. The woods had changed somewhat over the years, but Freddie knew that if he dug deep enough into the undergrowth, scratched away at the surface, he would find bits of that rotten rope.

The rain began to die down and the thunder seemed to be rumbling off into the distance. There hadn't been a lightning flash in almost two minutes, and Freddie thought the worst of the storm had passed.

He decided to take a short break—there was nobody up here, Wanda was wrong and he was starting to regret ever leaving the inn and getting piss-soaked in the process—and lit a clove cigarette. His throat numbed almost immediately as he took a long pull on it, and it crackled audibly like paper being screwed into a tight ball.

Planning to abort this mission as soon as he'd finished his cigarette, Freddie thought about the lamb he still had to slaughter that afternoon. He was no longer in the right frame of mind to do it; perhaps it could wait until tomorrow morning, when he was.

Just then, from somewhere to his left, there came a voice. Distinctly male. And then a second voice, followed shortly after by the sound of laughter. Freddie tossed his cigarette and rushed to the nearest tree wide enough to conceal his considerable girth.

Wanda had been right. She had heard men's voices, and they were right here, where she said they were.

Freddie's heart pounded in his chest as the voices approached. Quickly, he set about priming and loading the musket, carelessly spilling half of the iron balls and priming powder onto the forest fall in his excitement. He had a minute, perhaps less, to prepare, but he had decided that he would wait until the men were close enough to guarantee a direct hit. It had been a while since he'd fired this particular musket, and even then it had had a mind of its own, shooting balls off in all directions and missing the intended target completely. Close up it was deadly; at a hundred feet or more, you were taking a massive risk.

With the burning match clipped into place, the musket was ready to fire. Freddie took deep, deliberate breaths and pressed his back to the trunk of the tree.

There were two of them. That's what Wanda had said, and Freddie could hear two voices now. This meant that he would have to engage one of them physically. There would be no time to reload the musket after shooting the first man. The second man would rush him, try to take him down, but Freddie had his knife in the sheath strapped to his belt. When the second man came for him, he would plunge the knife deep into the man's neck. It would all be over in a few seconds, and even though it pained Freddie to have to dispose of outsiders so brutally, he could almost feel the sense of relief already washing over him.

The voices were close now. Freddie knew that if he were to take a little look, he would see the men, wandering through the trees, unaware that they were about to be ended. But he couldn't take a little look, not just yet. The men were there, and who was to say that they weren't looking in his direction as they ambled blindly through the forest?

There was, Freddie reminded himself, always the small chance that the men were villagers. He knew of at least one homosexual couple that came up here to take care of each other. Lucas Thorne and John Wexler had tried to keep their affair under wraps for many years, but there wasn't one villager who didn't know about it, that they were deeply in love. That asshole Jack Lockwood had announced it a quarter of a century ago, made it clear how disgusting it was that two men should "seek solace in the comfort of each other's arseholes" at a town meeting which, fortunately, neither gay man had attended.

It could be them, Freddie thought. Hoped. The voices were distorted by the howling wind, but yes, it might be them.

Now he knew he had to be even more careful, for if he was to accidentally shoot a fellow villager, forgiveness would be hard to come by. There would be uproar; Freddie would be ostracised, perhaps worse. The villagers would call for his exile from the trail, and he would have to relocate to...*here*. Move into the woods and rebuild The Lair Beyond and live out his final days in excruciation desolation. They might even accuse him of being a homophobe, suggest that he had shot one of the gay men due to his prejudiced beliefs. No matter how hard he would try to convince them it was a simple error in judgement, that he had believed the men to be outsiders, they would denounce him as a bigot.

The thunder came rolling back around; it was almost as if it knew what was about to happen and didn't want to miss the spectacle.

Freddie listened, cocked his head so that the voices became clearer. They were moving away again, and Freddie sighed. The men had passed, had thankfully not seen him. It was now or never.

Slowly, he stepped away from the tree and began to move in the direction of the voices. There they were. He could see them now, two men, one wearing a waist-length beige coat, the other a black jacket. They were slowly descending the slope that would set them on the trail leading into the village. One of the men, Freddie noticed, had a thick head of black hair, while the second man's hair was almost shorn to the bone.

It was not Lucas Thorne and John Wexler, which should have relieved him but did not.

These men were outsiders, and had to be taken care of quickly.

Almost two years had passed since an outsider had found their way into Neverville, and now, in the space of four days, there had been four of them. Those two girls had come first, and now these men.

Kelly? That's what Wanda said they were calling. That and something else, a second name, perhaps.

Those girls had led these men here. They were searching for those girls, which meant that there might be others, a whole army of outsiders. Freddie shuddered at the thought, hoped and prayed that these men had come here alone and that no one else knew about it. The last thing anyone wanted was an all-out war.

Being careful not to slip on the muddy bank, Freddie went after the men, musket resting over the top of his left arm. He would get close enough to take out the younger man, the one with the head of thick, black hair, and then kill the older man with the knife. In theory it couldn't fail, provided neither of the men were carrying weapons of their own and couldn't retaliate.

He could hear them talking again now, made out the words 'fuck' and 'hungry' and something about 'mushed peas.' Neither man turned around, but Freddie was being careful, sticking to the trees, keeping himself hidden as best he could just in case one of them should suddenly turn.

When they were just twenty feet in front of him, Freddie knew he had to act, for in a moment they would be out of the woods and onto the trail, and if the villagers saw them, panic would ensue. Any one of them could drop down dead as a result of those outsiders being here, and it could happen at any moment, depending on how long it had been since those men crossed the boulders.

Those girls and their demise had been covered up relatively well. Freddie, Joan, Eric, Walter, and everyone that had been at the inn that night had all kept their mouths shut, because, as Alice Carson would have said, "What they don't know won't hurt them." Knowing how close two of them had come to death was not conducive, and it certainly wasn't necessary. The fewer people that knew about outsiders, the better.

Two men strolling into the village, looking for those missing girls, would cause un-necessary panic. No, it was better to take care of them here in the woods, before it ever got to that point and before any other villager cast eyes upon them.

Freddie stepped out from his current hiding place—a Y-shaped tree that he and Dennis had once dared each other to climb many years ago—and raised the musket, aiming it at the back of the younger man's head and hoping that when he pulled the trigger there was an explosion of skull and brain and thick, black hair.

With one final deep breath he squeezed the trigger.

"No, seriously," Mike said. "Mushy peas over curry sauce, any day of the week. And don't even get me started on the whole 'gravy' thing."

"Please stop talking about food," Sam said. "My stomach thinks that my throat's been cut, and you're just making it worse."

The woods were endless, or so it seemed. They had been walking for what felt like hours, but in reality it had only been ten minutes since they'd been sheltering from the rain.

"You're right," Mike said, stepping over a felled tree and almost snagging his trousers on a bramble. "Fucking swear to God this forest is trying to kill me," he said.

"You know the problem with the youth of today?" Sam said, lighting a cigarette as he continued to walk.

"Sure you're going to tell me."

"Too much whining," Sam said. "You've had it easy, mate. All day in a warm car showroom, basically writing your own cheques. I mean, look at your hands. When was the last time one of your fingernails turned black and fell off because you dropped something heavy on it?"

Mike grimaced. "Wait, that's a thing?"

"See," Sam went on. "That's why all the factories are going under. Kids like you are out there coming up with easier ways to do things. Get a robot to do this, build a machine to do that, why pay a man a basic living wage if fucking HAL 9000 can do it quicker and for free?"

Mike frowned. "I have no idea what you're talking about," he said. "HAL what?"

"Never mind," Sam said. "The point I'm trying to make is, no one wants to get their hands dirty anymore. The youth of today is more interested in university, getting letters after their name, working on these bloody computers that everyone's carping on about, putting tradesmen like me out of a job."

"Technology is inevitable," Mike said. God, he sounded like he knew what he was talking about for once. He didn't know a damn thing about computers, or HAL 9000, whatever the fuck that was, but he knew that if you didn't move with the times, didn't adapt to changes as they happened, then you would ultimately get left behind. Sam was one of the ones being left behind, and he clearly wasn't happy about it.

"I'm all for advancements," Sam said, pushing aside several thin, spindly branches and ducking beneath a spiderweb that, a second later, Mike would walk face-first into. "What I'm against is laziness. Yeah, let's build something that can heat up food at the push of a button. You know what? I already have something that can do that. It's called an oven, Mike. But that's not enough. Now we need to heat that food up in two minutes, because life is just too precious and time spent standing in front of the cooker waiting thirty minutes for a shepherd's pie is time wasted."

"That's not laziness," Mike said. "It's convenience."

"Conveniently taking up two feet of countertop," Sam said, and Mike knew he would not win this argument. "It's just bullsh—"

"Stop."

Mike turned around. He had heard something. A click, a snap, like two sticks being tapped together.

"What is it?" asked Sam.

Mike scoured the woods for any sign of movement. Other than leaves blowing in the wind and branches creaking as they moved back and forth, up and down, he saw nothing. "I thought I heard something."

Sam didn't seem to be concerned. "Probably just a fox," he said. "Or a squirrel. How hungry are you?" He snickered, but Mike was still searching the trees, for he had definitely heard something close by. What surprised him was that Sam hadn't heard it, but the man had been in the middle of an anti-technology, anti-student tirade.

"I don't hear anything," Sam said.

Neither did Mike. Whatever it had been—fox, squirrel, badger, bird—it wasn't there now. He decided to call out anyway. "Kelly?" He called her name three times before Sam placed a heavy hand on his shoulder.

"Come on," Sam said. "It's nothing."

Mike nodded. Sam was probably right; there was nothing out there but indigenous wildlife and bad weather. That's what he had heard, or a combination of the two.

They continued on down the slope, and Mike was grateful that the conversation about technological advancements and the youth of today was finished. It was time to refocus and concentrate on the job at hand.

With one final glance over his shoulder to make sure there was nothing there, Mike followed Sam through the trees, coughing as the smoke from Sam's cigarette stung his eyes.

Fuck! Fuck! Fuck!

The musket had failed him, useless piece of shit. He had dropped and rolled behind a tree that had fallen over a long time ago, and now found himself with his hand resting in a cold pile of dogshit while he waited for the men to come back and find him.

They probably didn't hear it, he tried to assure himself. There had been a click as he pulled the trigger and the serpentine cleared the pan, but nothing more. Albie Moss's relic of war hadn't fired, but Freddie knew that in its failure to take the top of the younger man's head clean off, it had made enough noise to alert them. And his suspicions were proven to be correct when he realised the men were no longer walking; they had stopped and were talking, no doubt scanning the forest as he sat cowering, dogshit up to his wrist and oozing between his fingers like cold tar.

All he could do was wait and hope they moved on, but for the first time in a long time he feared for his life. He wouldn't stand a chance against two men, and if they backtracked and found him hiding with a musket in his hand and a knife on his belt, there was no telling what they would do to him.

I've never been any good at hide-and-seek, he thought, which was a ridiculous thing to be thinking as his own life lay in the balance. It was, however silly, very much true. Before the rope, before The Lair Beyond, he and Dennis used to come to the forest and spend hours hiding from one another. Frannie Mills would play, too, when they let her, but she was terrible at hiding, worse even than Freddie, and would cry out clues just so that they would find her sooner and she would get a go at being the hunter instead of the hunted. Even as a child Freddie had been large. Not fat, but just big. Stocky, his mother used to call him. "He's stocky for his age. Gonna be a big fella when he grows up," she would say. And because of his stockiness, Freddie found it almost impossible to remain hidden for long. It didn't take a genius to figure out that he wasn't behind that thin tree over there, or that there was no way he could have dragged his considerable weight up that particular trunk, so that must mean he was hiding in that gigantic bush, or behind it, because that was the only feasible place.

Alice Carson had been right in her prediction. Freddie had grown into a big fella, and was no better at hiding now than he was back then.

Shit, they're gonna find me and that'll be that. As a precaution, he removed the knife from the sheath on his belt, slowly, being careful not to make any noise, and closed his eyes. Could he overpower them both? Was it possible that he could stab them one after the other, if they were close enough together? A double attack that they wouldn't be anticipating and therefore would stand a slim chance of actually succeeding?

"Kelly?"

One of the men was calling out now. Freddie was relieved that they remained in place twenty feet or so away from where he was hiding. If he had been Frannie Mills, he would have been calling back now, letting them know exactly where she was and to, "Come and find me if you can! I'll bet you don't know where I am!"

"Kelly?"

Oh, just fucking go away! Freddie ran the blade of his knife along the thick, silver hairs on the back of his left hand, scraping off some of the dogshit and trying not to gag. He hadn't stabbed anyone in years, and hadn't felt the urge to, either, which was always a good thing. He had never enjoyed killing people; it was just something that had to be done every now and again.

When the man called out that name a third time, Freddie feared the worst. They weren't going away. They were going to find him, just like he always used to be found. There would be a scuffle, and if he was lucky, he'd take at least one of them out. One villager's life would be saved, and his own death in the process would make way for the outsider.

A hundred souls, and not one more.

Freddie had resigned himself to the fact that the shit was about to hit the proverbial when there came the sound of footfall. And, he was relieved to hear, it was moving away from him. He wanted so desperately to look, to ensure that the men were leaving, but he knew how risky that would be. At least one of them was convinced they had heard the musket fail to fire, and Freddie knew there was a good chance he was still searching the trees for the source of that sound.

Scraping yet more dogshit from between his fingers with the blade of his knife, Freddie sat and waited. He waited as the voices faded into the distance, his heartbeat returning to normal, the useless musket sitting beside him next to the squashed pile of shit that, Freddie knew, would stink him up for the rest of the goddamn day.

When he was certain they were gone, he slowly emerged from his hiding place and glanced in the direction the men had wandered off in.

"Fuck me," he muttered, both relieved and anxious at the same time.

The outsiders were heading straight into the village, and there wasn't a damn thing he could do to stop them.

FIFTEEN

Neverville, 1974

Eve had laughed when Doc Renfield suggested they split up, that they would find Jack sooner if they each moved in a different direction, starting at the Lockwood house and moving out from there and leaving no stone unturned. She had laughed, and then she had asked him what would happen if she found him, or if her mother found him, and they were all alone. They wouldn't stand a chance against him, not in his current frenzy. It was clear that he either didn't know what he was doing, or that he did and that he didn't care he was doing it. Either way, he would murder Eve as soon as he laid eyes upon her; he had already taken a shot at Joan, and would think nothing of finishing the job.

Renfield had conceded it was a bad idea after all, and so they had decided to search the village together. Jack was there somewhere; it wasn't as if he could leave. He had found that out the hard way back in '53, and despite his current derangement, Eve didn't think he was stupid enough to try it again.

Although it was a long shot—he wouldn't go back there, would he? That was the last place he'd been seen in public before...but that had been over twenty years ago—they decided to visit the inn. Renfield had been there on that fateful night in '53, had seen Freddie Carson set about Jack with unmitigated fury and the subsequent cruel treatment Jack had been dealt by the hand of the landlord, Albie Moss, which may or may not have led to Jack's moment of madness.

"It was awful," Renfield told Eve and Joan. "I just remember him stalking out of there with empty eyes, and I knew he was going to do something stupid, but I didn't stop him. None of us did."

"So, you think he'll be going after Albie?" Eve asked.

"Albie, Freddie, probably me," Renfield said as they approached The Wheatsheaf. "In his mind he's never done anything wrong. It's us. It's we who have wronged him, and he'll be looking to get even with as many of us as possible."

His words sent a shiver down Eve's spine. To think that man was her father, to even consider him as anything other than the monster than he was, terrified her. How many times had her mother covered for this man? How many lies had she told Eve to protect him as he sat on that rickety old commode and shit? Eve knew about what had happened with Freddie that night, she knew that The Burden had made enemies of almost every villager in the years before she was born. And Joan had continued to love him and, before Eve had taken over the reins, had cared for and tended to him as if he were a good man.

All those times she had berated Eve for her hatred of him, and Eve had been right all along. He really was a motherfucker of the highest order. Finding him, Eve thought, was not for his own protection. She couldn't care less what happened to him, hoped he was drowning in a muddy ditch somewhere. It was for the safety of the other villagers, because Jack, her father, The Burdon No Longer Confined to the Bedroom, was capable of anything right now. That's what scared her.

They entered the inn, trying to appear inconspicuous, which was difficult because they seldom frequented the place alone, let alone as a trio. When he saw them, Albie Moss's amiable smile turned to something else. Eve thought it was confusion at first, but then realised it was suspicion.

"I'll get some drinks in," Renfield whispered to them as they made their way across the room to the bar. Eve knew that they wouldn't be staying long, and certainly not long enough to finish a drink, but she knew what Doc Renfield was doing. It was clever. Nothing out of the ordinary here. Nothing to see. As you were.

There was no sign of Jack in the inn. Eve didn't think there would be, but no stone unturned meant exactly that. They could cross The Wheatsheaf off their list and move on, but not just yet. Albie was suspicious enough without them just walking in and out. Dennis Wainwright seemed to be regarding them with the same curiosity from his stool at the bar, his eyebrows knitted together into a frown, his elbows locked in place. At the end of the bar, Wanda Frewer seemed to be in a trance, staring off into the middle distance as if she had the weight of the world on her shoulders.

Renfield ordered a moonshine and two gins before excusing himself. "Just going to the outhouse," he said, walking away from the bar toward the large, open door at the rear of the room.

He was going to make sure Jack wasn't hiding back there, making the perfect excuse to check. When Eve's gin arrived, she knocked half of it back in one gulp; Joan cradled hers nervously, looking about the place, searching deep into every corner of the room in case Jack had secreted himself away in a recess.

"Busy?" Eve asked Albie.

"Joking, ain't you?" Dennis said as he picked something disgusting from between his teeth and flicked it away. Behind the bar, Albie shrugged. *What he said.* "What brings you in here, young Eve?"

"Just getting out of the rain for a bit," Joan answered for her daughter. "Got caught out in it. There are worse places to shelter." She motioned to the room around her with her free hand and finally took a sip of gin.

Eve had never liked the inn. It was usually rowdy, full of drunkards capable of speaking out of turn at any moment, and Eve hated confrontation. Then there was the smell; a sickly stench of barley and corn mash, hops and stale cigarette smoke. She knew it was a place of community, a building where men came together to talk about hunting and farming and factory work, while women came to gossip and play bridge and drink gin. It was Neverville's second sanctuary, after the church, and the men and women who came here were seldom the same men and women who went there.

"That's a nice ring, Eve," Albie said, leaning across the bar so he could take a better look at the octagonal band on her finger. He took her hand—a move which did not sit well with her, but she managed to overlook it—and pulled it closer to his face. She could feel his warm breath on the back of her hand as he inspected the ring, and he was wheezing like a broken concertina.

"I'll say," Wanda chimed in as she temporarily emerged from her reverie. "Must have cost a pretty penny, too."

"It was a gift for Eve's birthday," Joan said, seemingly annoyed by Albie's unnecessary infatuation with the ring. Either that or she didn't like the way he had grabbed Eve's hand.

"Well, things like this are hard to come by," Albie said, the suspicion intensifying. Eve didn't know where her mother had 'come by' the ring, but Albie seemed more than a little interested. And Wanda also looked intrigued by it, perhaps wondering if it would fit on one of her own stubby little fingers.

"They're out there," Joan said. "You just have to know where to look."

And that was the end of that particular exchange. Albie let go of Eve's hand just as Doc Renfield returned from the outhouse. He gave his head a little shake—no sign of Jack out there—before picking up his moonshine. To Albie he said, "Someone's left something nasty for you."

Immediately, Albie turned his attention to Dennis, who looked shocked at the insinuation. "Don't look at me!" he said. "I haven't even been to the shitter today."

"Fuck's sake," Albie said, angrily, before leaving the bar to take care of whatever Renfield had found in the outhouse.

"Who's been in today?" Renfield asked Dennis, who was in the process of rolling already-burnt tobacco in a piece of paper.

"What is it with you lot and questions?" he said as he concentrated on his cigarette. "First it was Eve, now you? No, it's not been busy. You're looking at pretty much everyone who's been in here today, apart from Freddie Carson. Those miseries over at that table have been talking about stitching and whatnot since I got here and I've had to listen to it, and now you come in here with your silly questions. Come to think of it, it's not even raining anymore, so you're either being extra damn cautious or you're telling fibs." He lit the awful cigarette and waited for a reply, scanning each of their faces in turn.

"We don't need any excuse to use the inn," Joan said, "and we certainly don't need permission from you, Dennis Wainwright, so why don't you mind your own business and let us finish our drinks in peace."

Dennis leaned back on his stool and held his crippled hands in the air, his way of saying that he meant no offence. "Fair enough," he said, smoke coiling from his lips before disappearing into his nostrils. Wanda clicked her tongue then settled back into a silent stare.

After that, none of them spoke. Eve wanted to get out of there as quickly as possible, so finished her drink and silently urged her mother and Doc Renfield to do the same. Joan must have seen the desperation in Eve's eyes, and she knocked her gin back in one go before setting the empty glass down on the counter. Renfield exhaled deeply before pushing his half-finished drink toward Dennis.

"Finish that, if you like," he told the man. "Guess I'm not used to day drinking. Reckon I'll be asleep all afternoon if I have any more."

Dennis grinned, his rotten black teeth exposed. "Don't mind if I do," he said, pulling the glass toward him.

They left the inn before Albie returned from the outhouse, which Eve thought was a good thing. She wondered whether it had been Renfield who had left a little surprise for Albie, just to keep him busy so they could make their exit without further interrogation. If he had, it was a cunning plan, and also gross.

"Well, he's definitely not in there," Renfield said as they stepped out onto the trail. A horse and cart passed them by—John Wexler and Lucas Thorne trying desperately to look inconspicuous and not in love with one another as they rode along the muddy trail—but there was no one else around. The harsh weather was doing them a favour by keeping people off the streets. For now, at least, Dennis Wainwright was right. It was no longer raining, and the thunder had long faded into the distance.

"So where now?" Eve scraped her long blonde hair back away from her face, where it had been stuck by the rain.

"We keep moving," Renfield said. "I don't think he will, but there's a chance he's headed up into the woods."

Eve shook her head, for she hadn't considered that possibility. If that was the case, they would never find him. They might as well wait down here for him to come to them, and he would come to (for) them eventually. It was only a matter of time.

"Eric Majors," Joan suddenly blurted out. "Eric was the only one who didn't hate him." To Renfield she said, "When Jack tried to go over the boulders, Eric came to see him every day for weeks after. The only reason he stopped coming by was because…well, I thought it was doing more harm than good and told him as much. If Eric had been there that night at the inn, before Jack lost his mind, he would have sided with Jack."

"We don't know that," Renfield said.

"Eric told me," Joan said. "Said he would have helped Jack. Said Freddie had been out of line the way he lashed out like that. Jack and Eric were once as thick as thieves. If Jack still thinks the whole village is against him, then there's only one man he'll turn to, and that's Eric."

Eve shrugged. She didn't know much about The Burden's relationship with Eric Majors, had only heard snippets—how Eric had played a small part in getting Jack and Joan together, and how Jack had returned the favour by delivering a whole deer carcass to Eric's front door one autumn, a gift which had kept Eric in good meat for the best part of three month—from her mother about their camaraderie, but it seemed as good a place as any to go next.

"We can't just go asking Eric whether he's seen Jack," Renfield reminded them. "Or whether he's hiding him there. Discreet, you said, so that we don't panic the entire village."

"Then we find an excuse," Eve said. "A reason to be calling by." She thought long and hard for a moment as Renfield and her mother looked on. How could they find out if Jack had gone to Eric without bringing it up? It would have been a lot easier if Eric didn't still have his wits about him, but the man was as sharp as a tack, had always been one of the smarter elders. What helped was that he was also a deviant, even in his old age, often making sleazy remarks about just about every female villager—his years of loneliness and decades of pent-up sexual frustration perhaps taking their toll—and Eve thought she might be able to use that somehow to infiltrate both his house and mind.

"I've got an idea," she said. "And I'll know whether he's hiding something." By *something* she meant The Burden, but she was still loath to refer to the man as her father, no matter how much it irked her mother, and yet she couldn't keep calling him The Burden either, no matter how true that was.

"Let's try his house," Renfield said.

"Okay," Eve replied. "But when we get there, you two need to stay out of sight. I have to do this alone." She didn't want to, but nor did she want her mother to see what she was capable of, or at least what she *thought* she might be capable of. She had never had cause to exploit her sexuality in such a fashion, and she hated that she would have to now, but neither her mother or Renfield seemed to have a better idea.

They set off toward Eric Major's place, where one way or another Eve was determined to find where the most dangerous man in the village had gone into hiding.

The church was cold now. And completely silent. Rain no longer pattered against the stained-glass windows, which Jack had had time to study in detail for the first time ever. They had never appealed to him before, but the longer he looked at them, the more he realised they had a story to tell, and now he understood why stained glass was often called the poor man's *Bible*. Even the colours held a deeper meaning than Jack had ever understood before. Blues symbolised hope, heaven, and piety. Greens represented growth and rebirth. Pieces of yellow glass were used for Judas, the haloes of saints, and the gates of Heaven, while browns were used as a symbol of spiritual death and a renunciation of worldly things. There was, Jack realised, very little in the way of black glass, perhaps due to its connotations of death, but the more he explored the images in the windows set into the walls of the church, the more he realised that this place was cursed, not by what had happened just a few short centuries ago, but way before that. The moment religion came here, with its false hope and promise of eternal life in exchange for infinite worship. That was the curse of Neverville, and these images—Jesus crucified, beatific Mary, the saints, the cross, the dove, the golden chalice—were proof of that.

Jack had only ever come to this place to appease Joan. She was a believer, brainwashed by Calhoun, along with almost a third of the villagers. Every Sunday he had let her drag him here, not because it made her happy, but because it kept her off his back for the rest of the week. Before she'd finally relented and let him fuck her once again—the first time in years, and Jack shuddered as he remembered how that turned out—she would lie in bed and read passages of the Bible, occasionally coming upon something that deeply moved her or that she deemed worthy of narrating aloud for Jack. He would nod along, secretly wishing she would just die in her sleep so that he wouldn't have to listen to her any longer.

And then Eve had come along, and Jack had had months to prepare. The baby would die, because better that than the alternative, but when that bitch Alice Carson came in and sacrificed herself, everything was ruined. If God was real, then He had a fucked-up way of making His presence known.

Jack stood for the first time in almost an hour and made his way to the front of the church, where Father Calhoun continued to stare up at the high ceiling with a look of pure terror on his face. A pool of blood had stretched out beneath the vicar's head, and Jack was careful not to get too close.

He knew he had to clean this mess up; he didn't want Calhoun's body to be discovered before his plan was executed, and what a plan it was.

Firstly, at nightfall, he would head on over to Freddie's farm. It was only a twenty-minute walk, and Jack figured with the cover of night and by taking the right route along the edge of the woods, the chances of his being seen were next to nothing. He would avoid the inn completely, because once the sun set, that's where any villager not home would be. No, he would return to the inn later, when everyone had left, and Albie Moss wouldn't know what had hit him.

He knew that Joan and Eve had probably discovered the smashed window, that they were out there now, searching the village, but their time would come, too. He would return to them at the house once Freddie and Albie were taken care of, pretend that he was fine, just a little disorientated, and they would eat that up like the fools that they were, because he was Joan's husband, he was Eve's father, and they hadn't spent the past two decades keeping him alive just to see him suffer now.

By morning, and after convincing them he was okay and just needed to rest, they would both be dead. He would kill Eve first and make Joan watch, because that's how it should have been all those years ago. Eve was an abomination, had slipped through the gaps thanks to the sacrifice of one Alice Carson, but Jack would set things right and Joan would witness it before he finished the job he'd started earlier that day.

Then there was the conniving doctor. Renfield. He would enjoy that one, in particular. But why stop there? This curse had to end someday, and he considered himself a martyr for taking up the challenge. He could go door to door, killing them all until Neverville was finally released from its shackles. It wouldn't be easy, but he had all the time in the world. Everyone was old now—everyone except Eve—and wouldn't put up much of a fight. If he was careful, he could end half of the village before anyone even knew what was going on.

"What do you think of that, Father?" he asked the corpse at his feet. "Sound like a good plan to you?"

Sounds good to me, son. The vicar's mouth didn't move, but it was his voice that spoke to Jack, that heavy Welsh accent that echoed around the church. *But you might want to think about how you're going to end yourself when it's over. Don't want a repeat of last time.*

"Of course not," Jack said, frowning. "But maybe I won't end myself. Maybe I'll live here alone for a while. In peace. Knowing that they were all dead by my hand would offer me that."

Sounds like you've thought it all through, the vicar's voice said. Jack watched the dead man's face carefully for movement. But there was nothing. Was he really having a conversation with a corpse? *But you know they're together, right?*

"Who?" Jack asked. The corpse seemingly knew something he didn't. Or perhaps this wasn't real at all, his subconscious telling him something he deep down already knew. That was far more likely than Father Calhoun still imparting wisdom while he lay there, staring up into nothingness with his head caved in.

The doctor. Eve, your wife, and the doctor. They're together right now, and they're looking for you, Jack. They won't stop until they find you.

Jack's furrowed brow deepened. Of *course* they were together. Joan would have fetched the doctor almost immediately. *Come! Take a look at Jack! He's returned, but he's crazy!* Jack knew her real reasons for going to him, though. She was still enamoured by Renfield, their illicit affair continuing even to this day. He had been right about them then, and this only further proved it. "Where are they now?"

Calhoun's sigh was so loud that Jack winced. *You're talking to a dead man, son. All I know is they're coming for you, and the apple hasn't fallen far from the tree. Little Eve, Little Evil, has murderous thoughts of you, Jack. She wants to end you.*

"Of course she fucking does," Jack said through gritted teeth. "You think I don't remember what she said to me all those times in the room? I couldn't do anything about it, but I heard her in my mind. I heard everything."

You must kill her before she kills you, Jack. You mustn't allow her to succeed, because if she does, this curse will never end.

"I can take care of one little girl," Jack said. Of course he could. And it would be easy, because Joan wouldn't allow any harm to come to him. She might be fucking Renfield, Jack thought, but her love for him remained.

Stupid.

Stupid.

Stupid.

When Jack was sure the corpse had nothing more to say—if he had truly said anything at all—he dragged the body across the room and, with a little more effort than he'd thought it would take, managed to prop the body up in the confessional. In the back room, where many cakes and cups of tea had been shared amongst the brainwashed congregation, Jack found a cloth. He pumped water into a bucket and set about cleaning the blood from the floor in front of the altar, picking up chunks of grey matter and skull as he went. When he was satisfied, he unlocked the church doors. He didn't want anyone to get suspicious, and the doors to the church were always left open. God was available at every hour of the day; at least, Jack thought, Father Calhoun was.

If they were coming for him, like Calhoun said, he would be ready.

He would be ready for them all.

SIXTEEN

Neverville, 1974

Mike had never been more relieved when they reached the edge of the woods and stepped out onto what appeared to be a trail. There was a lot of horse shit—it was everywhere, stacked up in massive mounds that teemed with flies and all sorts of insectoid nasties—and hoofprints were embedded in the mud, suggesting at least one or two had come this way recently. Up ahead, rooftops peered over the brow of a hillock, but apart from the wind, which continued to whisper through the trees behind them, everything was quiet.

"Thank fuck for that," Sam said, lighting what must have been his twentieth cigarette of the day. Mike thought that if the drink didn't kill him first, the cigarettes surely would. "Thought we were never going to get out of those damn trees."

"I don't think that's Staylittle," Mike said. They were still a way from Barbara's house. But it was something, a village, which was more than they had a moment ago. If Kelly and Rebecca had come this way, they would have had to pass through whatever lay ahead along this trail.

"Wherever it is," Sam said through a fug of blue-grey smoke, "it's in our way."

Sam was right. They were still headed in the right direction—Staylittle was in front of them, for they hadn't deviated by much and would surely find their way back onto the road that led there—and that was enough for Mike.

"At worst," he said, "they might have a chip shop."

"Or a pub," Sam added. Mike tried not to let Sam see his grimace. The last thing Mike wanted was drunk Sam again. He hoped there wasn't a pub along the way, despite wanting a drink for himself. He needed Sam sober, and didn't think there would be much he could do to stop him if they did come across a bar.

Just then, a tiny figure appeared over the hillock on the trail ahead. "Look!" Mike said, nodding in its direction.

"It's a kid," Sam said. "It's just a kid."

"Come on," Mike said, and he started to walk again. Sam took one more long pull on his cigarette before flicking it away. "You know, you ought to quit smoking," he said.

"What are you, my mother?" Sam said.

As they neared the approaching person, it became clear that it was not a kid at all. As far as Mike was aware, kids didn't have silver hair, and they didn't waddle like ducks, either. It was an elderly woman, a dwarf of some sort, and when she saw them approaching, Mike thought he saw her expression change from one of blissful oblivion to absolute terror.

"Some kind of midget," Sam whispered, for the woman was almost certainly close enough to hear them now. And she had slowed her pace and moved onto the grass embankment at the edge of the trail, as if she feared catching something from them. "What's the matter with her?"

"I don't know," Mike whispered back, never once taking his eyes off the strange, little woman. He took out the photograph of Kelly, ready to question the woman. "I think she's scared of us."

"I'm scared of *her*," Sam whispered. He had taken to keeping his lips still, too, as he spoke. The world's worst ventriloquist. "Fucking goblin."

Mike shushed Sam, although part of him wanted to laugh. *Fucking goblin* might just about have been the funniest thing he'd ever heard.

"Excuse me," Mike said now that the woman was almost close enough to piss on. "Excuse me, sorry to bother you, but you wouldn't happen to know the name of this place, would you?"

The woman's terror was palpable, and she ignored the question completely. Her eyes were fixed upon something unseen beyond Mike and Sam. The trail, perhaps, or the trees from which they had just emerged. Either way, she was deliberately avoiding making eye contact with them, kept edging along the embankment as if her life depended on it.

Both men stopped walking and watched as the woman passed them by without so much as a sideways glance. Maybe, Mike thought, she was retarded. Or deaf and dumb. Or maybe she just didn't like strangers. Two men coming out of the woods might have put the fear into her. Who knew what was going on in her mind? One thing was for sure—and it was confirmed when Sam called out to the little, old lady and got no response—and that was that they were wasting their time trying to engage her. She was clearly having none of it.

They watched her as she moved along the embankment, eventually waddling back down onto the trail when she deemed it was safe to do so. And then she did look back, just once, but it was enough for Mike to see that the terror in her face remained as she quickened her pace, her little legs slipping this way and that in the mud as she practically ran from them.

"Well, looks like we've got a contender for the most fucked up person we've met so far today," Sam said. "Glad I never moved out of Montgomery. At least we don't have too many leprechauns there."

Mike turned to face the trail ahead, and this time he did laugh a little. "Come on," he said, glancing up at the thick, dark sheet of clouds hovering over them. "Looks like rain again."

The first drop fell on his head just a second later.

Great, he thought. Could this day get any worse?

Eric Majors pressed a jigsaw piece into place and cracked his knuckles in celebration. He was finally getting somewhere; the map of the world was almost half complete, and by the end of the week he would be breaking it apart, ready to start all over again.

How many times have I finished it? he wondered. The same puzzle—and he was lucky, for it was the only one in the village, a hand-me-down from his ancestors, and wouldn't any one of the villagers love to get their grubby little hands on it?—completed in perpetuity. Yet it never got any easier. Maybe it was a sign of his failing functions, his declining dexterity. He never grew bored of it, though. It gave him purpose, a reason for continuing, and although he was only sixty-eight, one of the youngsters of Neverville, he thought about the mortality of man, of his own approaching cessation of life, more than most.

He pushed another piece into place—he was on a roll now, with almost half of Europe complete—and relaxed back in his chair for a moment, his back and shoulders aching from leaning over the board for almost an hour without intermission.

Eric thought about death a lot, perhaps more than was good for his health, but he knew it could always be worse. To be Jack Lockwood was unthinkable, up there in that bedroom every day and night, unable to move, not knowing what was happening all around him. That poor bastard had it worse than any of them.

With that incomprehension, though, came something that Eric longed for. While it was terrible, unimaginable, unthinkable, even, he envied Jack. Jack didn't know about those poor girls from just a few nights ago. Jack didn't know how many outsiders Eric and the others had buried up there at Freddie's farm. Jack didn't worry about when the next ones would come stumbling by. He was just there, oblivious, sitting in darkness in his room while all this horror went on around him.

Eric had to live with it every day, which was why he completed the puzzle over and over. It was to take his mind off the terrible things he had done to protect Neverville and its residents. Those horrible images—young girls pleading for their lives as they were skewered with pitchforks and blood spilled from their mouths and throats, young men running away as arrows thumped into their backs and they fell to the trail, gargling and moaning as the life drained from them, young couples who had come here for a dare and were now hogtied and set afire by hooded figures—still came to Eric at night, when he had no control over his thoughts. He would awaken, drenched in sweat and, more recently, his own piss, the nightmares still burned into the back of his eyelids as he tried desperately to blink them away.

This jigsaw puzzle was his escape from reality; he only hoped that, when his number was up, it was on one of the days he completed it. The thought of it sitting there on the table unfinished upset him, another reason why he constantly worked away at it. The more he did it, the less chance there was of his fears becoming reality and him dying in the middle of it. It made perfect sense to him, in a world that hadn't made sense in a long time.

The rain hammered at the window behind him. Fuck, would it never end? The whole day had been a washout, and there was no sign of it easing up soon. A flash of lightning confirmed this, the accompanying rumble of thunder the icing on the proverbial cake.

Weather had always been shit in Neverville. Doc Renfield said it was something to do with a meteorological enclave, whatever the fuck one of those was. The place was cursed, it seemed, in just about every way he could conceive. He couldn't remember the last time the sun shone down on the village. Perhaps when he was a child? Maybe the sun had come out just once, and only once, when he and Jack had hunted hares up in the woods with the huge knife Jack had stolen from his father. Eric couldn't recall the sun beating down on them as they'd skinned those animals—anything they could catch, anything stupid enough to get close enough to them in the woods—but he remembered the delight in Jack's face as he worked that blade.

There had been, Eric could remember, a lot of snow growing up. They would hurl little balls of it at one another, at other children who dared to get involved. Jack liked to put little rocks at the centre of his, so that they would inflict more damage and move more quickly through the air. Eric had done the same, and eventually none of the other children wanted to partake in the snowball fights. Those were fun times, but always with the bad weather. Always with the meteorological enclave. Always snowing or raining or thick with fog.

So long ago, Eric thought, and yet it felt like just yesterday.

With Europe almost complete, Eric decided to make a start on the good ol' US of A. He was reaching for a piece he saw had 'Col' printed on it—Colony of Louisiana, Eric thought, which was as good a place as any to start—when there came a knock at his door. His heart jumped into his throat at the suddenness and intensity of the intrusion.

"Who the hell...?" he muttered under his breath. No one had knocked at his door in years. No one had cause to, and that was the way he liked to keep it. If someone came calling, it usually meant something was wrong, and he hoped to God that wasn't the case now. He just wanted to work on his jigsaw in peace and forget about everything and everyone else. Was that too much to ask?

Apparently, it was as the knock came again.

Eric pushed himself up out of the armchair, his ageing bones protesting as he moved. With one final look at his jigsaw—he really was making progress, had crossed the halfway point and then some—he went out into the hallway to answer the door.

For a moment, Eve didn't speak, as if she had forgotten why she was there in the first place.

"Eve!" Eric said, for he had not been expecting anyone, but now that he'd seen who had come knocking, he no longer cared. She was a remarkable young lady, and he scanned her carefully, the way her knee-high dress clung to her body thanks to the rain, the mere suggestion of breasts beneath enough to cause stirrings where he hadn't had them for a while. She was remarkable, yes, and Eric would have given anything to spend just one night in bed with her. Of course, that would never happen; he was forty-something years older than her, and he wasn't sure he would even know what to do if the opportunity presented itself. It had been so long since he'd even kissed a girl—back in the thirties, perhaps, or even longer. Sexual desire would remain just that.

"Eric," she said, a faint smile tugging at the corners of her mouth. She ran a hand through her wet hair, moving it away from her face. "I'm so glad you're home. Can I come in?"

"Is something wrong?" Eric said, but then before Eve had a chance to answer, he added, "Yes, of course. Please come in." He stepped aside, allowing Eve to enter and make her way into the living room. He watched her go before closing the door. Had she walked like that on purpose? Slowly, deliberately, enticingly?

Stop it, you dirty, old bastard!

He joined Eve in the living room, where she was admiring the jigsaw puzzle.

"Ah, yes," Eric said, even though Eve hadn't spoken. "I know, it's silly, but it keeps me focussed."

"I don't think it's silly at all, Eric," Eve said. There was only one chair in the room—Eric's armchair, in which he had been sitting for so many years, it had been moulded into the shape of his body—and so Eve sat on the floor next to the table. She looked up at him, smiling, pulling the wet dress, which was sticking to her, away from her skin. He still had no idea why she was here.

"Can I get you anything?" he asked her. He knew he didn't have much to offer—the milk had soured that very morning, and the crab apples he'd picked from the garden were too bitter to eat—but it was the polite thing to do. He thought he might be able to muster up some hot tea; she certainly looked like she could use it.

"I'm fine," she said. "Actually, I came here to ask for a favour." She looked up at him with pleading eyes. Eric caught a brief glimpse of her tongue as she ran it along her bottom lip; he had to remind himself that the girl, Eve, was no more interested in him than he was in Frannie Mills. Nothing was going to happen here, to even think it was would be ridiculous. Still, it didn't hurt to fantasise.

"I'll help if I can," Eric said, stepping over Eve's crossed legs and sinking into his armchair. Eve was watching him carefully, but also looking around the room, out into the hallway. What was she looking for? What was she doing here?

"Mother and I are going to be out next week," she said. "Spending the night with Mae Creswell." She found something on the floor and picked it up. Eric saw that it was a puzzle piece. It must have fallen from the board. He watched as Eve examined the piece before slotting it effortlessly into the half-completed jigsaw in front of her. "Look!" she said. "It fits!"

Mesmerised, Eric urged her to continue. "And you want me to..."

"Well, it's a big ask, but we were wondering, *I* was wondering, whether you would come to the house and feed and read to my father on the night we are away." Her beautiful eyes pleaded with him once again, and for a moment he was lost in them. So innocent and yet so beguiling. Was she even aware of how beautiful she was? How much Eric wanted to ravish her, or at least wished that he still had it in him to do so? Eric wiped the spittle from his lips before speaking.

"Um, I'm not sure," he said. "I mean, I haven't seen Jack for a while. Suppose he doesn't want me there."

Eve laughed at this, but Eric saw, in her beautiful eyes, something else. Had she realised something? Was she telling the truth? What the hell was going on?

"Oh, don't worry about that," Eve said, and now she reached out and ran her fingers along Eric's ankle. "He doesn't know what's happening. The most you'll get from him is a grunt, but even then I think it's just a reflex."

Eric pulled his foot away from the girl. Reluctantly, he stood and walked across the room to the bureau in which he kept his important documents, his journals, his *Bible*. "I think I can do that," he said. "And your mother is okay with this?"

Eve smiled. God, she really was a siren! "It was my mother who suggested asking you," she said. "After all, you and my father were once good friends. You're pretty much the only man in the village that can be trusted with him."

Eric nodded. That was true. Asking any of the other villagers for such a favour would, he knew, prove fruitless. The ones that didn't laugh in Eve's face would laugh about it later, after telling her no, they could not take care of Jack Lockwood for the simple reason he was a bastard who deserved to rot in that bedroom.

"Okay, Eve," he said. "I will do that for you." But Eve was once again distracted, glancing toward the door as if she expected someone to come through it. "Is something the matter?"

Eve turned her attention back to Eric. "No," she said, smiling, or at least forcing one. "No, everything is fine." She stood then and, unlike Eric, her bones did not crack or protest as she straightened up. What he would have given in that moment to be young again. "So it's settled then," she continued. "It will be Wednesday evening from seven, if that's not a problem."

"That's not a problem at all," he said, leading Eve back toward the front door. He hoped to have the jigsaw finished well before then, and it would be good to see Jack again after all these years, even if the man was too demented to know he was there. And there really wasn't much to it, was there? Feed him, read to him, maybe talk to him about old times? A small part of Eric was already looking forward to it.

Eve did something then that he had not anticipated. She leaned in and gave him the sweetest peck on the cheek. "Thank you, Eric," she said.

Eric, taken aback, reached around Eve and opened the door. "Not a problem," he said once again. "I'll come over to the house before seven and you can show me what needs to be done."

Eve stepped out into the rain, but it didn't seem to bother her. She was already soaked through. A flash of lightning limned her beautiful body in the doorway, and Eric inwardly sighed.

"Sounds perfect," she said. "Thank you, Eric." And with that she turned and began to walk toward the trail. Of course, Eric watched her go, made a mental note of every movement, and when she disappeared behind the trees at the end of his path, he closed the door.

He reached into his trousers and began to stroke almost immediately, picturing her in his mind, imagining that she had come here for something else, and that thing was to be taught, to be shown how to fuck. She had wanted him, had gone down onto the floor like that so she could take him into her mouth. He imagined holding her head as she started to suck and lick him, then he was brushing the jigsaw off the table and throwing her down on it. She begged him to show her, pleaded with him to make her feel good, and he did. He thrust deep into her and she gasped into his mouth. He could almost taste her now, her sweet, sweet breath. And none of it was real, it existed only in his mind, but ultimately it worked. Pleasure coursed through his entire body and his legs threatened to give way beneath him as he orgasmed hard. He had to press himself against the wall for stability, breathing hard, smiling crookedly. He hadn't felt such intensity in a long time, and it had all started with an innocent knock on the door not ten minutes ago.

After he came, standing there in the hallway wiping semen on his trousers, he felt a little ashamed, but it didn't last for long.

He returned to his jigsaw, both satisfied and still frustrated at the same time.

"I don't like this," Joan said. They were standing on the other side of the trail a hundred yards away from Eric Majors' house, the trees hopefully providing adequate cover. Eve had been gone only five minutes, but already it felt like forever. "Why did she want to go in there alone? I don't trust that sleazy old fucker around my daughter. If he lays one finger on her I swear to God I'll—"

"Eve can take care of herself," Renfield said as he pulled a leaf from a low-hanging branch. He rolled it into a ball and flicked it away. "She's a lot stronger than you think. Than you allow her to be."

"Don't you tell me what's what, Doc Renfield," Joan said. "And what if Jack is in there, huh? What if Eric is hiding him there? Eve won't stand a chance." She shook her head. "No, we should have gone with her. It's too dangerous."

Renfield plucked another leaf from the branch, rolled it, flicked it. There was a flash of lightning, and a rumble of thunder. "Trust me," he said. "She knows what she's doing, even if we don't."

That did little to comfort Joan. Why was all this happening? Why was her husband suddenly awake and on the loose? Where was he hiding, and what was he going to do next? She could almost feel his hands wrapped around her throat again, could feel his hot, rancid breath on her face as he cursed at her through gritted teeth, his eyes mad and wide.

Of course, that morning hadn't been the first time he'd hurt her. Jack had always been physical, lashing out whenever he felt threatened. Even before they were married, he had punched her, kicked her, but she had endured it because she loved him so much and wanted to make it work. It wasn't as if there were too many alternatives, back then. You had one, maybe two opportunities in Neverville to find love; after that you were fucked. So she had accepted his violence, taken his outbursts with a pinch of salt, and things had eventually got back to normal.

Until the next time.

And the time after that. But Joan grew used to it over the years, and so did Jack. They were the epitome of young love. Toxic, inexperienced, fiery, but they had each other, which was more than most of the villagers could ever hope for. Apart from Joan and Jack, Mae and Walter Creswell, Lucas Thorne and John Wexler, and a few other married couples—though of course Lucas and John had never married or even announced their adoration for one another in a public forum—the village was populated by widows and geriatric singletons.

But isn't that what you've been for the past twenty-one years? Technically she was still married, but Jack hadn't been there, not really. She had been a widow, the same as some of the others. And now there was a chance she could rectify that, but Jack would have to first calm down and come to his senses, and she didn't know whether that would ever happen.

And what if he didn't? What if he was out there killing right now, in a frenzy? A witch-hunt would ensue, the end to which would be inevitable. She would be widowed for real, because the villagers would kill Jack, and she knew that some of them would actually enjoy it. Freddie, Albie, maybe even Doc Renfield, who was now plucking a third leaf from the branch, rolling it between thumb and forefinger, flicking it.

Then there was Eve. Joan knew there was no love lost between her daughter and Jack because there had never been any love to begin with. Joan had seen the hatred there, brewing beneath the surface, even when Eve had been a child. She used to ask who the man in the bedroom was, and when Joan told her it was her father Eve would laugh, as if it was the most ridiculous thing she had ever heard. To a six-year-old child, it probably *was*, because fathers don't just sit there, drooling and shitting themselves.

Fathers *do* things. They play with their children; they protect their family. They don't almost choke on mashed potatoes or vomit beets all over themselves. To Eve, the man in the bedroom—The Burden, she had started to call him when she got into her teenage years—was not her father, had never been her father, and would never be her father. He simply *was*. A coward who existed in near-darkness; a horrible man whose entire life had been dedicated to bringing misery upon anyone who knew him.

Would Eve join the villagers on their witch-hunt? Would she take up a pitchfork and go after the man responsible for her own existence? Joan hoped not, but Renfield was right: Eve was strong. Too strong for her age, and that scared Joan. She was capable of great things, capable of anything, and she had time on her side to succeed, unlike the rest of them. She loved her daughter dearly, but to think of her siding with the rest of the village against Jack was almost unbearable.

"Perhaps we should go and check on her," Joan said, glancing nervously in the direction of the Majors' house. "It's been too long, Doc. Anything could have happened."

But they didn't have to go and check on her. Renfield was in the middle of telling Joan why that was not a good idea when Eve stepped out onto the trail and came walking toward them at pace. She didn't seem to be hurt.

Thank God, Joan thought, her heart racing, her palms sweat-coated with worry.

"He's not there," Eve said as she ran the final few yards in order to get out of the worsening rain, almost slipping on the trail in her urgency before regaining her balance and grabbing on to Renfield's shoulder to recompose herself.

"You're sure?" Renfield tucked Eve under one arm and pulled her beneath the cover of the trees, where very little rain penetrated the leaves above them.

"I'm sure," Eve said, scraping her wet hair back and knotting it into a rudimentary ponytail. "Eric was in the middle of a jigsaw puzzle. I made up a story that would have, if he had anything to hide, given him away, but he wasn't hiding anything."

Joan cursed under her breath. She had convinced herself that Jack would have gone to Eric for help, and now what? Where the hell was he?

There came yet another flash of lightning, and this time the accompanying thunder was enough to rattle Joan's insides.

"We can't stay out here all day," Renfield said, his countenance one of fear. "For all we know he's watching us right now, waiting for the right moment. We need to regroup."

"We need to find my husband," Joan said.

"And we will," Renfield said. "But we need to be smarter about it, draw him out instead of...instead of *this*." He waved a hand vaguely through the air. "He can't have gotten far, that much we know—"

"And what if he's gone to the boulders again?" Joan said. "What if he's up there right now? He could already be lying there in the woods, dying. He's not in the right frame of mind to be wandering around the village."

Eve placed a hand on Joan's shoulder. It was a simple gesture, but it meant the world to Joan. It said, 'Everything is going to be all right, Mother.'

"Doc's right," Eve said. She took her hand away and wiped a droplet of rain from her cheek. "We've ruled out Eric and the inn, and I'm pretty sure that if he'd been spotted elsewhere, we'd already know about it. Which means he's found someplace to hide. We could search for him all afternoon and have no luck, because he's not going to come out in daylight, and especially not in this weather." She had, Joan thought, become the mother, while Joan had regressed.

Stronger than you let her be.

"Okay," Joan said. "So we wait. Until dark. But we need to prepare, because you know that's what he's doing right now, don't you? Wherever he's hiding, wherever he is, he's running it through his mind."

Renfield sighed. Joan took this as an acknowledgement. "We know he's on a personal vendetta right now," he said. "Or at least at the start of one. None of us is safe, and won't be until we have Jack under control." He sighed again. "One way or the other, this has to end tonight."

While Joan didn't like Renfield's choice of words, she agreed. They had to get Jack under control, back in his room, and checked over. They had to figure out why he had returned now, wakened from his stupor. They had to save her husband before it was too late and before Neverville even discovered he was out there, roaming free and with deranged thoughts driving him.

Just then, there came a shout, and when Joan turned and saw Freddie Carson limping frantically toward them down the trail, she feared the worst. Had Jack gone after Freddie at the farm? If so, what of Jack now? Joan quickly realised that Freddie was coming from the west, from the opposite direction to his home and farmstead, which was to the east. Freddie was coming from the woods.

"What is it?" Renfield asked, clearly just as concerned by Freddie's sudden appearance and panic-stricken countenance as Joan. "What's the matter?"

Breathless, doubled over and clinging on to what looked like Albie Moss's eighteenth-century musket, Freddie said the word they all dreaded. "Outsiders. Two of 'em." He straightened up and clutched at his side, as if he had a stitch. "Got away from me in the woods. This fucking thing," he held the musket aloft and stared at it with something akin to pure hatred, "didn't fire. I lost them, but they're here."

Joan couldn't believe what she was hearing. Two outsiders, today of all days. They really weren't having any luck. "How long?"

Freddie shrugged and slung the apparently useless musket across his back. "Shit, I don't know, Joan," he said. "For all I know they've been camping up there. Could have been here all goddamn night."

Eve gasped. Joan thought her daughter might pass out, was almost surprised when she didn't—just stood there with her eyes wide and her bottom lip quivering.

"This is bad," Renfield said. "This is very bad."

"No shit, Doc," Freddie countered. He looked tired, Joan thought. Then again, Freddie Carson always looked tired, and probably was, the number of hours he put in up at the farm.

"Did they see you?" Joan asked. "With the gun?"

Freddie shook his head. He was finally getting his breathing under control. "No," he said. "It was close, though. Thought they were gonna find me for sure."

Now was not the best time to tell Freddie about Jack; they had other things to worry about, like those two outsiders and what would happen if they weren't taken care of quickly. "They come looking for those girls, you think?"

Freddie sighed. "Pretty sure that's it," he said. "One of them kept calling out. A girl's name. Kelly."

"What girls?" Eve said, for she had no idea of the horrors that had transpired in Freddie's barn three nights prior. Joan had made a faux pas. The less Eve knew about these matters, the better. Strong she might be; willing participant she was not.

"Doesn't matter," she told her daughter. To Freddie she said, "We need to do this properly." Then to Renfield she said, "Call a meeting, brown robes only."

"Mother, what girls?" Eve seemed to be stuck on that, and it annoyed Joan greatly. She ignored the question and hoped Eve would not ask it again.

"I hope we're not too late," Freddie said.

Joan hoped so, too. Any one of them could drop down dead without warning at any moment. Until those men were dead, their own lives and the lives of everyone they knew hung in the balance.

Before morning, two people would be dead.

Joan did not know, in that moment, there would be a lot more than two.

She pined for easier times, like just a moment ago when Jack was the only thing they had to worry about.

"I'll fetch Eric," Renfield said. "Everyone at the inn in an hour." He set off across the trail to the house Eve had just come from.

This, Joan thought as her daughter stared at her with more than a modicum of concern and Freddie began to limp off toward The Wheatsheaf, was not happening.

"Go home, Eve," she said. "Mother has work to do."

For a moment she thought Eve might argue, or at least ask further questions, but she didn't. Good. Joan didn't think she had the strength for it. As Eve trundled off in the direction of home, Joan caught up to Freddie, who seemed to be in the middle of a heated argument with the faulty musket strapped to his back.

"Fuck!" he said, spitting a green wad onto the trail, where the rain washed it away almost immediately.

Joan silently concurred.

Fuck, indeed.

SEVENTEEN

Neverville, 1974

The horse and cart came barrelling toward them at great speed, and Mike knew it wasn't going to stop. Its two passengers, male, whooping and hollering like cowboys from the Wild West, must have spotted them walking slowly toward the village proper and decided that they were going to have a little fun.

Maybe they're travellers, Mike thought as those horses galloped toward them. They would get close enough to Mike and Sam and then veer off or stop completely. Everyone would have a good laugh, and that would be that.

But the horse and cart didn't veer off, and it didn't slow down. Sam, frozen beside Mike, made a guttural sound. He knew, too, that the men weren't going to stop. They were going to plough straight through Mike and Sam as if they weren't even there. Mike didn't know why they would do that, why anyone would do that, but he wasn't just going to stand there and be trampled by horses.

As the horses and the cart they pulled drew closer, Mike grabbed Sam by the arm and dragged him to the side of the trail. The men howled and whipped the horses with the reins, urging them to go faster. They were intent on running Mike and Sam over. It was like something out of a bad horror film.

With nowhere to go—there were no buildings to run to, no trees to strategically place themselves behind—Mike knew the only way they would avoid a collision was to wait until the horse and cart was close enough and then dive out of the way. It wasn't much of a plan, and he didn't even know whether Sam could do it or if he was thinking the along the same lines, but they were all out of options, it seemed.

A field stretched all the way down to their left, at the bottom a row of tall trees stood, a wooden fence separating the field from the trail. Mike thought it was too far away; they would be lucky to make it halfway before they were chased down. Mike didn't think the rotting wooden fence would hold up well against these horses and the cart they were pulling. To their right there was a stone wall, too tall to scale. With nothing but the trail ahead and the crazed men bearing down on them, Mike launched himself back into the middle of the road, surprised to find that Sam remained alongside him.

"Kill them!" one of the men cried, and the second man, seemingly motivated by his passenger, aimed the horses right at them and, with murder in his eyes—that's how close they are, Mike though—began to frantically lash the horses with the reins.

With the maniacs almost upon them, Mike dove to the left while Sam went to the right, and it worked. The horses, the cart, the lunatics went right through the middle and, unable to stop immediately, kept on going for almost a hundred yards.

Mike and Sam were back on their feet and running in the opposite direction. The trail was muddy, slippery, and it was all they could do to remain on their feet. Rain came down in sheets, making the terrain even more difficult to negotiate.

"What the fuck? What the fuck? What the fuck?" Sam was in near hysterics as they ran as fast they could. Mike glanced over his shoulder, saw that the men were turning the cart, trying to get the horses around on the trail which, fortunately, was not wide enough for a regular three-point-turn. He could still hear the lunatics, braying excitedly. If they were travellers, they didn't have an accent.

They ran alongside the tall wall until it stopped completely. Mike saw the steeple first, a split second before Sam said, "Church!" and they raced toward it.

The lunatics had managed to get the horses and cart around and were pointing back toward the village, toward Mike and Sam. With one more deranged howl—coupled with the wind, it sounded like the riders were Legion—they came again.

The church, Mike thought, was their only hope. He took the steps at the front three at a time, leaving Sam clambering up behind him. When he turned the handle and the heavy church door opened with a loud creak, Mike grabbed Sam by the shoulder and dragged him in, slamming the door as hard as he could behind them. There was a key in the door; it was a huge iron thing, but Mike wasted no time in turning it. It clicked as the lock slid into place. Mike listened to the thunderous beat of hooves on the trail as the horses cantered toward the church, the manic howls of the depraved men as they drew nearer.

With the church door locked, Mike was satisfied that the men couldn't get in, but his heart continued to race inside him, a mixture of fear and adrenaline and the fact he really needed to renew that fucking gym membership. Sam paced nervously back and forth along the first few metres of the aisle, rubbing rain from his wet head and muttering something only comprehensible to himself.

The horses had fallen silent outside, but Mike knew the men were still there, had probably disembarked from the cart. He had to give it to them; they were tenacious.

Suddenly, there came a thump on the door, followed by a muffled voice that had an accent Mike didn't recognise. "It'll do you no good," one of the men said. "We'll burn it down if we have to."

Sam looked to Mike, his eyes wide. He stopped pacing.

"As soon as they know you're here they'll come for you." It was the second man, who spoke with a much higher pitch, his faint voice coming through the door all the same. Mike didn't know if it was a mistake responding to them—they were both quite clearly out of their gourd on something—but he wanted to know what the hell was going on, why they had tried to trample them with the horses.

"What do you want?" Mike called back. His voice echoed around the interior of the church.

Sam placed a hand on Mike's shoulder and shook his head; *don't say anything else.*

"What do we want?" the first man said. Mike didn't know for sure, but he thought the man might have been smiling as he spoke. "We don't want *this*, but it has to be. So why don't you be a good little boy and let us in? We'll make it quick, we promise."

What does that even mean? It has to be? What has to be?

Despite Sam's insistence not to make another sound, it was he who spoke next. Mike was surprised that Sam didn't sound scared at all. Angry, sure. Vengeful, more than a little. Sam had clearly taken the stampede out on the trail as more than just village hijinks; it was an attempt on his life, on both their lives, and these psychopaths were fucking with the wrong crowd.

"You'd better get the fuck out of here right now!" Sam yelled. "I swear to God, I'll fuck you up and feed you to your own fucking horses, you hear me?"

The men fell silent. Mike thought he heard faint muttering, as if they were deciding what do to next. Either way, he hoped Sam's outburst had the desired effect.

After a few moments passed—Mike and Sam stood stock still at the church door, breathing heavily—the doorknob rattled violently. They were trying to get inside, had clearly not been deterred by Sam's threat.

"Fuck off!" Sam cried, balling his fists and hammering hard on the church door. "Just fuck off!"

The doorknob stopped rattling and then the second man said, "Have it your way," as if that was much worse than having it their way. "You're not going to make it through the night. They'll come for you. We'll all come for you."

Mike silently waited for this to be expanded upon, but there was nothing further from either of the men. A minute later, there was an audible "hyah" and the sound of hoofbeats moving away from the church and wheels squeaking as they slowly rolled through the mud. The men were going away, but the threat remained. The man's final words echoed implacably around Mike's mind.

As the hoofbeats and cartwheels faded into the distance, Mike turned to Sam. "What the fuck is going on here?"

Sam shook his head. "No idea, but those fuckers are going to come back. And it sounds like they won't be coming alone."

Mike couldn't believe what was happening. It was all so surreal, first with the midget back there on the trail, then with the hollering maniacs on the cart. Things like this didn't happen in real life. Not to him, anyway. He had seen a film just two years before, had taken a girl to the cinema—it had developed into yet another non-relationship in a long string of them—because of all the good reviews the film was getting. In it, Jon Voight, Burt Reynold, Ned Beatty and Ronny Cox were on a canoeing trip when the locals turned against them. Turned out the vacationers hadn't reckoned on the hostility of the natives, an error they would come to regret as the film played out.

Something was going on here, just like it was in that movie. Mike and Sam were in the middle of something quite terrible. Was it a gang thing? Had they encroached upon someone's—the resident pimp's, perhaps—territory and now had to pay the price.

"What was with the fucking horse and cart, Mike?" Sam asked. It was a good question, but Mike already had an answer for it.

"Gypsies. There must be a site not far from here. That's probably what they meant when they said they were going to bring more. The whole fucking gypsy community are going to come after us."

"I don't think they were gypsies," Sam said. He sat on the edge of the back pew, hands on his thighs. Mike knew what Sam was getting at: that the men hadn't spoken with an Irish brogue. But Mike knew that travellers came from all over. A few years back, a community of travellers had descended upon Bunker's Hill—a large, grassy patch not far from his mother's house in Montgomery—and set up camp there. They were cockneys, which had surprised Mike at the time, and remained until the council eventually moved them on almost three months later. All they left behind was an accumulation of empty gas bottles and detritus, and it took the council almost another three months to make that area fit for public use again.

If those men were travellers, and they very well could be, Mike knew the trouble they were about to find themselves in.

"Fuck, Sam," Mike said. "We can't hide in here all day." He knew they should be out there looking for Kelly, and Rebecca, asking around whether anyone has seen them. He hoped the old racist had been wrong, that the girls hadn't climbed over the boulders and come to this place, because if the welcome Mike and Sam had received since their arrival was anything to go by, it didn't bode well for the girls.

"Yeah," Sam said, lighting a cigarette. Mike didn't think it was very respectful, smoking in a church, but he didn't say anything. They had bigger things to worry about than an irate priest or a disapproving deity.

That was another thing. Where was the priest? The doors had been unlocked, but there was no sign of a clergyman. Surely they would have heard the commotion at the doors, come to investigate.

But the church was empty. Not one worshipper. Not a single vicar in sight. The rain had no doubt kept the congregation away, but surely someone had to be here to keep the ship afloat.

"I don't like this place," Sam said, flicking the ash from his cigarette onto the church floor, another reason they were probably both getting turned away from Heaven. At first Mike thought he meant the church, which was completely understandable. Mike had never been a huge fan of them, either, only attending for weddings and funerals and, reluctantly, once when his cousin was christened. But Sam wasn't talking about the church; he meant the whole place. The village.

Mike didn't like it either. It was...eerie, inexplicable. He had felt it no sooner than his feet made contact at the boulders, a thickening of the atmosphere, an emptiness within himself, but he had put that down to hunger, and Sam's subsequent bout of nausea down to alcohol withdrawal. But it had been more than that. This place was unnatural, somehow, and now that they had met some of the locals, his worst fears had been somewhat confirmed.

Mike called out a hello, hoping that a vicar would appear from somewhere. His voice once again echoed around the church, but there was no reply.

"No one's home," Sam said.

"Doesn't that strike you as a little odd?" asked Mike. "I mean, shouldn't there be?"

Sam seemed to consider this for a moment as he stared down at the burning cherry of his cigarette, his hand shaking slightly, which he fought against by gripping it at the wrist with his other hand. "Maybe it's an open church," he said. "You know, open all hours, if you're homeless you can come here and spend the night. Doesn't need to be someone here all the time."

Mike thought about Yorkshire; they didn't have open churches there. At night they were locked up, just the same as everything else. Sure, if you were homeless there was a soup kitchen every Monday and Wednesday, but that was as far as the church's charity went. Mike guessed they didn't want tramps stinking out the place at night, ready for the morning worshippers, which is why they shut the doors at seven and kept them shut until nine the next day.

"I don't know," Mike said with a sigh. All he could think about was Kelly and their search being unceremoniously halted thanks to a couple of assholes who may or may not be on their way back to their wider community right now to "saddle up, boys, we've got ourselves a couple of fresh ones." She was still out there somewhere, or had come this way and had encountered the same resistance as Mike and Sam. If that was the case, then anything could have happened to them.

"Well, you're right about one thing," Sam said as he stood and walked along the aisle. "Two things, actually. Firstly, there's no one here but us, and secondly, we can't stay here all day. I'm not hiding from those pricks."

Mike admired Sam's tenacity, but he wasn't a fighter. If it came down to a brawl with a group of incensed travellers, he knew he wouldn't fare well. Sam was bigger, stronger, could probably take care of himself if it came down to it, but he was getting on in years. Perhaps Sam hadn't accepted that, still believed he was able to take on a man half his age. Charles Bronson he was not, despite his apparent courage.

"Maybe this place has a telephone," Mike said. "We could call the police. Tell them what just happened."

Sam shrugged. "Police aren't going to come all the way out here just because we've been threatened by a bunch of gypsies. And besides, we had to climb a fucking boulder just to get in. We don't even know if there's an opening, or where we even fucking are."

Good point, Mike thought. "We could tell them it's by Pennant," he said. "They must know the place."

"Yeah, we could tell them it's the fiftieth boulder on the right, go straight ahead when you see the silent goblin, and we're in the church with the angry pikeys outside it." Sam's trenchancy, Mike thought, was unnecessary. They were after all in the same boat, as they had been since the start of this thing. They just had very different methods of dealing with things. Sam's way was to be caustic and sardonic, angry and impulsive. That was just the way he was, and Mike was getting used to it.

"I'm going to check anyway," Mike said. If there was a telephone, maybe he could call his mother back in Montgomery, let her know the current state of affairs, that they were lost and could she please try to find out where they were? Somewhere between Pennant and Staylittle, a small village that had a church, a forest, and lots of fields.

But it hadn't been on the road atlas he'd looked at. Whatever this place was, wherever it was, it wasn't clearly marked, and his mother had never been great at simple things like map-reading. She had only recently learned how to turn off the smoke detector—he'd installed one for her after she almost burned the house down making a cottage pie—and he knew she didn't cope well under pressure. She would panic, get flummoxed and then angry, before Mike managed to calm her down again and tell her not to worry, they would figure it out eventually.

"Wasting your time, Mike," Sam said, taking a pew at the front. He wasn't going to help look for a telephone, was probably just thinking about what he was going to do, or attempt to do if his body allowed it, to those two fuckers if they returned.

In the back there was a small room. At its centre there was a table and four chairs. Old, ornate, and probably worth a couple of quid, Mike thought, to someone back in the real world. On the table there was a single cup, which also looked like an antique. It was made of bronze or brass or something like, and its contents were half-finished. There was a *Bible*, a candle that had burned all the way down, and at the edge of the room there was what looked like a hand-pump. This place didn't have hot and cold running water, it seemed. Of a telephone there was no sign. Hanging on the walls were various framed religious paintings, and someone had attempted a Fresco of The Virgin Mary that was not just terrible but also a very good reason to hire a decorator and pronto.

The room had no windows; the room was gloomy, only partially lit by the open door behind him. There were, Mike noticed, no electrical outlets, which would have been strange if it were not for the fact the church had to pump its own water. It had been left in the dark ages.

Satisfied there was no telephone in the room, Mike made his way back out onto the corridor. A thin hallway led off to the right, and Mike decided to take a look. Maybe the vicar lived here, had his own quarters somewhere on the premises. He thought about calling out; the last thing he wanted was to give anyone a heart attack.

At the end of the hall was a door. Large, arched, it looked like the sort of door you read about in fairytales, a door leading to an alternate reality. Wonderland. Narnia. The Emerald City. Mike laughed to himself, imagining that the woman they had passed on the trail earlier was not merely a dwarf; she was a munchkin, had escaped the clutches of the wicked witch and come through this door and was now on the lam.

Mike opened the door, which was heavy and groaned on its hinges. At first, he wasn't sure what he was looking at. The room was massive, almost another church. A large, flat stone sat in the centre of the room. There were windows in this room, although they could hardly be called that. They were holes in the walls, around a foot long and half a foot wide. Mike counted ten in one wall and six in another. There was no glass in them, which meant the rain was coming in, dripping down the stone walls and forming puddles on the ground at the edges of the room where it was uneven.

Around the strange stone monolith in the middle of the room, candles were strategically placed. They were half burned down, white wax trailing away from their bases. There was a strange smell in the room, too, a mustiness that could have been the rain or something else.

Mike walked around the stone table and saw, on one side, an iron loop. There was one on the other side, too. Both were embedded deep in the rock, and it took a while for Mike to understand what they were for.

They were to feed straps through.

This wasn't just a stone table. It was a restraining platform. People had been tied down here, but for what reason? Upon closer inspection, Mike could make out scratches. A lot of scratches in the grey stone where the bound person's hands would have been. Whatever had gone on here wasn't consensual.

"This place just keeps on getting better and better," he mumbled sarcastically.

Turning, he noticed that chains hung from the wall behind him—all four walls, in fact—and at the end of each chain was an iron loop, just large enough for a human wrist to fit through. These were dungeon shackles, and Mike suddenly didn't feel well.

What had happened here? Why did this place exist? Counting the shackles along one wall, Mike estimated there were over a hundred in the room. Perhaps even more.

"Fuck," he said, suddenly wishing he was somewhere else...*anywhere* else.

It was then that Sam started shouting, bellowing Mike's name as loud as he could. Mike's whole body contracted, but for a moment he was stuck, unable to move, wanting to run to Sam but completely incapable of doing so.

Sam yelled his name again, and now Mike could move. He had to, and he ran as fast he could along the thin hall toward the door leading back into the church, his heart pummeling inside him, for he feared the two men had returned with backup and were once again trying to get into the church, only this time they would succeed. They would force the door down or, worse, set fire to the building in order to draw them out.

When Mike saw Sam, he realised that things were much worse. Sam stood in front of the confessional box, the only thing keeping him upright was the pew to his rear. When Sam saw Mike he simply pointed at the confessional, visibly shaking, mouth opening and shutting but nothing coming out.

"What?" Mike said, rushing down the aisle toward Sam. He stopped suddenly when he saw what Sam was pointing at, what had put the fear into him. "What the fuck!"

A man sat on the bench in the confessional. His eyes were wide, and he stared out at them, seemingly imploring them to get him out of there. His head and face were bloodied. Part of his skull was visible, even in the dim light of the church. The way he sat, Mike thought he'd been there for a while; rigor mortis had already started to set in.

Mike saw the cassock, the dog collar, purple preaching scarf, and knew immediately that they had finally solved the mystery of the missing vicar.

"This is so fucked up," Sam said. He'd begun to pace again, something Mike realised he did when he was nervous or scared. And Mike was nervous and scared, too.

"We need to find a phone," Sam said. Then repeated, "This is so fucked up, Mike!"

"There's no phone here," Mike said, but Sam had already known that. "I found something in the back, though. Some sort of chamber. I think they were keeping people here; it's some kind of prison, or dungeon, or something." Weren't dungeons usually underground? Mike didn't know the ins and outs of medieval penitentiaries, but he knew that was what he had found.

"In a church?" Sam said, incredulous.

"I think so." Mike was still looking at the dead man propped up in the confessional, his lifeless eyes, his head cracked open like a coconut. He didn't look real, sitting there. He looked like a special effect from some low-budget horror movie. Mike was a fan—the cheaper looking, the better—and had only recently watched a double-bill of *Bloodthirsty Butchers* and *Flesh Feast*. The man in the confessional looked like a prop from one of those movies.

"We need to get out of here," Sam said. "We need to get help." He lit a cigarette and continued to nervously pace back and forth. Unlike Mike, he seemed unable to look at the corpse in the confessional. He had seen enough.

"We do," Mike said, his hopes of ever seeing Kelly alive again evaporating by the minute.

Just then, a bell began to ring somewhere off the distance. It wasn't an alarm or a siren, but an ordinary handbell, as if the village had a town crier. Mike and Sam looked at each other as if one of them might have an explanation.

The bell continued to ring as they stood there, terrified, with a dead man sitting in the confessional next to them, neither man having a clue of just how bad things were about to get.

Jack watched the men from the chancel. He had heard the hoofbeats on the trail and had decided to crouch, for a moment, behind the organ, in case anyone should enter the church, and he'd been right to do so, for a minute later the two men had come through the door in a state of panic and locked it shut behind them.

It became immediately clear that they were outsiders, even though he could barely make out their faces through the gloom; one of the men had jet black hair and was much younger than any of the men in the village. They wore strange clothes, too, a style that Jack had never seen before. The young man's trousers were wide at the bottom; the older man's jacket was almost puffy, as if it were stuffed with something. He had watched them carefully, listening to the conversation taking place between the outsiders and the men on the other side of the door. Then the men's pursuers had gone away, and the outsiders had begun to explore the church. One of them said something about a tallyfone, whatever that was, but Jack was more concerned with staying out of sight.

Part of him was happy the outsiders had arrived when they did. It was fortuitous, for it meant that the villagers would be preoccupied. Jack knew they would be running around like headless chickens trying to hunt these men, and while they were doing that he could move around almost freely.

One of the men went off to the back, where Jack knew he would find nothing of use. But what if he came across the chamber? It didn't matter. That old place hadn't been used in centuries, the last time being the night the curse was placed upon the village. There was nothing, and certainly no tallyfone.

Jack watched as the older man, now alone in the church, mumbled incoherently to himself. Something about pike-ee bastards. Again, Jack was at a loss, but it seemed to be some sort of slur, and he could see that the man was visibly trembling.

This was perfect. These men would distract the entire village, although it wouldn't last long. They would find them and they would kill them—they always did—but it would hopefully take them long enough. These men, these unfortunate fucking outsiders, would draw out the deceitful—Freddie and Renfield and Albie, Joan and Eve and anyone else who had ever crossed him—and he would pick them off one by one. It would be easy, but he knew he would need a knife or a garrote, something that wouldn't make too much noise, and he still hadn't figured out where he was going to get one from without being seen.

Calhoun's cane was good for striking, but it was quite heavy and one strike did not guarantee death. He had had to hit the vicar a dozen times before he had fallen silent, and another six times before he stopped moving completely. A knife across the throat would be quicker, deadlier quieter. A garrote would be even better.

The older outsider stood then and walked up and down in front of the altar. Jack watched him, rapt. For a moment Jack thought he had been seen, peering out from the darkness behind the organ, but the man only glanced in that direction for a moment before looking away again.

Then, and this for some reason delighted Jack, the man's attention turned to the confessional, and he walked across the church toward it.

He was going to find Calhoun; of that Jack had no doubt, and the ensuing tumult would be amusing to behold. The men would shout and panic, and Jack would have to stifle his snickering. He hoped he could control himself, but at the moment, there didn't seem to be a lot he was in control of.

Jack watched as the man stood motionless in front of the confessional for a moment, as if trying to figure out what it was, but then he opened the door and recoiled in horror before shouting at the top of his voice, and Jack pressed a hand tight against his mouth as the inevitable mirth threatened to give away his position.

The other man came running in then and saw Calhoun propped up in the confessional. It was remarkable how quickly this had escalated. Jack loved it. God, it felt good to be alive again. After all, he had spent so long in that personal purgatory, it was enough to drive a man insane. But Jack wasn't insane. He was as sane as a man could be. And this was delicious.

The men were in complete shock. Jack could see that by the way they stood, their posture, their expressions, the way the older man began to pace back and forth.

He remained low, out of sight and in the shadow of the organ. He didn't think they would find him there, or even come looking. He expected them to leave, to try to escape the village, but the village would never let them leave, the villagers wouldn't let them live. These men were dead the moment they set foot on Neverville soil, but they had yet to realise it.

Just then, the older man—Jack placed him in his fifties; he was a big guy, though, broader than the young lad—lit a cigarette. The young man muttered something to the older man.

And then the bell started to ring. Jack hadn't heard that damn sound in forever, but it was exactly the same as it had been back then. Tinny, discordant, and whoever was ringing it was giving it their all. It was to summon the brown robes to the inn, where they would discuss tactics and arm up. He had been there alongside them on many occasions, when he himself was a brown robe. That was a long time ago, though, but some things, it seemed, never change. Jack wondered how many brown robes there were now; twenty? Twenty-five? Back in the early fifties, before Jack was incapacitated by stupidity, there had been almost fifty tasked with hunting down outsiders, but he doubted that was the case now. Many of them would be too old for such physical exertion; others would have simply decided to hang up their robe, electing instead for a quiet life, without the undesirable assignment of necessary murder hanging over them all the livelong day.

As the bell continued to ring, Jack grinned, broadly.

The men, the outsiders, confused and scared, had every reason not to do the same.

And Jack's grin only widened when he realised he had an opportunity, for his daughter would be all alone now. Unless she had grown up to be a brown robe, like her mother. Jack didn't think that Little Evil would have wanted that. She probably wants to be a princess, or a mermaid, or a nun. Not a murderer.

Jack waited, willing the outsiders to go away so he could put his plan into action. He knew they wouldn't remain in the church; that bell was already worrying them, he could see that.

It was only a matter of time.

Jack could barely contain his excitement.

EIGHTEEN

When Eve heard the bell toll, she knew it was bad. Worse than just a couple of outsiders wandering into the village. The bell was reserved for potentially problematic outsiders; the brown robes summoned only when things were already out of control. But what separated these two men from the other outsiders? Eve didn't understand it, nor did she know anything about the two girls to which her mother alluded out on the trail, but Eve was smart, and it didn't take her long to figure out a possible connection.

The two men were here looking for the girls. Maybe fathers? Brothers? Searching for missing loved ones? That would explain why the brown robes were being called for; these particular outsiders were here, not by chance. They were actively looking, and here in Neverville actively looking was not a good thing. People who did that ended up the same as the others, Eve knew that. The brown robes were well-versed in the hunt. That was, after all, their job. To maintain the established hundred, to ensure the villagers' safety was protected, to kill any outsiders as quickly as possible. The village wouldn't sleep until those men were dead. Eve was just as much at risk as everyone else, and could drop down dead in the next five seconds, if it was the will of the curse. She had never heard of such a rapid death, though. Usually they had hours to end outsiders, sometimes as long as a day, but rarely longer than that. It was almost as if they were being thrown a lifeline by the curse. Either that or it liked to toy with them, keep them guessing. It was far scarier not knowing when it would happen, or if it would be you. The only thing Eve knew was that two people would die. It all rested upon whether the brown robes acted fast enough.

The bell continued to ring.

Eve went to the kitchen window, glanced out at the trail. There they were, passing on horses, some rushing along on foot—if you could call that rushing; one of them was limping fast   but they all had one thing in common.

Walnut brown hooded cloaks. The garb used to separate the willing killers from the villagers who preferred not to butcher. These men and women had volunteered to take up arms against any man, woman, and child that threatened the continued existence of Neverville and its current hundred residents. The brown robes had been sworn in, had pledged their allegiance, and had no reservations about killing. Eve was not a brown robe and had never had any ambition or compulsion to become one. The thought of taking a life didn't sit well with her, no matter if it was imperative. She didn't even think she could do it, if she should find herself in that situation. You were either born a brown robe—ruthless, ugly, able to switch off emotions at will—or you were not.

Eve was not.

Standing there, she counted at least ten. Then there were those coming from the opposite direction, who would not pass by her house. So many, she thought, for just two lost souls. They certainly weren't taking any chances.

Eve knew her mother was one of them. Joan Lockwood had always revelled in the bloody festivities that the outsiders brought with them. That's not to say that she wanted them there, risking her life and others; just that she didn't exactly dislike the art of killing, had gotten pretty good at it over the years and decades. Eve didn't fear for her mother's life when she was out there, hunting. She always returned home, blood spattered across her face and already drying to a crust, and she would sigh with relief and drop languidly into her armchair before falling into a deep sleep, as if she had just come home from a hard shift at the mill.

Freddie and her mother were at the inn now, awaiting the arrival of the other brown robes. Albie was, Eve surmised, probably the one ringing the bell that summoned them. It was the same bell he used to call time at the end of a night's drinking, although he seldom used it for that purpose, which was why the inn often remained open until the early hours.

Eve suddenly felt exposed. Her father—The Burden—was still out there, still hiding somewhere amongst them. An enemy too close for comfort, he would hear that bell. She didn't know if he knew what it meant—he'd been away for a long time, so to speak—but even as a child Eve remembered it. A ear-splitting clang that, no matter how near or far you were, always arrived at the same volume. If Eve remembered it growing up, chances were that it had been used before she was born, when Jack was still very much an active and functioning member of the community.

He knew.

He knew what that bell meant. He had, after all, been a member of the brown robes. And, according to her mother, Jack Lockwood was one of the deadliest, singlehandedly taking care of half a dozen outsiders in 1949, and then another group in '50. He preferred, it seemed, to work alone, which terrified Eve even more. Her father was working alone now, and had a lot of pent-up aggression to express.

He might use this to come for me, Eve thought, knowing it would be perfect, perhaps his only real opportunity to get her alone.

All at once Eve was beset with fear, and quickly rushed to the door to make sure it was locked. It was, although she didn't remember locking it when she entered. It had been automatic, and she was glad she had. She checked the door at the rear of the house, too, and was pleased to find that locked, too. There was no way in, apart from the smashed window on the first floor of the house, and she didn't think her father would be able to climb up the wall outside, unless he had transmuted into something otherworldly.

She was safe, for now, but part of her still feared that he would somehow get in. He would get in and murder her while the brown robes were out murdering two outsiders.

Eve checked the locks once more and lit a dozen candles, placing three in each ground floor room.

If he was coming, she wanted to be able to see him.

Just then, the bell stopped ringing, its final clang fading to silence. An unnatural silence, Eve thought, as if her eardrums had been pierced by something sharp, leaving her forever deaf. She could hear her own shallow breaths, though, which convinced her that she was simply being overdramatic.

The brown robes were all in, and in a moment the meeting would commence.

Eve suddenly wished she was anyplace other than Neverville.

After instructing Walter Creswell to close and lock the inn door, Albie started the meeting, as he always did, with a prayer. Hooded heads were bowed as Albie mumbled his way through the same prayer they had heard many times before.

"Father, we have sinned against You, and are not worthy to be called Your sons and daughters. Father of mercy, like the prodigal son, we return to You and say: we have sinned against You and are no longer worthy to be called Your children. Christ Jesus, saviour of the world, we pray with the repentant thief to whom You promised paradise. Lord remember us in your kingdom. Holy Spirit, fountain of love, we call on you with trust. Purify our hearts, and help us to walk as children of the light. Amen."

A chorus of 'Amens' sounded around the crowd in unison, and heads and weapons were once again raised and hoods lowered, for it was time to get down to it.

Freddie, standing beside Albie at the bar, tried not to look nervous, but the events that took place in the woods that very afternoon had affected him. He had come so terribly close to a two-on-one situation, and not in his favour, and now realised he'd been stupid to go out there on his lonesome. But what had been the alternative? Dragging Dennis Wainwright's gout-ridden carcass around with him? Maybe interrupt Edith Frewer and Liz Slocombe's tête-à-tête about fabrics and which stitches were best, hand them both a knife, and tell them to get a move on, because, "Those fuckers aren't gonna slaughter themselves!"? No, he had had no choice and, at the time, had thought he could handle it on his own. Had it not been for Albie's faltering musket—he'd let Albie know just how pissed off he was about that, and Albie had apologised profusely and offered Freddie free moonshine for the rest of the month by way of atonement—he might have taken off the young man's head, might have overpowered the second man and stabbed him once or twice before running his blade across the man's throat. Might have.

Woulda, coulda, shoulda.

"As you are all aware, that bell can mean only one thing," Albie said with the same air of authority he always exuded during these speeches. "We once again find ourselves in great peril. There are currently two outsiders within our walls, their arrival placing our village in imminent danger."

"Just point me in their direction!" Wanda Hill cried from the edge of the room, where she stood on a table so she could see what was going on at the front. "Don't like the way them boys looked at me," she said. "Reckon I owe 'em for that."

The villagers began to mutter impatiently. Someone told Wanda to, "Shut the fuck up, half woman!" which was perhaps, Freddie thought, a little harsh.

Standing on the other side of Albie was Eric Majors, and he held his hands up in a placatory fashion, trying to pacify the unsettled brown robes. "All right, all right, everyone just calm down," he said. He had to raise his voice to be heard above the commotion. "We must maintain some semblance of order, so if everyone could please, just settle down, we can continue."

Freddie didn't like Eric—even less after the way he'd spoken to Freddie a few nights prior—but this was something he was good at. He was in his element right now, and Freddie had to hand it to him: he knew how to control a crowd.

"It's just two men," Eric went on. "Of course, we would have preferred this to be a loner, but we've dealt with multiple outsiders before, many times, so there is no need to panic. Everything is under control."

Albie addressed the crowd once again, his head now fully visible. "As far as we understand, these men are here for a specific reason. A few nights ago, two female outsiders were discovered in the village, and were dispatched efficiently and without losing any of our own. We have reason to believe that the men are somehow connected to those girls, and have come to Neverville to find them."

More impatient muttering followed, for this was the first some of them were hearing about those girls, and it wasn't going down too well. Brown robes didn't like to be kept in the dark about outsiders.

Still furious about Albie's malfunctioning musket, and raising his voice to be heard over the protesting horde, Freddie said, "I've seen them, and would have ended them if not for..." He glanced toward Albie, decided not to besmirch him in front of his fellow brown robes. "Anyway, one of these men is young. Early twenties, perhaps. The other is older, but he's bigger. Shouldn't be too difficult to take them out, but we need to work together. They're here for a reason, determined to find those girls." Of course, they would never find them, not unless they dug up the new patch at the back of Freddie's farm. "That makes them dangerous. There will be no pretending to be a normal village on this one, no acting. We're going to hunt them and kill them on sight. We have the upper hand. There are eighteen of us against two of them." He had performed a perfunctory count as the brown robes entered the inn, hoping for a better turnout. There were more than a few faces missing. There was no sign of Father Calhoun, and the gay boys had apparently given it a miss. Freddie put that down to the bad weather; the rain continued to lash the windows of the inn, lightning flashed intermittently, thunder roared overhead.

"So, this is going to be a straightforward hunt," Eric said, inspecting the blade of his machete, his weapon of choice. Freddie's knife was much smaller, but it had never failed him. Unlike that damn musket.

Every brown robe had their preferred weapon. Walter Creswell had his bow; the quiver of arrows was strapped to his back. Walter favoured killing from a distance, and he was a damn good shot, thanks to years of practice. Joan Lockwood used a knife, Doc Renfield a machete—although his was slightly shorter than Eric's, its blade wider—and Frannie Mills a morning star flail. Albie would usually use his musket, but after Freddie's unfortunate incident in the woods, had opted for an axe. Dennis Wainwright, Freddie saw, was relying on his trusty crossbow, although how he could operate it with the way his hands were all twisted was beyond Freddie, and Wanda Hill had been holding her ancient war hammer aloft since she'd arrived. There were more knives, a couple more machetes, every brown robe armed and ready to wage war.

"We are unsure of their exact time of arrival, however we know they have been here for some time, so we must deal with this promptly and methodically." Eric lowered his machete and, although he didn't single Freddie out, the next part was meant for him; Freddie was sure of it. "There is little room for error, so no mistakes, please, lest we suffer unthinkable consequences. We must—"

There came a sudden thump at the door. Followed by another, equally as urgent. Every man and woman present turned to face the door. Weapons were raised, and then lowered again when a voice said through the door: "Albie! Eric! It's just us!"

With a nod from Eric, Walter turned the key in the door and allowed Lucas Thorne and John Wexler to enter, before shutting and locking it behind them. They were drenched, their brown robes almost black with rain,

"Sorry we're late," Wexler said. "But when you hear what we've done, you're gonna thank us."

Freddie was intrigued, along with the other brown robes. A silence descended upon the room as they waited to hear just what Wexler and Thorne had done.

"We were on our way back from the pond when we saw them out there on the trail," Thorne said. "Just walking along without a care in the world, but we changed that, didn't we John?"

"We sure did," Wexler said, smiling. "Tried to run them over, for sure, but they got by us. Managed to reach the church, they did. Locked themselves in. We even spoke to them, didn't we?"

Thorne nodded. "Right couple of bastards," he said. "Won't feel bad about taking these two out, will we?"

"Not at all," Wexler said.

"Where are they now?" asked Eric. Freddie could see the veins in his forehead throbbing, the cords of his neck tautening. He was clearly angry that Thorne and Wexler had left the church unguarded.

"Still there, probably," Thorne said with a shrug. "Reckon they're too scared to come out."

"If Calhoun's in there, he's probably already taken care of them." Wexler smiled again; Freddie could see the cavities in the man's teeth from where he stood across the room.

"We can't be sure of that," Freddie said. "Or that they're still even there, thanks to you two morons." Wexler and Thorne frowned as if they didn't know what he was talking about. "Calhoun's absence from this meeting might be a good thing," he said, for if the vicar was not here then he was at the church, and if he was at the church then there was a chance he had already gotten to the outsiders, saving them all the trouble. That, however, was conjecture, and it was far too risky to assume such things. "A party will head for the church first of all."

"Yes," Albie said. Eric agreed, too, albeit with a grimace. Freddie thought it was because he had lost control of the room for once.

"Walter, Doc, Wanda, Lucas, John, Freddie, and myself," Eric said, pointing at each man and the dwarf as he reeled off their names. "We'll head on over to the church. The rest of you separate here. Spread yourselves far and wide. If we do not end them on the outskirts, we'll drive them toward you."

Casting a large net was perhaps the best way to draw this to a suitable conclusion, although Freddie would have picked Albie over Wanda. It was at times like this he missed Jack Lockwood. The man was an absolute hornswoggler, but he was brutal. That fucker knew how to take care of outsiders, and had no qualms when things got down and dirty. Unfortunately, that was all he had been good for. Mindless killing of unarmed drifters. Still, Freddie would have swapped three Wandas for one Jack Lockwood.

Those whose names had been called out gathered near the door while the rest of the crowd made way for them. Someone patted Freddie on the back, which he didn't appreciate too much, since he was still aching from his earlier encounter with the men whom they now all hunted. Eric continued to hand out instructions to the remaining brown robes; Albie was to lead two men and a woman to the east of the village, where they were to form a line. Once established, they were to search every house and cottage, including their own, in case the men had left the temporary sanctuary of the church and gone elsewhere. Joan was assigned three men and instructed to move north, toward the mill. Dennis, with two men and two women at his disposal, were to move south toward the pond, since Dennis knew that area well. Twenty men and women, each with a direction to move in, every one of them determined not to be the person mourned at the end of this.

Albie silenced the crowd, who were seemingly eager to get out there, despite the storm. "Lord, You are almighty," he began. "You hold the final authority over all of us who stand here. No one can stand against the might of Your hand. You have always protected us and taken care of threats. We stand in Your presence once again because of these outsiders. We call upon You because we know You can hear us and will save us. Thank you, Lord, for Your saving power. Amen."

There were Amens from the horde as they crossed their hearts, but Freddie didn't join in. Neither did Joan Lockwood. Freddie had noticed her strange demeanour throughout the meeting. She was both in the room, and yet not at the same time, as if something plagued her. Was it that Jack was not here for this? Or that Eve was alone at home? Freddie didn't know, but there was something fighting for Joan's attention. He could see it in her eyes and the lackadaisical manner in which she gripped her knife.

Eric instructed Walter to unlock the door, and they moved out onto the trail in their small groups. It was going to be an eventful night. Freddie could feel it in the atmosphere. There was something different about this, something wholly unusual was in the air. He had felt it once before—many years ago, on the night Jack Lockwood had been exiled from the pub and had gone to the boulders. Freddie's bones vibrated, his eyes watered, his heart was already racing, even though he was yet to exert himself in any way.

He had felt it back then in '53, and he was feeling it again now, but why? He wondered whether it was just him experiencing such strange discomfort, and glancing around at his fellow brown robes as they gathered around, formulating plans and repeating Eric Majors' instructions, confirmed nothing.

Perhaps it was just adrenaline.

"Freddie," a voice said. Freddie turned to find Eric moving toward him at pace, his feet squelching in the mud as he approached. He came to a halt less than a foot from Freddie, leaned in, and said, "You've got a lot to atone for. What happened with those girls the other night, what happened at the woods today." Freddie didn't have a chance to argue about that before Eric continued. "If those bastards are still up at the church, we'll be lucky, so I suggest you get your head straight before we set off. Are you ready?"

Freddie nodded. He was ready, despite feeling a little off-colour. The strange sensation forced down deep, he said, "I'm good to go." So was everyone else. Those with horses were mounting them, those without horses pacing excitedly around.

"Come on then," Eric said. "The sooner we get this over with, the sooner we can all go back to our normal lives."

That, Freddie thought, was a joke. They had never known normal lives. Not one of them could say they had. What they had was an existence, sheltered, quarantined away from the rest of the world where they survived on a day-to-day basis, as their parents had before them, and their parents before them. It was an infinite loop of survival. The trick was to accept it would never change and get on with it. And this, killing innocents, was just another part of that.

"Okay, you all know what needs to be done," Albie called out as he made sure the inn doors were properly locked. It was already getting dark; the thick black clouds above muting what remained of daylight before its time. "Let's get to it."

They each went their way. Freddie joined up with his group and set off for the church, where he hoped the men were still holed up. Those idiots Lucas Thorne and John Wexler had made a huge mistake leaving that place when they had them cornered. If anyone had to 'atone' for anything, it was those two. Freddie was still livid with Eric for implying this was somehow all his fault, that none of this would have happened if it weren't for his losing track of those girls the other night, or suggesting that he was wholly responsible for Albie's musket not firing. Of course these things had been beyond his control, but Eric didn't seem to agree, had taken it upon himself to place the blame squarely upon Freddie. That sonofabitch.

With a dry throat and stomach still turning over, Freddie gripped the handle of his knife and fell into line between Doc Renfield and Walter Creswell.

Toward the church they marched in silence, weapons drawn and only blood in their eyes.

NINETEEN

Neverville, 1974

When the outsiders finally plucked up the courage to leave the church—the young one didn't seem to think it was such a good idea, while the other, the older man, was adamant they would be safer outside—Jack was almost falling asleep. He had listened to them talking for almost an hour, maybe longer, and their dulcet tones had made him sleepy.

They were going for help, that was the gist of it. They would find somewhere with a tallyfone and they would get help, but Jack knew better. The brown robes would be out looking for them now. They were as good as dead.

Jack had given the men a head start. He wasn't going after them they were not on his itinerary. He wanted them to get far enough ahead so that he could also leave the church without being seen. When he was sure they had been gone long enough, he came out from behind the organ and slowly made his way down the aisle toward the doors.

The church was even darker now, and Jack wondered if he had fallen asleep at some point. Maybe he had. Maybe it was nighttime now, in which case the outsiders were most definitely dead.

The longcase clock at the rear of the church ticked and tocked, its pendulum moving side to side, and Jack saw that only three hours had passed since he'd arrived, less than two hours since the outsiders came. The darkness outside was a mere illusion caused by the weather. It was only five twenty-five.

Jack made his way out of the church, sticking to its walls for the first ten metres before concluding there was no one there, either on the trail ahead or coming across the field opposite. He quickly made his way across the road and over the fence there. Soon he was darting between trees and underbrush, knowing exactly where he was going and making sure he was always out of sight should anyone come along the trail to his right.

He had been right to stay off the trail, for a group of brown robes came along when he was halfway to his destination. He concealed himself within a thorny bush, hissing as the tiny spines jabbed into his skin and tore at his soiled clothes. Some of the brown robes were on horseback. The one at the front (Jack couldn't see his face) carried an oil lantern, its tiny flame flickering frantically.

Amongst them, Jack was certain he heard Doc Renfield's unmistakable voice. He was talking to someone tall—again, Jack didn't know who it was for certain, but it definitely wasn't that midget, Wanda. She was at the rear of the group, waddling to keep up.

From the bush, Jack watched them pass, listened to the hoofbeats fade as they pressed on further along the trail. They were going to the church, he had no doubt about that. Those two men would have returned to the village and told them that's where the outsiders were. So now they were going to check, but the outsiders were no longer there. Oh, what a farce! What an absolute joy to observe!

Satisfied that the brown robes were gone, Jack tore himself free of the bush's spines and continued along the tree line. Once that group had ascertained the outsiders were no longer at the church, they would come back this way, return to the village. Jack knew he had limited time to get this done. Part one of a multi-chapter tome.

This was the quickest way home.

The fastest way to get to Eve.

Little Evil. He grinned as he moved, leapt over branches, pushed through nettles, slipped through mud. *I might be an old man*, he thought, *but I'm not dead yet.*

I'm not dead yet.

Busying herself had helped. First, Eve had cleaned up the broken glass in the bedroom. Most of it had gone onto the grass outside and below, but there were a few shards here and there on the floorboards in The Burden's room. After that, she had decided not to take any chances, and had set about boarding up the broken window with the wood they had used on the door earlier. She had cut her hand on a nail still protruding from one of the planks, and hoped it didn't get infected. Renfield could take a look at it later, when all of this was behind them, but for now she worked furiously to get the window boarded.

As she worked, the house made noises behind her, but she knew it was only the weather. Still, when a gust came through the broken window and suddenly slammed the bedroom door shut, she almost screamed out, for she was certain her father had found a way into the house, had crept up the stairs—avoiding the third, seventh, ninth, and tenth steps, for these were the ones that creaked—and was just seconds away from committing filicide. How relieved she was to find no one standing there in the room, yet how pathetic and small she felt at the same time.

A group of brown robes made their way past the house, and she watched them through a crack in the boards. She couldn't see their faces; their hoods were up. But she knew her mother wasn't amongst them. She knew the way her mother walked—listing ever-so-slightly to the left and with her arms tucked into her body at all times, as if she was afraid of somehow losing a hand if she wasn't careful. None of these brown robes moved like that. She recognised Dennis Wainwright's rickety gait, though. That man couldn't walk right if his life depended on it.

They were moving in the direction of the pond, which was, Eve surmised, where they had been instructed to go by Eric Majors. She thought about him, sitting there, his head working frantically as he searched for puzzle pieces that would fit, thought about the way he had looked at her earlier, and now he was out there playing General, leading the brown robes into an uncertain battle against two men none of them knew.

Once the group were out of sight, Eve went downstairs. She needed the outhouse desperately, had held her bladder for as long as humanly possible, but the time had come to just get it over with.

She unlocked the door at the back of the house and, after first checking the trees to her left and the field to her right, ran as fast as she could toward the small, wooden structure at the bottom of the garden. Rain pelted her, whipped at her exposed legs like tiny daggers, but she didn't stop, nor did she look back, for if she looked back, she knew she would see him standing there. Grinning. Drooling. Murderous and maniacal.

She flung open the outhouse door and yanked it shut behind her. Almost in tears by the time she undid her dress, it took a full three minutes before Eve could urinate, by which time she had calmed down and assured herself that she was still alone.

She thought about staying there in the outhouse until her mother returned; her father, should he come for her, wouldn't think to look there, would he? Was she not safer, tucked away in a box at the bottom of the garden? Was it not better than the house, where her father knew every crevice, every hiding place, every little detail?

Almost ten minutes passed, and Eve decided to compose herself and return to the house. She would arm herself and wait. Maybe a knife or a hammer. If her father found a way in, she would be ready. She wouldn't hesitate to bring that hammer down on the top of his head, wouldn't think twice about driving a knife through his stomach. She could almost picture it, could almost visualise perfectly his contorted face as he dropped to his knees as blood poured from his broken head. It shouldn't have made her smile, but it did.

She didn't run back to the house. She walked along the tree line, listening for movement, holding her breath as she drew closer and closer to the back door.

That was when she realised she'd made a big mistake. The door was slightly ajar. Through the crack, candlelight flickered. She had not locked the door behind her before rushing to the outhouse, had simply taken off for fear of being caught and butchered.

He could be in there now. He could be in there, waiting for me. How could she have been so stupid? In the ten minutes that she had been in the outhouse, her father could have returned, made himself a slice of bread and butter, picked his weapon, and slipped into the shadows to lie in wait.

Eve knew, though, that she couldn't stay in the garden all night. Not only was her father on the loose, but there were two outsiders roaming free, and who knew what they would be capable of once they found out the whole village was out to kill them.

The thought of returning to the house was no more terrifying than the idea of standing out in the rain until morning. If The Burden didn't find her, the outsiders might, and if they didn't, there was a very good chance she would succumb to hypothermia. The rain looked set to continue. If the thunderclouds were anything to go by, it could last a while.

A flash of lightning sent her running for the door, and when she reached it she didn't stop. She yanked it open and pulled it shut behind her, fingers already gripping the key in the door before it was even fully shut. Breathless, she locked the door and, from the washstand, retrieved a large knife her mother must have used earlier to slice bread.

Turning, Eve found shadows dancing across the kitchen walls, a hellish nightmarescape of cavorting figures, silhouettes prancing along the cracked paint, always moving, always changing. She realised it was an illusion from the flickering candles, but she was on edge, and even though she had the knife, she half-expected her father to come running into the room, screaming like a madman with an axe in his hand.

The rain pattered heavily against the kitchen window, and Eve wanted to get away from there. If her father or the outsiders came around to the rear of the house, they would surely see her through the window; the candlelight would make her stand out like one of the silhouettes sashaying across the walls.

She moved into the living room, slowly, gingerly, and on tiptoes. She was still reprimanding herself for not locking the back door when she peered out into the hallway, and that was when a huge hand wrapped around her throat and squeezed. She tried to scream, but nothing came out.

How stupid! Eve, you fool! Now you're going to die because you couldn't hold your water any longer, you silly, silly girl!

"Don't *hurt* her!" a voice said from the shadows. Her assailant, to her left, hadn't spoken, was simply pinning Eve to the hallway wall and holding her there. This voice had come from Eve's right.

"I'm not bloody *hurting* her," her attacker replied, easing up a little on Eve's throat. "She's got a bloody knife." He was holding her hand down, making sure she couldn't raise her arm and slash at him with the blade. To Eve he whispered, "I'd drop that, if I were you. We're having a pretty shitty day. Be a shame to make it any worse."

Eve stopped struggling. There were two of them, the outsiders, and she knew she had very little hope of escaping them. But was it worse that the outsiders were here instead of her father? She would shortly find out.

"Okay, okay!" she gasped, allowing the knife to drop from her hand. It clattered on the floorboards, and the man holding her by the throat kicked it down the hall.

"All right," he said. "I'm gonna let you go now, but if you scream, if you make one sound, I'm going to kill you. Do you understand?"

Eve nodded. She had no intention of screaming. No one would hear her anyway; they were all off looking for these men.

"Is there anyone else in the house?" the other man asked as he stepped out of the shadows. He was young, Eve saw. Perhaps the same age as her. Quite handsome, too, in an unconventional way. Eve had never seen a young man before, and it was strange now. To cast eyes upon a man devoid of wrinkles, a man whose hair was dark and thick, it was more than a little surreal.

Eve shook her head. "Just me," she managed. The man's grip had loosened a little, and she was no longer being pressed against the wall. "My mother, she's out," Eve added, as if this information would be extracted from her anyway, so she might as well put it out there and let the outsiders decide what they were going to do with it.

"Okay, Sam," the young man said. "Let her go. I trust her not to make a noise."

"We don't even know her," the man, Sam, replied. "She might be crazy."

"Are you crazy?" the young man asked Eve.

Eve, once again shaking her head, said, "I'm not. A little scared, but not crazy." It was true. She feared for her life. These men clearly knew that they were not wanted in Neverville, had perhaps survived an attempt on their lives already, which was why they were taking no chances with Eve, and why they were in her house now, laying low for a while until they figured out what to do next.

The one called Sam released her neck and she rubbed at the sore heat and blinked away the stars that had appeared in her vision.

"My name's Mike," the young man said. *He has kind eyes,* Eve thought. *A little sad, but kind.* "This is Sam. We're not going to hurt you, but we're in trouble and we need to get to a telephone."

A sudden crash of thunder made them all jump; now that it was growing dark, the lightning had become more intense. The hallway was illuminated for almost three seconds, in which Eve managed to get a good look at the outsiders. Sam was older than Mike; his eyes weren't kind, just angry. He had every right to be angry, too. It wasn't every day someone tried to kill you, let alone an entire village.

"I don't know what that is," Eve said, confused.

"A telephone," Mike repeated. "We need to make a call, get some help out here." He seemed frustrated, and frantically gestured with his hands as he spoke.

"Make a call?" Eve said. What did 'make a call' mean? This was some outsider thing, a creation from beyond the boulders, and she knew she could not help them with something she did not understand.

"She doesn't have a phone," Sam said, rubbing his balding head anxiously. "This place doesn't even have electricity, Mike. Look around." He stepped into the living room and motioned vaguely to his surroundings. A candle crackled momentarily before blinking out.

"These things are all Mother's," Eve said. She didn't care for the armchairs, the rug, the trinkets on the mantelpiece, but she wasn't about to allow these men to come in and make snide comments about them, either.

"Must be a power cut," Mike said. To Eve he added, "When did the power go out? How long have you been without electricity?" His frustration was seemingly exacerbated by Eve's confusion.

"We don't have elec...electrishty," Eve said. It was close enough that Mike seemed to understand her. "You are from beyond the boulders, yes?"

The two men looked at one another; they seemed to know what the other one was thinking, although Eve did not. The one called Sam said:

"Yes, we climbed over the boulders. Then we came through the woods. Then a couple of idiots tried to mow us down with their horses. Then we found a dead fucking vicar in that church of yours, and now—"

"Father Calhoun is dead!?" Eve gasped, cutting the man off mid-sentence.

"We didn't get his name," Sam said. "All we know is that someone smashed his head in and stuck him in a confessional box."

Several emotions overtook Eve then. Fear, sadness, loss, confusion, anger, she felt them all at once. And she knew it was her father who had killed Calhoun, which meant that he had gone to the edge of the village. She hoped he was still there, far away from her and the rest of the villagers, but knew that was unlikely. And now the brown robes were out on the trail, looking for these outsiders. Surely they would search the church; her father would not wait around for them to come, would be on the move, sticking to the darkness and hiding himself away as much as possible. He was, according to her mother, a smart man, an intuitive man, not the kind of man you could easily get the better of. He was, by all accounts, not a fool, which was why Eve was so wary of him and what he was capable of.

"She knows something, Mike," Sam said. "She's not telling us something."

Mike turned to Eve, and when she saw his expression—as if he no longer trusted her—she took a step back. "What's your name?" he asked. She had not been expecting that. In this place, where everyone knew her name, it was a question she hadn't heard in forever. Maybe this was the first time ever.

"Eve," she said. "Eve Elizabeth Lockwood."

Sam laughed as if she had said something funny, and maybe she had. Maybe Lockwood was a curse where these men came from, and she had just blurted it out as if it were nothing.

"Well, Eve Elizabeth Lockwood," Mike said. "We're going to need you to tell us what the hell is going on here. Where is this place?"

"Neverville," Eve said.

"Neverville?" Sam said.

Eve nodded. "Yes, but it is not like the places you have ever been before," she said. "And it is not a place you can ever leave, not now that you're here."

The one called Sam shrugged and allowed his arms to fall heavily to his sides. "See, Mike? Did you hear that? You can never leave. She's obviously just as fucked up as the rest of these people."

Mike didn't seem to hear Sam, or had chosen not to. "What do you mean by that, Eve?" he asked. "When you say it's a place we can never leave, what do you mean?"

It was strange talking to new people, and Eve was struggling. "It's a curse," she said. "An old curse. Once you come across the boulders, it won't let you leave. We've been here forever, our families before us, and theirs before them."

"Fucking wacko," Sam spat. "Mike, there's something in the drinking water around here, I'm telling you."

"All water is drinking water," Eve said. "Except for the stuff Freddie gives to the animals. I wouldn't drink that if you paid me a guinea."

Mike took something out of his coat pocket, glanced down at it for a moment, then held it toward Eve. It was a picture of a girl, younger than Eve. She was beautiful, but Eve didn't know what she should do next. She waited for Mike to speak.

"Have you seen this girl?" he asked. "Might have come through here a few days ago."

Eve hadn't seen anyone, but knew that she was one of the girls her mother, Freddie, and Renfield had been talking about on the trail in front of Eric Majors' house. She was the reason these men were here.

"I haven't seen her," Eve said, taking the picture from Mike. She looked down at it and was amazed by the accuracy of the image. "This is remarkable!" she said. "Who painted it?"

"No one *painted* it," Mike said. "It's a photograph. I think it was taken a few months ago."

"A fertograf?" Eve said, turning the picture over and examining the back. It was difficult to see through the gloom, but someone had inscribed a date on the back of the picture in blue ink: 5/3/74.

"Look, we don't have time for this," Sam said, stepping closer to Eve. She wanted to take a step back, but the armchair behind her prevented her from doing so. Fear returned, brought on by the angry man. "Yes, it's a photograph," he said. "A fucking picture from a fucking Polaroid camera." He snatched it out of Eve's hand and thrust it toward Mike, who tucked it back into the pocket of his coat. When he turned back to Eve he wasn't looking at her face, but at her hand, which was still extended. For a moment he didn't speak, remaining silent even as he grabbed her by the wrist and turned her hand over.

"Sam," Mike said. "Let go of her."

"Rebecca's ring!" Sam said, pulling Eve's hand closer to his face. "Mike, this is Rebecca's ring. I bought it for her fifteenth birthday." His face was so close now that the fine hairs on the back of Eve's hand tickled and a droplet of rainwater from his face stubble landed on her knuckle.

"My mother gave it to me!" Eve said, trying to pull her hand free of the man's giant grasp. "It's my birthday this week! It was a gift!"

Mike came closer now and took a look at the ring, frowning, one hand on Sam's shoulder. "How sure are you?" he asked.

"Mike, I'm fucking positive!" Sam said, still refusing to let go. "H. Samuel, we were walking past the window. She went crazy for it. Mike, I know it's hers, I know it's the same fucking ring." He turned to Eve, anger knitting his eyebrows together, his bottom lip quivering with rage. "You fucking cunt, tell me where she is? I'll kill you! I'll kill you all!"

Eve panicked then. She didn't know what else to do, but Sam was enraged, so much so that he was barely human. His teeth were bared, his eyes wide with rage, and he was snarling like a wild animal. She kicked out, hoping to connect with his groin, but her foot hit him hard in the thigh and he caught it, spun her around, and threw her down onto the armchair. Mike was trying to placate him—Eve could hear him, although the armchair cushion was muffling him somewhat—and pull him off and away.

"She's got Rebecca's ring, Mike!" Sam cried. "My Rebecca! My Rebecca's fucking ring!"

"Sam, please, let her up!" Mike yelled. "She's no good to us dead, is she?"

Eve struggled and bucked, hoping to throw Sam's weight off her, but he was strong, and he was determined, and she knew she wasn't getting up until he allowed her to. Fortunately for Eve, Mike's words seemed to work and she was unceremoniously pulled back to her feet and tugged around by the arm so that she faced them again.

"You're going to start talking, girl, or I swear to God you die here, in this room." Sam walked out into the hallway. When he returned he was holding the knife Eve had had only a moment ago. When Mike saw his friend—partner, uncle, father?—with the knife, he staggered back himself a few steps, which Eve didn't think was a good sign. If even his companion (yes, that was the best word for it) was shocked and confused by Sam's actions, then Eve should have been terrified, and she was.

"Look, Mister," Eve said, her eyes darting from Sam's enraged face to the knife in his hand and back again. "I'll tell you, but you need to understand that what happens here in Neverville, it can't be altered. It can't ever be changed, and the people who live here, myself included, are good people." She thought about her father, who wasn't good people and had never been good people, but for the most part the villagers were inherently virtuous.

Sam's expression didn't alter. He was so riled up by Eve wearing his daughter's ring—*thanks for that, Mother. Thanks for gifting me a dead girl's jewellery!*—that Eve doubted his incensed expression would ever fade.

"I'm going to tell you something terrible first. You will want to kill me, and might, for what I am about to say is the last thing you want to hear." She knew those girls were dead, had been dead for days. Someone—her mother, Freddie, Eric?—had killed them, for there had been reported deaths among the villagers, and the girls were still missing. If Sam should stab her out of sheer rage, then so be it. They themselves would be dead soon. She at least would die with that knowledge.

"They're dead, aren't they?" Mike stepped forward and, through the gloom, illuminated now by only two candles, Eve saw the change in him. He was not angry, not like

Sam. He was sadness in human form, a man who could accept dying himself in that moment, would welcome it just for the misery to end. Eve wanted to go to him and hold him, but she was terrified. And besides, Sam's tremulous hand still held onto that knife, and Eve was anticipating it coming up and slashing at her, cutting bits of her away until nothing remained. He was, she thought, more than capable of that, and very much within his right.

Eve nodded. "I'm afraid they are," she said. She closed her eyes, and with the darkness came a sensation of calm. She waited for the pain, the agony as the blade tore through her flesh, renting her apart, perforating her until blood sprayed out in all directions.

Peace.

Silence.

Calm.

She clenched her eyes tighter, watched as tiny red stars danced across the space between her eyes and her eyelids. Her heartbeat didn't rage, as it should have in that moment. The certainty of death, the inevitability of this new information sending Sam into an impassioned frenzy, made her placid, accepting of her fate. Eve had spent years contemplating death, what it would be like, what might come after, if anything. All her questions were about to be answered; she just prayed for it to be quick.

A sudden clatter made her open her eyes. It took a while for her vision to adjust once again to the dimness of the room, but when it did, she saw Sam kneeling there. He had stepped away from her and had dropped to his knees. The knife lay on the floorboards to his right. Mike's hands were on his fallen companion's shoulders, and he massaged them slowly, and whispered words that Eve couldn't quite hear. Sam, Eve realised, was sobbing silently. Tears trailed down his face, glistening in the candlelight. He looked like a glass bust, all agleam, and he shook uncontrollably.

They remained like that for several minutes. Eve didn't know whether she should speak, and so remained silent. Nothing she could say would make things better; she knew that. Their loss could never be repaired by words, or anything else.

After a while—Eve didn't know how long it had been, but one of the two remaining candles had fizzled out, and the room had fallen further into darkness—Mike helped Sam to his feet and steadied him, for he looked liable to fall over without assistance.

The fury had disappeared from Sam's expression, had been replaced by something much worse. He was inconsolable, broken, helpless, but worst of all, his eyes were devoid of life. Eve had seen those eyes before, had stared into them as she forced potato into the thin, drooling slit beneath. Had wanted to stick things in them just to elicit a response from the dormant man taking a runny shit in front of her. They were The Burden's eyes, lifeless and empty.

"I am truly sorry," Eve said, no more than a cracked whisper.

Mike looked up at her, seemed to accept it. Did he know that she was not complicit in the deaths of those girls? Could he see that she was not capable of such an act of brutality? Eve thought he did, but she knew she had to explain to them, had to make them understand what was happening to them now and why they were destined to never make it out of Neverville alive.

It would be a while before the brown robes came; she had time to tell the story of the curse, the way it had been told to her by her mother when she was a child, the way it had been told to every villager.

"It was 1764," she said, slowly taking a seat on the armchair to her rear. "A leap year. The third George ruled the country, and the Seven Years' War had just ended…"

TWENTY

Neverville, 1764

"Make more room if you must." Edmund Ladock slammed the cell door and turned to Father Calhoun. The screams from the other side of the door intensified, a cacophony of high-pitched wails that reminded Ladock of the time his cat fell down the well at the back of his cottage. "Put more chains up. The night is young, and they're coming out like rats escaping an inferno. We mustn't allow any of them to escape."

Father Benedict Calhoun sighed. Ladock noticed it and immediately reproached him. "This village has been under siege for years," he said. "You would allow them to continue? To pursue their desire for darkness? To live amongst us and thrive, and stand by as their unholy acts go unpunished?"

The priest shook his head, as if the very thought offended him. "I do not think that," he said. "But there are so many of them. So many, this church can no longer hold them all."

Ladock shrugged. "And there will be many more," he said. "You summoned me, did you not. A letter was sent requesting I immediately come here, to this forsaken place, and rid it the evils crawling through its fields and forests. These demons in the shape of women that have blighted your fair village and turned it into the Devil's garden."

Calhoun nodded. "Yes, but we didn't realise there were so many," he said, exasperated. "And how certain can we be that they are all witches? Where is the proof?"

"The proof, Father, is at the end of this blade." He removed a dagger from the leather scabbard on his belt. The priest looked at it with some confusion. "Come, let me show you." Ladock unlocked the heavy, wooden door and threw it open. The women chained inside immediately fell silent, perhaps fearful of reprisal for their relentless wailing.

Posthaste, Ladock paced across the room, sidestepping the stone monolith at the centre. "Pick one," he said to Calhoun. "Anyone will do."

Calhoun, seemingly even more confused, said, "I do not understand."

"Oh, come, come," Ladock said, smiling. "Just point at one and I will prove it to you."

The women, all eighty of them, made themselves as small as possible, pushed back against the stone walls of the dungeon. Iron chains rattled against the ground and wall; some of the women whimpered.

Father Calhoun pointed at one in particular. A raven-haired woman whose face was smudged with grime. She must have been seventeen years old, Ladock thought. Maybe even younger. A witchfinder's work was never done, and with witches getting younger and younger, he knew it never would be. "That one," he said. "Prove it to me on that one."

Ladock looked at the girl, for she was no more than that. Barely old enough to bodily love, but yet old enough to know better than to become engaged in witchcraft. "Good choice," he said. "I shall prove to you that these women, all of them, are witches."

He made his way slowly toward the girl, who watched him with fearful eyes. The tear rolling down her cheek did not fool Ladock; he had seen it all before, was unaffected by their lies, their pleas.

"What is your name?" he asked the girl as he came to a halt in front of her. He could see her chest rising and falling slowly as she sobbed. It was, of course, all for show. An act that would gain her no sympathy from Ladock.

"Idony," the girl said, glancing up at Ladock.

"Leave her be!" one of the women called from across the room. This was met with further screeches and appeals from the other chained women, but when Ladock turned and glowered, they all fell silent once more.

He turned his attention back to the girl.

"Idony," he said. "Give me your arm."

The girl looked up at him again. This was, Ladock thought, only going to end one way, and that way was his. The girl could fight him, struggle, scream the walls done, but she was giving him that arm, even if he had to take it off at the shoulder.

"I will not ask a second time, Idony," Ladock said, remaining calm. He did not have all night; there were more of them out there, and Ladock wanted to get as many as he could before dawn, when the element of surprise would be forever lost. This was an all or nothing hunt, and the High Priestess was yet to be captured, despite his men's best efforts.

Idony reluctantly raised her arm. She knew what came next. It would not physically hurt her, but it would be irrefutable proof that she was a witch, and that would be more painful, because once that was established, there was only pain and suffering to look forward to.

"What are you doing?" Father Calhoun was beside Ladock now, but Ladock attributed that to the fact he didn't want to be anywhere else in the room, where an outstretched talon could snatch at his ankle or a mouth full of sharp teeth could snap out from the walls and latch onto his thigh. These women were dangerous, and the priest knew that as well as Ladock did.

"Simply proving it to you," Ladock said, taking Idony by the arm and pressing the blade of his dagger down hard into it. He ran it all the way from elbow to wrist, and a thin slit appeared. Flesh separated, but it was like slicing into a brick of butter. Skin went one way, fat another, but there was no blood, no arterial spray. After a moment—Idony was still crying, but looked away, no longer interested in what was being done to her—the wound closed itself up again. Fat was sucked back into the girl's arm, and then it sealed, not even a scar to suggest it had been wide open a second ago.

Satisfied, Ladock released the girl's arm. "See?" he said. "A witch. They are all witches, and I could make my way down this line and prove it in the same manner, but since you selected this girl at random, I trust you believe me when I say they must all be burned."

The priest nodded. "I shall place my trust in the Lord," he said.

"Very well," Ladock said, somewhat bemused. "And I shall place my trust in this." He held out his dagger for the priest to inspect before sliding it back in its scabbard.

Outside, heavy rain continued to fall. It had been raining interminably for days, and Ladock wondered if it would ever stop. The moon was full and seemed to be watching them as they set about their task. Ten more witches were captured over the course of the next three hours, and brought to the church, where they were processed accordingly. There would be no long-winded trials for these women. The justices of assize were not going to hear anything of this. As far as Ladock was concerned, these women, every one of them, had committed acts of maleficium. People had died as a direct result of these heretics of Christianity. They did not deserve a trial, fair or otherwise. They deserved to die in the most agonising way imaginable.

Which was why pyres were currently being constructed in the field opposite the church, huge pyramids of wood and combustibles. At the apex, there was room enough for ten witches, which meant they could stake and burn them *en masse*, which meant they wouldn't be out all night, suffering under the incessant storm.

The rain would make the pyres difficult to light, but they would get them going. Ladock had already instructed his men not to attach the customary container of gunpowder to the heretics to expedite their deaths, for he wanted them to suffer as much as possible. "Those demons don't deserve to explode," he had announced in his speech earlier that evening. "Make it last as long as possible. I want them still screaming when the sun rises and they're nothing but teeth, bones, and cinders."

Another ten witches came in, and Laddock felt something as one of them was ushered past him. It was *her*, he knew it. His hackles were up, and he immediately pounced upon her, dragging her away from the men leading her into the church and forcing her to the ground.

"You!" he cried. "It's you!"

The woman laughed, seemingly unperturbed by this sudden act of violence. Her mouth was filled with mud, and she spat it out before speaking. "If you say so, Edmund Ladock," she said, her voice hoarse. Her breath was rotten and coiled upward, making Ladock gag. "If you say so."

Ladock climbed off the High Priestess and pulled her up by the neck. He so wanted to snap it, to hear the bones break as he twisted and pulled. Perhaps, he thought, her head would come off entirely, but that was no way for a witch to die. She must suffer. She must feel everything, and it must last for as long as possible.

"She is the one," he told the two men, who took her by the arms again. "Make sure her teeth are removed. And her finger- and toenails. Strap her to the stone table and get it done. I think we can move ahead with the burning."

The witches died in varying states of pain. Some of them screamed like banshees as the flames licked at their flesh, while others simply whimpered, eyes fixated on their executioners. Several of them decided to utilise their final seconds by dancing lustfully, thrusting their bodies away from the stake, licking their lips and moaning as if in the throes of orgasm. Once again, Ladock believed it to be for show. They felt the pain just as much as the others, and when the life finally left their bodies, their charred expressions said as much.

They had burned ninety before the sun began to rise. Only ten remained, and amongst them the most dangerous witch of all: Clemence Landrake. Her teeth had been pulled out and her nails had been removed, but no one was taking any chances. The High Priestess had been placed in special silver shackles before being led out of the church. Father Calhoun walked alongside her, reading from the *Bible*. It seemed to keep her under control, and cause her quite a bit of pain at the same time. Was that smoke Ladock perceived crawling from her bosom in thin wisps? She was wholly naked, the thick, dark thatch on her pubis looked more like twigs than hair. She was so thin, every bone was pronounced; her desiccated skin pulled taut. As she grinned a toothless grin, Ladock wondered how she had enchanted so many men, how she had led them to their deaths and used them for purposes only the Devil would ever understand. She was abhorrent, physically disgusting, her breasts sagging, her sharp bones threatening to pierce her skin as she moved.

The nine witches walking in front of Clemence were all terrified of what was about to happen, the pain they were about to endure before the darkness came, but Clemence Landrake looked no more concerned than if she was out for a mid-morning stroll. She positively revelled in the festivities. Danced, even, swinging her boney hips rhythmically to music Ladock didn't hear, didn't want to hear.

"These are the last ones," one of the hunters informed Ladock. He was an ugly man, somewhere between a rat and a frog. Ladock couldn't decide which he resembled more.

"I know that," Ladock said, trying to ignore the man's rodent-amphibian features. "Why has she been stripped?" He pointed at Clemence, who was now whispering something incoherent into the ears of one of her captors. Ladock hoped it wasn't some incantation; she was powerful enough to turn the man into a killer, send him home tonight to murder his family as they slept peacefully. All it took was a few words spoken in the correct order, and that was precisely what he would do.

"She did it herself," the unattractive man said. "She bit her own tongue off when we were pulling her teeth."

Not necessarily a bad thing, Ladock thought, no longer fearing for the unfortunate man leading Clemence toward the one remaining unlit pyre. Her words would be gobbledygook without a tongue.

The nine pyres raging off to their left emitted great heat and the stench of burnt flesh and hair was beyond terrible. Ladock thought a little more space should have been left between the huge pyramids, for he was dripping with sweat now, unable to even look in the direction of the pyres they had already used, and the ninety witches still burning there, or what remained of them.

Ladock gave the go ahead to set the final ten in place. He wanted Clemence at the centre. "She deserves to see these women dying on either side of her," he said. "That will be the last thing she sees as she burns away."

Clemence must have heard this from the top of the pyre, where she was being bound to her allotted stake, for she laughed. It was a cruel laugh that made gooseflesh creep over Ladock's entire body; she still wasn't scared of what was about to happen to her. Her evil knew no bounds.

With the final ten witches strapped in place atop the tenth and final pyre, Father Calhoun began to recite from the *Bible* in his hand. It was then that the *Bible* must have caught an ember, blown from one of the burning pyres, for the book went up in flames so fast that Ladock didn't even see it happen. He heard Calhoun bellow, and then the burning book was flying through the air, leaving a trail of smoke and bright orange sparks in its wake.

Two hunters stamped on the book until the flames went out, by which point it was covered in mud, rain, and was almost burned to a crisp. The *Bible* had been rendered useless. From the pyre, Clemence laughed again, a throaty cackle that sounded like many voices all at once.

Had she caused that? Had she made that happen with her wicked powers?

"Never mind that," Ladock said, motioning to the ruined bible at the feet of the breathless hunters. "Get this fire started. I want screaming witches in less than three minutes, do you understand?"

The hunters—twenty in total, all milling about doing something Ladock had no doubt instructed them to at some point in the evening—confirmed that they would make that happen with ayes and nods.

As five men managed to get the fire started on the left side of the pyre, seven men worked on the other side. Within a minute even the rain couldn't douse the flames, although it threatened to. The conflagration crawled up and up, through and into the pyre, slowly but surely edging closer to the witches, most of whom were screaming as the crackling heat intensified.

Ladock watched, his gaze falling upon Idony, the raven-haired witch from earlier, who had been strapped in place to the left of Clemence Landrake. She no longer appeared scared, as she had been when Ladock's blade sliced through her arm to provide evidence to the priest that she was, in fact, a witch. Was it that she had accepted her fate, or simply that she was home, where she always knew she would end up, beside the leader of their coven atop a pyre?

As the flames licked at their ankles, the witches hissed. Gone were the screams, the terrified faces. This was, Ladock knew, when their true selves made an appearance. All the hatred, the venom, all bubbled and rose to the surface, where it manifested for a few moments before the pain hit them. Their hisses, their sneers, their rage-fuelled curses, none of it meant anything to Ladock, who smiled as the smell of singed flesh began to fill his nostrils. But Clemence was shouting now, and Ladock paid attention to her because of who she was.

"Pati!" she cried. "Pati in aeternum!"

Suffer for eternity. Ladock's Latin was not great, but he knew enough.

The flames were up to her naked waist now, the hair of her pubis catching instantly and fizzing and turning orange and floating away on the wind. She was in pain, severe pain; Ladock could see it in her eyes. She was no different to the others, and this pleased him.

"Centum!" she hissed, her voice still a chorus of voices, her eyes rolling back in her head until only the whites were visible. "Tantum centum animas!" Then the flames were crawling all over her, setting her hair ablaze, and she disappeared behind the bright orange tendrils as they whipped and coiled and stabbed at her blackened flesh.

As if on cue, there came a crash of thunder. Some of the men who had been watching the burning ducked for cover, their gaze turned to the dark sky above. Ladock, however, continued watching the blaze. None of the final ten witches was visible now. There was only fire, flames, smoke. And that should have satisfied Ladock, but for some reason he felt uneasy.

It was those final words, the last sentence uttered by Clemence Landrake, for he had heard it clearly and had managed to decipher it in his head.

One hundred...

One hundred souls, and not one more...

What did she mean by that? It was certainly a strange choice of final words.

Centum...

"Sir!"

Ladock turned to find the rat-frog man running across the field toward him, a look of shock and fear painted across his face.

"What is it, man?" Ladock asked, impatiently.

The breathless witch hunter, clutching his side, said, "It's Archibald, sir! He's just dropped down dead!"

Archibald Winton was one of Ladock's finest hunters, and he had indeed dropped down dead at the edge of the field. "What happened?" Ladock asked the bearer of bad news, whose name was Timothy Rampart, or Rapport, or something. Ladock wasn't quite sure.

"I don't know, sir," the man said, nudging Archibald with his boot as if to make sure he was in fact deceased. He was, and his wide, staring eyes said as much. "He was just standing here, making a note of something in his journal, when he went over. Didn't make no sound or nothing. Just went..." The strange little man demonstrated how Archibald had gone down; Ladock pulled him back to his feet and reprimanded him for his foolishness.

The fires burned and raged behind them, the heat almost unbearable, the smoke stinging at Ladock's eyes.

"I find it strange that this man, a healthy witchfinder with no prior ailments, has all at once dropped down dead without so much as an—"

He stopped there, for the rat-frog man—Timothy Rampart, Ladock had decided—fell to the mud with a thump. When Ladock tried to pull the man to his feet again, cursing his insolence and foolishness once again, he was met with resistance. Rampart was a dead weight. In fact, Ladock concluded, Rampart was dead. As dead as Archibald, and with no apparent explanation.

"What in the name of all that is holy and pure!" Ladock staggered back, away from the two dead bodies lying in the mud at the edge of the field. And that was when the screaming began. It came from all around, from everywhere at once. Men and women, calling for help, shrieking with fear, wailing mournfully.

Later, Ladock would learn that almost two-hundred villagers had dropped down dead over the course of that first hour, but in that moment he was oblivious to the extent and severity of the situation.

"Sir, what's going on?"

The question came from Peter Lockwood, Ladock's second-in-command. He was a tall, wiry man, with shoulder-length silver hair. For this reason, Ladock had given him the nickname: Wizard.

"I don't know," Ladock said. "But we must find out. The village is still under attack, it seems. We have seemingly failed to curb this evil at its source."

"Cut off the hydra's head and two more shall grow in its place," Lockwood said. There was something poetic about that, Ladock thought, but not until much later, when the dust had settled and the reparations began. "Sir, I heard what she said. Centum. One hundred souls and not one more."

Ladock nodded. Lockwood hearing the same confirmed that his own ears had not deceived him.

"A curse, sir?" Lockwood asked as a piercing shriek penetrated the night, went straight through Ladock's skin and flesh and bones, leaving him trembling as if he'd just emerged from a freezing lake.

"Perhaps," was all that Ladock could manage. Lockwood sensed this, and hurried away, disappearing into the church on the opposite side of the trail.

Between where Ladock stood and the church doors, Ladock counted ten dead bodies, all men in his employ, witchfinders, damn good men, fallen where they had stood alive and well only a minute earlier.

The church was the same. As Ladock entered, he saw the bodies. Some had fallen in the aisle, others were draped across pews, as if they had been walking when death had come for them. Lockwood and a few others were at the altar, staring out at the inexplicable scene before them, discussing something that, when Ladock approached them, came to a sudden end.

Outside, villagers continued to cry and moan, and Ladock now knew why. This wasn't just happening to his men; it was widespread, all across the village, maybe even farther than that.

Centum...

One hundred souls and not one more...

"Sir, have we made a mistake here tonight?" Lockwood asked.

"We have done our jobs," Ladock said. "And she has brought Hell up to meet us, it seems, but ultimately we shall prevail." He didn't know whether his words would inspire confidence in what remained of his men; he didn't know who he was trying to reassure, them or himself. What he did know was that great leaders don't panic in the face of adversity.

"It *is* a curse, sir," Lockwood said. "My wife, my children are in the village. We were put up in the inn for the night, sir. What if they are in danger? What "

"Go to your family, Wizard," Ladock said, for he had no further need of assistance. The witches were dead. The curse, whatever it was, had already been set in motion. If Ladock had had a family, he too would have returned to them. Fortunately, he was alone. It was better that way. Easier to look after oneself than concern yourself with the welfare of others.

Lockwood gave thanks and rushed out of the church, almost tripping over bodies as he went.

The two remaining witch hunters, Forrest and Bosworth, regarded Ladock with something bordering on contempt. Did they blame him for this? For what was happening in that moment throughout the village? If they did, they were making a huge mistake, and one that Ladock would not stand there and accept.

"I will charge you both with fucking treason!" he yelled. Their expressions softened. Bosworth looked almost apologetic. "Now, both of you, get the fuck away. Find me some water or something. And you, Forrest. Go into the village. I want numbers. I want you to go door to door if you have to, but I want to know how many are dead. Don't come back here until you know the exact figure."

"But that could take—"

"Yes!" Ladock interjected. "It could, couldn't it! So, I suggest you get moving. If you're not back by sun-up, we will leave this place without you, and you can spend the rest of your days here, burying the fallen."

Forrest sighed. "Yes, sir," he said, and was gone.

Ladock was, apart from the corpses all around him, alone in the church. He went along the hall and into the cold cell where the hundred witches had been kept, shuddering at its emptiness. Next to the stone monolith at the centre of the room, sitting on a wooden tray on the floor, were Clemence Landrake's teeth, her fingernails and toenails, and the stub of tongue that she had bitten off herself. There was, of course, no blood.

Ladock sat upon the stone table and sighed. Anguished cries continued out in the night, and Ladock listened, for he had failed these people, had brought yet more pain and tragedy to their village. The only good thing about it, he thought, was that come dawn, he and the remainder of his men would be riding out of here.

And Ladock couldn't wait.

Upon his return to the inn, the innkeeper—a frightfully rotund old man with no manners, whatsoever—let him in, and admonished him as he raced up the staircase, but Lockwood was not paying him any mind. All he wanted was to make sure his family were safe; his wife and daughter were all that he had. Perhaps it was time to stop allowing them to accompany him on these perilous expeditions. His daughter had only just begun to walk unaided; witch hunts were no place for a baby.

He entered the room at the end of the hall, and relief washed over him when, from the gloom, his wife, Grace, appeared, carrying Ann in her arms and bouncing her up and down. Ann was cooing and gargling, the way she always did when she was happy and safe and in her mother's warm embrace.

"What is it?" Grace's worry was palpable; Ann continued to giggle and blow bubbles, oblivious.

Lockwood rushed across to his wife and pulled her close. He would never allow anything to happen to them, not as long as he should live, and even then he would watch over them and protect them from beyond the grave.

"I heard the screams, Peter," Grace said, her voice muffled by his shoulder. "It woke Ann, so I went to her. What is happening out there?"

"I don't know," Lockwood said with a sigh. "But we are leaving as soon as the sun rises and not a moment later." He wanted to put as much distance as possible between his family and Neverville, and they would never return to this place. It was the Devil's land now, and the rent was long overdue.

"You're scaring me," Grace said, pulling away from Lockwood. Ann might have squeaked "Daddy" for the first time, but Lockwood didn't notice it. He was far more concerned about what was going on right now, how that High Priestess had left behind a little gift before departure. More suffering. More pain and loss. But to what end?

"I am sorry," Lockwood said, stroking Grace's arm. He took his daughter from her and cradled her close. "There is nothing to fear, my love. I am here, you are safe. I love you, Grace. I love you, Ann." He kissed his daughter's warm, round, head. Her fine hairs tickled his nose.

"I can still hear them, Peter," said Grace. Lockwood could hear them, too; he wished they would shut up or just hurry up and die, for they were scaring his wife.

"It will stop in a moment," he promised her, even though he wasn't sure that would happen. He didn't know in that moment that people would continue to die all through the rest of the night and all through the following day.

Hundreds upon hundreds of men, women, and children, the life just snatched from them by invisible, callous hands.

Centum, Peter Lockwood thought as he settled his daughter in her crib and held his wife through the night.

Centum.

Ladock didn't sleep a wink. With all the noise going on outside the church, it was impossible. Even when he staggered along the hall to the front pew of the church and collapsed there, closing his eyes, all he saw was Clemence Landrake's sneering face, her crispening features as flakes of her came away and were carried off by the wind. It would be a miracle if he should ever sleep again.

Resigning himself to the fact, he got up and headed out into the morning, where the fallout of the previous night became immediately apparent.

Bodies lay strewn across the trail. Horses galloped freely across the fields, enjoying for a moment this temporary freedom, unburdened by carts or cargo. As Ladock walked into the village, he saw familiar faces, men and women who had, the previous day, recounted their experiences and encounters with the witches. Only now they weren't giving information, pointing Ladock in the direction of the accused. Now they were lying face-down in mud, or staring vacantly up at the sky, from which a fine drizzle continued to fall. A child—Daniel, he had introduced himself as; Ladock remembered him well only because of his precocious manner—sat on his stoop, sobbing. His parents were inside, both dead, according to Daniel. He had tried to wake them that morning, but, "They weren't breathing, sir! I tried, but they weren't breathing!"

Ladock didn't know what to say. He couldn't help the boy. He flipped a coin in the boy's direction and continued along the trail toward the inn.

The Wizard was outside, loading luggage onto the back of his cart. His wife stood at the doors to the inn, cradling a baby. How she's grown, Ladock thought, for Ann had been no bigger than a ball of yarn the last time he'd seen her.

"Sir," Lockwood said, acknowledging the witchfinder, but he didn't stop loading up the cart. He seemed to be in a rush to get out of there.

"Have you seen Forrest?" Ladock asked.

"I haven't, sir," Lockwood replied. "Nor Bosworth. I assumed they were with you."

This was wholly unusual. Neither man had returned in the night, and Ladock doubted it would take that long to tally up the dead in a village so small. And Bosworth was sent for water, not the Holy Grail.

"I think we should leave together," Ladock said, watching as Lockwood threw another bag onto the cart. "Right this minute. My horse appears to have gotten loose in the night." He motioned to the field that was barely visible from where they now stood. A tiny, four-legged shape frolicked and danced across the grassland. "We can leave as soon as I have captured her."

Lockwood nodded, but said, "Without sounding insubordinate, sir, we really would like to leave as soon as possible."

Ladock told him that he understood, and yes, it was in their best interests to vacate the village quickly and without further delay.

He found both Forrest and Bosworth on his way to fetch the horse. Bosworth was nestled in a bush at the side of the trail, his face already half-devoured by foxes or some other starving nocturnal creature.

Forrest was slumped against the doorframe of a cottage a little farther along. The woman dead next to him, the owner of the cottage, had fallen in such a way that the two were now holding one another. In Forrest's left hand was a leatherbound book; the right hand gripped onto a quill. The page he was turned to was smudged with ink, but Ladock could see that he had tallied almost two-hundred people dead when he himself was taken.

Had he managed to count this woman before succumbing? It was an incongruous thought, and one that Ladock pushed away immediately.

After getting his horse under control—it took a lot longer than he had antici-pated, and he hoped and prayed that the Lockwoods hadn't left without him—he made his way back to the inn, and was relieved to discover they had waited.

"Thank you," he told Lockwood.

"Did you find them, sir?" Lockwood asked. He held his wife close, as if fearful of her drifting away from him and becoming just another mark in Forrest's unfinished census. "Forrest and Bosworth?"

"I found them, Wizard," Ladock said, and left it at that.

They rode away from the village slowly. The trail was littered with corpses; it was impossible to gather any real speed. When they reached the church, Ladock saw that the pyres were still smouldering. There was a terrible burnt smell to the air, an all too familiar odour that was neither wood nor fuel. It was acrid, rotten, the stench of flesh lingering on the breeze.

When Ladock looked back—for he had taken the lead, now, and was steering them all toward the trail that exited this hellhole—he saw that Lockwood was looking at the pyres, too, perhaps wondering what had gone so wrong. Ladock had thought of nothing else all night, yet it wasn't that he blamed himself. It was that he had learned a valuable lesson. Witches could still recite devilish incantations without their tongue.

"Not much farther!" Ladock called across his shoulder. "I can see where the trail forks just beyond—"

Lockwood looked to the pyres. Grace squeezed his leg, perhaps in an effort to distract him, but it didn't work. He couldn't believe what he had witnessed the previous night, the aftermath he had awakened to this morning. So many lives lost, so many unexplained deaths. It was a curse, of that he was sure. Clemence Landrake had cursed this place before dying. That was the only explanation, and it was terrifying.

Ladock, riding a few metres ahead, turned on his horse and said, "Not much farther!" Lockwood knew this already; they had reached the edge of the village. "I can see where the trail forks just beyond—"

But that was as far as he got before he thumped into something invisible. The horse continued onward beneath him, but he was thrown backwards, somersaulted, landed on his neck. His legs folded up unnaturally above him.

"Peter!" Grace cried out, but Lockwood had seen it with his own eyes. He had seen Ladock bounce off thin air, had watched him fold up into a shape never before made by a human.

Lockwood brought the cart to a stop and climbed down onto the trail. The mud squelched beneath him. It was so slippery it was all he could do to stay on his feet.

"Honey?" Grave whimpered from her seat on the cart. She looked positively terrified. "Peter, what happened to him?"

Lockwood shook his head. He didn't have any idea, but it was so strange. The way he fell, the way he twisted and folded like that. It was so freakish, Lockwood had never seen anything like it before. And he knew, even before he reached Ladock's crumpled form, that he was dead.

"It's okay, dear," Lockwood called back to his wife, but he didn't take his eyes off Ladock. His horse had continued, disappeared somewhere along the trail ahead. He could no longer see it, but its hoofbeats were still faintly audible. "Just stay there."

As he got close enough to Ladock to see that he was correct, the witchfinder was as dead as could be, his insides began to thrum. Sweat beaded on his brow. It all came on so suddenly, it almost knocked Lockwood from his feet.

"Don't come any closer," he warned his wife. "Keep Ann with you. Do not let go." For some reason this all seemed very important in that moment. His family were being threatened by some invisible force; another part of Clemence Landrake's malediction?

Ladock's head was entirely flattened along one side, his features pushed across as if there was no more space on that particular side for them. It was as if Ladock had gone barreling into a stone wall at full speed and had met it face first. There was not an unbroken bone in his body, it appeared. He was a tangle of limbs and flesh and bloody pulp. Lockwood's stomach finally gave way, and he retched and then dry-retched until there was only an empty pain left within him.

Stomach raw, Lockwood straightened and turned to find his wife staring at him. She couldn't see the extent of Ladock's injuries from where she sat on the cart, but she must have noticed Lockwood's frightened countenance, how he had been sick all over the trail, and that was enough.

"Peter, is he dead?"

Lockwood nodded. "I'm afraid so," he replied, wiping thick, warm drool from his lips and chin.

"What did he hit?" Grace screeched. "What could have done that?" She pulled Ann tighter, if that were indeed possible. Fortunately, Ann was sleeping peacefully, wholly unaware of anything going on around her. And how much would she understand if she were awake?

"He hit the air!" Lockwood said, a little more excitedly than he expected. "Grace, I saw him, he hit thin air, and that...*that* did this to him."

Grace was off the cart, Ann cradled tightly in her arms.

"I told you to stay over there!" he said, and she stopped moving, the rage and confusion in his voice enough to convince her to do as he said. "Grace, I don't know what's happening here, but please, don't come any closer."

Not only did she not come closer, but she took a couple of steps back.

Good, Lockwood thought, for he wanted his family safe. It was his job to protect them from...whatever this was.

The sickness continued to flood through him. His blood felt as if it were turning to mercury; an ice-cold chill surged through his veins, despite the sweat now dripping from his nose and forehead.

"We can't go any farther," he told his wife, who was now whispering to Ann, perhaps reassuring her that everything was going to be okay, that there was nothing to worry about, and to keep sleeping, for it was safe there, in her dreams, wherever that may be.

"We must leave, Peter," Grace said. "We cannot stay here. This place is wrong."

And that, Lockwood thought, was only the half of it. "We can't leave," he told her again. "We won't be allowed to."

How he knew this, he wasn't sure. Just that if he stepped forward, into the invisible thing that had taken Ladock off his horse and folded him up like a bedsheet, he would die. They would all die. The nausea he felt now was from being so close to the thing, the imperceptible line preventing them from continuing along the trail toward home, toward sanctuary.

Toward freedom.

They got back on the cart and returned to the village, where the chaos had continued in their absence. Lockwood soon realised he was the only surviving witch hunter. People continued to die all around, seemingly from nothing at all.

A kindly old couple, the Carsons, took Lockwood and his family in, gave them a room at the top of the house, and fed them well as Lockwood continued to try to figure out what was happening. Would they all die eventually? Would the curse only end when the last of them succumbed to it? What horrible malediction had Clemence Landrake unleashed upon this place?

Villagers died at the border. Panic sent them there, and their slowly rotting bodies marked their graves all along that unseen boundary. People quickly came to realise that they couldn't leave. Passersby could come through, but once they were in, they, too, became cursed. If they didn't fall down dead within a day or two, someone else did.

At a meeting called by Father Benedict Calhoun—the church was the designated gathering point, and was filled to the rafters, as the meeting had been deemed mandatory—Clemence Landrake's curse became clear to Lockwood.

"One hundred!" Lockwood cried from where he stood with his family. Calhoun had been in the middle of a sermon, but Lockwood didn't care. He had figured it out.

Centum.

Lockwood pushed his way through the crowd, and the villagers grumbled and groaned as he did so. Somewhere behind him, Grace tried to call him back, for she had no idea what he was about to say, either.

"It's one hundred!" Lockwood said as he reached the altar. "That's what we have been cursed with! One hundred souls and not one more!"

"What are you talking about?" someone shouted. Lockwood thought it was Robert Wainwright, but the muttering crowd made it hard to be certain.

"That's what she said!" Lockwood replied. "Landrake cursed this place before she burned. *Centum.* One hundred souls and not one more. Don't you see? I counted as you came in. There are exactly one hundred people in this room at this precise moment, myself included."

The villagers fell silent.

"We can't leave. Those who have tried have perished. Those who have come through here have replaced them. When there are more than one hundred souls in Neverville, it takes someone at random. That is what I have perceived over the past week."

"As crazy as that sounds," Father Calhoun said, "it's true. When you came in," he pointed toward the Moss family—Jacob, Elizabeth, Roger, and Victoria—who were apparently not too comfortable at being singled out, "four villagers died the same afternoon."

"Are you saying that was our fault?" Jacob Moss said, angrily. "We were on our way to Elizabeth's mother's. This was the only way through."

"It is not your fault," Lockwood said. "None of this is anyone's fault, but it is happening, and we must do something to make sure we remain safe and alive."

"Like?" Father Calhoun asked.

Lockwood considered for a moment their limited options, none of which were pleasant, all of which meant death and misery and an existence that no one would want.

Picking out the face of his wife in the crowd and sighing, Lockwood began to explain the only way Neverville could survive this terrible thing.

TWENTY-ONE

Neverville, 1974

Mike, now seated in the armchair across from Eve Elizabeth Lockwood, shuffled restlessly. Sam, still on his knees on the floor—at least he had stopped sobbing, and he had listened well to Eve's recounting of what had happened all those years ago—moved so that his legs were out in front of him, before pulling his knees up to his chest. It was, Mike thought, the way a child might sit. Sam had regressed; the helplessness he now felt had turned him into an adolescent.

"Those hundred decided to kill anyone who came in," Mike said, not a question. He understood now; Eve's story, while both terrifying and unbelievable, had made it clear there was only one way to protect the village. It also explained why there was no electricity in the village, no modern technology. This place hadn't been sent back to the dark ages; it had never left them. That was why the furniture was all old and threadbare, that was why people were riding horses, that was why there was a dungeon up at that church. This place was almost medieval.

"Anyone who came in after that meeting," Eve said, "yes. It was voted upon, and with the ayes at seventy-nine and the nays at twenty-one, it was decided that outsiders would be executed, for it was easier to dispose of someone you didn't know than to lose someone you did."

"Dispose of?" Sam said. "Is that what happened to my daughter? You disposed of her?"

Eve shook her head. "I didn't know about your daughter," she said. "To the villagers, it's a necessary evil, one that we have coexisted with for centuries. There is no way to end the curse. At least, none that we have found. All this village knows is death and sadness and loss and mourning. It is a haunted place, lost forever."

Mike thought about Kelly, her face all smeared with icing and pastry, that dog kennel in which she hid at a birthday party that wasn't hers. It was heartbreaking, but she was gone. He knew that now. She and Rebecca were both gone, and now he and Sam were at risk of the same.

"So we will die here," Mike said. "One way or the other, we are never leaving this village." Again, these weren't questions, but simple facts spoken aloud. To speak them was terrifying; to actually believe them—and Mike did—was enough to send a man spiralling into the abyss.

Eve considered this for a moment. "You said that Father Calhoun was dead," she said. "You saw him at the church."

"No coming back from that," Sam said. "Yes, he's dead." His voice was still tinged with anger and sorrow. Mike knew it would get them nowhere fast.

"Then only one more must die," Eve said. "Of course, the brown robes don't know that, but I saw a group heading toward the church. They're going to find Calhoun. Maybe they'll realise it and let one of you live."

"Maybe?" Mike said. "Let one of us live? Lady, that's not a great option for either of us."

"There are a hundred-and-one souls here," Eve said, crossing her legs. She had become a little more relaxed since starting her story, and was now completely at ease. "One more than is allowed. Someone will die. If not you, then one of us."

"How can you talk like this?" Mike said. "I mean, it's as if you're not talking about human life. It's as if you're trying to figure out whether to put a dog down because it's started to shit too much."

Eve shook her head. "No," she protested. "It's not like that at all. I value every single life more than anything else. Think of it this way: if you had to choose between killing Sam, or a complete stranger, and you had no other alternative, who would you kill?"

Mike was dumbstruck. "I...that's..."

"The people in this village, the couples still in love after all these years, the men who fish together and drink together, the women who play bridge together, they are connected. We are all connected, united in a way that is greater than any one single being here. I was born and shouldn't have been. A woman died, sacrificed herself, on the day I came into this world. Life is precious, exceedingly so, but it is more precious when you have a connection to the people whose lives are at risk and a choice has to be made. Either them or us. That is the way it is, and that is all we have ever known."

Sam stood then and dusted himself down. "I've heard enough of this bullshit," he said. "Fuck me, witches? Invisible force-fields? Killing innocent people. And then what? Trying to justify that? You're all sick. Crazy. And you killed my daughter so that one of your old fucking farts didn't die? Is that what you're telling me?"

Eve pushed herself back in the armchair, watched Sam carefully. Did she think he would go for the knife again? Only one more had to die, that was what she said. Was Sam about to kill Eve and bring the number down to one hundred again? Mike didn't know, and in that moment, he wouldn't have stopped Sam from doing what he saw fit.

"I think I know a way we can make this right," Eve said. "A way that you don't have to die tonight."

Sam scoffed at this. "Really? Because I'm running out of fucking patience here. I'm trying to decide whether to kill you all or just kill myself right now."

Mike knew that he meant it, too.

"How?" Mike asked Eve. "How can this be made right?"

Did he want it to be made right? Spending the rest of his life trapped in this place with these people didn't appeal to him in the slightest. Killing innocent, what was it she called them, outsiders? Killing outsiders as they came through because that was what was best for the village? He hadn't thought about it until now, but he would never see his mother again, never walk into that impossibly warm car showroom and try to convince some city-dweller that they needed to buy the new, top-of-the line Escort because it would make the women fall at their feet, never drive his Marina again—which was probably up on bricks and graffitied all to hell back at that dilapidated car-park—and never order a Chinese takeaway from The Golden Harvest on those nights he was simply too exhausted to prepare anything himself. If Eve's story was to be believed, if what she had told them was true, then life as Mike knew it was over. So, did he want it to be made right?

"My father is out there," Eve said. "He is out there right now, and needs to be stopped. He is dangerous and crazy."

"No shit," Sam said, lighting a cigarette. Eve coughed a little, more for show than anything else. "You're all, what's the right phrase? A little fucked up? Yeah, that's it." He purposely blew smoke in Eve's direction, and she waved it away with her hand.

Eve told them what had happened with her father, how he was despised by almost everyone, how he had tried to go over the boulders, cabbaging himself in the process, how she had reluctantly cared for him, how she wanted him dead, how she had thought about it thousands of times over the years, and how he had come to and tried to murder her mother before going on the run.

It was the second seemingly far-fetched story she had told in succession, but Mike once again believed every word of it.

"So, you're suggesting that the villagers will somehow listen to you. Instead of killing us, they'll settle for your father. The number's back down to one hundred, everything's fine and dandy, and we can all live in perfect harmony forever and ever." God, Sam's cynicism was rubbing off on him.

"I'm not saying they will listen to me," Eve said. "But right now, he's out there and you're in here. They will be coming for you. I don't know what to do. My father is a very dangerous man. Even when he was unconscious, I feared him. And now that he has murdered Father Calhoun, they will want to bring him to justice. The Calhouns have been here for more than seven centuries. The Lockwoods have not. This village will be better in my father's absence, and so yes, I think they will listen to me."

A trick? Was Eve buying time until the brown robes—the hunters out there right now looking for he and Sam, the sonsofbitches who had killed his sister and Sam's daughter so heartlessly and without hesitation—came knocking and found them here? Mike didn't know, but something told him to trust Eve. What other choice did they have?

"What are you suggesting, Eve Elizabeth Lockwood?" For some reason, calling her by her full name seemed appropriate. Perhaps it kept things formal between them, for they were never going to be friends. Mike couldn't imagine befriending any of the villagers, no matter how much time passed, not after what they had done to Kelly. They were out there hunting him right now; how could you possibly forgive and forget something like that once the dust settled, if it ever did?

Eve said, "He will come for me. Of that I have no doubt."

"Yeah," Sam said. "And so will *they*. We can't just wait here for the door to be busted down. So, if your daddy's on his way, he'd better hurry the fuck up and get here before *they* do."

Eve shook her head. "You're right," she said. "We can't stay here. I can try to talk to them, but not until I've got you someplace safe." She stood up for the first time in a while. When she did, Sam bent down and picked the knife up from the floor. This didn't elicit a response from Eve. She had seemingly come to terms with her own mortality. Either that or she trusted Sam would do the right thing. Mike wasn't so sure.

"Where did you have in mind?" Sam said, waving the knife through the air. He wanted her to know that, even though she was the one with the plan—however outlandish it turned out to be—he was the one in control. Mike didn't think he could even stop Sam now.

We're in the same boat.

Yeah, but riding different storms, Mike thought. And Sam's boat had sprung a leak.

Eve told them where she would take them, and even Sam agreed with her, lowering the knife long enough to tell her so. "Okay," he said. "How far to this farm?"

Jack watched them through the kitchen window, crouched low and stifling a laugh as the older outsider threatened Eve with the knife,—*go on, stab her! See if I give a shit!*—and watched as she sat down and began to talk to them as if they were normal people, of all things. The outsiders. They were annoying, these two. Wherever he went, there they were. Now they were here with his daughter, and all he wanted was two minutes alone with her, plenty of time to beat her to death with something dull, more than twice as long as he needed to slit her throat.

Hell, he thought, *give me thirty seconds and I'm good.*

The men were listening to her, but Jack couldn't quite make out her words through the window. He tried to read her lips, but it was dark in the house, and even darker outside. A candle flickered somewhere out of view in the living room, providing just enough light to discern simple shapes and outlines, but lip-reading was out of the question. He couldn't even see her lips.

But oh, how Jack had laughed as the older man had dropped to his knees. The young outsider had consoled him the way a lover might, massaging his shoulders, rubbing his neck. It was, Jack thought, a ridiculous display of affection. It had brought bile into his throat.

Just kill her already, he'd thought. *Just get it over with and save me the trouble.* But he didn't want that, not really. He wanted to be the one to do it; he wanted to kill Little Evil. Why should they get to do it? What had they done to deserve that privilege? She hadn't ruined their lives, had she, the way she had ruined Jack's?

The outsiders continued to listen intently as Jack watched, peering over the windowsill like some devious voyeur. His heart was racing, though in that good way, that strangely wonderful way before something remarkable happened. He found himself both anxious and relaxed at the same time. Part of him wanted to rush in there and take his chances against all three of them, while the sensible part of him (if you could call it that) told him to hold steady and play the waiting game. It was nice to have the choice, to be in control of his destiny once again. He had spent so long unable to move, unable to even shit when he felt like it, in that world where everything had already happened a thousand times and never veered off course no matter how hard he concentrated, that he was never taking that feeling for granted again.

He was almost falling asleep, pressed against the rear wall of the house, when Eve stood and the old outsider picked up the knife again. It jerked him back into the present, and he pushed away the fatigue he felt and watched their every move.

Eve was talking again, and then she went off to somewhere else in the house. Jack heard a steady thump, thump, thump, and decided she had gone upstairs. The outsiders talked amongst themselves for a while, but again Jack had no idea what was being discussed. The old guy looked irate, waved the knife around to emphasise his point, the young man looked placatory, hands held out in front of him, composed and calm. When Eve returned, she was carrying something in an old sack that Jack recognised almost immediately.

"My robes," he said quietly as she removed them from the sack. There were six robes in there—it was amazing how quickly they became soiled or bloodied, and so each brown robe had several deep stains—and she passed one to each of the outsiders.

Jack knew what she was doing. Wolves in sheep's clothing, that's what they were going to become. She was certainly no daughter of his; this apple had fallen so far from the tree, it had landed three fields over.

A sudden clap of thunder made Jack crouch lower at the window. His legs were beginning to tire, but he knew he couldn't take his eyes off them for one moment, had to know what they were doing, and where they were going next.

As they put the robes on—they were big on Eve, swamping her almost—Jack made his way around to the side of the house and waited in the shadows. He needed that outsider's knife, and would take it from him at the earliest opportunity.

Then he would paint the village red.

TWENTY-TWO

Neverville, 1974

Freddie had not known Father Calhoun as well as some of the others. They had exchanged pleasantries here and there and, as was their wont, discussed banal subjects like fishing or weather or farming—the priest had a patch of vegetables at the rear of the church, to which he tended regularly when he wasn't busy genuflecting or edifying the masses. He was, Freddie thought, a good man, a righteous man, and now someone, those bastard outsiders, had caved his head in and stuffed him in a confessional.

"Well this is just excellent!" Eric said, sarcastically, as he glanced down at Calhoun. "The last of the Calhouns. The death of religion here. Might as well turn the church into a...fucking fishmongers. Freddie's Fishmongers! Has a lovely ring to it, don't you think?"

Freddie knew what Eric was alluding to, and how dare he! "Are you saying Calhoun is dead because of me?" Of course he was. Eric was placing the blame on Freddie for this entire thing. "That damn musket failed to fire," Freddie continued. "Those sonsofbitches would have got this far no matter what, and Calhoun would still be dead."

"He must have tried to kill them." It was Wanda, who had sidled silently up to them and was now picking at something between her teeth that she couldn't quite find. "Reckon they overpowered him, I do. Reckon they got the better of him, for sure."

"Thank you very much for your input," Eric said, forgetting for a moment about the machete in his hand. He almost took Wanda's face clean off. "Go search the back room. Take Walter with you, and tell Renfield to check the cell."

"They're gone," Freddie said. He knew they would be; they all knew they would be.

"Just check anyway!" Eric told Wanda, and she waddled off toward the rest of the group, who were standing on the other side of the church. Lucas and John were searching the grounds, the small cemetery at the back of the church, the trees and hedges to the right of the building. Freddie wasn't sure they were capable, but it kept them out of his way.

"We must have passed them," Eric said, composing himself once again.

"They had plenty of time to get to somewhere else," Freddie said. "Probably already at the village. Eric, this is bad. Too much time has passed."

"You don't think I know that?" Eric rubbed furiously at his balding pate. "I've never given up, Freddie. Never. But this time, part of me knows that we aren't going to make it. We're going to lose two of our own because of those men."

"One," Freddie said, nodding in the direction of the murdered priest. "Only one." As if that made it any better, for they had still lost two, whichever way you looked at it. The fact that Calhoun didn't die at random, though, did make some sort of difference. The other victim would be chosen by fate. And perhaps fate would be kind and take one of the outsiders. Perhaps it would be even kinder and finally give Jack Lockwood the peace he didn't deserve. Those were the best-case scenarios, but fate was seldom kind, and Freddie knew that better than anyone.

"Just one of us is one too many," Eric said, his voice low, his sadness palpable. "We have to get back to the village, check in with the others, and pray to God that those men have been found and taken care of."

"Nothing in the back room," Walter said.

Wanda, beside him, added, "Probably already heading back the way they came. The old priest no doubt spooked them when he attacked them. That's what I reckon, anyway."

Freddie didn't think so. If he'd just been attacked by an old man, who was then killed in the melee, the last thing he would have done was head on out to a dark forest in the pissing rain. They would be panicking by now. Looking for help. Lucas and John had already put the fear into them, and now Calhoun had made an attempt on their lives and failed. It was only natural that they sought help.

Renfield returned then. "Nothing in the cell," he said. "God, I hate that place. Do you know how much better it would be if you let me turn it into a library?"

"Not now, Doc," Eric said, pacing toward the aisle. "Come on. Stay close. We're going back."

They fell back into something resembling a formation and headed for the village.

Freddie knew things were going to get much worse before they got better.

Mike was scared. Terrified. For the first time in his life, he felt as if his life was in someone else's hands, his future uncertain. The hammer that Eve had given him once he had the robes on offered him little hope, but it was better than nothing. Sam still had the knife, which was not much better than a hammer, Mike thought, but the difference was, Sam would have no compunction using it if it came down to it. Could Mike bring that hammer down over some old man's head? He wasn't sure, and hoped he didn't have to find out the hard way.

Eve led them along the edge of the trail. She seemed to know exactly where she was going, where the shadows would be thicker, always staying close to some tree or outcrop that they could, if they were discovered, hide behind or make a run for. But still Mike felt exposed.

Two dozen brown robes, Eve had said as they'd prepared to leave. Twenty odd maniacs with weapons out here in the darkness, hunting them like wild animals. Their only saving grace was age. Eve had told them that not one of the villagers, apart from herself, was under the age of sixty-five. Her father was that age, and so was the village doctor. Some of them were touching eighty. These people were slow, their reactions not as immediate as they once were. They were riddled with ailments, couldn't run for more than five seconds without coughing up a lung, and most probably would have a heart attack if you angrily shouted at them when they weren't expecting it.

They were zombies, Mike had thought, like those shambling, mindless creatures he had seen in a black-and-white Romero pic a few years back.

While Mike and Sam had that on their side, those hunters had numbers. Twenty-something lunatics with knives and bats and whatever else they were carrying, no matter what speed they were coming at, was a terrifying prospect. Mike imagined what it would be like to be swarmed by them as they stabbed and beat at him, their emaciated old bodies crawling all over him like skeletal grotesqueries. He would surely put up a fight, but it would be to no avail, the end result the same.

"Mike," Eve whispered. She had come to a stop ten feet ahead and was ushering Mike to the side. He didn't like the look on her face, but did as he was told. Sam, behind Mike, followed suit. When he reached her, Mike saw what they were hiding from.

There were three of them, brown robes, spread out evenly and walking the perimeter of what looked like a massive pond. The moonlight reflected on the water, making it easier to discern the hunters as they moved slowly around the water's edge.

"I count three," Mike whispered.

"Me, too," Sam said.

"There could be more," Eve added, which didn't make Mike feel any better about the situation.

"Any way past?" Mike didn't know where they were headed. Just that it was a farm, and that the farmer, Freddie, was a brown robe and wouldn't be there. He was too busy out hunting like the rest of the brown robes. Eve said they would be safe there for two reasons. It was big enough to lose yourself in, and it was at the edge of the village. They could only be attacked from one side, so if they put their backs to the border, they would see anyone coming. Eve would come back here once Mike and Sam were safe, and she would try to talk to the brown robes, tell them about her father, and convince them that it would be easier to kill him and end this hunt that way, rather than continue to go after Mike and Sam. That was the plan, if you could call it that, but they were about to fall at the first hurdle, it seemed.

"If we go around it'll take longer," Eve said, "but if they're all down there, and stay down there, we should be able to get past without being seen."

"Keep your voice down," Sam said. Eve's whisper had apparently become a little too excitable for his liking. Mike didn't think she was doing it on purpose.

"Okay," Mike said, the hammer in his hand feeling all at once heavy. He glanced behind him, thought he saw something move back there across Sam's shoulder, but there was nothing. "Let's keep moving."

Just then, a man appeared on the trail in front of them. A brown robe, although he had lowered his hood for reasons Mike didn't know. He had seen them at the side of the trail and was making his way over. The way he walked, he didn't seem worried.

"Find anything?" the man asked.

Mike's heart jumped into his throat. *He doesn't know it's us,* he thought. *He thinks we're allies because of the robes.*

They all stepped out onto the trail; there was no point trying to hide from this man, who was still walking nonchalantly toward them. It was then that Eve lowered her hood, and when the man saw her face he frowned.

"Eve?" he said. "Little Eve Lockwood? What are you doing out here? Let me guess, Eric made you an honorary brown robe for the night, huh? Going to get your first kill under your belt, is that it?"

Eve smiled. Mike had to hand it to her, she was a great actress. Unless, he thought, it was them she was playing, in which case she had chops enough for Broadway or the West End.

"Vic," she said, still whispering. "Keep the noise down, will you?"

By way of an apology, the old man, Vic, held his hands up. "Any sign of them," he said, but now he was looking across Eve's shoulder, trying to figure out who she was with. It wasn't realisation Mike saw in the old man's face, not at first. It was intrigue. Eve was out here when she shouldn't be, so who was hunting alongside her? It was a perfectly reasonable assumption that they were also not bona fide brown robes, and if not, who the hell were they?

"No sign of them, Vic," Eve said. "Keep on looking, though, yeah?" She went to walk past him, and Mike was about to follow when Vic threw up an arm and stopped her in her tracks.

Mike wasn't sure what happened after that, but later he would piece it all together and wonder how it all escalated so quickly, so brutally.

As the old man's hand came up and nudged Eve's shoulder, Sam rushed past Mike, almost knocking him to the ground, and brought the knife down hard into the old man's skull. There was an audible crack as Vic's cranium split, and he stood there for a moment, blood dripping into his eyes, mouth wide open, unable to speak or cry for help, until his legs crumpled beneath him and he dropped to the floor like a set of clothes without anyone inside of them.

An arrow thunked into the tree next to Mike's head. He didn't know what it was at first—he felt the wind of it, heard its squeal as it whipped past in front of his face—but when he saw the fletching bobbing up and down in front of his eyes, he knew he needed to move quickly.

"Go!" he said, just as a second arrow whizzed past his head.

Sam was already running. It took Eve a second or two to realise what was going on; she was still looking at Vic's twitching body when Mike grabbed her by the arm and pulled her away. Where they were running to, Mike had no idea, just that they needed to run as fast as they could, to escape these elderly lunatics or risk ending up like Vic, Rebecca, Kelly, and countless others before them.

"Over here!" someone called out. Mike, still running, turned in the direction of the voice to find a man bounding along through the trees. He was the bow-and-arrow man, and he seemed to be struggling to keep up. Every step on his right foot threatened to send him crashing to the ground, and so he seemed to be bouncing along rather than running in an effort to lessen the pain he was suffering.

"Dennis?" a voice to Mike's right responded. "Dennis, have you found them? Get 'em, Dennis. Fucking get 'em!"

Mike didn't look back again. He didn't dare, in case one of them was quicker than him. Mike hated being chased. As a kid, whenever Kelly had set off after him in a pursuit, he would erupt with laughter and stop, and she would catch him, ask him why he hadn't carried on. He wouldn't do that now, but he hated being chased, nonetheless.

Just then a brown robe leapt from out of the bushes in front and to their right. He thumped into Sam and wrestled him to the ground, screaming and flailing limbs. Sam managed to throw the man off, and his hood came down to reveal it wasn't a man at all, but a woman. She must have been seventy years old, and looked like anybody's grandma: all gums and wrinkles and knobbly features.

Mike didn't stop running, but brought the hammer up, ready. As Sam got back to his feet, almost slipping in the mud—the rain was never going to stop coming down, Mike had already accepted that—Eve latched onto him and dragged him forward.

That was when the old woman raised what looked like an axe, only bigger. Something from Norse mythology, Mike thought, as his momentum sent him speeding past her. He swung the hammer at the static woman's head, connecting perfectly somewhere at the base of her skull. She grunted once before slamming down face-first onto the trail, but not before Mike got a good look at her head and the damage he'd done to it.

"Esme!" the would-be Robin Hood croaked, mournfully. *Fuck Esme,* Mike thought. *Fuck her and her stupid, big axe!*

Another arrow suddenly split the air between Mike and his two running companions, and he thought, *How many fucking arrows does this guy have?* Luckily, it seemed he wasn't a great shot, otherwise they'd all be kebabs by now, skewered against a tree.

And now he did look back to find two more brown robes in pursuit, albeit lagging behind and the distance growing between them. The archer—although that was perhaps doing other archers an injustice, since the guy couldn't hit water if he was standing on a boat—had stopped to help Esme, but Mike thought he was wasting his time. He'd hit her with so much force that one of her eyes had come out; she was not getting up from that.

"This way!" Eve said, no longer whispering. It wasn't necessary. They had been careless and had been found. There was no point shutting the barn door now the horse had bolted.

She led them off the trail and across a field. Mike could still hear the water as the wind brushed over the top of the pond to their right. Ducks were quacking, too, apparently disturbed by this sudden display of violence and action.

Sam was slowing down, now, and Mike had a feeling he wouldn't be able to run for much longer himself. A stitch was already stabbing at his right side, and his legs were burning. Eve looked fresh, able to run all night, although her blonde hair was matted from where it had been stuffed into the hood of her robe, giving her an almost feral mien.

He could easily picture her running through that forest at the other side of the village, dragging deer down with her bare hands, tearing at the meat with teeth and claws. Maybe that's what she did to let off steam every second Sunday of the month. Who knew with these people?

They reached a fence, and Eve flung herself over it without slowing down. Sam fell over it with all the grace of a drunken sailor, picked himself back up from the ground on the other side. Mike did something in-between, and was surprised when he landed on his feet.

"Go!" he urged Sam, who was breathing heavy and spluttering a little. "We are not fucking dying tonight. You hear me."

Sam nodded. "Loud and clear," he said, wiping white foam from his mouth. He kept up the pace, but neither of them could match Eve, who was almost out of sight in front of them. Behind them, there was no movement. Mike hoped they had lost the brown robes, but they would have seen the direction they were heading in, and there couldn't be much this way. It wouldn't take a brain surgeon to figure out where they were going.

"Eve!" Mike yelled, hoping she would stop and wait for them to catch up, or even slow down a little. She seemed to have forgotten that only she knew the way to the farm. If they lost her, they lost everything.

As he leapt over a nettle patch—his trouser leg rolled up, and the little wet bastards stung him just the same—he saw her up ahead, and was grateful that she had heard him, even though the rain was deafening and the thunderclaps had gotten louder.

"Not much farther," she said. To Sam, who was doubled over and sucking in huge lungfuls of air, she said, "You didn't have to kill him. Victor Swain was a good man."

Mike didn't mention what he'd done to Esme—that eye had popped out like a gumball from a penny machine—in case it pushed Eve over the edge and they lost her as an ally forever.

"I don't care if he was the future Pope," Sam said, straightening up. "Like you said back at the house, us or them. Them or us. I'm always going to choose us, and if you don't like that, then you might as well—"

"Let's just take a breather and calm the fuck down, yeah?" Mike knew what Sam was about to say and decided it would do none of them any good to fall apart right now.

"I was doing you and your people a favour," Sam said to Eve, ignoring Mike's plea for some sort of accord. "Hey, that guy's dead. Guess what? Number's down to a hundred. I might have just saved your life, girl."

Sam was right. He might have just saved Eve's life, or Eve's mother's life, or the life of someone else that Eve cared about dearly, but that wasn't the reason Sam had embedded the knife in that old man's head. Self-preservation was all that mattered right now, and Sam, in a moment of brutality and disorientation, had just saved his own ass. Saved Mike's ass, too. These people weren't going to kill Eve if they found her harbouring outsiders, stealing them away in the night. But they sure as fuck weren't going to hesitate to put as many arrows in Mike and Sam as they could.

"No more killing," Eve said. "They're not bad people. *We're* not bad people." She stepped forward then, turned the ring around on her finger a few times before it slipped off her hand. She held it out toward Sam. "Take it," she said. "It was your daughter's. It was never mine."

Sam took the ring from Eve, and after trying to find a finger it would fit—they were all far too big, even his pinky—he slipped it into his coat pocket. Mike remembered the hair bobble from earlier, that neon green band that Rebecca used to tie up her hair, and thought Sam was building up a little collection of his daughter's things in his pocket. He had nothing of Kelly's, just vague memories.

Icing, kennel, confusion, Bakewell tart, birthday party...

"Not far to go," Eve said, turning and pushing past a tangle of thin twigs.

Somewhere behind them—off in the distance still, which Mike was grateful for—the brown robes were calling into the night, summoning back-up as they mourned for their fallen comrades with plaintive howls and enraged bluster.

He had to get past the brown robes. Eve and the outsiders were getting away, and even though he knew exactly where they were going—Freddie Carson's farm was the perfect place to hide, with its myriad outbuildings, stone enclosures, overgrown heaths, and troughs and ditches—he couldn't afford to lose sight of them.

He stepped out onto the trail, where Dennis Wainwright and Anne Worth were crouched next to the dead bodies of Vic and Esme. Pete Cole was walking toward them, shaking his head. He had given up his pursuit of Eve and the outsiders.

"Hey there!" Jack said, smiling. It was so informal, so incongruously out of place amongst the carnage, it stupefied the brown robes enough for Jack to get close.

When they saw who it was, they stopped mourning. Pete Cole came to a sudden halt, and Anne—who was looking so old now, Jack wanted to get her out of the rain before she wrinkled up to the point she imploded on herself—whimpered something before crossing her heart with a trembling hand.

"Jack?" Dennis said, squinting, blinking rain from his eyes. "Is that you, Jack Lockwood?"

Jack smiled. "Sure is," he said. Noticing they were all momentarily unarmed, except for Pete whose dagger was sheathed, Jack moved quickly, lunging for the axe that Esme had dropped when the old outsider rattled her brain. He snatched it up from the mud and brought it around in a wide arc. There was a meaty thunk as it stuck into Dennis Wainwright's shoulder, and then Dennis's entire arm came away and slipped down his body, bounced off his boot, and landed in the mud.

Dennis screamed in agony and shock, staggering away and staring down at the place his arm had been a second before. Esme screamed; Pete came at Jack, but Jack was already swinging again, this time in an upward direction. He took a step toward Pete and the axe went through the man's stomach, chest, chin, and finally his head. Pete stopped coming then. His feet lifted off the ground and he went back, landing on the trail, gargling and groaning. His momentum spinning him around, Jack saw Esme as she began to make a run for it, crying and begging and shrieking and panting.

Jack threw the axe, watched as it went blade over handle through the rain before burying itself in Esme's back. Not quite between the shoulder blades, but close enough. She went down almost immediately, and Jack ran to her and pulled the axe free before bringing it down again. As her head rolled away and nestled against a tree trunk, Jack turned his attention back to Dennis, who had seemingly given up all hope and was sliding through the mud on his backside, his legs and remaining arm pushing him back through the puddles on the trail.

"Ja...Jack." Dennis, as pale as an albino, could hardly talk. Jack almost felt sorry for him. Almost. But Jack didn't feel sorry for anybody. You start doing that, you open yourself up to a world of hurt. And Dennis Wainwright's lifetime affinity to Freddie fucking Carson made him as much an enemy as anyone.

"Save it," Jack said, raising the axe over his head. "You've had a decent run. We all have, if you think about it."

Dennis closed his eyes as the axe came down.

TWENTY-THREE

Neverville, 1974

Joan heard the cries of her fellow brown robes from the trail. They had just finished searching three cottages belonging to the Masons, Richard Flockhart, and Henrietta Stone respectively. She had just headed out of the Mason's cottage when the shouting and crying began.

"What the hell is going on down there?" Alan Horseman was the youngest of Joan's assigned deputies. With his white beard, moustache, and hair, he looked like a shorter, slimmer version of Freddie Carson. She had often wondered whose son Alan was, but had never asked him outright. Perhaps he and Freddie had more in common than just looks.

"I have no idea," Joan said, "but it sounds like they found something. Get the others. We're going to have to go see."

The others—Richard Fowler and Henry James—were knocking on the next cottage door a little farther along the trail, this one belonging to Harriet and William Locksley. Alan had only been gone two minutes when all three of them returned, and it appeared that Alan had already told them about what they had just heard.

"Do you think they're in trouble?" Fowler asked, the first words out of his mouth since setting off from the church earlier. He looked frightened, nervous, and loath to go looking for anything that might be dangerous. Joan wasn't sure how many hunts Fowler had been on—she had never worked with him before, she had never even seen him out of his brown leather dungarees which he wore to the mill—but part of her wanted to tell him to pull up his robe hood and stop whining.

"I guess we're going to find out," Alan said before Joan opened her mouth to reply.

They made their way along the trail. The pond, where the other group were searching, was about a quarter of a mile. It would only take a few minutes to get there, but everything seemed to have fallen silent once again. No screams. No shouts. Just the howling wind and the roaring thunder. After a few hundred metres, Richard Fowler began to hum a church hymn to himself—'Come, Let Us Join Our Cheerful Songs', Joan thought it was, but it was so out of tune and half-hearted that it was impossible to tell for sure—and Joan had to tell him to keep quiet. He was singing because he was terrified of what they were about to find, and filling the horrible silence with something set him at ease. It was like nails down a chalkboard to Joan, who was having none of it.

Off in the distance. A dog began to bark. Joan didn't know if it was coming from Neverville or the other side of the boulders. Not that it mattered; sometimes she forgot there was anything beyond those walls.

They edged past the pond, which was on their right, but there was no sign of the second group. Dennis Wainwright's group. Either he had finished up here and moved on, leading his men and women to a different area—which wouldn't please Eric, Joan thought, if he found out—or something had happened. That question was answered a few seconds later when Henry James said:

"Is that...is that what I think it is?"

Joan looked at the trail ahead, saw what Henry James had seen, and dry-swallowed. "Oh, my God," she said, not wanting to look but unable to look away.

There were three bodies, arranged in such a way that they formed a cross in the middle of the trail. As they drew closer—Richard had moved to the back of the group, where he probably hoped he would be the last to die, should anything bad start to happen, when in fact it was more likely they would be attacked from the rear, in which case he was a chump—Joan saw Dennis Wainwright's contorted face first. It was split almost entirely in half down to his lips, but it was definitely him. The other four, Esme Loomis, Peter Cole, Anne Worth, and Victor Swain completed the macabre cruciform, their bodies fully stretched out as if they had decided to take a nap and enjoy the rain and clouds while they lasted.

"Why would they do this?" Henry asked, nervously twisting his sodden moustache between his thumb and forefinger.

Joan didn't know. Perhaps they had made the mistake of taking these outsiders for granted. Maybe out there, beyond the boulders, they were a formidable duo, killers, soldiers of some recent war, or simply not sound of mind. She couldn't look at the mutilated bodies in front of her any longer, though. *Such a shame,* she thought. *Such a terrible shame.*

"I think they went this way," Alan Horseman said. He had drifted off to the creepers at the edge of the trail and was staring through the trees there. "There's footprints in the mud here, here, and here," he added, pointing at the imprints left by several pairs of boots.

Joan took a closer look at the prints, which were already fading as yet more rain came down and filled them up. "Could be anyone," she said. "Could be Dennis's group left 'em."

"Maybe," Alan said. "But I don't think so. I think those bastards were caught going somewhere by Dennis and his group. There was a skirmish here and those sonsofbitches killed 'em all before hot footing on out of here and up thataway, and there's only one thing thataway. I used to cut through myself whenever I ran low on milk. Course, I don't anymore. Go all the way around, on account of all the stingers in there and me not being as steady as I used to." He pronounced it *ustah*.

Joan knew what was that way, too, if they moved as the crow flies. "The farm," she said. "But they don't know it's there, do they? Freddie's place?"

"They're just running blind," Alan said. "Anywhere's good as long as they're still breathing." He motioned in the direction he believed they had moved in. "If they're going to the farm, we can get 'em cornered. Ain't no way out of there except past us."

Richard came across to them, looking as nervous as ever. "Does this mean no one else is gonna die?" he asked, pointing to the grisly cruciform created from their former neighbours and fellow brown robes.

Joan nodded. "Not by the curse," she said. "But those boys need to be taken care of before they do to us what they did to them." She pushed past Richard, and Alan followed her. After calling Henry over—he was walking up and down the trail, swinging his machete at overgrown vines—she said, "We sure we've got them on the run that way?"

"Has to be," Alan said. "Nowhere else for 'em to go."

Joan nodded. Alan was right. If those sonsofbitches had come this way, they hadn't altered course. They were going to get to Freddie's, and when they did, they'd have all manner of potential weapons to work with. Up there, Freddie had more sickles, shovels, pitchforks, and axes than you could ever use in a lifetime, even if you switched up once a week. They would be armed to the teeth, which was not a good thing since they were clearly deranged and not afraid to retaliate.

Joan knew what needed to be done.

She stepped onto the trail and howled. She howled as loudly as she could. Alan joined her and did the same, and before long, all four of them were howling into the night. It didn't matter that the outsiders would hear them and would know their position. All that mattered was that the other brown robes heard them, and answered the call.

They needed everyone.

Those damned outsiders wouldn't know what hit them.

Albie Moss was leading his group toward the woods when the call came. They all stopped and turned in the direction of the noise, which was distant—perhaps half a mile away, but it was hard to tell with the wind howling the way it was and the rain coming down in sheets.

"Joan," Albie said. He had heard her call before, many years ago, a mix of wolf howl and fox mewl. "Sounds like it's coming from over by the pond." Again, it was just conjecture, but they were definitely over that way somewhere.

"That's where Dennis's group were searching," Archie said. "Why are they all together? Eric'll be pissed about that."

Archie was a tall guy, all limbs and elongated torso. He was almost two feet taller than Albie, and thusly his robes came up short, like a child who had outgrown his learning uniform. He was smart, though, and he was right about Eric. But there had to be a good reason for Joan to abandon her position.

The call told Albie there was.

"We need to get down there," he said. "Either they've found them, or things have gone south."

"Shit!" Frannie said, covering her mouth almost immediately. As a woman of faith, she scarcely swore, and when she did, she made a big deal of it, either by slapping a hand to her mouth or following up the curse with an apology or a "pardon my Latin."

Albie sighed. This night was not going to plan at all.

He began to howl and the others followed suit.

Eric's group had reached the inn when he heard Albie's call. Freddie instructed John and Lucas to silence their horses, and they brought them off the trail onto the grassy stretch opposite the inn, where they cantered for a moment before stopping. Wanda was now riding with John Wexler, since she was struggling to keep up and was slowing the rest of the group down. She hadn't complained much when Eric told her to do so; she had been flagging ever since they left the church, moaning and complaining and generally reminding them all that her legs weren't as long as everyone else's.

Freddie listened carefully. There were two groups howling, one off to the left and one further ahead on the trail. Albie's group were answering Joan's, and Joan was the group nearest the trail but farthest away. Freddie put two and two together.

"Head toward the pond," he said. "Sounds like that's where it's coming from."

Eric nodded, even though he didn't seem to like the fact that Freddie had deduced that by himself. Did he think Freddie was vying for leadership? If he did, he couldn't have been more wrong. Freddie didn't even want to be a brown robe anymore, let alone be in charge of the whole damn party.

"Okay, you boys ride ahead," Eric told Wexler and Thorne. "Don't take any chances. You see someone that isn't one of ours, take them down, and I mean, on sight. No fuck-ups."

The riders galloped away, their horses kicking up mud from the trail and Wanda Hill clinging on to John Wexler's waist for dear life with one arm, her war hammer hanging down the side of the horse, unintentionally whacking its flank as it ran.

Eric began to walk after them at pace, and Freddie, Walter, and Renfield kept up.

"You think they're in trouble?" Renfield asked, his expression telling Freddie that he already knew the answer.

"I think we all might be," he said, and left it at that.

"Holy shit!" Walter said.

"I'll be damned," Albie added.

"They couldn't have done this," Freddie said. "I mean, a couple of outsiders wouldn't have done this."

"We don't know a damned thing about those men and what they're capable of," Eric said, moving around the five bodies lying at the centre of the trail. To Joan he said, "They were like this when you got here?"

Joan nodded. "'Course they were," she said. "We didn't put 'em like this."

Eric pinched his nose between thumb and forefinger, as if he was thinking or suffering from a terrible headache. Freddie didn't feel too well, himself. The day had started off decent enough, with Eve's visit to the farm, but it had all been downhill since then. The woods, the musket misfiring, Eric being a grade-A asshole, and now this, and he had a feeling it wasn't going to get better any time soon.

"They did this," Eric said. "Just like they did that to Father Calhoun back at the church."

"Did what?" Joan latched onto Eric's arm, yanked him back slightly. "Did what to Calhoun?"

"Don't tell me the fucking priest's dead," Albie said.

Eric nodded. "The fucking priest's dead," Eric said, in exactly the same tone Albie had used. Freddie wanted to clobber him upside the head for that, but managed to keep his temper under control. They were all under enough stress without in-fighting.

Frannie Mills crossed her heart and sighed. "May the Lord have mercy on their souls," she said. "Or may they rot in Hell for an eternity."

Make your damn mind up, woman, Freddie thought. He was so angry at what was going on all around him, it was all he could do to remain calm. And now those fuckers were up at his place doing God knows what, and he was tired and wet and feeling like he was going to upchuck at any given moment. Were any of the others feeling it? That something was not right tonight? Or was Freddie just spooked by the whole situation? Getting too old for this shit? They all were, and it couldn't last forever. It wouldn't.

"We're dropping like flies tonight," Albie said, which wasn't conducive at all. "I mean, this has been one bad night, even by Neverville's standards."

"Albie," Eric said. It was a warning. That that was not the kind of thing he wanted to hear right now in the middle of a hunt.

"Okay," Joan said. She was sheltering from the rain as best she could beneath a huge oak, but she was already a drowned rat, her hair clinging to the side of her head so that her ears stuck out. She looked so rodenty, Freddie wondered why no one had tried to trap her yet. "So what's the plan, Eric?" There was still something she was keeping from them. Her usual calmness, her composure, it was all gone. She was more concerned than Freddie had ever seen her before, and Joan Lockwood didn't worry on hunts. Joan Lockwood got things done on hunts. Freddie still hadn't had a chance to ask her what was wrong yet, but he would. He would make time once this was all over. Not because he gave a shit, but because it paid to know what was going on in the village at all times, or as much as possible.

"Okay, we hit the farm from every angle," Eric said. "Freddie, anything up there we should know about?"

Freddie wasn't quite sure what he meant by that, so he replied with a shrug.

"We ain't gonna end up caught in some steel jaw-trap we don't know about?"

Freddie considered this for a moment. He had set some traps, but they were out wide, and while they were enough to keep a fox down, Freddie didn't think they had the snap to hurt a person. He told them about the traps anyway, just in case. He didn't want little Wanda Hill getting snared. Damn things would probably kill someone that small.

"We all here?" Eric asked.

"Looks like it," Albie said. "What's left of us, anyway."

"Okay, no horses," he said to those riding. "We go up there on foot, quietly."

This was met with some discontent, but those with horses dismounted and sent their animals back off along the trail toward the village with a swift smack on the hindquarters. They would gather them up later.

If, Freddie thought, *there should be a later.*

"Let's get moving, folks," Eric said. "This night ain't getting any younger, and there's two fucking maniacs on the loose. Three with that bastard, Jack! I want them found, I want them dead, I want to go home to my bed."

Very poetic, Freddie thought, sarcastically. *Just what we need right now. Eric bloody Shakespeare.*

TWENTY-FOUR

Neverville, 1974

The farm was pretty much what Mike had expected. Stables, pens, wooden out-buildings, a large house that would have cost something in the region of a quarter of a million back in Yorkshire, that now faraway land he would never return to. He hadn't yet come to terms with that, but it niggled away at him like a sore tooth. It seemed so unreal, like a nightmare from which he couldn't snap himself out of no matter how hard he tried. But it wasn't a nightmare, he wasn't waking up in his own bed covered in sweat, he was never sleeping in that bed again, and that hit him hard as stupid, banal things kept coming into his head. I'm not going to be able to pay the rent, so I'm going to get evicted! Work are going to be so pissed off at me when I don't even call tomorrow morning to let them know I won't be in! My beautiful Morris Marina, no doubt destroyed by now! It was ridiculous, because none of it mattered anymore. They were being hunted by geriatric lunatics in brown robes in a village from which they could never escape, but all Mike could think about was whether his mother would be okay when the smoke alarm ran out of batteries.

That was when the howling started, and Mike forgot all about work and bed and Yorkshire and the fact he'd never eat a Nestle's Dairy Crunch bar again. Those howls were terrifying, and brought all three of them to a halt in front of the farmhouse.

"What the fuck is that?" Sam asked, catching his breath

"They're calling to each other," Eve replied. "It's their way of communicating, letting them know where they are."

"What are they, fucking dingoes?" Sam, Mike thought, was just as unsettled by the noise as he was. He hadn't smoked in almost an hour, which probably didn't help, and Mike wondered if he'd finally run out of cigarettes. If he had, his crankiness was only going to increase from here on, and Mike doubted they sold Marlboros in twenty-packs back in the village. It was something Sam might have to come to terms with if they survived the night.

Just then, Eve sighed. It was a sad sigh, and Mike didn't like that one bit.

"What?" he asked.

"We should keep moving," Eve said, turning back around. "This way."

Eve seemed to know the farm inside and out, and took them around the back of the huge farmhouse. Chickens grew flustered and began to *buck-buck-buck* as Eve led them past a coop, and Mike thought, *Yeah, you and me both.*

"I don't like this, Mike," Sam whispered. He was still at the rear, but was doing his best to keep up. "I mean, where the fuck is she even taking us?"

Mike knew they had to trust the girl; what choice did they have, really? She said she would get them someplace safe, promised them she would do her best to talk to the brown robes and get them to call the hunt off, convince them there didn't need to be any more bloodshed, not tonight, and although Mike didn't trust her completely—she was angry at Sam for killing that old guy back by the pond, and had every reason to change her mind about helping them—they were all out of options.

"I *can* hear you," Eve whispered back before Mike had a change to reply. "Like I said, I'm getting you somewhere safe."

"Well, forgive me for being a little fucking suspicious," Sam whispered back, "but I've seen *The Godfather*. Not everyone who smiles at you is your friend."

There was a momentary silence and Eve stopped moving for a second. She glanced back and whispered, "Who's the godfather?"

"It doesn't matter," Mike said, keeping his voice low. It was hard to believe that this girl had never been beyond those boulders, had never experienced the world beyond Neverville. She was as much a victim of all this as they were, only she had been thrust into it straight from the womb, knew no different than what had been set before her and told to her by her ancestors. She wouldn't know who Marlon Brando was, or Al Pacino. This whole village had paused in the 18th Century, which was why this farm had no tractors to plough or cultivate or harvest, no balers for the hay, no machines to spread manure. It was why the village had no electricity, no hot and cold running water, no telephones. It was why these people were so fucked up in their archaic beliefs, hoping that one day the curse would just come to an end and they wouldn't have to kill any more.

And now we're among them, Mike thought.

Welcome to Neverville, the village of a hundred. What was the Latin for that again? *Centum*? Such a nice word, and yet so much misery and death had been caused since Clemence Landrake uttered it atop that burning pyre all those years ago. And what a lovely name for a village: Neverville. So fitting in this instance. As in Never-getting-the-fuck-out-of-here-ville. If that was just a coincidence, then someone—the god of fate? The lord of destiny? Some prophetic cartographer?—had a sick sense of humour.

They arrived at what looked like a wooden lean-to. Inside was a rotten wagon, its wheels removed; empty barrels were set out haphazardly, some of them lying on their side, discarded and no longer useful. As far as storage units went, Mike had seen worse, but it wasn't exactly the best place to hide, and could see from Sam's expression that he was thinking the same thing.

"This place hasn't been used in years," Eve said. "I don't even think Freddie remembers it's back here. I come here sometimes to get away from...well, when I want to read in peace."

To get away from Daddy, Mike thought but didn't say.

"Well this is just beautiful," Sam said, his cynicism returning full-force. To Mike he said, "Who do you want to be? Butch Cassidy or the Sundance Kid? I mean, I've always thought of myself more of a Paul Newman man, but—"

"Sam," Mike said, cutting him off mid rant.

"I don't understand," Eve said, looking genuinely hurt and confused. "Butch Sundance..." She trailed off there, frowning with confusion.

"Again," Mike said, "it doesn't matter. You think we'll be safe here for a while?"

Eve nodded, though she didn't seem too certain. Mike once again realised how innocent she was, how sad and alone she must feel, how oblivious she was to the world. And how beautiful she was. Far too beautiful to be a monster, far too virtuous to be exposed to all this madness. She reminded him, in that moment, of a Manson girl; so pretty and seemingly innocent, lost, following others' lead, living an unconventional life. But Eve was no Squeaky Fromme, or Leslie Van Houten, or Patricia Krenwinkel. She was Eve Lockwood, and Mike didn't think Eve Lockwood could ever kill.

"Then we stay here," Mike said. "If you're sure."

Eve nodded again. "I'll go back the way we came," she said, stripping the brown robe off. It was heavy and filled with water, and she tossed it into the corner of the shed, which sent a hiding rat skittering across the dirt and out through a small hole in the wood

"I will do my best," Eve said, mainly to Mike. She seemed to have given up on trying to appease Sam. "If I can get Eric to listen, tell him that you didn't kill Father Calhoun and that my father did and he's still out there, I might just be able to convince them to reconsider."

"Yeah, you let those assholes know we're not going down without a fight, as well," Sam said.

"Sam!" Mike had had enough. "How is that helping?"

"They killed her, Mike!" Sam said. "They killed my daughter, fuck's sake. They killed your sister, and now you want to what? Kiss and make up? Tell them it's okay, they were just doing their job?"

"I don't know!" Mike snapped. "I don't know what's going to happen, but I don't want to die here tonight. I don't want to...to just fucking end like this. Yes, Kelly is dead, and they did it. Yes, Rebecca is dead, and they did it. I'm trying to understand what's going on here, just the same as you. I didn't believe in witches...or, or fucking curses, or think any of this could ever be possible, but it is, Sam. It is, and it's happening to us. And we're stuck here, and Kelly and Rebecca would have been stuck here, no matter what these sonsofbitches did to them." He paused, tried to swallow but there was nothing but dryness in his mouth and throat. "Their lives, the lives they had before, ended here the moment they came over those boulders. Just like ours have. Whether we choose to accept that and survive is up to us."

Mike felt something cold brush past his neck and rest upon his shoulder, and when he looked around, saw Eve standing there looking sadder and lonelier than ever, her hand resting on him, he smiled a little. "I know it's not your fault," he said. "But you have to make them see. We don't have to die here tonight. No more of them have to die here tonight. We don't have to fight them."

Eve didn't respond. A single nod and the faintest of smiles and she was gone.

"This is fucked up," Sam said, throwing his arms up in disapproval. "You might not be ready to die, Mike, but I couldn't give two shits right now. I'm not going to shake hands with those evil motherfuckers, tell them I forgive them for what they've done, pretend that I'm okay with it and teach them all how to play Led Zeppelin songs on their fucking harpsichords, or whatever the hell they've got here."

"We don't have to do that," Mike said, walking the length of the shed, which took him all of three seconds. "But they're gonna keep on coming until we're dead unless Eve can talk them out of it." He kicked at a grain bag in the corner, and grain trickled out of a hole in its side and scattered across the ground. God knows how long it had been there, but the stench was atrocious.

"She's just as bad as them," Sam said. "I don't know why we're even giving her the benefit of the doubt, Mike."

Mike did. He knew exactly why. One, they had no choice, two, she was innocent in all of this, and three, well, three, Mike didn't want to die in the next half hour, regardless of what that meant.

Something else came to him in that moment, a terrible thought that hurt him far more than the pining for chocolate bars, losing his home and job, and the air conditioning in his Marina. He would never be able to contact his mother. She would live out the rest of her life believing she had lost two children, not knowing the truth, not knowing that they had both stumbled upon someplace strange that shouldn't exist and wasn't on any recent maps. It pained him to think of her, worrying when he didn't return, standing by telephone just waiting for it to ring. The police would come looking, but they would never find this place. Perhaps it went much deeper. Maybe the police did know about Neverville, and had sent officers over the boulders. These people would have killed them, until eventually the force steered clear altogether. Out here in the middle of nowhere, anything was possible.

"We're not just giving her the benefit of the doubt," Mike said, annoyed with Sam's tone of voice. "We're placing our lives in her hands, and so far, she's done nothing to make me think she won't try."

"Apart from almost kill me back at her house," Sam said, holding up the kitchen knife as if Mike needed reminding."

"She thought you were her father."

"Oh, yeah! And where is he, this mystery man who's coming after her, huh? This psycho killer who'll stop at nothing?" Sam glanced around the cabin in a mock search; of course Eve's father wasn't there. He was making a point.

"I don't know," Mike said. "But he could be—"

Eve's scream pierced the night. Mike turned and pressed himself to the wall as Sam stumbled clumsily across the shed, knife poised to penetrate anyone who came through the door. She was close, hadn't moved far from the rotting shed at all, and Mike didn't know what was more frightening, the scream or Eve's lack of progress.

If her first scream was chilling, the one that followed was enough to curdle blood, and Mike knew that the girl whose hands their lives rested in was in a great deal of trouble.

He could have just killed her, he knew that. He could have jumped out on her and jammed the axe in her spine, and that would be that. But Jack wanted it to last. He wanted to see the fear in her eyes when he did it, and hear her tiny, insignificant voice as she begged him not to.

He was surprised at how loud she screamed, though. She had a good set of lungs on her, and he almost dropped her as she wriggled and struggled to break free. He growled and threw her down, and she almost bounced back up from the undergrowth. He grabbed her again, this time from a better position, and managed to force her forward into a tree. Her head bounced off it, and after that she went still.

He turned her around and crouched, allowing her to slump across his shoulder. She might have been strong, but she was light—no more than a couple of sacks of grain, if that—and he had no problem lifting her. With Eve across his right shoulder, he retrieved the axe from the bush he'd been hiding in, wiped the wet, muddy blade on his trousers, and headed for Freddie Carson's house.

"You are not doing what I think you're doing?" Sam looked amazed, shocked even as Mike moved toward the shed door, but he didn't try to stop him. Maybe he knew better; maybe he was too tired to care.

"She's in trouble," Mike said. "I can't just stand here if she needs help."

After the second scream, there had been no third, and Mike was already fearing the worst. Eve was dead, lying in the mud, butchered by her maniac father who had been coming for her all along—following them from the church? Eve's house? the pond?—despite Sam's skepticism. And now he had got her, and any hopes of talking the brown robes around had gone out the window.

"If she's gone, she's gone," Sam said, and Mike hated him for that. Was it this place that stripped people of their humanity? Peeled their empathy away until nothing remained? Sam was starting to sound less human by the minute; Mike thought, if they made it through the night and somehow managed to get the villagers on their side, eventually Sam would find himself wearing one of those brown robes permanently, and not just as a ruse to escape unnoticed.

"You can stay here, Sam, but I'm not letting that bastard kill her." He thought about the priest and the gruesome manner he'd been concealed in the church confessional. If her father was capable of beating a clergyman to death with a blunt instrument—as it appeared he had—he was capable of anything. "Look, mate, this is all crazy, but it's going to end one way or the other, and I want to do the right thing before...before I go." Not because he feared going to Hell or anything of that ilk, but for his own peace of mind.

He considered this for a moment and then, digging deep beneath his robes and producing a crumpled cigarette packet from somewhere, he took out a bent smoke and lit it. "Last one," he said. "Looks like I'm quitting." He chuckled, humourlessly, stared down at the smouldering cherry of his cigarette and the smoke trailing up and around his tobacco-stained fingers. "Let's go get her."

He crushed out the cigarette between his finger and thumb and moved for the door. Mike nodded, glad all hope wasn't lost just yet.

TWENTY-FIVE

Neverville, 1974

There was no point messing around. Jack put Eve on the ground and shoulder-charged the door to Freddie's farmhouse until it gave, which was the third attempt. He dragged Eve into the house by her feet and pushed the door shut behind them, leaning the axe against the doorjamb. It was so good to finally get out of the rain, and even though his clothes were soaked through and his skin wet beneath them, Jack sighed with relief.

Eve moaned, but she remained unconscious as he took her by the arms and pulled her toward the staircase. If she did come to, he would punch her until she was out again. He couldn't have her waking up just yet, not until he was good and ready, not until he had her in place.

As he tugged and pulled her up the stairs, Jack wondered what had become of the outsiders. Where had she taken them? Where were they now? Jack had lost track of them for a few minutes, and if Eve hadn't come wandering back through the trees at the side of Freddie's land, he might still be out there in the rain looking.

Maybe she had done the right thing, after all. Led those men up here on false pretenses and then butchered them. It was a roundabout way of doing things, but in gaining their trust first, it would have made killing them all the simpler. But Jack knew, as this wonderful thought crossed his mind, he was being ridiculous. Eve was far too nice, far too different from Jack, to have killed them, which meant they were still on the farm somewhere, hidden away so that the brown robes couldn't get to them.

At the top of the stairs, Eve began to breathe heavily as Jack dragged her toward the bedroom at the end of the hall. It was, Jack knew, where Freddie Carson's mother, Alice, had once slept, before she had slit her own throat. Jack knew that because he had been here once, a quarter of a century ago with Eric Majors. Eric had purchased a Jacobean oak chair from Freddie, and needed help to move it down the stairs to his wheel cart, and of course Jack had offered, for who knew what jewellery Alice had left lying around the house, ready to fall into unscrupulous hands?

Jack pushed his way into Alice's old bedroom—it was candlelit, and there was a shrine dedicated to Alice Carson in the corner of the room, which would have affected him if it weren't for the fact he hated the woman, hated her son, hated them, hated them, hated them!—and managed to lift Eve onto the bed. He quickly went back downstairs to fetch the axe he'd left by the front door. He raced back upstairs to Eve, for he didn't want to disappoint his precious daughter, now, did he?

She had moved a little—one arm was now resting on the pillow next to her head and her leg had been pulled up into an arch—but Jack was pleased to see she was still out cold. Her head was bleeding from where it had connected with the tree, and a crimson patch was already beginning to dry on her cheek, where it had been grazed.

Jack smiled. "My little girl," he said, the smile turning into a grin.

At the side of the room there was a wardrobe larger than the confessional Jack had left Father Calhoun in. Had that been just today? It felt, Jack thought as he searched through the wardrobe for something to tie Eve up with, like several eternities ago. Beneath a pile of nightgowns that were about as alluring as a mound of sheep shit, Jack found a stack of thin sheets.

He twisted them lengthways and set about wrapping them around Eve's wrists and ankles and binding her to the four corners of the bed. She was fitful, but remained unconscious as he worked. He pulled the sheets tight, making sure there was no way she could break free, and when he was done, he took a step back to admire his handiwork.

He was still grinning and nodding when a thick, heavy arm suddenly tightened around his neck and a voice said, "Sick fuck!"

Sam just grabbed the guy. No warning, no conversational foreplay, just threw an arm around his neck and yanked him back into the hallway. Jack Lockwood didn't even have time to react.

Mike didn't know what to do, so he just began to hit Jack in the stomach as hard as he could with the hammer. With each strike came a horrible exhalation of warm and acrid breath from Jack, but he made no sound as he struggled to prise Sam's arm from around his neck.

"Fucking...son...bitch..." Sam brought the knife he held up and tried to push it toward Jack's face, but Jack saw it and grabbed Sam by the wrist. He was strong, Eve had been right about that. Much stronger than most men his age, and definitely stronger than he had any right to be, since he'd spent the last twenty years near comatose.

Mike hit Jack hard in the left kneecap with the hammer, and Jack buckled momentarily before regaining his footing and throwing a leg up and out into Mike's midriff. It knocked the wind out of Mike and he staggered back, crashing against the wall behind him. But the force of the kick had also pushed Jack and Sam back to the wooden bannister, and before Mike realised it they were both going over, a mass of arms and legs and Mike didn't know whose were who's or what was happening until they were both out of sight.

There was a loud crash as they landed somewhere below. Mike rushed forward and glimpsed down through the darkness, but he could only see one foot from his vantage point. It was twitching spasmodically.

From the bedroom, Eve whimpered as she came to, realising she was bound to the bed and completely unable to move.

Mike was torn, for he didn't know who to go to first. That was a long way down, and whichever way Sam had landed, it would have hurt, but Eve was screaming now to be let up, sobbing and yelling for her father to release her.

Just then the foot Mike could see moved out of view, and Mike knew he had to get down there. Eve was safe for now, but Sam was not. He hurried along the hall and bounced down the stairs, taking them two and three at a time, hoping Sam was still alive when he got there.

"They're in there," Albie Moss said, pointing at the farmhouse. "The door's been broken open, see?"

Freddie could see, and he wasn't happy about it. They were in his house, his sanctuary, those two bastards roaming around on his property. He felt deeply violated in a way he had never felt before. "I want my house surrounded," he said, turning to the others. "Anyone except me, Eric, Joan, Doc, and Walt come out of there, you take 'em down and you make 'em bloody, you understand?"

The brown robes nodded in unison before separating and moving in small groups to surround the farmhouse.

Freddie turned to Eric and said, "You know as well as I do this doesn't end well for all of us. We might lose more. Those fuckers seem to know exactly what they're doing."

"We've already lost so many," Eric said, but he wasn't saying that he was worried about losing more; he was saying that these outsiders needed to suffer for what they had done, regardless of how many more were lost before this was over. He was saying it was worth it, just to see the looks on their faces in the seconds before they met their maker. And for the first time in a long time, Freddie agreed with Eric Majors.

Sam was on his knees, trying to get to his feet, when Mike made it down to the ground floor. He looked shaken and confused, but nothing appeared to be broken. Except for perhaps his ego, which, in the grand scheme of things, didn't matter all that much now. There was no sign of Jack Lockwood.

"You okay?" Mike helped Sam to his feet. Upstairs Eve continued to scream, only now she wasn't crying out for help. She was shrieking for her father to, "Get the fuck back here and untie me, you crazy bastard! I'll kill you! I'll kill you, you cunt!" She was, it seemed, no longer scared. Now she was just angry, pissed off that she had been blindsided and captured, and now livid that she was strapped to a bed from which she couldn't escape.

"Go," Sam said, picking his knife up from the floor. "I'll find him, just go and get her off that bed." Before Mike had time to argue, Sam spun and lurched for the open door at the end of the room. He was injured; Mike could tell by the way he walked. But that wasn't going to stop him.

Mike raced back up the stairs to Eve.

"Mike!" she cried as he careened into the bedroom and began to untie the sheets. "Mike, where is he? Where's Sam?"

"Sam's okay," Mike told her, hoping he wasn't lying. With her wrists free, he set about untying the twisted sheets from her ankles. "Look, everything's going to be okay, yeah? We're going to get out of here."

"Is he dead?" Eve asked, meaning her father. "Did you kill him, Mike?"

Mike shook his head. "Sam's working on that right now," he said. "But we need to be quiet, okay? He's still in the house. We need to go downstairs, and we need to get out of here, do you hear me?"

Eve nodded as the last sheet was loosened and she pushed herself up slowly from the bed. She was unsteady, still groggy from whatever had knocked her out, and Mike thought she would fall back for a moment before she steadied herself on the wall.

"We have to help Sam," she said. "He's in trouble."

"Sam'll be okay," Mike said, once again hoping he wasn't lying. "He's a tough guy, he can look after himself." Mike thought about the Sam he had known all those years ago—back then he had just been Mr. Jones, the big ol' factory worker whose cleft-lipped daughter was there to be made fun of and taunted and targetted with pebbles—and wished he had that man with him now. *That* man would have been okay going up against Jack Lockwood.

"Come on," Mike said, taking Eve by the hand and leading her toward the bedroom door.

That was when there came an almighty crash from downstairs and someone yelled, "You sonsofbitches came to the wrong fucking house tonight."

Eve gripped Mike's hand tighter. "It's them," she whispered. "It's the brown robes."

Jack waited outside at the back door. He had to get back upstairs to Eve and to the axe he'd left in the bedroom. He had to kill her, that was all he cared about. If he died doing it, then that was fine with him, but he had to kill at least her, the way she should have been killed twenty-two years ago. All of this—stupid, selfless Alice Carson's suicide, that night at the inn when Freddie bust his cheekbone and the whole village turned against him, twenty-something years of purgatory, his own private hellscape, Vic, dead, Esme, dead, Father Calhoun, Pete Cole, Anne Worth, Dennis Wainwright, all dead—was because of her.

She has to know. She has to see what she has wrought, what she has made of me!

That one outsider, Jack thought, had to be dead. Jack had landed on top of him, cushioning his own impact, but his weight would have caused serious damage to the outsider. At least he hoped it had; he hadn't stuck around to check for a pulse.

It was raining heavily again, and Jack could barely see through it, which was why when a voice suddenly shouted, "Get him!" he was completely taken aback. He spun around to find three faceless dark shapes lunging toward him. No, there was a fourth, but she was smaller, lower down. They must have seen who he was, though, for they hesitated, just long enough for Jack to react.

He hit the one at the front as hard as he could in the side of the head, and it snapped sideways, the morning star flail she was swinging rattling her own knuckles instead of its intended target—Jack's head. The brown robe's hood flew back to reveal his attacker as Frannie Mills. He reached up and snatched the flail from the brown robe as he brought a knee up into her side, but the little brown robe—had to be Wanda Hill—clattered the hammer into his thigh. She had been going for his groin, but he had avoided the agony of that by twisting his lower body away from her. As Frannie went down, Jack swung the morning star once around his head, and then out, whipping the spiked ball toward the little brown robe's head. It embedded there for a moment, and she froze until he tore it free. Then she fell to the side, blood spraying up and into the air, and hit the ground with a thud.

Brown robes three and four came at him together: Alan Horseman and Richard Fowler. And Jack was running on pure adrenaline by now, his body taken over by a survival instinct he had no control of. He swung the morning star flail at them both, and they paused for a second, seemingly assessing the situation. They were wielding machetes, but weren't willing to put themselves in harm's way unnecessarily,

"We're on the same fucking side!" Jack snapped, even though that couldn't have been further from the truth. Jack was on no one's side. Jack was on Jack's side.

Even so, his attackers waited, perhaps perplexed, but Jack thought at least one of them would recognise him. Horseman certainly knew who he was; they had once worked together, felling trees in the forest. That had been over forty years ago, but Horseman hadn't changed too much; Jack could make out his beaky nose now, and those almond-shaped eyes that were always just shy of a squint. He didn't care whether Horseman remembered him. He had what he wanted.

A second of uncertainty.

Jack brought the flail around in a wide arc and slammed it into Richard Fowler's jaw. Teeth erupted from his open mouth and rattled against the farmhouse wall as they bounced off, his lower mandible came away entirely. Fowler groaned as his lights went out for good.

As Alan Horseman thrust his machete toward Jack, the morning star flail's chain wrapped around the blade, and with one tug, the machete was pulled out of Horseman's grasp and flew across the yard. Jack spun and went low with the flail, and it stuck in Horseman's calf and swept the man off his feet. As he fell, the flail ripped out, and Jack brought it up and down. Before Horseman even hit the ground, the spiky ball was in his chest. Jack pulled it free and swung it down again. And again. And again. Until Horseman stopped grunting.

"Fuckers!" Jack said, surveying the dead bodies lying in the mud. They thought they had him. No, they thought they had one of the outsiders. They hadn't been counting on him at all.

But Jack didn't have time to celebrate his victory as, for the second time in ten minutes, he was attacked from behind. A body slammed into him, knocking him forward away from the farmhouse. He went down, rolled and rolled, ate mud and rainwater. When he got his bearings, he realised the flail was no longer in his hand. Standing in front of the farmhouse was that outsider, the older one, the one called Sam. He had a knife in his hand and an expression on his face that said not only was he not afraid to use it, he damn well wanted to.

"Will you just *die* already?" Jack snarled. "You're going to anyway!"

The outsider took a step toward him, bringing the knife up and jabbing it in Jack's direction. "Age before beauty," he said.

Jack lunged back, away from the blade, but tripped over Wanda Hill's leg. The dwarf was deader than Descartes, but it seemed she was going to have the last laugh.

He went down once again into the mud. By now he was covered from head to toe, every inch of him coated in thick muck. It was starting to slow him down, but he still had luck on his side, and that came in the form of Wanda's war hammer. She must have dropped it when he'd killed her. As Jack went down, his hand brushed against the cold, curved spike on the head of the hammer, and instinctively he reached down for the handle just as the outsider, Sam, landed on top of him and tried to bring the knife down.

With one upward swing—that was all it took; the weight of the hammer did most of the work—he knocked the outsider off. One of them was bleeding. Red filled Jack's vision for a second, until he blinked it away and got onto his knees.

He had been stabbed. The outsider had managed to get the knife down into his shoulder, and pain suddenly erupted where the blade had pierced his flesh and stopped as it hit bone. Hissing, Jack ignored the pain and the nausea that came with it and clambered to his feet, slipping and sliding in the mud.

The outsider was out cold. Jack stood over him, the heavy rain pattering his head, whipping at his ears like a thousand tiny needles, dripping into his eyes and off his nose.

"Sorry," he said. "Wrong place, wrong time."

He brought the war hammer down once, and as the outsider's head exploded like a busted watermelon, Jack sighed with ecstasy.

TWENTY-SIX

Neverville, 1974

Eve stood at the top of the landing, the stairs descending in front of her. "Freddie!" she called. "Are you there, Freddie?"

A pause. They were trying to figure out who had called out to them, and now they had and were wondering what Eve Lockwood was doing here and where her voice was coming from. Eve couldn't see them from where she stood, but she heard movement down there in the darkness.

Just then, her mother's voice called out to her. "Eve?" she said. "Eve, is that you?"

Eve sighed. Of *course* her mother was here; Joan Lockwood was basically third in command, after Eric and Albie. Maybe fourth, if you wanted to throw Freddie into the mix. But Eve didn't want her mother here, not now, not with her father down there somewhere, not at all.

"Mother!" she called back, and went to move down the stairs, but Mike threw up a hand to her right and she stopped. He didn't want her to go down there. Eve knew they wouldn't hurt her, for it wasn't her they were after. She was one of them, a constant villager, one of the hundred, and they would never dream of hurting her. But Mike seemed to think otherwise, or was at least worried enough to make her think twice. "I'm okay, mother," she said, sensing Mike's unease in her periphery. "Mother, you must listen to me. This isn't the outsiders. They didn't kill Father Calhoun."

"What are you talking about, Eve." It was Eric Majors now. Something clattered down there, and Eve took a step back. Maybe Mike was right; she needed to be wary. While she didn't believe they would intentionally hurt her, they might if it meant getting to Mike, and where was Sam? Was Sam okay?

"It was my father," Eve said, for there was no point hiding it any longer. "Mother, father killed Calhoun. And he's here. He's still here, somewhere, and he tried to kill me, just like he tried to kill you this morning."

There came confused muttering from the gloom below. Questions were being asked, and Eve heard her mother trying to explain. Doc Renfield was here, too. Eve could hear him trying to explain why they had kept her father's sudden resurgence, his inexplicable rebirth, a secret. "We were going to tell you," her mother said, no doubt to Eric. "We were trying to control the situation."

Eric was having none of it. Eve heard him cursing, then Freddie telling him to calm down. At the side, Mike became even more unsettled. It was his life that still hung in the balance, and Eve wasn't doing a great job of keeping him safe just yet. The unexpected news of Jack Lockwood's presence and the subsequent murder of Father Calhoun had only made things worse. Sam killing Vic was the icing on the cake. If the brown robes were on edge before, they were positively rattled now.

"Are they with you?" Eric called up to Eve. He sounded even more irate now, and Eve didn't think she had the power to talk him back down any longer. She thought about the old man, leaning over his world map puzzle, searching for the next piece. But this puzzle was far more difficult; none of the pieces would fit, no matter which way he turned them. "The outsiders, Eve? Are they up there with you?"

"If they're up there," Walter said, "you have to give them up, Eve. You know there is no other choice."

Eve cast a glance across to Mike, who didn't seem to know the best way to proceed either. He simply stared back at her, eyes wide, his grip tightening around the handle of the hammer. Eve had to make a decision and quick, for they would come upstairs, regardless, no matter what she told them or how long she delayed.

"One of them is," Eve said, not much more than a whimper. Mike nodded, seemingly agreeing with her decision. "The other has gone after Father, that bastard." Almost as an afterthought, she said, "They're good men, the outsiders. We don't have to kill them, Eric. Mother, we don't have to. We are below one hundred. They don't have to die. We can talk."

More silence as they considered it. Eve didn't know whether it would work, but she had at least given them pause for thought, an option they hadn't yet contemplated. They had, until then, only had death on their minds, the execution of Mike and Sam. But now they had Jack Lockwood to worry about, and that changed everything. Or nothing. Eve had no idea which way it was going to go.

Mike moved toward her then. And when he spoke, his voice was soft, measured. "We're sorry," he said. "We would never have come here if...if we had known. But please, we don't deserve to die. We can...things can be changed." He shook his head, as if he couldn't believe the words coming from his mouth. He was trying to convince the brown robes why he and Sam should be spared, why their lives mattered. It must, Eve thought, have felt ridiculous to him. He came from a world where this was not an everyday occurrence, a place where you could probably go your entire life without pleading for it to not be taken away.

"Let my daughter go. You hurt her, we'll make you suffer even more than you have to." Her mother sounded stressed, which was never a good thing. And, of course, she hadn't listened to a word either Eve or Mike had just said. Her eyes were on the prize, and there was nothing coming between her and that.

"Mother," Eve said. "I am not a prisoner. I am helping them willingly."

"Then you are a fool," Eric said.

"She's not." It was Freddie, and Eve loved him for that. "She's just not like us, or any of the other fucking crazies in this godforsaken village."

"Watch your tongue!" Eric said. Eve wished she could see the look on his face. Perhaps the same look he got when he couldn't locate a particular piece of his puzzle. Eric hated being stood up to, loathed being put in his place, and in doing so, Freddie had truly rattled his cage.

"I will not!" Freddie's voice said. "Eve is right! Too many have died, and this—"

But that was as far as he got before all hell broke loose downstairs in the darkness.

Jack burst in through the door, machete already swinging through the air, cutting through the semi-darkness like warm butter and hoping one of them was close enough to hit. He had listened to them arguing from the other side. Freddie Carson, Eric Majors, Doc Renfield, Walter Creswell, and that bitch wife of his, Joan. The only one he would regret butchering was Eric, but this was a war, and in war there are always innocent casualties. He wouldn't lose too much sleep over it.

"Fuck!" Freddie said, bringing the knife up but moving away from Jack and the swinging machete. Doc Renfield, who had been closest to the door when Jack came through it, was not so fortunate, and Jack altered the direction of the blade, brought it back the other way.

It sliced through Renfield's throat, cutting a line all the way down to his shoulder. He spun around, and Jack slashed again, this time horizontally the other way. Renfield fell forward, hissing and gargling as the life escaped him.

Eric drew his machete then. Joan backed away, terrified by her husband. She fucking should be, Jack thought, but he didn't have time to linger on it. His machete clinked against the blade of Eric's. Walter came around the back of Jack and tried to pull him backwards, but Jack was too strong for him. He threw up an elbow and sent Walter sprawling to the floorboards, Walter's bow flying across the room and the arrows in his quiver leaping out and skittering away.

Eric brought his machete up, and Jack took a shallow cut to his already painful shoulder. It did nothing to slow him, though. In that moment he was a God. He *was* GOD.

Something hit Jack in the abdomen and bounced off. Freddie, across the room, had thrown his knife, but it had hit Jack's handle first, as harmless as could be. Jack was already swinging his blade again, and this one caught Eric perfectly in the temple. Eric's body did something strange—a stutter, a stagger, his arms dropping down to his sides and the machete he'd been holding falling from his grasp as if he no longer had the strength to hold it—and then he slumped to the floor, Jack's machete blade slipping free as he went.

Freddie came at him then. Jack didn't have time to swing, and so the machete was only halfway up when Freddie's fist caught him in the jaw. He saw stars—dancing red stars, a bright white light, the feeling he was no longer on his feet but flying through the air—and then he snapped back to the present, on his back, arched over the still-twitching corpse of Doc Renfield.

"Don't hurt him!" a voice said, which made Jack laugh, or would have if he wasn't in such agony, for the woman who loved him, who had said 'I do' all those years ago, even though she knew what he was, what he could do, was trying to protect him, to prevent Freddie from hurting him anymore than was necessary. *Bless her*, Jack thought. *Bless the stupid cunt.*

Jack pushed himself away, but Freddie grabbed his ankle and pulled him back into the centre of the room, twisted him this way and that, as if he was trying to yank Jack's entire leg out of its socket. With his free leg, Jack kicked up, and must have caught Freddie under the chin, for the man immediately let go of Jack's leg. There was a thud and a grunt as Freddie hit the ground in front of him. Jack got to his feet, steadied himself, picked up the machete, blinked away blood and forgot all about the throbbing pain in his blood-soaked, rain-soaked shoulder.

"Jack!" Joan cried. She was scared, and coming toward him with the knife in her hand raised. Her expression was exactly the same as it had been earlier that day, when his hands were pressed tightly to her throat, squeezing, squeezing, squeezing the life out of her, and that look—stupid, blank, full of love despite everything that was happening to her—remained as Jack thrust the machete toward her. She walked onto the blade almost in slow motion. There was a sickening wet sound as her torso swallowed up the machete, almost a crunch as it came out the other side, and Jack leaned in so that his face was close to hers. He wanted to see the light go out of her eyes as she died. Her breath was salty, hot, not quite rancid but not pleasant either.

For the longest time she just stood there with the machete skewering her, searching Jack's eyes, imploring him to say it one last time; that he loved her and he was sorry. That he hadn't tried to kill himself at the boulders all those years ago while she was at home, tending to their daughter, Little Evil, that he hadn't meant to hit her all those times, that he had not been in the right frame of mind that morning, when he'd tried to strangle her as she slept opposite him.

Jack simply grinned, for he hoped that was exactly what she wanted from him, and he would never give her the satisfaction.

Instead, he told her, "Don't worry, Joan." Closer now, licking the blood from her nose and tasting just how bitter it was. "Eve will be with you shortly, wherever you go next."

He pulled the machete blade out of her, but not before twisting it a little, making sure he inflicted enough damage to put her down and keep her down. She moaned once and then hit the floor at his feet. If she wasn't already dead, the pool of blood already blossoming out beneath her suggested she would be in a few seconds.

Something smashed upstairs then, and Jack knew what was happening. That outsider, the young one still dressed up as a brown robe, had freed Eve and they were going out of the window. But Jack wasn't stupid enough to go rushing up the stairs to try to stop them. Instead, he made for the door. He would get them outside, before they hit the trail running.

When all hell broke loose downstairs—there had been a sudden bang, followed by grunts and gargles and wet smacking sounds like meat being thrown repeatedly down on a butcher's counter—Mike had grabbed Eve by the wrist and dragged her toward the bedroom door. She had resisted, perhaps a little more than he had anticipated, but he managed to pull her through and into the bedroom.

"My mother!" Eve had cried as Mike pushed the door shut and pulled a heavy, oak dresser across to barricade it. "Mike, my mother!"

Mike didn't know what to tell her, but he knew that her mother was probably already dead. Was it Sam? Had Sam come back into the house and set about the brown robes? Mike hoped so, because the alternative was unthinkable. If it was Eve's father, then Sam was probably dead, and that thought hit Mike harder than it should have, since he'd only known the man properly for thirteen hours, or thereabouts. But in those ensuing hours they had been through so much together. God, he hoped Sam was okay.

"We have to get out of here!" Mike said. Whatever was going on downstairs, it wasn't going to end well for Mike. If it was Jack Lockwood and he slaughtered the brown robes, as he was no doubt capable if Eve was to be believed, then he would come for Mike and Eve next. If the brown robes ended Jack Lockwood down there, then they would come for Mike next. Eve would probably be spared, despite her treachery. Either way, Mike was fucked.

On the dresser now blocking the door there lay a crucifix. Mike snatched it up and was surprised at how heavy it was. Bronze, he thought; whatever, it was heavy enough to knock someone out. There was something inherently blasphemous about hitting an old person with a crucifix, but Mike thought that if there was a God, he would surely understand. He handed it to Eve, who looked down at it with puzzlement.

"It's better than nothing," he told her. He had the hammer, she had the cross. What Mike would have given for a gun. He had never fired one before, had never even held a real one—as a kid, he'd had a few cap guns, a spud gun, a space gun that lit up red and made an electronic racket whenever the trigger was pulled—but how hard could it be? Point, aim, fire, and the person standing in front of it took a bullet. But he didn't have a gun. He had a hammer. The only good thing was that those berobed maniacs didn't have guns either.

Mike went across the room and, with one swing of the hammer, smashed the bedroom window. Eve stayed close to him as he continued to knock the remaining glass out of the pane. A flash of lightning blinded Mike momentarily, and he had to wait for his vision to return before carrying on.

Everything had fallen silent downstairs, which Mike didn't think was a good thing.

"It's too high," Eve said, but Mike thought she was wrong. He had jumped from higher places before. Sure, he was older now, but it didn't look that far down. He could see bushes below, which might cushion their fall, and beyond that there was thick, long grass. Stretching out as far as Mike could see was a field. Trees stood, swayed in the wind, at the end of the field. That was where they would run to.

"You'll be okay," Mike said as he started to climb up onto the windowsill. "Just drop. And when I catch you, start running straight. What's in the trees?"

Eve shook her head; she didn't know. "Never been there," she said.

That was good enough for Mike, because if Eve, with all her curiosity and wanderlust, hadn't been there, the chances were the brown robes hadn't, either.

"Okay. Don't hesitate. Up on the sill, and then down. Don't look down of it helps, but I'll catch you. Okay?"

She didn't look okay; she looked apt to upchuck without warning, but Mike knew she understood and would do exactly as he'd instructed her to.

Mike turned, lowered himself as much as he could out through the window, and let go, his backside sliding off the slippery, wet sill, and then he was falling. Less than a second later, he landed on the grass in front of the bushes, for he had missed them entirely. His legs bent up and he kicked himself in the arse. It hurt like a sonofabitch, but he was okay, and wasted no time getting back to his feet.

He looked up to the window just as Eve started to ease out through it. She looked almost pleadingly toward Mike, as if she wanted him to come back up and look for another way down. Rain filled Mike's vision as he said, "Don't hesitate. Just drop."

Eve brought one leg up and out, and then the other. Mike envisioned hands suddenly appearing, wrapping around Eve and pulling her back into the bedroom. She needed to hurry up.

Luckily, the option was snatched away from her as she slipped on the sill, gave a little whimper, and then dropped toward the bushes below. Mike lunged for her, but she was just out of reach, and he only managed to catch her once she'd landed. She was shaken, but didn't appear to be injured.

"We have to go," he whispered as he helped her to her feet. He dragged her by the hand for the first couple of metres, but then she pulled free of him and they were both running, racing for the trees at the end of the field. They looked so far away, Mike thought, now that they were at ground level. It was raining heavier now than it had been before. Crashes of thunder came every few seconds, and the lightning was like nothing Mike had ever witnessed.

Eve was trailing behind him, but as Mike glanced back, he was glad to see her running at full pelt, her wet hair whipping left and right, her soiled dress clinging to her body as if it had been painted on. And then Mike saw what was behind her, and he knew she was in trouble.

There was Jack Lockwood, bearing down on his daughter, a rictus grin pulling his whole jaw back and giving him the appearance of some wild animal. He must have been waiting for them, knowing they would come out through the window. And what of Sam? Where was Sam? And a voice whispered into Mike's ear that, "Sam is dead, mate.

Sam is dead," and Mike somehow knew that the voice—and it was Sam's voice, which made everything so much worse—was telling the truth.

Beyond Eve, beyond Jack Lockwood behind her, a line of figures was also racing across the field. There were perhaps six of them, seven, no eight, spread out equally like some coordinated seaside aircraft display. The brown robes running as fast as their old, wasted bodies could manage. Mike knew then that Eve was going to be caught. By her father, who would finish her off before the brown robes reached them. Then Jack Lockwood would be killed. That seemed to be the only way it could go, and Mike felt so bad about it because Eve was innocent in all of this, at least as innocent as she could be.

And now she would die, and there was nothing Mike could do about it without committing suicide.

Mike turned and ran toward the trees.

He was getting too far ahead. Eve's legs were already burning, and she couldn't keep up with him. She had hurt her right leg in the bushes back there, could feel the scratches burning, and it was slowing her down.

This was not a good plan at all. Eve didn't know what was in those trees ahead. She'd never come this far onto Freddie's land before, and had assumed this was just another grazing field for his beasts. They were running toward the unknown, and that was just as scary, Eve thought, as running away from an uncertain future.

Mike, still running, turned and looked back at her. He was checking she was still there, still with him, and also perhaps letting her know that he was still there, and hadn't forgotten about her despite the distance increasing between them. When he turned and began to run faster, Eve pushed harder to keep up. She didn't want to lose him. Once they got to the trees, if they were separated it might be impossible to find each other again.

Eve was digging deeper, running faster, when something caught onto her ankle and sent her sprawling face-first into the thick grass. She came down heavy, and it took the wind right out of her, but she quickly rolled over onto her back, and that was when his full weight was on top of her, his head right above her, his terrible breath—hot, stale, what death's mouth might smell like—hitting her hard in the face

"No need to run, Little Evil," he said, gasping for breath as the rain bounced off him. He had her pinned down at the wrists, but Eve continued to struggle, more so when he let go of her left wrist to pick up the machete he'd dropped as he'd wrestled her to the ground.

Eve slapped him hard across the face with her free hand, but he took it as if it were nothing. She tried to bring her knee up into his groin, but only succeeded in knocking him further up onto her belly, which he was now fully straddling.

"That's my girl!" he said, grinning. "There she is!" Lightning illuminated his face, and for a moment Eve thought she had caught a glimpse of his skull beneath. "The Lockwood you could have been if I'd stuck around. If you fucks hadn't ruined everything!"

"Fuck you!" Eve cried, trying once again to push him off. He was too heavy, too big, and Eve knew she was in big trouble.

"Fuck me, right?" he said. "Pity you'll never know what a fuck feels like. It's a beautiful thing. Your mother used to love a good fuck, Eve. Before you came along. You put an end to all those good fucks, girl."

She could barely hear him over the rain and thunder, and then there was something else. Someone was shouting. She thought it was Freddie, but it could have been anyone. "Walter!" the voice yelled. "Now, Walter!"

That was when her father leaned back and raised the machete. Eve slapped at him, at his body, at his face, did anything she could to stop him from bringing that blade down, but she knew it was fruitless. She would lose fingers in the process of trying to hold him off, and ultimately, she would die.

I hope Mike makes it, she thought, reaching up for her father's wrist one last time.

Mike ran into the trees without looking back. Jack Lockwood had her; she was gone, and there was nothing he could have done to help her.

The arrow came through her father's face so violently and unexpectedly that Eve didn't know what had happened until seconds later, when he slumped on top of her. The arrowhead sticking out of her father's cheek by six inches or more came down beside her neck, scratching her slightly before it buried itself into the grass beside her head. Then he just lay there on top of her as the rain came down on both of them and Eve, tired and sore and confused and sad—not about her father; never about her father—looked up to the darkness above and waited.

Sickness. That's what Mike felt now. So sick he wanted to stop running. He couldn't see the field any longer. Just more trees, and dancing white lights flitting in front of him like fireflies. Sicker now. And tired, but he knew he couldn't stop. He had to get somewhere they wouldn't find him. Eve was dead, of that he was almost certain. And Jack was dead, for the brown robes wouldn't have allowed him to live. Which left him.

Sick, exhausted, alone, Mike Denver, who would never see his sister again, never see his mother again, never go to work or drive his Marina again. Just plain ol' Mike from now on, surviving in this place where there was no place, and never would be, for the likes of him.

Just an outsider, he thought, as the sickness became too much to bear and he doubled over, clutched at his stomach, and brought up nothing of substance.

And then he saw the rope. Half-buried in the dirt, rotten and old, and he staggered forward on his hands and knees, crossing it. A second later, there was only darkness.

It was Freddie Carson who pulled her father off. "Help me, Walter!" he said. "I think she's okay."

Eve looked up into Freddie's eyes and knew that, while she wasn't really okay, she would be. She could talk to them, could make them see that Mike didn't have to die. If she could convince Eric Majors and Albie Moss—she thought she could convince Freddie to do just about anything; he'd always had a soft spot for her—that Mike could be one of them now, then maybe, just maybe...

"Mother," Eve said as Freddie and Walter helped her to her feet. "Where's my mother?"

Freddie sighed.

He didn't have to say any more.

EPILOGUE

Neverville, 1980

Eve stood in the kitchen, waiting for the potatoes to boil and staring blankly out through the window at the mid-morning sunshine. It was going to be another nice day, she thought. It hadn't rained in almost a week, which was almost unheard of, and everywhere she looked there was green. The trees were beautiful, the grass a lush carpet of emerald, even the rotten outhouse—which she had once sobbed in, hiding from The Burden as he stalked the night—looked majestic.

Remembering the events of that night were never easy for Eve, and she often embellished them in her own mind, made them more palatable to herself. But as Freddie always told her: "What happened happened. We are not what happens to us; we are what we choose to become." That was one of his mother's, and whenever Freddie used one of her sayings, he always did so with a little smile.

It had been Mae Creswell's funeral yesterday, and everyone had been sad, but such was life. Walter had sobbed so much that Eve didn't think he would last long without her. Was it possible to die of a broken heart? Eve thought so. Just like when Lucas Thorne had died two years prior, and John Wexler had lasted just a month before following him into Heaven. Eve had been close to death herself, once she had time to think about her mother, about Doc Renfield, about Sam the outsider, who had come here only to find his daughter and had found her in the afterlife for his troubles.

But Eve had a reason to go on.

She had a purpose.

The potatoes were done and she mashed them as best she could with the fork. There were a few lumps, but nothing dangerous. She hoped Freddie's harvest was good this season, for she was almost out of everything. After this, she would go to the farm for milk, and Freddie would rustle up a pint from somewhere. He always did.

She made her way upstairs and into the bedroom, and was that a smile she saw on his face, or at least the hint of one. Probably not, but she liked to think so.

She sat across from him, where she always sat when she fed him, read to him, talked to him about banal subjects, no doubt bored him to distraction with her many philosophical musings, and said:

"I'm here. Sorry it's potatoes again, Mike. Open wide."

She began to feed him.

The Beautiful Outsider in the Bedroom.

THE END?

Not if you want to dive into more of Crystal Lake Publishing's Tales from the Darkest Depths!

Check out our amazing website and online store or download our latest catalog here.
https://geni.us/CLPCatalog

We always have great new projects and content on the website to dive into, as well as a newsletter, behind the scenes options, social media platforms, our own dark fiction shared-world series and our very own webstore. Our webstore even has categories specifically for KU books, non-fiction, anthologies, and of course more novels and novellas.

AUTHOR BIOGRAPHY

243

Adam Millard is the author of twenty-nine novels, thirteen novellas, and more than two hundred short stories, which can be found in various collections, magazines, and anthologies. Probably best known for his post-apocalyptic and comedy-horror fiction, Adam also writes fantasy/horror for children and Bizarro fiction for several publishers. His work has been translated for the German, Russian, and Spanish markets. He lives in Newcastle-Under-Lyme, UK, with his wife, Dawn, and her cats, which were not his idea at all.

Readers...

Thank you for reading *The Village of C*. We hope you enjoyed this novel.

If you have a moment, please review *The Village of C* at the store where you bought it.

Help other readers by telling them why you enjoyed this book. No need to write an in-depth discussion. Even a single sentence will be greatly appreciated. Reviews go a long way to helping a book sell, and is great for an author's career. It'll also help us to continue publishing quality books.

Thank you again for taking the time to journey with Crystal Lake Publishing.

You will find links to all our social media platforms on our Linktree page.
https://linktr.ee/CrystalLakePublishing

Follow us on Amazon:

MISSION STATEMENT

Since its founding in August 2012, Crystal Lake Publishing has quickly become one of the world's leading publishers of Dark Fiction and Horror books. In 2023, Crystal Lake Publishing formed a part of Crystal Lake Entertainment, joining several other divisions, including Torrid Waters, Crystal Lake Comics, Crystal Lake Kids, and many more.

While we strive to present only the highest quality fiction and entertainment, we also endeavour to support authors along their writing journey. We offer our time and experience in non-fiction projects, as well as author mentoring and services, at competitive prices.

With several Bram Stoker Award wins and many other wins and nominations (including the HWA's Specialty Press Award), Crystal Lake Publishing puts integrity, honor, and respect at the forefront of our publishing operations.

We strive for each book and outreach program we spearhead to not only entertain and touch or comment on issues that affect our readers, but also to strengthen and support the Dark Fiction field and its authors.

Not only do we find and publish authors we believe are destined for greatness, but we strive to work with men and women who endeavour to be decent human beings who care more for others than themselves, while still being hard working, driven, and passionate artists and storytellers.

Crystal Lake Publishing is and will always be a beacon of what passion and dedication, combined with overwhelming teamwork and respect, can accomplish. We endeavour to know each and every one of our readers, while building personal relationships with our authors, reviewers, bloggers, podcasters, bookstores, and libraries.

We will be as trustworthy, forthright, and transparent as any business can be, while also keeping most of the headaches away from our authors, since it's our job to solve the problems so they can stay in a creative mind. Which of course also means paying our authors.

We do not just publish books, we present to you worlds within your world, doors within your mind, from talented authors who sacrifice so much for a moment of your time.

There are some amazing small presses out there, and through collaboration and open forums we will continue to support other presses in the goal of helping authors and showing the world what quality small presses are capable of accomplishing. No one wins when a small press goes down, so we will always be there to support hardworking, legitimate presses and their authors. We don't see Crystal Lake as the best press out there, but we will always strive to be the best, strive to be the most interactive and grateful, and even blessed press around. No matter what happens over time, we will also take our mission very seriously while appreciating where we are and enjoying the journey.

What do we offer our authors that they can't do for themselves through self-publishing?

We are big supporters of self-publishing (especially hybrid publishing), if done with care, patience, and planning. However, not every author has the time or inclination to do market research, advertise, and set up book launch strategies. Although a lot of authors are successful in doing it all, strong small presses will always be there for the authors who just want to do what they do best: write.

What we offer is experience, industry knowledge, contacts and trust built up over years. And due to our strong brand and trusting fanbase, every Crystal Lake Publishing book comes with weight of respect. In time our fans begin to trust our judgment and will try a new author purely based on our support of said author.

With each launch we strive to fine-tune our approach, learn from our mistakes, and increase our reach. We continue to assure our authors that we're here for them and that we'll carry the weight of the launch and dealing with third parties while they focus on their strengths—be it writing, interviews, blogs, signings, etc.

We also offer several mentoring packages to authors that include knowledge and skills they can use in both traditional and self-publishing endeavours.

We look forward to launching many new careers.

This is what we believe in. What we stand for. This will be our legacy.

Welcome to Crystal Lake Publishing—Tales from the Darkest Depths.

9 781957 133881